Praise for Carol Wo

SUMMONING

"What can a werewolf girl and a demon have in common?
Only the need to save the earth from the Eater of Souls and the
planet-shaking power of the World Snake. And where else to
do it but Darkest Los Angeles? In *Summoning* Carol Wolf
gives us a story rich in mythic lore and as tightly woven
as the mesh of fate itself."

—Douglas Rees, author of *Vampire High*

"Thank gods this isn't actually a lyrical 'paranormal romance'!
It's a fast-moving adventure full of surprises and delights including several richly imagined women of power, yet not slight-
ing the men (or the bears). Our heroine, Amber, is convinc-
ingly tough, confident, and resourceful, no bluster but plenty
of heart, which makes her a pleasure to spend time with—or,
rather, try to keep up with. The story moves, like its protago-
nist, boldly, unhampered by any emo blithering, to an unusual
and satisfying conclusion. I hope there's more coming!"

—Suzy Charnas, Hugo, Nebula, and James Tiptree Jr. Award–
winning author of *The Bronze King* and *The Ruby Tear*

"Lone wolf Amber is a character any reader
will enjoy discovering."

—Linda Wisdom, national best-selling author of *A Demon
Does It Better*

"Carol Wolf's *Summoning* is a fast-paced, colorful romp
through a supernatural Los Angeles full of demons, witches,
soul stealers, and plenty of supernatural hi-jinks to delight
lovers of Urban Fantasy."

—Matthew Kressel, World Fantasy Award nominee
and founder of *Sybil's Garage*

Binding

Other Books by Carol Wolf

Summoning: Book One of the Moon Wolf Saga
(Night Shade Books)

Coyote Run
with Eric Elliott
(Fast Forward)

Playwriting: The Merciless Craft
Comprehensive Techniques of Beginning, Intermediate, and
   Advanced Playwriting
(Ambush Books)

Binding

BOOK TWO OF THE MOON WOLF SAGA

CAROL WOLF

NIGHT SHADE BOOKS
NEW YORK

Night Shade Books may be purchased in bulk at special discounts for sales promotion, corporate gifts, fund-raising, or educational purposes. Special editions can also be created to specifications. For details, contact the Special Sales Department, Night Shade Books, 307 West 36th Street, 11th Floor, New York, NY 10018 or info@skyhorsepublishing.com.

Night Shade Books® is a registered trademark of Skyhorse Publishing, Inc. ®, a Delaware corporation.

Visit our website at www.nightshadebooks.com.

10 9 8 7 6 5 4 3 2 1

Library of Congress Cataloging-in-Publication Data is available on file.

Jacket art by Tony Mauro
Interior layout and design by Amy Popovich

Print ISBN: 978-1-59780-534-6

Printed in the United States of America

For lost friends:

Steve Henderson
Sir Stephen MacEanruig, KSCA
Carolyn Wellington
Mom

This candle burns for you

CHAPTER ONE

A wolf caught in a trap has been known to gnaw her own leg off, rather than remain in captivity. I couldn't get to my foot, but I could reach my upper arm, and that would do it. But the question that I had was, at what point does the balance tip between hope and death? How do you know when the moment has come to start chewing?

I saved the world. Well, not the whole world, just the greater Los Angeles area. But that's the whole world to some people. When the World Snake, devourer of Herakleitos (you never heard of Herakleitos, have you—that's why) and Atlantis, threatened Los Angeles, I'm the one who turned her. I'm the one who made sure that she would never devour a human city again. So you'd think after that, there would be celebrations and congratulations, feasts and toasts and speeches of thanksgiving, a victory lap and autographs. Instead, someone shot me.

I woke up in a cage. I was manacled by my right wrist to one corner, and by my left hind paw to the opposite corner. I reached up with my free hand to test the chain, and saw my left foreleg pawing uselessly at the handcuff. And as I tried to understand that I was in both forms at once, human and wolf, like in some bad dream, my thoughts blurred, and I was drawn down into unconsciousness like a puppy being drowned in a bucket.

I am a daughter of the wolf kind, who can change form at will. I ran away from home—for good reasons!—about eight months ago, and made a place for myself in Los Angeles. My driver's license says my name is Elizabeth Beaumont. It also says I'm 19. Ha. My cousin, who was also running away, bought an I.D. for me when she got one for herself. I answer to Amber, but that's not my true name either.

Pain brought me back awake, and I clung to it. My hip ached. It felt swollen and stiff. But that wasn't all that had been done to me. I yanked on my chains and darn near let out a whimper. I wasn't just bound. Something was jabbing deep into my manacled wrist and ankle. There were surgical bandages under the cuffs, hung with the smell of blood and pus, new and old, and something else, something metallic. I'd been there awhile, then. A day or two, at least. And it wasn't just pain and stiffness clouding my brain. Something kept pulling me down into unconsciousness.

I lifted my lip in a frustrated snarl, and gathered myself to change, because of course my right wrist would slip the cuff when I was a wolf, and then I froze in surprise at the pain that flared out from whatever was stabbing into me under the cuff. I paused, and then tried again. Changing is easy. It has always been easy. You do it the first time without even realizing it. I tried harder, and convulsed as the pain rode upward, matching my efforts, heading off my attempt, flowering into agony. The world went black and I thought I would faint, but I still hadn't changed. And it wasn't the pain that was stopping me.

I tried to think. My mind was cloudy, sluggish. Maybe the cage was bespelled to keep me in this crippling dual form. I couldn't sense any wards, any shaping of power into intention and will, coming from the bars or the latch. There was something… and I could study it much better from outside. With all my strength, I attacked the cage, trying to tear it apart, bend it open, break the corners, twist the bars. I gritted my teeth in a snarl as my wrist and ankle flared in renewed pain, and the wound in my hip throbbed. I'd been shot in the hip. I remembered the involuntary yelp and twist of my head to grab at the dart and stop the agonizing pain. My hip hurt as though I'd been stabbed by a spear, and now the wound was bleeding. I tried again.

The cage shook under my onslaught, but it held. Stretched out as I was, I didn't have the leverage I needed to bend the metal bars. I could see the cage door. This was an animal cage, designed to hold a large live animal. There was just a latch holding it shut—not even a padlock! Someone sure thought I was helpless like this. The latch holding the door shut was outside the bars, of course. Fingers might reach it, but not a wolf's paw. I tried to change again, riding the increasing pain like a ladder, to where it would top out, and I could keep going and make myself whole again. This time I did black out.

When my senses returned, the room was lit by indirect sunlight. The cage lay between a big black iron stove and a dirty beige wall with cracks in the paint. I lay staring at the coils of thick smoke surging through the bars near my head. It took me a few minutes to understand that the stove wasn't lit. The smoke was coming from underneath it. By tipping my head I could see a carved wooden box for burning incense, set on its side, with most of the little ornate holes blocked, except the ones aimed at me. The bottom of the stove held the smoke just at the level of my face, until it reached me before dissipating into the room. The smoke coming from it was thick and odorous, a tang of metal overlaid by something heavy, cloying, almost nauseating. It pressed its way into my throat and the back of my nose, and pulled my mind back into oblivion.

It was the smoke. I came awake again with that thought, and shifted in the cage as much as I could, welcoming the pain from my wrist and ankle, and my wounded hip, as it helped to keep me from sinking back into unconsciousness. I repositioned my head to try to avoid the smoke. There was an annoying sound coming from across the room, a repetitive squeaking that started and stopped at irregular intervals. Beyond the stove, on the other side of the room, a young man was silhouetted against a sliding glass door, where he was meticulously cleaning the glass. His too-short t-shirt rode up with the movements of his arm, and his cutoffs sagged.

He had his back to me. That pissed me off. I let out a long, low growl, almost below the threshold that a human can hear, but just audible enough to remind him that for a long time, humans were our prey. This is the sound of being alone in the room with a wolf.

He paused, his shoulder blades tensing, and I grinned to myself. Then, without turning, he began buffing the glass again. Huh! My growl got louder, but he paid no further attention. That was strange. He gave out no sense of being dangerous, or powerful, but he wasn't enough afraid of me to turn around when I threatened him. My eyes should have turned gold just then, as I narrowed in on the need to teach this guy an important lesson. But I was having trouble holding on to my anger. I shifted my head and exhaled toward the smoke.

I was sure of one thing. I wasn't trapped in this cage because someone thought I was easy to deal with. I was chained up, drugged, and imprisoned, because someone didn't want me loose. Now, that was respect. And it wasn't window-cleaner over there, who thought of me as furniture, who had done this to me.

Someone else lived in this house. I huffed into the smoke again, turned my head and opened my jaws, taking in the scents of the room. Ugh. Someone around here used a lot of cleaning chemicals.

I could feel a residue of energy in the room, here and there, like splashes of paint or spills from a broken jug, sudden and messy, but with no shape or pattern. The room didn't have the feel of a place where a great power wielder lived. That kind tend to organize the energy around them. What I sensed was small, and slap-dash.

A woman lived here. Middle-aged, former cigarette smoker— that smell never goes away, no matter that you changed the curtains or painted the walls—not happy, some kind of problem with her teeth. I could feel a few small residues of energy, but she didn't feel like a great power wielder to me.

So that meant whoever had done this to me had left me here. Why? For how long? And if not the woman who lived here, then who was my enemy?

I pulled at the manacles, just to see if it still hurt the way I remembered. It did. The blood and pus was caked on my bandages. Huh. No one had changed them while I was unconscious. I turned my head and blew at the smoke. I concentrated, as I'd never had to in my two-natured life, and tried to change. I threw myself at that place where my wolf form ducks under and my human form rises up, but now there was a barrier there, one that receded the harder I approached it. Agony flared out from my wrist and ankle the closer I tried to go. This was impossible. This was unheard of. No one could stop you from changing. Shaking with pain and rage, I pounded at that barrier, finally stopping just at the edge of the convulsion brought on by the pain. I lay shaking and panting, soaked with sweat, still trying to avoid the smoke. Squeaky window-washing man was listening to me, I could feel his attention, but he didn't turn around. I wanted to kill him.

I had to get out of this trap. You can cut off a foot and still run away. A wolf can survive on three legs. But if I started gnawing, I was going to have begin with my right upper arm, which was all

I could reach with my jaws, and then chew off my left hind paw. I wasn't sure how viable I would be after that. Especially when I stood in my two-legged form. And I really wanted to meet whoever did this to me while I was still dangerous.

When I arrived in Southern California, all the local power raisers were in a frenzy to try stop the World Snake, destroyer of Thrace, devourer of Atlantis, who was on track to take out greater Los Angeles. They held meetings and tried to make plans to work together to avert the common threat. Power raisers working together is like organizing an all-cat marching band. You call the first meeting, and hope they still admit to playing an instrument, if they even show up on the right day. Then the auguries revealed—to folks who believed in them—that I was fated to be a prime mover in that fight. This seemed unlikely, even to those who thought they knew who and what I was. But it was true. And I won. With the assistance of a demon who'd taken service with me... okay. After circumstances—which I had a lot to do with—got my demon all his powers back, I ordered him to turn the World Snake, to keep her from destroying this, or any other city, and he'd done it at my command. Crisis passed, the good guys won, hooray. The trouble was, no one believed me.

I called him Richard, because you don't go speaking a demon's true name where anyone can hear it. He'd been trapped here in the form of a beautiful young man about my age, with golden hair, white skin, slender, muscular body, deep blue eyes... the shape imposed upon him by the magician who caught him and rendered him powerless four hundred years ago.

Richard chose me to defend him from the enemy he feared. He and I ran and hunted, fought and played together, while we worked to save the city and set him free. And I missed him. Since he left, all I wanted to do was moon around the places where he and I had talked and laughed and made love, while everyone kept demanding I call forth my demon and do great battle and destroy the World Snake and on and on, and didn't listen when I told them and told them, it was already done.

My gift to Richard, in return for his love, was to release him from this world. He wasn't my demon anymore. He was gone, and it was over, and nobody would let me alone about it.

I lost my job because I didn't want to miss a minute of my last two weeks with Richard. I wasn't in love. It wasn't really love. Richard only looked like a man, smelled and tasted like a man. But he wasn't real. You can't really lose something you never had. Funny how it feels just the same, though.

Why didn't I keep him? I wouldn't be in this mess, for one thing, if I had. But twice I'd seen him in his demon form. In our last two weeks he took good care to appear just as human and sweet and attractive as he could. But the wolf in me remembered, and I knew in his true form he was unfathomable, and dangerous.

Window-wiper passed into my view again. I must have fallen asleep. The light had changed. It was sharper, the room was warmer. I'd forgotten to blow away the smoke. He wore a blue and white bandana squared neatly on the top of his head. With a spray bottle in one hand, and a soft cloth in the other, he went around and buffed every piece of furniture from top to bottom, even the metal lamp stand.

He stood staring up at the wall for a long time, and I noticed the clock. When it was exactly two o'clock, cleaner guy hurried to put his stuff away, took off the bandana, and curled up on the couch and took a nap. I didn't blame him.

I came awake again when the vacuum cleaner roared past my head, as the young man proceeded to scrape over every inch of the sandy carpet, twice. He avoided my eyes, where I lay glaring at him. I waited until he pushed that thing near my head again, and I sprang at him, as though I could leap right through the cage. I fell back in agony, but it was worth it. He'd jumped back open-mouthed, hands open, almost squatting in terror.

When he saw I was just as trapped as ever he looked around, picked up the vacuum cleaner, and resumed shoving it right where he'd left off. I lost sight of him when he went to other side of the stove. The sound of the vacuum cleaner changed, and the smoke got thicker, was moving faster. He was blowing it at me. I yanked my wrist hard to try and stay conscious. The smoke was the problem. And I'd smelled it before. I held on to that thought, my eyes closed, waiting for cleaner guy to go away.

My friend, Yvette, leaning out of the window of the car she was driving, "See you tonight at the party!" So I went, driving up the 405 freeway through the stop-and-stop afternoon traffic.

I went to the party because when they invited me I thought it meant that people had figured out I was right, the crisis was over, and everyone wasn't angry and stupid and wrong anymore. Plus, once they realized I'd won, there should be thanks and speeches, praise and affection. So I told myself I'd been invited to this party because some of that was coming my way. And I'd gotten to like the gatherings with music and drumming and dancing, lots of good food, and people I was starting to know.

The directions took me to Malibu. A dirt parking lot. A path leading down to a private beach. Honey, a guy I knew from the Thunder Mountain Boys, manning the gate.

I didn't know anyone at the party. Yvette wasn't there. But everybody seemed to know me. I assumed Yvette and the other drummers would come later.

There was a bonfire. Yes, and there was smoke, that same smoke, not from the bonfire, but from a brazier on the picnic table, and people coming up to me, talking to me, standing so that I stood in the smoke. They were all so attentive, so friendly. They were watching me. And someone called for a toast to victory, and I was handed a glass, and I raised it to drink and I felt a sudden tension in everyone around me, everyone looking at me or care-fully not looking at me and smiling, all my new friends smiling, and I could smell that the drink they'd given me was bad, that it had something in it that didn't belong there. I lowered my glass. I looked around the circle of people, and now all of them were looking at me. All my new friends. And I raised my glass again and smiled back at them, and poured the drink out onto the sand.

The tang of fear, tension, and excitement rose from the crowd, like a dog pack that's found the family chicken loose in the yard. What did these people think I was, their prey or something? My smile widened, showing my teeth, and it was not my nice smile. I decided I didn't want to be at this party anymore.

A couple of people near me said something, placating lies, pretending the drink was not poisoned or drugged, offering me another, offering me food, and other delights to come. I started away from the fire, stiff-legged, wondering if I should bite someone before I left, and who it should be. A couple of guys, egged on by the others, stepped into my way, held out their hands, and I'd had enough. I changed. The guys coming at me backed away, but not very fast. I realized that while fear spiked off them and the others, shock or surprise did not. They had expected me to change—not that a lot of them weren't darned amazed nonetheless, because when I change, it's that impressive. I stepped forward in my wolf form, looking around to identify the ones responsible for bringing me here.

People backed away as I turned, and I was about to give up and charge up the dirt road to my car, when I smelled the gun. Everyone was still. I turned, and I saw the barrel of what looked like a shotgun, a woman in the shadows raising it to bear, too far to reach in time. I managed one leap away toward the hopeful darkness when I heard a whoomph, and my hip exploded into agony. I spun in the air, snapping at whatever was causing the pain, and dropped awkwardly to the sand. I scrabbled to my feet, turning to look for the gun. Not a shot gun, a vet's dart gun. The woman, her hands shaking, was reloading. I tried to bare my teeth. I tried to start toward her and stumbled. I think I blacked out before I even hit the sand.

And here I was, in both forms at once. How was that even possible? I'd never heard of such a thing. The throbbing pain in my hip—that was where I'd been shot with the anesthetic dart. And there was something that felt like it was hooked through the tendons of my wrist, and my hind foot. And the smoke was keeping me stupid, making me pass out. And someone had done this to me. Someone arranged the party, doctored the drink, laid the fire, ignited the smoke. Someone from the party? The woman with the gun? Or someone else, who had devised this trap, and the means to hold me helpless in both my forms. I moved my head away from the smoke and breathed as shallowly as I could. First, I had to defeat the smoke. Then, I had to get free. I brooded on hope. I lay my head on my aching and swollen right arm, stretched out my left hind leg as far as I could, and waited to kill someone.

CHAPTER TWO

A woman stomped around the kitchen, plopping food from one pot into another, talking to herself. No, talking to the cleaner guy. Cleaner guy stood by the counter and watched her every move. He had a terrific body: lean, taut and muscular, a long, straight nose, high cheekbones, curly black hair. He watched her with shining eyes, his mouth slightly open. I knew from her scent that she was the woman who lived here. She came over to me, walking heavily, stirring canned chicken and mushroom soup into the pot of noodles she held in her hand while she stared down at me. Cleaner guy turned to watch her, but didn't move from his spot.

"You're awake!"

When I am angry, my eyes turn yellow. You don't want to see that. It bothered me a lot that right then I didn't seem to have the energy. I just looked at her. Old corduroy jacket, scuffed and dirty boots, worn jeans, denim shirt, short, graying hair, none too clean, and the smell of sheep, and horses. A rancher. I was on a ranch. She bent over me, not touching the bars of the cage. Bad breath. I was right about her teeth.

"Can you hear me?" She turned to the cleaner guy and her voice sharpened. "You keep the thing burning, right? She's not supposed to be awake. This is not good." She leaned closer, still not touching the cage. "Can you hear me?"

I rolled my eyes back and closed them. I didn't need her upping the dose.

"Baz, get that for me." Baz hurried over to her, got down and reached under the stove. He handed her the incense burner, holding it with two hands, as though he were offering her the Grail. She walked out of sight and came back adding a little dark brick to whatever smoldered in there already, holding it away from her face, and then handed it to Baz to get down and push back under the stove. I slept again then. I woke when a door banged open, and I heard her tromp into the kitchen with a flashlight in her hand. It took me a while to realize that it was night, because the room reflected the glow of a high-powered critter-be-gone light through the glass doors and the window.

"Get in here," she said, calling to the cleaner guy. He hustled in after her. She came toward my cage, and I shut my eyes. She pushed the incense burner with her foot, so it was closer to my head. "Come on, Baz," she said, and left me in the dark. The smoke thickened, and I went out again.

Baz washed the kitchen cupboards the next day, the bandana square on his head. He'd put his t-shirt on backwards today. It was annoying. At noon he ate two pieces of toast that had sat waiting for him on the kitchen counter all day. Just before two he stood staring at the wall clock again, and at two o'clock, he put everything away, and went to the couch for his nap. I waited until he had just settled down, and then I growled, "Baz! Ge' off the couch!" He slunk off before he realized who was ordering him around. Then he turned on me, his lips open in what would have been a snarl, if he weren't in the form of a man. I knew it. I knew it! Baz was a dog.

He came over to the cage, his lip still raised. I leaned into the smoke, pretending to suck it up. "Oh, yes," I tried to make my sleep-thickened voice sound like a moan. It sounded distorted, whether because of the smoke, or the weird shape I was in, I didn't know, but I made sure he understood my meaning. "Give me that smoke, it is so good." I looked up at him sharply. "Don't you take any of that. *She* gave it to me. It's not for you, you don't get any. *I'm* the one who gets it, all of it. Not you."

He stood looking at me, his mouth open. I knew I had him when he turned to look out the glass door. I went into my moaning act again. I closed my eyes partway, and watched under my lashes as he opened the burner, broke off a big chunk from the gray brick smoldering inside, and removed it. He paced to the glass doors and back. He went to a shelf next to the television and brought down a wooden box and pawed through it carefully and took out a little square of incense that resembled the stuff in the burner. He switched it out, and wrapped the purloined piece in a dampened paper towel. Then he looked around, and stuffed it under the couch. He gave me such a look! I thought he was going to turn his back and scrape dirt at me. I closed my eyes, smiling.

In less than an hour my head cleared. Baz polished the heavy, slightly lopsided wooden table, right down to the feet. He set up a stepladder, and wiped down the top of the cupboards. He cleaned and chopped a busload of potatoes and carrots. I felt exhausted just watching him.

I woke from a doze to hear the woman on the phone. She was standing over me. I kept my eyes shut.

"She's fine. She's asleep. Yeah. I thought she was waking up yesterday—she just opened her eyes. But she's been out all day. Come on, Elaine, I can't keep her here."

Ah, hah. I knew it wasn't her. Elaine. I would remember that.

The woman continued, "How much longer before he gets back?"

This I wanted to hear.

"Friday? Three days? You owe me, you so owe me. And Cecil owes me double!" She snapped the phone shut, grumbling to herself. "What does Holly think I am, a zookeeper? Her and her stupid Cecil." She stomped around some more, and then called, "Come on, Baz!" and the two of them went out.

Well, I was certainly going to be out of there in less than three more days. I pulled at my manacles, wrist and leg at once, and stopped, gasping with the pain. Okay, I thought. Okay. Not by strength was I going to get out of here. Figure this out. I was in both forms. Right. So, I could reach my manacled right wrist with my left forepaw, but a paw wasn't of use to get me loose. And my right foot wasn't able to loose my left hind paw. The chains were strong.

Nine tenths of magic is distraction. Richard told me that. The smoke wasn't the magic. The smoke was a drug to keep me asleep, to keep me stupid when I wasn't asleep, and make me sleep most of the time. Asleep, they didn't think I was dangerous. Okay, so I could beat this if I was awake, and if I was smart. And I could beat this if I was in human form, or in wolf form, but not in both. Right.

The manacles would not work if I was in wolf form, because I could slip out of them. The cage would not work if I was in human form. The cage and the manacles were not what were keeping me a prisoner. They were merely a distraction. So it was necessary that I remain in this strange hybrid form, in order to be a prisoner. What was keeping me like this? As if in answer, the tendons throbbed in my wrist and my heel. Yes, that something that was hooked around them. Something cold, or hot, or both. And it hurt. Everything else was a distraction. This was what was keeping me prisoner. This was what I had to beat.

I let myself slip into sleep again, but this was a wolf nap, not unconsciousness. I registered the woman and her… companion…

coming in again, and the aggressive rattle of pans and cutlery as she heated up rice and canned stew, and slopped it in a bowl. And suddenly, I was really, really hungry. Something in the smoke must have kept my metabolism quiet. I hadn't eaten in days, and didn't notice until just now. And more than that, I was suddenly, overwhelmingly, painfully thirsty.

"She's drooling," the woman said. She was standing over me, shoveling food from her bowl into her mouth. "Did you top up the fire? Smoke seems thin." Baz must have responded satisfactorily. She peered down at me, but didn't ask him to reach her the incense burner. "Huh." I kept my eyes closed, and slowly let my mouth relax. "Drooling in her sleep," the woman concluded, turning away.

"C'mere, Baz!" She handed the guy the bowl, and he stuck his head into it and scarfed up her leftovers. She sighed heavily. "All the stuff you can do, and you can't use a spoon. Stupid dog." But her voice was forgiving, caressing, even. I let myself fall asleep again as the two of them curled up on the couch and turned on the television.

I snapped awake when they came in from night rounds, and Baz turned off the lights, and followed the woman down the hall. He had an annoying prance to his walk. It made me want to bite him. It was an hour before all the sounds died away. I suppose I shouldn't have been surprised. It made me wish for a bit more of that smoke, though. Honestly.

At last the house was asleep. It was my time.

I needed my left foreleg to be my left hand again. Then I could deal with the bandage that held the hook into my wrist. So, all I had to do was change… But I couldn't change. I tried again anyway, because that was me, that was my power, and if I gave it everything I had, it had to work somehow. I gathered myself, aimed for that place where the change always happened—and broke into a cold sweat as the place receded infinitely and the tendons of my wrist and ankle went from a cold dull ache to a sudden, breathtaking, fiery flare.

Okay. That really wasn't going to work. I lay still, panting for a bit, trying to think. This was the heart of the magic that held me bound. I wasn't supposed to be able to change. Or rather, I was stuck, changed both ways at once, and held there, by these hooks. For a hook to work, it has to be the right size. And one thing I'd learned, during my recent adventures, is that I can be just about any size I want. So, all I had to do…

I made myself small, in both my forms. The hook in my tendons flamed a little, sensitive to my powers but not geared for this. Then I stifled a cry as my arm and leg were stretched against the hook and the manacles because I was nearly too small to reach the edges of the cage…

Okay. I went back to my usual length, about five feet nothing as a human, about the same as a wolf. And both at once. I breathed for a few minutes, summoning my anger from the place it lives just above my heart. When I thought of this cage, and lying here practically helpless, and someone doing this to me— my fury peaked and I got larger, curling as much as I could to keep from breaking out of the cage right away. I didn't want the dog waking up or the woman interrupting my escape. I wanted this to be quiet.

When my wrist and hind leg were pressed hard into the cuffs, and the tendons were three times their normal size, I felt the hook slip from the enlarged tendon of my rear paw, but it did not quite dislodge itself. I made myself even larger, ignoring the bite of the cuffs, scrunching down to make more room, and then felt the hook slip from the tendon of my right wrist. I felt a huge wave of relief, and took in a deep, involuntary breath, and reverted to my usual size. Whatever this device or spell was, it was leeching into the heart of my power, of my self, and it had been doing it for days. And now I was able to change, and it was easy, as it should be. I took my wolf form, feeling the power of my wolf nature engulf me. I slipped my right forepaw from the manacle, and pulled my left hind foot free too. I ripped the tape off my wrist with my teeth.

Under the tape and the surgical bandage I was wearing a tight braided leather band, woven with copper wire. The wires all met and threaded through a silver eye that pierced the leather bracelet and then, I assumed, me. I bit at it, feeling the tingle of power on my tongue, and managed to part the strips of leather, but the wire held firm. I nudged at it with my muzzle, but that wasn't going to do any good. I stopped, and changed back to my human form, ripped the tape from my left ankle, and found another bracelet there, humming with power. I reached my fingers through the bars and unclipped the latch of the cage. The door opened.

I was naked. Huh. Whoever had taken me prisoner had taken my clothes off when they put me in the cage. When my kind changes, ordinarily, we take whatever we're wearing next to our skin with us, and it comes back—mostly—when we change back. So someone had stripped me while I was in human form. I looked forward very much to meeting whoever that was again. On my terms, this time.

I nearly fell back when I lifted my right leg out of the cage. The wound in my hip where I'd been shot was deep though not wide. It started to bleed again. It smelled of blood, pus, and tar. A livid bruise rose round it wider than both my hands, and it hurt like mad when I stretched my leg.

The bright porch light reflected through the windows. I limped into the kitchen and found a sharp knife in the dish drainer. I sat down on the floor, favoring my right hip, and sawed away at the bracelet on my ankle, and when it fell loose, I gently pulled the silver hook out of the wound. Oh, what a relief. I cut the one off my wrist as well, and sat for a moment examining them.

The copper wire was twisted into curious patterns, and wound around the bloody little silver hook. It still tingled to the touch, alive with the power, whatever it was, that had worked on my ability to change. I pulled them apart, tore the wires into a tangle and then balled them up. The silver hooks still tingled. That was the spell. The leather bracelet, the copper wire, were just a distraction. And I was losing time. I needed to get rid of them. And I needed to get away.

I unlocked the glass door and pushed it open gently. I slipped outside into the open air. Whoever had wanted me naked, helpless, drugged, caged, manacled, and bespelled, had better watch out. I was the hunter now.

CHAPTER THREE

I stepped out onto a wide porch made of splintery pine boards that hadn't been painted in years. The brilliant porch light, besieged with bugs, made it impossible to see further, but I could smell... sheep. The night was cool, but not cold. After the smoke, the cleaning fluids, the cooking odors, the dog, and the woman's fetid breath, the open air tasted wonderful. I limped to the steps and down into the yard to get out of the light to where I could see, and get a sense of how to get out of here. On the right, a beat-up old pick-up and a dented green hatchback stood parked on a sparse layer of oily gravel. It was too much to hope that my car had been brought here as well. But I would be happy to take one of hers.

She had not conveniently left the keys in either the truck or the car. And the doors were locked anyway. What an untrusting nature. Beyond the cars, a dusty gravel drive sloped up the hillside between two fences, and around a bend toward the ridge beyond. The sound of traffic, never distant anywhere in the greater Los Angeles area, came from beyond those hills, and a little to the south. A pale smudge in the dark sky indicated the direction of the city.

My feet were bare. They're fairly tough, but probably not up to miles of gravel road. My ankle hurt, my hip ached, and I was limping hard to favor them both. Blood was dripping from my ankle and wrist, though the puncture in my hip had closed up again. I would be slow, easy to track. Wounded and naked as I was, it would be hard to blend in once I reached traffic and habitation. Walking away up the road was not my best option.

Across the yard a large building loomed in the shadows from which emanated the scent of horse, hay, and old wood. I limped on past, because from beyond I caught the scent of water. I was so thirsty it hurt. I changed with relief to my wolf form and dropped into the brimming horse trough on four feet. I hunkered down, lapping and lapping, letting the water wash my sores and clear my head as I filled my stomach. The darkness was not very dark. I was in a shallow valley, northwest of Los Angeles, not far from the ocean. The ridges all around were dotted with lights indicating scattered houses. Heading off toward the darkest ridge was probably my best bet. My ankle throbbed at the very thought of so much walking or running, but it was a better choice than the road, at present.

I stood up on two feet and stepped out of the trough, which was much quieter than heaving out on all fours. The dog might be man-shaped, and sated with sex, but I didn't want to risk being heard. Once out of the trough I changed again to my wolf form and shook off the water. I padded along the side of the barn until I reached the fence where the sheep pens began. I opened my mouth to draw in the delicious scent of many, many sheep, of wool and lanolin, manure, milk, and blood… and lambs.

It was the tail end of lambing season. The pen right in front of me held about two dozen big fat ewes on the verge of dropping the last lambs of the season. Half a dozen dim solar lights, strung on fence posts, gave just enough light to see if there was a new lamb. The sheep lay about the yard in little groups, sleeping or chewing. One was off in a corner, wandering back and forth. Probably about to drop. My mouth watered.

I changed back to human form so I could go on past the lambing pens without rousing all the sheep, which would be bound to wake up the dog, and probably the woman as well. She was a shepherd, after all. I walked slowly toward the rutted lane that led along the fence to the gate into each field. The next pasture was scattered with bales of straw built into square pens where new lambs lay curled up with their mothers. The field beyond stretched all the way across the valley and up the slopes of the hills. Here the rest of the flock, the ewes with older lambs, the yearlings, and a few rams, lay in groups scattered over the field.

I stopped and leaned on the fence post. My hip was a little less sore for the exercise, but the wounds on my wrist and ankle were bleeding again. The ridges beyond the sheep fields seemed a long, long ways away. I am much faster on four legs than two, but being wounded in two opposite legs was really going to slow me down. Besides, crossing the field in wolf form was going to cause a sheep riot. After all, we've been teaching the woollies for thousands of years what it means when a wolf shows up in their midst.

In front of me, a little lamb, his frame still hollow and curled from his time in the womb, trotted from ewe to ewe, crying for his mother. A nicker, a surge, and mom charged up to him, trailing her other lamb, and nosed him all around while he went straight for her udder and head-butted it hard. He grabbed a teat and started sucking like he was starving. He probably was. I certainly was. He smelled so good I wanted to cry.

I started down the lane that ran along the fence of the sheep pastures, heading for the hills across the bowl of the valley. I caught the scent of dog, and stopped. On the other side of the barn stood three adjoining chain linked dog kennels. I opened my mouth to catch a whiff to see if they were occupied, but a moment later in the ambient light I could just make out three, no, four border collies. Two lay on top of the old oil drums that served as den and shelter for each of them. Two more lay in the corner of the kennels. All four stared out at the sheep. Not good.

I was down wind, for the moment. The breeze had changed directions a couple of times since I'd stepped out into the night. They hadn't seen me, but if I continued along the lane they were going to, and then there would be a whole lot of noise. If the shepherd heard the ruckus, and loosed them, I'd have to be really fast to get up into the hills before they ran me down. And at the moment, I was very decidedly not fast.

I could probably kill them if they came at me. I would face them in wolf form, after all. But four of them, all at once, meant I would probably get bitten, even if I did kill them all in the end. I was already wounded. They would know that; they would smell the blood, see from the way I stood and moved, and they would attack me where I was weakest. I would end up hurt worse than I was already. You don't see crippled wolves. Crippled wolves die. It's a mercy that they do. I was not getting out across the sheep fields. Not tonight.

I retraced my steps to the barn and pulled open the door just enough to slip inside. I felt the presence of power as I entered, as though someone had given the air shape, and organized it. Huh. The energy centered on the workbench against the far wall of the barn. A peg board of neatly organized tools stood above an ancient table. Someone had been raising a fair amount of power here, and for a long time.

The hair on my neck stood up as the still air stirred. I smelled my scent on that table, and my blood. That was where they had done this to me.

I had an impulse to leap over there in my wolf form and snuff out every trace of evidence of who was there, and what they were.

Being wounded and sore gave me a moment to think about that. I couldn't feel any wards that would alert the shepherd to my presence if I touched them. It was possible, though, that whoever had bespelled me over there on that table, had the power to make wards sneaky enough that I wouldn't sense them. I did walk over close enough to try and see if any of my clothes were there, but I didn't see them.

To the right, bales of fresh alfalfa were stacked high. Old sacks of feed and dog food stood next to them. The rats and mice had been at them. I grinned to myself. I limped along the wall toward the pair of stalls on the left. One was lit by a dim bulb hanging from a loop of wire above the door post. A tired old horse stood inside with his head lowered, not bothering to mouth his wisps of hay. In the stall beyond, the shepherd had piled broken farm tools, stacks of lumber, tailings of wire fencing, twisted tee posts, and old animal cages of various sizes. The old horse watched me as I poked around, looking for a discarded pair of boots, a rag made from a shirt, paint-splashed overalls. There was nothing.

A pair of cats stared down at me from the darkened loft. I didn't bother looking up. A heavy, crusted blanket hung over the stall door, but that wasn't going to be any more use than the worn saddle and mended tack.

To ride out of here on my captor's horse was a pleasing thought, but while there are few down sides to being one of the wolf kind, this was one. We do not ride horses. Bad things happen when we do.

I went back to the water trough and slipped into it again. I drank and drank, looking up at the few stars that shone through the hazy sky.

The cage, the manacles, the hooks, the drugged smoke, the spells, were all part of the trap. This valley was another part of it. Just getting out of the cage did not mean I was free.

If I went into my captor's bedroom and found a way to kill both her and her dog, then I would have time to find clothes, search out car keys, and get out of here. In my present state, attacking both of them was not the best of plans. For all I knew, the woman slept with a gun under her pillow, and would sic Fido on me while she placed her shot. I could kill the dog quickly, but to win, I would have to be lucky. And that was not a good way to plan.

If I killed her and got away, I would not know who had shot, bespelled and captured me. Whoever it was knew who I was, had known how to find me, divert me, attack and capture me. If I left now, whoever it was still had all that knowledge and power, and I was still their prey.

I shook myself and went back to the house. In human form, I let myself back in. I found the box of incense, and switched out the drugged blocks for some that were the same size. I rubbed them with the drugged ones, so they would have the right smell, at least to a human nose. Then I distributed the drugged ones in hiding places around the room, deep in the couch cushions that hadn't been cleaned in years, under the fridge, in the ashes of the stove, behind the pristine set of Reader's Digest condensed books, where some mouse long ago had cached a supply of dog kibble.

I lit the plain old ordinary incense and set it under the stove. I would not be drugged again.

I wrapped my wrists again in the gauze and tape. I got back in the cage. The next bit was tricky. I have changed from my wolf form to my human form and back again thousands upon thousands of times, hardly thinking about it. To stick halfway, half human, half wolf, wasn't something it would ever have occurred to me to do. But I'd been held in that form for several days, so it was possible. I tried changing and changing back at the same time. That didn't work. I tried changing one part of me at a time, and that didn't work at all. After what seemed like hours of trying I learned that I could hold part of myself in one form while I took the turn that brought me into my other form... and there it was. One wolf paw, one human hand. One wolf hind foot, one human foot… and then I had to start again because I'd gotten it wrong-way round. I slipped the manacle loosely over my wolf hind foot, and then my human wrist.

I hadn't destroyed the silver hooks, or the wire and leather wristbands. I'd hidden them so that even the dog couldn't suss them out. I needed them. They were evidence.

I lay back, exhausted, uncomfortable, my wounds aching, and tried to rest. I heal pretty fast. In three days, I should at least be much faster than I was tonight. The cage, the manacles, the drugs and the spells were an illusion now. Sometimes, there is a wolf in a trap. And sometimes, the wolf is the trap. Let them come.

My next job was to deal with Baz.

Shepherd woman was called Sarah. I learned this the following day when a delivery man banged on the door to the back porch and called her name. Baz the dog in human form stood at bay in the kitchen with his mouth slightly open, while the delivery guy called to him over and over to come and sign for the damn thing. Baz bolted for the bedroom and didn't come back until Sarah mounted the steps, told off the delivery man for not knowing she was out with the sheep, signed, and dragged the box into the house, still complaining. The delivery man tore off up the drive, gravel spraying under his wheels.

She burned her eggs cooking breakfast while she was trying to get the thing out of the box, and then stood there cursing for a long time. Then she cursed into her phone for awhile, having to do with whoever had delivered the box not being willing to come and get it again. Then she got Baz to pick up the box and carry it outside. She came back and dumped the burned eggs in a bowl, set it out for Baz, and then shoved him back in the house and locked the door after her. The motor of the truck started up, and then receded. This was promising.

Baz stood by the door looking out, changing his angle to look out farther up the road. He went over and mouthed up the eggs, and then stood licking the bowl while he stared out the window. Then he harrumphed, and went over to the couch.

I waited until he had plumped down, scratched at the couch pillows, turned around, curled up and closed his eyes. I waited a little longer until his limbs relaxed. I slipped my manacles, unhooked the cage door, stepped out and into wolf form. I didn't let him get a whiff of me until I was on top of the couch, looming over him, grown so huge my head was almost as big as he was. As I hit the couch his eyes flew open and I leaned down and snarled into his face.

So, he could make a sound! It was a delicate little shriek as he spun off the couch onto the floor and tried to run on four legs to the bedroom. I stepped off the couch, avoiding the damp stain he'd left there. He'd been very frightened indeed. I smiled as I thought how much trouble he was going to be in, and stalked down the hall to the bedroom.

I hauled him out from under the bed by one leg, rolled him over and grabbed his throat in my teeth. I did it carefully. My plan did not include leaving a mark on him, but he didn't know that. He clutched himself, his eyes rolled back, his tongue came out and he licked his lips again and again.

I let him go and stepped off, and he ran off again. He'd left a puddle this time, big, stinky, and messy. My plan was working very well indeed.

I set off after him, hauled him out from under the table, dragged him around a bit until he rolled on his back and his tongue came out again. Little, powerless canine to big, imposing canine: you can kill me if you want, but please don't. I let him go, let him run, and caught up with him again. Big canine to little canine: I know. The next time, he tried to climb into my cage, and I started laughing, and almost tripped into my human form. When I let him go the next time, he didn't move, but just lay there staring at me. Lesson learned. For the moment, at least.

I sniffed around the house for anything that belonged to me. My clothes would have been nice, but there was nothing. I went into the bedroom, rummaged through the drawers until I found some sweats that would fit me. I stashed them in the back of a bottom drawer where I could find them easily in the dark.

I came out into the living room in human form, but Baz didn't get up. Good enough. I went to the kitchen and made a search for the car keys, but I didn't turn up anything. She must have them all on one ring or something. I went through the fridge, helped myself to some leftover rice, some cheese, some overcooked meat. I don't think I would have noticed what a lousy cook she was, but Richard cooked for me for nearly a month, and he had standards. In his memory, so had I. It didn't stop me from scarfing up anything I could find. I was starving. It just meant I despised the woman while I did it.

Baz's head came up before I heard the sound, but I trusted his hearing. I closed the fridge, hopped back into the cage, latched it, and bound myself up again. Baz jumped up and ran for the bedroom. I grinned after him. Then I panicked as I realized that getting into both forms was not quick. It had taken me what seemed like hours the night before. And the truck was coming back, I could hear it now. And I couldn't remember how I'd done it. And I realized I'd forgotten to look for the woman's gun; she was bound to have a gun, and probably a shotgun as well. Then the truck came to a stop outside, and her footsteps fell heavily on the porch, the back door opened, and I was still in human form.

Sarah walked into the kitchen, and I was still frantically trying to change into the right two parts. She paused a moment, stepped into the living room, sniffed, found the stain on the couch and began to scream. I got ready to come out and kill her, which would involve getting out of the damn cage and then shifting to wolf form—but then she charged down the hall to the bedroom, shouting at Baz. I relaxed. I would have plenty of time to figure this out. It would be a few minutes before she had a thought for me. Sure enough, there was a renewed scream when she saw the puddle Baz had made in the bedroom.

I got myself sorted out, listening to the rather disturbing sounds coming from down the hall. Poor guy. Even in human form, it was still a dog's life. When she came back into the room, dragging Baz by the arm, I seemed to be chained up, muzzily awake, staring out at the noise, but she charged right by me and out the door.

When she came in again after awhile, Sarah was on the phone. "Sick? It could be." I heard the fridge open. "Well, shit, he got into a bunch of leftovers... I was going to throw that round steak out. Yeah, he might just be sick. When can you come?"

She'd called the vet on Baz. A vet who made house calls. The fridge door slammed. "Not until tonight? Elaine, what if something's gone wrong?"

Huh. My eyes opened wide for a second. I'd heard her talking to Elaine before, about me.

Sarah wandered into the living room, but didn't spare me a glance. My eyes narrowed. Good thing she didn't see the look, or she would have known I was about as drugged up as she was. But that she could have me—me—caged up on her floor, and not think about it, well. Somebody needed a lesson. And I was looking right at her.

Sarah went out again, still talking on the phone. I took a nap. I didn't open my eyes when Sarah, talking sweet and syrupy, tried to get Baz to come in the house. She probably wanted him to clean up his mess. It was getting pretty ripe in the living room. I grinned and went back to sleep.

Later on there was the sound of scrubbing. Sarah stood over Baz, on his hands and knees with a bucket and scrub brush. His little blue and white bandana was on his head, but perched askew. He was watching me as he worked. Sarah was not. I opened my eyes, let them go gold with my fury and power, and closed them again as Baz yipped and knocked over the bucket.

Okay, I probably shouldn't have done that, because the next thing I knew Sarah was standing over my cage, with the phone in her ear again. "I'm not sure," she said. "The smoke is all right, I checked. She's in the same position. But I swear, Baz saw her move or something. He's freaked out, Elaine. He's under my bed and I can't get him to come out."

I did not betray myself by smiling. But it was close.

"I don't care what you do to her. I want her out of here. Tonight."

What? What had I missed?

"Because she's bothering Baz! That's how I know! He's never done anything like this, not since he was a puppy. Well, yeah, he was sick that time—. Okay, he did throw up in your car."

Sarah covered her mouth with her hand. I almost did the same.

"All right," she snapped. "You take a look at Baz, and then we'll see." She bent over the cage as she closed the phone. I tried some heavy breathing, as though I were so deeply asleep the sound didn't even disturb me.

"Baz? Baz, sweetie…"

She turned on the television and listened to the evening news as she banged around the kitchen making dinner. Then she stood at the counter, eating a tuna fish sandwich and yelling back at the announcer. Baz was back in the barn. She called up Elaine again when she made up a bowl for Baz, to ask her what she should feed him, and why wasn't she here yet, and when was she coming. She put it on speaker phone, so I heard both sides of the argument. Elaine told Sarah not to give Baz anything, if he was sick, and Sarah talked her around to some kibble with tuna oil, a bowl of milk, and the cheese stick he got as a treat. Good thing he was a dog, or he really was going to be sick.

Elaine sounded stressed. She was late because she had to make another house call. She would come soon. She would bring with her everything she needed, to take care of Baz, and me.

My eyes opened. She would be here soon.

I wasn't going to stay for this. That was not a good plan. Sarah was a magic user. This Elaine vet woman might have even more power, more than I could take on. I lay there and thought for awhile. It was getting dark when the heavy truck came down the drive and pulled up with a tinking engine next to the house. I heard Sarah call a greeting and then their voices dropped as they talked outside. If they came in here and Elaine planned to "take care of me" first, I was going to kill them both. If I could. Because I didn't think I could get out of any deeper a trap than I was in already. I barely had a hold on this one yet. So it was a good thing that I heard their voices recede, as they headed out to the barn.

I made myself small in my human form, slipped out of the cuffs, unlatched the door, left the manacles closed tight, latched the door after me—if magic was nine tenths distraction, I could use every bit that came to me tonight.

I let myself out of the front door, which put the house between me and the barn. It was dark outside, but the light on the back porch was so bright the reflection lit the front of the house as well. When I reached the corner of the house I paused and looked across at the barn. Sarah had shoved open the door, talking to a tall, spindly woman in a bulky jacket, open at the front, her hair in a heavy braid down her back. Elaine wore round glasses and carried a black box by its handle, leaning a little to counter its weight. Sarah went into the barn, calling Baz's name in her sugary voice, and the vet followed. I thought I recognized her form, though she wasn't close enough for me to catch her scent.

I moved quietly along an uneven brick walkway, skirted some spindly trees, crossed a bare patch of weeds that had once been a garden, and reached the lambing pen. I opened the first gate wide, then hurried down to the next field. I was in human form, and I'd come from the house, so the border collies, who must have seen me by now, were not barking. Yet. I opened the next gate. It wanted to swing shut so I propped it with a rock so it wouldn't close.

I hurried to the next gate, stepping long on my good leg, and favoring my ankle, hoping my bruised hip would warm up again soon. It hurt, but not as much as it had last night. I reached the big field, and dragged wide the double gates. They opened into the rutted lane I was following. Beyond the lane on the left a huge field had been cut to stubble after the last harvest of alfalfa. Far across it, up the hillside a ways, behind the fences of the next farm, dogs were barking.

I reached the farthest gate and opened it wide. The sheep, who had been fed and settled for the night, watched me incuriously. That was about to change. I looked back at Sarah's house and barn. I'd gone about a quarter of a mile. This next part needed to be fast, or it was going to end badly. If I did it right, there was going to be a whole lot of distraction working in my favor.

CHAPTER FOUR

I changed. I leaped into the sheep field at a bound—and almost crumpled. I'd gotten used to favoring my ankle. I'd forgotten about my foreleg. I started forward more tentatively, but the hysterical barking of the border collies across the way reminded me that what I did next needed to be done as fast as possible.

I loped across the field toward the house, and the sheep, sweet, beautiful sheep, high-tailed it away from me. I sent them bounding toward the double gates, and they galloped out, charging off in a panic into the dark, empty field beyond. I got to the second sheep field, and charged across it as well, and all the ewes and their little lambs ran out into the night. Most of the lambs ran at their moms' heels, but of course a bunch of them were slow to get up, or facing the wrong way, or ran into the fence instead of the gate, and were left behind. They trotted around, crying pitifully like the babies they were, but the moms didn't stop. It might have been a hundred generations since they'd caught the scent, but they remembered, and they knew what it meant when a wolf was in the pen. Ewes with newborn lambs, penned in squares of hay bales, found it in them to leap straight out and follow the herd, leaving their little lambs bawling behind them. I nearly tripped over one of the little sweeties, who banged his head into my leg, and nosed around, crying and looking for mom, and milk, and comfort. He smelled so good, I could have just eaten him up. But I couldn't stop yet.

I almost crawled over the fence into the lambing pen, where the heavy ewes rolled their eyes and jounced toward the gate and off into the lane. I followed them, and oh, how they ran. You wouldn't think anything so big and encumbered could lumber so fast.

The border collies were barking hysterically; Sarah and Elaine emerged from the barn. Sarah ran for the house and after a minute returned to the yard with a shotgun—I knew there would be a shotgun! I ducked around the house, and came out behind them, just off the porch, in the shadows by the cars.

"What is it?" Elaine called. "What's out there?"

"I don't know," Sarah said, sounding deadly from behind her gun. "But I'm going to find out."

Sarah ran for the kennels. I thought that's what she'd do. I sloped across the yard behind the trucks so I could watch from the far side of the barn. Sarah let out the first dog, and before she gave him a command he went charging toward the open field where the sheep had scattered and were only now beginning to slow down. She whistled at him and he stopped and lay down, trembling. She let out the pair that shared one kennel, and then sent all three of them to make a huge loop around the field, two going one way, one going the other. The fourth dog yelped and whined at her.

"Get down, Polly, you're not going." Sarah patted the fence and then told her sharply to be quiet. I was close enough then, and on the right side of the wind, to know why this dog was locked up by herself. She was in heat.

Elaine came over to the kennels with the flashlight.

"Did you see anything?" Sarah asked her.

"Just the sheep. I don't see any down."

"Spook and Joe will bring them back," Sarah said.

"Why'd you let Tally out?" Elaine asked. They were walking away from me, toward the field where the dogs had circled out after the sheep and were gathering them up.

"Might as well give him a run," Sarah said. "He won't do any harm."

When they crossed the lane, I changed to my human form and slipped up to the last kennel. Polly didn't seem very interested in killing me. She stared out at the moving herd in the distance, caterwauling, her voice rising and falling in excitement and frustration. I opened the latch on her kennel.

"Go get 'em, Polly!"

Polly shot out of there, leaped over the fence into the lambing pen, and took off across the field. I closed the latch on her kennel and ducked behind the barn just as I heard Sarah shouting. "Polly! Leave it! Come! No, no, Joe, get out of there, Spook, lie down LIE DOWN! Polly! Polly, come here right now you goddamn idiot bitch!"

I grinned. In six weeks, there were going to be unlawful puppies.

When I rounded the back of the barn, I saw the flashlight bobbing in the big open field, and heard Sarah yelling and whistling to her dogs. I started to limp across the yard back to the house when another border collie came out of the barn. I stopped. He stopped. If he barked, Sarah would head back here with her shotgun, and I would be in big trouble. If he attacked me, it might slow me down enough to attract attention. I gathered myself to change, leap on him, grab him by the neck, when the border collie dropped to the ground and rolled over, sticking his tongue out between his lips. Oh. That border collie. Baz was almost all black with a silly white blaze in the form of a crescent across his face, white stockings, and a white tip on his tail, which he wagged hopefully, just a tiny bit. Good dog.

"Get in the barn, Baz," I said. Then I changed to my wolf form, and he was gone. There is great satisfaction in a job done well. Respect is an important lesson.

I limped heavily on both bad legs over to the house. They hurt like hell. I was not going to be able to run or even walk much farther tonight. I had to avoid the dogs, and I had to get out of here. I looked out across the field where the mass of sheep were being trotted back toward the gates to their pens, hurried on their way by one of the dogs. No sign of the other three. Ha. Sarah was still going to have quite a time getting the sheep back in the right paddocks, with the correct lambs. I had to get out of sight before she got back. But first, I needed some supplies.

I changed again as I reached for the doorknob and went into the house. I grabbed the sweats I'd put aside earlier and pulled them on. I swiped a bandana out of the same drawer. I stopped in the bathroom to drink as much as I could hold. I went out the front door, since Sarah didn't use it much, and most of the light was in back.

At the side of the house I tucked the bandana into the pocket of my sweats where it would probably stay, and changed to my wolf form again. I gathered myself and unleashed my fear, my pain and my anger all at once, making myself big enough to leap onto the roof. I nosed around and found the little silver hooks in the leather bracelets, still smelling of my blood and pus, where I'd tossed them the previous night. Up on the roof, the dogs wouldn't find them. I figured it wasn't likely that tonight they'd find me there either.

I changed to my human form, retrieved the bandana and used it to wrap up the bracelets, wire, and hooks. I didn't want them in my pocket. Our clothes go with us when we make the change from human to wolf and back. We don't usually lose things out of our pockets, though it's been known to happen. But I was not going to risk having those bespelled hooks near my body when I changed. For all I knew, one of them could end up in my brain. I let myself get small again, leaching out my passion and fear. I lay down on the roof to enjoy the show.

I must have dozed off, out of relief at being in one form at a time, out of exhaustion from the trek I'd made on my damaged legs. Sarah woke me, shouting and carrying on in all directions down in the yard, about Polly being out—she was still out—the sheep being all mixed up, and me being gone, and yelling that I had to be responsible. Well, she got that right. She came up on the porch with the dog Spook, and one of my bandages, told him to "find" and sent him off into the dark. I'd been looking forward to this. He nosed around the yard, circled the barn, went into the barn, and came back to the porch. Yup. That's where I'd gone in my human form. She must have given him the gauze from my right wrist. Elaine came out next with the other gauze, and they had an argument over whether it would make a difference—Sarah outshouted her, but Elaine was right. Of course it would make a difference! Wolves smell different from humans. Really, they do.

"Sarah, please, just try it. What harm can it do?"

"Harm? What are you talking about? Do you know how many lambs I've lost tonight?"

She hadn't lost any, so far as I knew, but it was fun to lie there and listen to her carry on about it.

Sarah talked herself around after awhile, and gave the other border collie, Joe, the scent of the other piece of gauze. Joe took off across the lambing pen, hopped over into the next pen, hopped into the big field and ran almost to the end of it. I lay there grinning. Sarah must have thought for a few moments that Joe was after me, and would catch me, just before he came through the gate, ran down the lane, and back to the house. He was tracking me backward.

There's no way to tell which way your prey went from a scent trail. You have to figure out in the first place if they were coming or going, before you go after them. I'd gone in a circle. That's always fun. Back home, when I was a kid, my brothers and cousins and I used to play hide and seek. One game could take hours, as our range included a seventy-mile valley, two ridges of mountains, and a long black beach. Those were the days. And that was not quite two years ago, before my dad disappeared. But that's another story.

Sarah put one of her dogs back in the kennel, went back into the house, and then back out to the field to try and pair up the right ewes with the right lambs, before the little critters cried themselves sick or starved to death. I made use of her absence. Elaine came out of the house in tight-lipped fury, opened the cab door, and tossed her vet bag onto the front seat. She came back, hoisted the big live-animal cage that had been my prison into the back of the truck and climbed into the cab. Sarah hadn't done much to make her feel friendly. Funny, I felt the same way. Elaine drove off very fast down the drive. And that was fine with me because by that time, I was in the backseat of her big truck. Trusting soul, she'd left the door unlocked.

We bounced down the gravel road, climbed the far ridge, got on to blacktop and sped down the hill in the darkness. Elaine's bulky jacket didn't disguise her thin shoulders. Her boots smelled of dirt and sheep muck, of course. Her jeans smelled of—camel? She turned on her CD player and yelled along with the singer who also had someone who'd done her wrong and gotten her mad and needed shooting right now. She trapped her long braid against the seat to keep it from swinging around as she rocked the music.

I sat curled up in the footwell behind the driver's seat, which is the least likely place for her to notice me if she happened to glance in the back. A gun case lay on the back seat, on top of a hairy old blanket that smelled of all kinds of critters recently, and one old dog from a long time ago. When I found the small plastic box in the other footwell, I was pretty sure I knew what was going to be in it.

The truck slowed, made a sliding California stop, and turned right. Then it gathered speed, the interior lit now and then by street lights. We were closing in on civilization, and I didn't want to do that yet.

I sat up, poking my head between the two front seats. "Hi!" I said. "Do I know you?"

"Oh my God oh my God oh my God!" Elaine jerked, the truck swerved, and the left front tire smacked up onto the median.

"Hey! Careful!"

"Oh God oh God oh God—" Elaine swung the wheel wide to avoid driving right over the median, and plowed across two lanes. What a good thing there wasn't any traffic just then.

"Watch out! I couldn't find the seatbelt back here."

Elaine held the wheel in a death grip. "Help me please—"

"Turn off that noise!" I told her.

Hand shaking, Elaine turned off the CD player. "—please please please please help me—"

She wasn't asking me, I was pretty sure of that. "Pull to the right," I said. We were on a big wide street, two lanes each way with a median strip planted with bushes. On either side, housing developments rose above the ramparts of their sound walls, their security gates, and the landscaped slopes of their future mudslides.

The car kept going straight. Elaine's mouth was open, but she wasn't yelling anymore. Her eyes rolled my way, her round glasses glinting in the light reflected from the street lamps, and she put her foot down. The car leaped forward. I touched the point of one of the darts from the plastic case to her neck. Elaine gasped and lifted her chin. "Do you know what this is?" I asked, but obviously, she knew exactly what it was. She lifted her foot from the gas pedal.

"Slow down, and pull over."

I could read the tension in her arms, in her jaw, like a newspaper. "Vet Crashes Truck After Late Night Sheep Riot!" I leaned in to speak into her ear. "Do you know how much it hurts to have one of these things stab into you? Go on, ask me how I know." The truck slowed a little more. "That's right, because I'm going to hold this dart right here and not move until the truck is stopped. So, it would be good if we didn't hit any bumps or anything."

She drew in her breath, as though she'd been holding it for a minute. "What do you want?"

"What I want is to have the last five days of my life back. Any chance of that?"

"I didn't—I mean, we weren't—"

"And," I added, since there was no limit on what I could wish for, "I'd also like it a whole lot if I didn't have a dart wound in my hip, and if my wrist and ankle weren't still bleeding, and they didn't all hurt so damn much!"

She winced away from my voice, and the truck swerved again. "I—"

"Yes. That is what I want to talk about." Just ahead a narrow road met our thruway on the right, leading up a barren hillside where development had not yet been committed. "Turn right there," I told her. "Not too hard, because you don't want to jerk my hand or anything." She made the turn as gently as that big truck could.

"Where are we going?" Her voice was not quite steady. In a rising tone, she asked, "What do you want? What are you going to do?"

I couldn't help it. I grinned. "I'm so hungry. I'm going to eat you for dinner, my little pumpkin!"

Okay, the screams were fun, but the truck weaving out of control, not so much. I was careful not to poke her with the dart, because I really did want to have a conversation, not watch her bleed all over the place. And again, it was lucky for us there was no traffic on that lane going either way because we would have nailed them all. I slipped into the front passenger seat and put a hand on the wheel to steady the truck. Her screams rose into hysteria. Then she got a good look at me, and they began to taper off.

I made myself look small. There are times when wearing the aspect of your second nature like a spirit superimposed over your head, or changing to a wolf so large she hardly fits in the room, and her head looks big enough to swallow someone whole, can go a long way to focusing a conversation. But just now, I didn't need Elaine any more crazy, and I knew that making myself small didn't mean I was any less dangerous. It just allowed her to believe it. For the moment. She stopped screaming and stared at me.

"But—you're just a kid!"

"Yes," I said. "I'm the kid that you *shot* the other night. Pull over here."

She pulled into a wide place in the road and stopped. I reached for the keys, turned off the engine, and pocketed them.

"Now," I said, and I let myself grow larger. "You get to explain why you shot me."

She leaned away from me until her back was to the door. I thought she was going to grab the door handle and make a run for it into the night—and I have to say that the thought of running her down in my wolf nature made me forget, just for a moment, the towering pain in my wrist and ankle, which meant all I could have done was hobble after her anyway. But she didn't run. Her right hand groped for the end of her braid. I wondered if she had some kind of weapon stashed there. All I could see was a small dark metal clasp. She grabbed it, held it up to me, and made a warding sign with her other hand. "Avaunt ye, demon! Begone!"

I heard a sound like a marshmallow popping, and felt a tiny rush of air. She shook the clasp at me. "Thing of darkness! I command you to depart!"

"Um. No."

"You—demon—begone!"

"I'm not a demon."

"You're…" Behind her specs I saw her blink. "You are a demon. I saw you." She shook the little charm at me. "This should be working."

I plucked the clasp from her fingers and leaned forward to examine it. She didn't try to stop me. She just leaned away as far as her braid would let her. The clasp was a Celtic knot, cast in bronze. I could feel the twinge of a ward there, but it wasn't very strong. This was supposed to dismiss a demon? Richard wouldn't have bothered to swat it aside, even before he got his powers back.

"Where did you get this?" I asked her.

"I don't have to tell you."

"No?" I lifted a lip at her. "Well, it won't work on me." I tossed it and her braid back to her.

"I saw you! I saw—"

"What did you see?"

She swallowed. "You changed into a wolf. You couldn't do that if you weren't a demon."

I smiled, and it was not my nice smile. She leaned back as it turned into something wider, with too many teeth, and she stopped talking. I made that twist in my mind that allowed my other aspect, my wolf self, to rise up and superimpose itself above me, until I wore both my natures at once. A little trick I'd learned from a friend of mine of the bear kind. "Only all my life," I said. I leaned in to her, and she shrank. She must have been a head taller than me, but now she was the one who made herself small. I asked her, "Have you never met one of the wolf kind before?"

She licked her lips. I wondered if she meant it the same way Baz did. "The wolf kind?"

"One of the two-natured folk, who wear one aspect while the other waits." She looked over my human head, where my wolf head loomed over her, eyes gleaming, mouth opening. "Well, most of the time."

Her mouth opened, too. She stared, first at one of my heads, then the other. I could only see her out of my human eyes, since the wolf head wasn't really there. But it's still a cool trick. She swallowed a couple of times. She started to lift a hand, but then thought the better of it, which is a good thing because whichever head I'm wearing, it bites.

"That's just…"

What? Amazing? Cool? Beautiful? Terrifying. Yeah. I grinned.

"They said—they told me there's a demon in Los Angeles, who has the power to stop the World Snake, but she won't." She stared at me over her glasses. "You've heard of the World Snake."

"Oh, yes." I had heard too damn much about the stupid World Snake.

"And that it's coming here. And that it's going to swallow this whole section of California. That's what you heard, right?"

"Yes, but it's over. It's taken care of. She's not going to come."

"Oh? That's not what I've heard. There's a demon, or a girl who's possessed by a demon—"

"Look," I told her, "there is no demon. It's gone."

"Then there was a demon!"

"I told you—"

She leaned forward. "How do you know it's really gone?"

I sighed. Oh, Richard. "Believe me. He's gone."

She looked over her glasses at me. "I have a very good friend, who can tame this demon, and use its powers for good."

I leaned my head back against the seat. Telling her things just didn't seem to be working.

She went on. "Cecil, that's my friend, said he could do so much more with this demon if he had it. So, Holly and I—Holly's my sister—decided we would get it for him, for his birthday."

"And that is why you shot me?"

"I didn't…"

"You want to see the hole?" It still really hurt.

"I thought I was shooting a demon," she said quietly. "Holly asked me to get it for Cecil."

"For his birthday. And who's this Cecil who wants a live birthday present that bleeds?"

"No—not you, just the demon, I told you."

"And shooting me was just a means to an end."

"We were trying to save you!"

"Couldn't you have asked me first if I needed saving?"

She took that in for a moment. "All right," she said at last. "I'm sorry. I'm sorry I shot you."

There! Was that so hard? Except, now that she'd finally said it, it didn't seem like anywhere near enough. All of a sudden, I really wanted to bite her. I wanted to taste her blood, and then spit it on the ground.

"So," I said, in a voice that really meant, *I want to kill you right now*, "tell me about Cecil."

"It was his birthday on Saturday."

"Who is he?"

She turned wide eyes on me. "Cecil. You never heard of him? No? He's the leader of the Order of the Higher Nature of Tantric Karma."

"You're kidding me."

"He has a group of followers in Malibu, and he teaches them meditation techniques for advancing upon the Way. Cecil is the Noble Master, the Teacher, the Great-Souled One. He is the incarnation in this century of the Universal One."

She said all those words, but her voice had spit in it too.

"You don't believe that," I pointed out.

"I used to."

"Then why do you want to give this guy a birthday present?"

"I don't. Holly does. My sister. And—I told her I would help."

"Because you had the gun."

She looked at me. "Because I have experience with large animals. I'm a large animal vet."

Oh. "So that's why you smell like a camel?"

I swear she flushed. "Yes. There's a camel who's going to drop her calf anytime now. I had to… I gave her a check-up today."

I looked down at her arm and sniffed. So she had. "And what does Cecil want with a demon?" I asked her.

"Holly said Cecil could use the demon to stop the World Snake."

"That's done. We did it already."

"Yeah. Anyway. Cecil says the demon could teach him things about the world that would save him a whole lot of incarnations."

"But you don't believe him."

"I think Cecil's full of shit," she said.

"And you still shot me?!"

"I said I was sorry! And anyway, I shot a wolf. I really big wolf!" She looked at me sideways. "You didn't look like you do now."

It's true, in my wolf form, I have almost my full growth. And in my wolf form, I am pretty big. I almost smiled at her for noticing.

She went on, "Anyway, I'm sorry that you were stuck in the cage for so long. Cecil was supposed to be back on Saturday, and Holly planned a big party, but he was out of town."

"So you were planning to keep me drugged and chained up for how long?"

"Until Cecil got back and could safely remove the demon." Her glasses glinted again.

"There is no—" I started, and she held up her hands.

"I know, I know!"

I didn't think I had convinced her. I didn't know what more I could do about it except start chewing on her, and somehow

I didn't think that would convince her either that I was not possessed, or that the demon had gone. I should have tried harder, but I hurt, and pain makes you stupid. I let it go. And boy would I be sorry later.

"All right," I said. "Tell me about these." I reached back into the footwell, grabbed the bandana and opened it up. The leather bracelets, the tangled wires, the delicate little silver hooks, were still smeared with my gore.

She wasn't surprised to see them. She knew exactly what they were. All she said was, "How did you get them out?"

"How do you think?" I snarled. I wasn't going to tell her all my ways.

"You're the first who's ever done it."

And suddenly I was very large indeed. She shrank back, gasping again. "Do you mean to tell me," I said, low in my throat, "that you do this to folks all the time?"

"No—no, that's not what I meant. I meant—"

"Oh," I was tired, which made me slow. I realized, "Baz couldn't get his out. He's not two-natured. He's just changed. Who changed him?"

"Sarah. My aunt, Sarah. She's always been able to do that."

"That woman can change people into animals?"

"And animals into other animals." Elaine got a little reminiscent smile on her face. "It's fun."

"Fun?"

Her smiled faded. "It can be fun."

"Who else has she done it to?"

"Did you see her horse?"

"The old bay in the barn?"

For a moment she had a trace of a grin. "Aunt Sarah tells everyone her ex just walked out on her. And he did. In a way."

"And you help her with this?"

"No, no, I just treat them."

"Who put these in me?" My wrist and my ankle still hurt, badly. You don't want to be lame, if you're a wolf. You really, really don't. As my anger rose, I began to grow.

It took her a moment, her fear peaking again strong enough for me to smell it in my human form. She curled back against the door and almost wailed, "I did. I wanted to help get the demon— for Cecil." She added, "I'm sorry." But that wasn't enough. "Oh, God. It's all fucked up now."

It isn't usual to change form without deciding to, but I found myself staring at her through my yellow wolf eyes, my butt crunched up against the door as I took up more than half of the cab. Elaine crouched down against the door with a cry, turning away from me, warding me with her hand. I contemplated the sheen of sweat on her neck. I though how easily I could pierce the the cartilege of her throat with my teeth, how the blood would stream, and that it would taste good. If I killed her, I would be certain that she never hurt me again. Or I could at least bite her a little. I could hurt her the way she hurt me.

I changed back. It took her a few moments to stop crying in fear, and sit up again to look at me. I held out the bandana. "Did you make these things?"

"No, God, no. I don't have any magic. I'm just a vet."

"An evil vet. Just what I need. So, who does make these things?" I lifted up one of the little hooks. I could still feel the tingle. Whatever it was, it was still working.

"I don't know if I should tell you."

"Listen, evil vet, I just spent five days locked in a cage. If you don't want to be the one to pay for that, tell me who is."

She lifted her hands. "All right. I can't tell you his name."

"You can't?

"He's a metallurgist. He teaches metalwork at Pasadena City College. Holly—my sister Holly knows him."

Something was cockeyed about what she was telling me, but in the shape I was in, I wasn't sharp enough to figure it out. I wrapped up the silver hooks, the wire and bracelets in the bandana, and put them in my pocket. Pasadena was not that big. I was going to find that guy.

Elaine said, "There really was a demon, though. Wasn't there?"

I looked out into the darkness. Shapes of bushes and a few trees were silhouetted against the sky. In the back of my throat I still remembered the scent of Richard in his wolf form. I remembered him running in my tracks, fighting by my side. The demon had played me in every possible way, and wooing me in wolf form was just one of his wiles. But it was still real. He had been there. "He's gone," I told her.

"Can you get him back?"

"He's not coming back. Look, if you don't believe in your Cecil guy, why do you want the demon anyway?"

"Holly says that with the demon, Cecil thinks he can bring us peace on earth in our time." She looked at me, and her glasses glinted again. "I think that's worth a try, don't you? Even if Cecil is a king-sized, asswinding jerk."

I tried to imagine Richard instructing a great-souled leader of Tantric meditation in the nature of the universe. Not Richard as I'd known him, the beautiful youth, trapped and powerless, but the writhing conscious mass of weighted and spiraling darkness he became, when he recovered his powers. The hair on my neck rose, remembering his demon form. Maybe he'd laugh. Or, maybe he'd just make lamp oil out of this Cecil, to make a pinprick of light in whatever universe of blackness he dwelled in now. Or he might bring us eternal peace. Very still, very quiet, and very dark. That would be bad. I said, "I don't think you want to study the One True Way from a demon. No."

She rubbed her hands. It was late. The cab was cold. In the east, the gibbous moon was rising, eight days past full. My wounds ached.

"Where are my clothes?" I asked. "And where is my car?"

She said Holly had thrown my clothes in a dumpster, because there was blood on them. The bitch. My car was still parked in the dirt lot where I'd left it at the beginning of this adventure. Elaine drove me to the lot above the private beach where I'd been lured to the party, that was not a party after all, but just a trap. I added a couple more people to the list I had to talk to. Honey, from the Thunder Mountain Boys. And Yvette, who I'd thought was my friend.

My keys and my wallet were gone, but one of the things my kind always does is stash spare car and house keys. We can usually hold on to the stuff in our pockets when we change, but every now and then something doesn't come back with us when we change to human form. I found the magnetized box in the wheel well, and the keys were there, and the car started just fine. I made Elaine get out of the truck and give me all the money she had, for taking my wallet. And that wasn't a bad haul, since her camel patient had paid her in cash. I also made her give me her tennis shoes. They didn't fit, but I scrunched her socks up in the toes, and that worked all right.

Before I left her, I pulled out her vet case, and scrounged out some things I would need. Then I took the keys from her once more, lined up the truck, put it in gear, got out and released the handbrake. I had planned to aim it over the cliff and into the sea. But since I'd been talking to her for nearly an hour, and we'd gotten all chummy and looked into each other's souls—even though she still didn't understand what she'd seen in mine—I just sent the truck down the steep dirt path and sank it nose first in the sand on the beach. I'd angled it just right, so it made the first hairpin turn before it fell off the path. It was going to take a tow truck hours to haul it out. They might have to use two winches. I hoped it would cost her five days of anguish, but I don't think it gave her that much. The gun, though, I did throw into the sea, though she squawked that it was county property. And it served her right.

I left her running awkwardly down the dirt road after her truck, barefoot, shouting at it, and yelling curses back at me, angry and cold, frustrated and afraid. But unharmed. I still had three holes in me, and I was pretty sure one of them was bleeding again. She hadn't even offered to bandage my wounds. She was an evil vet. The bitch.

CHAPTER FIVE

The only up side to driving away from Malibu toward home was that at that hour, there was no traffic to speak of. My black Honda Civic is a manual drive. Shifting, with my right hand, flexing all the muscles of my aching wrist, and pressing my wounded left foot down on the clutch, hurt. Every time. I used my right foot for the gas and brake, so once I got onto the highway I was able to stretch out my left ankle and let it rest.

Far across Los Angeles, my apartment in Whittier drew me on, offering bed, food, water, especially bed. I headed down the 10 freeway at exactly three miles over the speed limit.

It wasn't long before I realized that if people were still after me, Holly, the metallurgist, Cecil, or any other of his ambitious idiotic acolytes, that was where they would look. If they shot me through the window, I could wake up in a better-guarded cage, and never see them coming.

My foot lifted on the gas. I put it down again. They were all across the valley behind me in Malibu. I just wanted to be home.

But one of the people who had set me up worked in Pasadena, just up the 605 and a ways along the 210 from Whittier. My friend Yvette had decoyed me to the party. She lived in Whittier.

I skipped the turn-off to the 60, and stayed on the 10. I needed sleep. I needed safety. I needed to tend to my wounds so they would heal quickly, and not get infected. I skipped the turn-off to the 605. I was not going to Whittier tonight. Soon after, I followed a bright attractive sign and pulled off the freeway into the parking lot for a motel. The parking lot was crowded even though it was the middle of the week. The long, two-story building looked well cared-for. I would use my well-gotten gains from the evil vet to buy a room for the rest of the night, and the next night too, maybe, and wash and sleep, and sleep…

I hadn't even gotten out of the car before I realized that without my precious fake ID, no one was going to rent me a room. At least, not at a place where I could be sure of getting through the night without an unpleasant interruption. Wearing sweats that didn't fit, bruised and wounded as I was—I hadn't had a chance to check but it was likely that just then I looked like a pretty suspicious person.

I started the car again. I winced as I put it in gear. Every time. I trolled down the main drag until I saw a 7-11. I wasn't going to stand out there. I wandered in and bought stale sandwiches, packages of jerky, chips, more jerky, a Danish, a couple of bottles of water, and some more jerky. You just can't have too much jerky. The zombie store clerk didn't raise his eyes to me.

I drove back toward the motel, into the parking lot of the even bigger one next door, and chose a remote parking spot, not right at the back, but an inconvenient walk from or to anywhere. I ate and drank. While Richard was with me, he'd done the cooking. He had strong views on processed food, on the necessity of fresh meat and condiments. I liked the sound of his voice, and the way he looked when he talked.

I kept reminding myself that he hadn't been real. He'd been Dr. John Dee's fantasy, overlaid with every other of his masters' fantasies, for he altered himself, as a good servant does, to suit. The last had been me. Well. Not everyone gets a fantasy for their first love. If they had any idea what it was like, the people who were after me for my demon would want him so much more. I know I did.

So I ate my stale food and thought of what Richard would say about it. Then I changed, hopped into the back seat, and licked my wounds. And slept at last.

At first light I worried open the crusted scabs on my wounds and licked them until they didn't smell bad anymore. It's difficult to make detailed plans while wearing a wolf's brain. I changed and lay curled in the back seat, trying to think of what to do. I could leave Los Angeles. That might be safest. But I'd have to go the Whittier to recover some of my cached money, and that was out. I needed somewhere not too far away to lay low until I healed, and could defend myself again.

It occurred to me that I knew of such a place, where the welcome was inscribed on a stone beside the path that led up to the house. Welcome. Friendship. Safety. I needed them all, right now. I wrapped my wounded wrist and ankle in the gauze and bandages I'd taken from the evil vet. I bought gas, and headed east on the 10 freeway for Mt Baldy.

When I was well and strong, there were people I would track down and deal with. You do not shoot one of the wolf kind, you do not cage, bespell and wound the Daughter of the Moon Wolf. There were people out there who needed this lesson taught to them. I would need all my strength to do it.

Mount Baldy is warded by a bunch of paranoid Buddhists up at the priory. I was forewarned this time, and only took one wrong exit and two wrong turns before I managed to point my car up the mountain and follow the roaring creek all the way to Baldy Village.

I parked in one of the few remaining spaces at the trail head for Cedar Creek Canyon. A crowd of Japanese hikers, wearing the same-style snazzy clothes, and carrying identical high-tech metal water bottles, were just setting off up the trail. A big Hispanic family was sorting out itself, and their dogs, and they wandered up the trail next. I sat in my car, telling myself I was waiting until I could make the hike in solitude. In fact, I was hoping my ankle would stop throbbing.

When they were gone I got out of my car. There wasn't any reason for me to wait for the trail to clear. I wasn't going to be loping up it in wolf form. Not that most people would notice. A surprising number of people will tell you that what they saw was a dog; a big dog, but still a dog. A huskie, usually. Or a wolf hybrid, which is true in a sense. Or even a German shepherd, for the gods' sake. There are a fair number of hikers, where I grew up. But being lame on two legs, I would not be making the climb as a wolf.

I picked up a discarded walking stick and started up the rocky trail, flapping in my too-big shoes. The roar of the creek, filling its banks at this time of year, flooding the trail in places, blocked out the sounds of the other hikers. If not for all the various and informative fresh scent trails, I could almost believe myself alone.

I'd forgotten that the trail was so rocky. And steep. Cedars lined the canyon, together with pines. Flowers grew in the crevices between the rocks. Every now and then a cabin could be seen perched on some rare flat ground up the slope from the creek. The walls of the canyon rose high on either side, the tree line giving way to steep slopes of scree, until the trees commenced again at the top of the ridges.

The scent of cedar, water and clean air was a balm. I'd chosen the city when I left home. But after all those months, I'd forgotten what air is supposed to taste like. It was a pleasant hike, which was good, because I was very slow.

A pack of serious hikers strode up from below and passed me, offering cheerful greetings. I nodded to them, stopping off the trail so none of them noticed and commented on my limp. If you are wounded, after all, it's best if folks don't realize it.

The cabin I sought wasn't far. Beside the trail there would be a large rock with a flat side facing the trail. On it were inscribed the signs I knew, Friendship, Safety, Welcome, entwined in Celtic knotwork, with wards repeating the same messages. These were beacons to the two-natured kind that help would be received there, if asked. Across the creek and high up the bank a cabin stood in a grove of cedars. The memory came to me with the scent of beef broth, and two women who had been kind to me. And to Richard. I could rest there. I could hide there, and heal up.

The day was clear and bright, chilly between the canyon walls. I climbed slowly, looking forward to getting off my ankle, and sleeping off the wounds in my hip and wrist. There'd still been snow on the ground when Richard and I tore up this path only a month ago. When I found myself in trouble, Marge had invited me into their cabin, and helped me out. Marge and her friend Andy had made me welcome.

I passed by the stone without sensing the ward. When I saw the big cedar ahead, where I'd discovered the scent marker of one of the folks hunting me, I backed up, as I had the last time I'd been here. I found the rock. The signs, painted and etched on the surface of the stone, were smeared with mud and gook from the stream, scratched through with a pointed stone. The wards had been marred and dispersed. I looked up at the cabin, barely visible on the far ridge above the stream. Gray Fox stood there watching me.

Oh, shit. And I couldn't even run.

"Come up," he said. Even from so far away, he didn't raise his voice for me to hear him.

I hesitated. Herald, scout, henchman, adviser, the gray fox kind have been allies of my family from time out of mind. When I left home, I knew they would seek after me. I'd left trails that led into the mountains, to make them think I was living as a wolf in the wild. There are thousands of square miles of mountains in California. It gave them quite a lot to search, while I made a place for myself in the city, where my trail was obscured every day by a million people and a million cars. But now, after only six months, Gray Fox had found me.

"Come up, Lady," he said again. He gestured, and I felt the compulsion he put behind it.

I made my way over the board Marge and Andy used as a bridge across the creek, and up the steep path to their cabin. I tried not to limp. Gray Fox was watching me. I hoped he didn't notice my shoes. When I reached the top, he was gone. The back door to the cabin stood open. Smoke rose from the chimney. I turned my head slowly from side to side, my mouth slightly open. Traces of Marge and Andy's scents were everywhere. They'd been using this cabin for years. But none of the traces were recent.

As I looked around, Gray Fox emerged from the cabin carrying a tray. I smiled at him, as though I'd only been taking in the cabin and its surrounds. Anxiety is a weapon in your enemy's hand. I needed every advantage I could hold on to, against Gray Fox.

He set the tray down on the weathered wicker table that stood in a stone-lined space on the ridge above the creek. Marge and Andy had decorated the make-shift patio with colored rocks and shards of broken plates set into concrete. Gray Fox set the bigger of the two chairs for me, and stood holding it for me. I moved toward him and he bowed.

I stopped. "How's Mom? Is she all right?"

"Your mother is well, I assure you. Please, sit down."

I went to the chair and sat down and I did not limp or wince. Gray Fox wore a dark green waistcoat, an old tight-fitting tweed jacket, heavy brown pants, and a faded white handkerchief tied at his throat. His gray hair always curled slightly at the ends, no matter how short he kept it cut. It struck me for the first time how odd he looked, dressed in such old fashions. At home, that had always been how Gray Fox looked. Now that I'd been away for awhile, he looked quirky to me, rather than familiar.

His eyes looked like they were too close together. They held his usual expression, that he was thinking of a stupid joke about me, but was too polite to repeat it. You got the impression that even in his human form his ears were pointed, but if you looked closely they weren't. His brows were gray. I'd never noticed that before. I wondered how old he was.

He actually waited by his chair until I motioned him to sit down. He poured hot tea in both our cups, gave me a plate, and then offered me my choice from the platter of meat, cheese, bread and pickles that he'd brought out.

"Where are Marge and Andy?" I asked him.

"Who?"

I looked around. "The women who own this cottage."

He shrugged, lifting his brows as though this matter were too unimportant for him to consider. "I've no idea. The cabin was open when I came. I've been borrowing its amenities while I waited for you." He waited for my reaction. I decided not to give him any. He smiled slightly, as though in approval. "You found my scent marker. I followed your trail back down, and out to Redlands. If you want to know, I haven't found your den there yet. But I will." He looked smug.

He always looked smug, I thought. I chewed on a big bite of bread, beef and pickle. His voice sounded like molasses ought to taste, sweet and rich, lovely to listen to. I'd always liked his voice, but now it sounded affected. I'd never been to Redlands. Marge's daughter Hannah had made a scent trail out that way, to obscure mine, when I'd stupidly blundered onto Gray Fox's scent marker. I hoped that my chewing kept him from seeing any reaction I might have made.

"You're hurt?" he asked.

"'S'nothing," I said. "Just a hunting accident." I grinned at him, and he obligingly grinned back. He had a lot of teeth.

"How's Luke?" I asked. My younger brother, the only one of us left at home. My older brother, Carl, disappeared when my dad did.

"He's surviving," Gray Fox said lightly.

I felt a wave of guilt. Since my mother brought home Ray, as our new stepfather, I'd been Luke's protector. I realized on the heels of that wave of feeling, that Gray Fox meant me to feel guilt, just by the way he'd answered me. My attention rose a few more notches. Then I tamped it down. He could read focus, any hunter can read focus. And this conversation was, I realized too, another kind of hunt.

So I didn't ask him what he was going to do, now that he'd found me. I asked him, instead, something I wanted to know.

"Where is my dad?"

He smiled, lifted a hand. "Please, Lady. Don't ask me questions you know I'm not allowed to answer."

"I go by Amber here."

"Very well. Amber."

"And I will ask you anything I damn well please."

For just a second he was taken aback. Great, something that wasn't in his script. Then he bent his head to me. "As you wish, L—Amber." He showed his teeth for a moment as he replied. "You will excuse me if I don't always answer you."

I nodded, as though it wasn't a big deal. As though this wasn't a kind of battle.

"Are you staying long?"

That brought a smile. "Lady, we have been hunting you for six months."

"You have a message for me?"

"Of course." He opened his hands. He wasn't eating anything, I noticed. I wondered if I should have surreptitiously sniffed the food more carefully, to see if he'd doctored it. That would be a point to him, though. "'Come home.'" His eyes glinted. "'Now.'"

I put my sandwich down. This was serious. "Okay," I asked. "Who sent you? My mother?"

He looked at me gravely for a moment, and shook his head. "Ray sent us. All the fox kind. He wants you back." He grinned, showing his teeth. "Right now."

I grinned back, but I was lying. I wondered if he was. I didn't ask him what my mom said, because I didn't want him to tell me. My mother is the Moon Wolf, Lady of the Wolf Kind, and I am her Daughter. Disobeying a direct summons from her, well, that was something I wanted to avoid.

"Ray wants you back," he continued, turning his mug in his hands, "because by the time of the next Gathering he must be seen to be in control."

I nodded. It didn't take much figuring to know that.

"The Rapsons have left the valley," he continued.

I raised my brows.

"The Shorburns went last month. The Ipsitts are selling up." He sipped his tea, watching me. "And your cousin Claire left about the same time you did."

"Did she?" I sipped my tea, too.

"Yes," he smiled. "She did." He put his cup down and opened his hands. "I must tell you, Lady—Amber, I don't like Ray's sudden appearance, his faction, nor his influence any more than you do."

I studied the dregs of my tea. It was not possible that this was true. Gray Fox had not lived in Ray's house. He had not been a girl who Ray and his sons believed needed to be taught a lesson. Needed to be taught her place. Needed to be taught this as often as necessary. There was no one who wanted Ray gone, who wanted him dead, more than I did. And his sons with him. When I lifted my head, Gray Fox almost started back. My eyes had gone gold. "Oh," I said, "I'm not so sure about that."

He nodded understanding.

"If you try to take me back there now, I will fight you."

He shook his head. "But, Lady, have you considered what your absence means to your family? Your mother, pardon my bluntness, is not considered to be a strong leader. Her acceptance of Ray, her allowing him and his cloddish sons to throw their weight around—"

I cracked a laugh. "Sorry. That's what we've always called them, Luke and me. The clods."

Gray Fox leaned toward me for emphasis. "The line depends on your mother's successor. We all look to you. Grow quickly, grow strong. Be wise. It may be sooner than you think before everything depends on you."

Tears pricked my eyes, so I looked away. I couldn't figure out why his words made me so angry. They were true, of course they were true. But something was wrong about how he said them, or why. Or that he brought it up now.

"I have to report back," he was saying. "But, thanks to the way in which you escaped, I have a lot of ground to cover before I must do that." He smiled at me. "One would not want to leave any trail unchecked, for where you might have gone, or what you might be doing. That would leave my report incomplete, after all."

I almost smiled back. "I need a year. I will be eighteen a year from August. I need until then."

"I can't give you that long," he said, his voice filled with regret. "I'll need to bring back word before the Gathering."

I nodded. I had until the fall, then. Unless he was lying. Why did I feel that he was lying?

He checked the teapot, then rose, gathered it up together with my cup and his, and said, "I'll make more tea. You look like you could use some."

He went into the cabin before I could figure out a polite way to tell him I didn't much like his tea. It had a strangely bitter aftertaste for something with so little flavor. I thought in a moment I would get up and go after him, just to get a look inside the cabin. I wanted to go in and sniff my way around, to find out what I could about what had happened to Marge and Andy. If their dead bodies were rotting inside the door, I could certainly smell that from here, even in my human form. As a wolf, I could sort out all the old traces of their comings and goings, from the last time they left. I might also be able to tell if they were frightened when they went. I could tell which way they went. I could check the stone by the path, and find out who obliterated the wards, and smeared out the signs.

I badly wanted to know all that, but I realized, looking after Gray Fox, that I very much didn't want to change in front of him. I didn't want him to see how badly wounded I was. If he'd watched me come up the trail, and I assumed he had, then he'd seen me limping on two legs. I wouldn't let him see me limp on four. I was forming some plan of how to find out all I wanted to know, that became entwined at the back of my eyes with the Celtic knotwork that connected the three signs on the stone by the path. With a start I sat up and opened my eyes. Gray Fox sat across from me, pouring the tea. He smiled. "Here. This will help." His smile looked smug.

I didn't need to change to my wolf form to know that he had touched me. He'd checked my pockets, moved my keys. I didn't look at him. I didn't want him to know that I knew. I cleared my throat and said, "What will you do now?"

He laughed. "Don't you know better than to ask the Fox his business?"

Ask the Fox a question and he will waste your time. "I told you, I'll ask you whatever I want."

"Very well. Amber. I will be here for awhile. I have several scouts out, who will report to me here. If you need anything, come and see me. I'll do whatever I can."

"You're staying in the cabin?"

He shrugged. "It's convenient. It has a few wards. The nearest neighbors are…" he lifted his nose, "a quarter mile away."

I didn't drink any more of his tea. I got up to take my plate into the cabin, thinking I could at least get a look inside that way. I headed for the door.

"Leave that," he said, not quite sharply. I turned and looked at him, and he lifted a hand. "I'll get that in a minute. Come," he gestured. "I'll walk you down."

As he started down, he changed to his gray fox form. The fox kind, like the wolf kind, take no time at all to change. He set a foot down as a human, and the next foot down as a fox, sliding from one form to the next like water from one vessel to another, almost too quickly to follow. Then he turned and looked at me. Strange. I'd never noticed before how small he was, as a gray fox. He was above average height as a human. I wondered if he took pains to make himself look larger than he was.

He stood looking at me expectantly, his bright eyes challenging. He wanted me to change as well. I pretended I didn't see the look, and continued down the slope after him, picking my way along the rocky path, and trying not to limp. Aside from not wanting him to see the shape I was in, if I changed, I was sure I'd lose those damn stupid shoes.

In any case, when we got to the creek, my decision seemed prescient instead of defiant, because at that moment a crowd of hikers came laughing and chattering up the trail. A few of them waved. I waved back and smiled. When they had passed, I turned to look for the Gray Fox, but he was gone.

It was a long walk back down the trail. Hikers passed me every few minutes, going either way. My ankle hurt, but I couldn't limp too much to spare it. Gray Fox was out there somewhere. He would be watching me.

It was a good thing I'd lost my I.D. He'd have gotten my address from it, and my new name. I tried to feel grateful that he promised to hold off before telling my family where I was, but I didn't. It was a while before I realized he'd promised no such thing. He'd given the impression that's what he would do, but he hadn't said so. Then I realized what he had done. He had offered to deal with me, separately from my stepfather, but most of all, separately from my mother. He was playing me, as though I were a piece on a board that belonged to him. And that was just wrong.

When I thought it through like that, then our whole meeting made a lot more sense. I must be growing up. I could see what he had done. Like a good hunter, he had separated me from any allies I might still have at home. He had blocked me from my covert. He'd gotten me into the open, and now he would watch me and see where I ran. He was hunting for himself, and I was his prey. When he was ready, he would drive me to his chosen ground, and then he would come in for the kill.

CHAPTER SIX

I got to the parking lot without seeing Gray Fox again, but that didn't mean he didn't follow me every step of the way. I was very glad to sit down in my car and get my weight off my ankle, but the wound in my hip had begun to hurt. I'd probably torn all the newly-healed tissue in the three miles of hiking that rocky trail. Clenching my hand on the stick shift made my wrist ache again. I was one sorry pup as I headed off that mountain, with no place to lay my head.

I drove out to Redlands, about an hour to the east on the 210. I didn't know if Gray Fox was shadowing me, or if one of his many tribe was tracking me, or if he could scry me, but I did not want him following me home to my place in Whittier. Since he was so sure my den was in Redlands, that's where I went, and hopped off a couple of the exits, circled the neighborhoods, and hopped back on again, then got on the 10 and drove back toward L.A. Then I caught the 215 and headed south.

It's difficult to scry someone on the freeway, because freeways all look alike. I hoped to obscure the trail enough so that when I eventually went to ground, I would be pretty hard to find. I had one last place where I thought I could ask for help. If she was in town, if she was at her shop, Madam Tamara might help me.

I pulled around back into the parking lot for the World Music: Ethnic and Tribal Instruments store in Costa Mesa. Parking lots look pretty much the same to scryers as well. I sat in the car for a few minutes, resting my wrist, getting up the strength to stand on my bad foot again.

I could hear the drumming from inside the car. Some folks were jamming on the little patio beside the store. Toots and bells, honks and whistles played among the drums, and I thought I heard a fiddle as well. The music had a joyful buzz to it. The residue from the many magical workings that had taken place at Tamara's store over the years gyred in the air, and music or dancing, or sometimes just conversation fed into it, caught the buzz and expanded in its resonance. I was the farthest that I'd ever been from wanting to dance, but as I passed the music makers, heading into the store I felt my heart and my breathing respond. I saw a few faces I recognized, but no one I really knew. A couple of them nodded at me, friendly.

A bear was sitting on the wall to the patio, drinking coffee. He was in his human form, a big black man with a heavy face and eyes that seemed sleepy, but noticed everything. I nodded to him. It pays to be respectful to the bear kind. They will make you pay if you are not.

"Aaron," I said, greeting him.

He nodded back.

"Is Tamara here?"

He pointed to the store with his chin and I headed for the door.

"You look a mess," he said, as I passed him.

"It's a gift."

Coming out of the bright late April sunlight, I paused inside the door of the shop. A group of women clustered among the bright silks, the African pattern cloth, the Indian muslins set with tiny mirrors. Wafting traces of ginger and sesame oil, they draped one another with colorful textiles from the various racks, posing, exclaiming, twirling in front of the mirrors. Along the next aisle a couple of giggling children made rude noises with some wooden whistles. An elderly man methodically sorted through a box of old sheet music, frowning over his glasses.

Tamara stood behind the counter, watchful over everyone in the store, while she wrapped up and boxed a painted mask for a burbling customer. Madam Tamara wore a sky blue turban, vivid against her dark skin, and a flowing yellow, blue, and black dress that set off her angular frame.

She saw me as I came in, looked me over and motioned me to the back of the store, without breaking off her side of the conversation. I went through the curtained doorway, the wards parting for me as I reached it, passed through the office and collapsed in the first chair I came to in the back room. I shoved a stack of catalogs on the long table out of my way and put my head down on my arms.

The next thing I knew, Tamara had my right wrist in her hand, and was washing the wound with a cloth over a bowl of scented water.

"There you are," she said, when she saw I was awake.

She looked tired. I remembered suddenly that I'd been off the map for five days. "How's your mom?" I asked. Tamara's mother had been in a coma since she danced up a spell for me. Tamara's dark eyes hardened and grew distant, and I knew I had not been forgiven.

"The same," she said. "Now what have you been up to, girl?"

"I was taken prisoner."

She thought I was joking. "By who?"

"Well, supposedly, by the disciple of some nut up in Malibu who thinks he should have my demon."

"Ah," Tamara bent her head. "Has this happened before?"

My gaze on her sharpened. What had she heard? "Has what happened?"

She met my eyes. "Has someone tried to take your demon from you?"

"Twice." I winced as she touched my wound with her cloth, and tried not to show it. She felt it though. Her touch became more gentle. I told her, "Couple of weeks ago, this guy called Joachim offered me money for my demon." Richard had already been gone by then. I'd almost taken the money.

Her brows rose in amusement. "How much?"

"Not enough," I snarled. "He's one of the Holy Workers out near Chino." She nodded to show she knew the group. "Another guy tracked me down in Whittier and tried to mug me for him."

She stopped and looked at me. "What did you do to him?"

I shrugged. "I dissuaded him. But that was nothing compared to this latest bunch."

"How so?"

"They shot me!"

Her head came up again. Her eyes were amused this time. "Oh?"

"Knockout dart. Veterinary gun."

"You were in your wolf form?"

"She still shot me." What did it take to get some sympathy?

"And then they took you prisoner?"

"They were planning to give me to their guy Cecil for his birthday."

"Cecil?" Her voice rose in what sounded like amusement.

"You know him?" I don't think she liked the way my eyes narrowed, or my jaw tightened, or my mouth was suddenly all too full of teeth. It's an impression I give when I'm thinking about killing something.

"Oh, yes, I know him." She lifted a finger at me. "I didn't say I liked him."

I backed down. "Cecil told his disciples that he should have my demon, so they set it up so they could deliver me to him." I hissed out my breath as Tamara smeared some ointment into my wound.

"I told you having that creature was dangerous," she said, her concentration on what she was doing. It was more than just cleaning and bandaging. I could feel the warm energy from her hands dull the pain in my wrist.

"If I still had my demon," I pointed out, "they couldn't have held me prisoner."

Her eyes met mine, arrested for a moment, then disbelieving again. "It is only you who say he had any more powers than he needed to read tarot for us."

"Okay, fine. But he did have enough power, as you say, to walk in, hit people on the head and let me out of that cage. But he's gone. So I had to do it myself." I reached into the pocket of my stolen sweats, and took out the bandana and laid it in front of her. "While I was unconscious, I was forced into both my forms at once, and then held there. Look." I opened it, and showed her the leather bracelet, and the silver hooks. "Have you ever seen these before?"

Her head went back as she felt the magical charge they still held. Then Tamara leaned over, examining them. She looked again at the wound on my wrist, her face grave. She held out two fingers and, not quite touching, passed them over the bracelets and the hooks. She touched her finger to her tongue, and passed them over the hooks again. "I've never seen such things. What did they do?"

I told her how I'd woken up in the cage, pinned and chained. "I think they are bespelled to hold you in one form."

That got her full attention. She turned over the bracelets and the hooks, using the bandana so she wouldn't have to touch them, concentrating, sussing out the flow of energy in the device.

She held her fingers over my wrist again, to see if any of the spell lingered in my body. Then she wrapped the hooks up again, and passed them back to me. "Monstrous."

I told her about the dog, and watched her face swell up as she tried to hold on to her indignation. She finally burst out laughing. I grinned back at her. "Her ex-husband's in the barn. She turned him into a horse."

Tamara chortled and tried to look stern at the same time. There are rules about using magic, and Sarah was breaking them. Still, from a certain point of view, it was funny.

Tamara interrupted my story only refill her bowl with warm water from the sink in the bathroom. She added some powder to it from a white ceramic bottle above the sink, and brought it back steaming, to go to work cleaning the wound on my ankle while she listened to my adventures. Some of my adventures. I didn't tell her everything. I didn't tell her what I'd done to the vet's truck. It's harder to sound like you need help if you've already committed a major act of vandalism. Even if the evil vet had deserved it. I thought I'd see if I could get the help first.

"Sarah is the changer. But she had help. She didn't make these things. The vet said there's a guy who works metal, up in Pasadena, and he might have done these. Do you know him?"

Tamara did not look at me while she thought. I wondered what she was deciding not to tell me. As she spread salve on the wound in my ankle, and a pleasant warmth dulled the pain I'd felt for days, I thought even if she lied to me, just for the present I'd have to let it go. At last she said, "I know someone who can do this. I don't know if he is the one."

Well, that was all right. "I'd like to talk to him." I added, my voice growing grim, "In fact, there are a number of people I'm planning to talk to."

"Oh? And what do you plan to do to them?"

"Just talk," I said, with all the innocence I could muster.

She gave me a look. It's not her wide jaw, her high cheekbones, or her deep-set eyes that make her face so expressive. The powerful spirit, the wellspring of her magic, blazes out her messages through her dark eyes and makes them impossible to miss. In her expression I read, "Who do you think you are? You're in no condition to *talk* to anyone right now." And, underlying everything, "You've been nothing but trouble since the day you first walked in here, bringing a demon with you into my presence."

Under the weight of her gaze, I added, "I don't plan to kill anyone."

"I'm so happy to hear it."

But that was the question. What was I supposed to do to these people? I couldn't just let them get away with setting me up and attacking me. If I did that, it meant what they did was all right with me. So I had to do something. And the longer it took me to recover my strength, the more dire that something should be.

I didn't want to discuss all this with Tamara just at present, so in order to skip the whole tedious conversation, I asked, "Who is this guy? Where can I find him?"

She shook her head, exasperated. "This is not important now. It can wait for a more opportune time. Why don't you concentrate on the crisis at hand?"

"I have told you and told you—"

"Yes. I know. You keep saying that the fight is over, that the Worm We Do Not Name has been defeated."

"Not defeated," I tried to explain one more time. "She's been turned. Richard turned her. She's not coming."

"But Richard is gone."

"Yes. He's gone. I freed him." I had to look away. I don't cry. I don't. But I was tired and wounded and in pain, and I missed him.

Tamara lifted her hands. She moved like a dancer, with a dancer's grace. "And yet no one has been able to verify what you claim. People are growing desperate."

"Look, if the World Snake was coming, would I still be here?"

She made a sign of aversion at the name. "Child, that only means you believe what you say. It doesn't mean it's true. Your demon is a being of trickery and deceit. Eight million souls depend on your word, and no one knows if your word is good."

That made me burn. My eyes flared but Tamara didn't react. Here, in her own holding, within her own defenses, she wasn't afraid of anything I could do. I was supposed to be a big player in this crisis. And I had been! I'd won the war. Being a big player with a small voice is frustrating. But it was true, about Richard. He'd been a master of manipulation and deceit even when he was powerless, because these are the stock in trade of a slave. Once his powers returned, and he was free, he became something unfathomable.

I watched Tamara's hands spread ointment on my ankle, that hardly hurt anymore. And I wondered, just for a moment, if Richard had lied to me. I shook my head so hard Tamara looked up at me. According to the rules of his presence here, Richard was not allowed to lie to me, or disobey a direct command, while I was his master. So I could trust that he had done what I asked. Getting other people to understand all this, now that was the problem.

"What can I do?" I asked Tamara. "I thought if I waited, and the World Snake didn't come, then people would finally believe me. Instead, I woke up as someone's multi-mammalian experiment. I was a couple days away from being tied up in a bow and offered as a birthday present when I got out of there."

She finished tying off the bandage on my ankle. "Where were you shot with the dart?"

I peeled back the sweat pants from my hip, revealing the huge purpling bruise emanating out from the crusted angry puncture wound. No wonder my walk was stiff. It was the biggest bruise I'd ever had.

"Oh, my!"

"Yeah," I agreed. "That hurt."

She cleaned and anointed it like the others, and left something warm and tingling working in the wound when she bandaged it. Then she laid a hand on my head. When she took it away a moment later, the pain of my wounds had receded, and my tangled situation felt less daunting. "Thank you," I said.

"Go home," Tamara said, gathering up the detritus of her doctoring. "Rest. I've thought of someone who may be able to help. I'll see if she will come and help us. I'll send for you when I'm ready."

"I can't go home," I told her. "People know where I live. There's nothing to keep them from taking me again, if they shoot me while I'm not looking."

"No one will do that again. I'll talk to them."

I wasn't sure I could trust her word to that extent either. But that wasn't the only problem. I'd kept my personal affairs private thus far. But I needed Tamara's help if I was going to stay out of further trouble. It was time to share. I said, "My family has found me. I think they're tracking me. I can't let them know where I live."

"Your family?" Tamara took me by the shoulders and looked into my eyes. "Just how old are you, my girl?"

I shook my head. "I can't go back home. Not until I'm older. And stronger."

She held my gaze a moment longer, and then said, "What is it you want?"

"If you could tell me how to keep them from scrying me, now that they know where to look—"

"They can't scry you here," she assured me. "There isn't anyone I know who can get through the wards around this place." She thought a moment, and then seemed to give way to a remedy that did not entirely please her. She sighed. "Stay here. Rest. Get well. Then, we'll see. Come. I'll show you where you can sleep."

Tamara and her mother lived in the house that stood across an empty lot from the music shop. The dark little clapboard bungalow, with peeling green paint on the porch, had two downstairs bedrooms. Tamara's mother had long ago built a studio on the upstairs floor where she did her workings. I could feel the charged air coming from up there as we passed the stairwell. Tamara's mother was a sorceress of considerable power, as I had reason to know. But she wasn't home now. She lay in a hospital, undertaking who knew what journey, into another kind of night than the one now falling outside. She'd saved my life. She'd given me what I needed to save the city, and I'd only spoken to her once.

Tamara showed me to a tiny spare workroom at the back of the house, where a narrow bed stood against the wall, made up with a pillow and an old handmade quilt. The pine tree pattern was threadbare in places, and the colors had faded, but it held a sense of comfort and peace, worn into the cloth by three generations of women. Tamara and her mother had both curled up in it many times, and another girl as well. Before that there had been another woman, who had slept in it, wept and bled into it, a long time ago.

Tamara rummaged in a narrow closet and brought out a couple of pairs of jeans, more stylish than any I owned. One of them fit me, if I rolled up the legs. Everyone is taller than me. She found a t-shirt for me as well, and some underwear. The girl who had owned these clothes was the other girl who'd slept wrapped in the quilt, but I didn't say anything. It wasn't my business, and besides, I was too tired. I peeled off the sweats that smelled of the shepherd, back in the days when she'd been a smoker, and kicked off the stupid shoes. I wrapped myself in the quilt that smelled so good, dropped on the bed and fell into blessed sleep.

I woke once from troubled dreams where I was pinned to the dirt by a giant silver hook while Gray Fox stood over me, looking at me like I was his dinner. I blinked away the vision as Tamara entered the room with a jar of ointment and fresh bandages. The windows were dark, and Tamara's shadow was cast by light from the kitchen beyond. She did not speak to me, but sat on the bed and checked my dressings, humming under her breath. I fell asleep again before she left, but the warm imprint of her hand on my forehead stayed in my consciousness even as I subsided again into dreams. This time I walked through a forest of pine trees, drawn by some necessity toward a lighted glade, and a small intense figure dancing there. She turned as I broke into the light, her dark eyes bright, smiling fiercely, and said something, and I woke up with her voice in my ears.

It was not yet dawn. I lay listening, thinking that Tamara had brought her mother home, and it was her voice I had heard. But the house was silent. The voice, like the figure, had been part of the dream. I went in and used the little bathroom, and drank from the tap until my stomach was full. I went back to bed, but before I fell asleep again I got up on top of the covers and changed, pawed and turned around until the conformation of the bedding suited me, and then dropped down again and fell asleep in my wolf form. My wolf brain was not troubled by disturbing dreams. I woke later in the day because there was a bear in the room.

"You want me to feed you in here, or you want to come eat in the kitchen?"

Aaron loomed in the doorway, his deep voice resounding between the walls, though he did not speak loudly. "Come on, get up. Tamara's brought someone for you to talk to."

I changed on the bed to my human form so I wouldn't have to drop onto my right forepaw with all my weight. Oh, how I ached. All my bruises had seized up, and my wrist and ankle felt like the hook was back in them, big as a pipe, throbbing, and with spikes. I put on my new borrowed clothes and hobbled barefoot toward the kitchen. Then I pulled myself together, slowed and shortened my steps so I was only limping a little when I entered the room. Two other bears, Sol and Jonathan, small compared to Aaron, but big compared to anyone else, seemed to take up all the room around Tamara's kitchen table. Sol was already tearing into the second of the six huge all-meat pizzas, and Jonathan was chewing efficiently, and already reaching for his next slices.

I helped myself to three pieces, knowing that if I took them one by one, the bears would have finished the food before I got my second piece. Do not wait on bears when it comes to food, or you will go hungry.

I didn't see the fourth bear. "Where's Jason?" I asked with my mouth full. If you stop eating, they think you don't want that other piece you have, and you can't argue about that when they've already starting chewing on it.

"Where is Yvette?" Jonathan asked in return, cocking a heavy brow at me.

"Ah." My friend Yvette the drummer had taken up with Jason a few weeks ago. She knew he was one of the bear kind. It hadn't been a problem yet, but then, he hadn't taken her home to meet the family, either. "If you see her," I told the bears, "I need to talk to her." There was the little matter of her inviting me to the party at which she did not appear, but I got shot.

"So we heard," Aaron said.

Tamara opened the door to the kitchen and came in trailed by two others, just as the bears were tearing into the last box. The bears stopped, big hands still outstretched over their claimed portions as she came and stood over the table. "Any left for us?" she asked pointedly.

Sol, the littlest bear, still over six feet, his big frame just a little more wiry than the others, was the last to withdraw his hand.

"Sure," Aaron said, getting up. "Come and sit here. There's plenty left," and he stepped back as though he didn't have two pieces cupped in his huge palm.

Sol and Jonathan perched on the counters, Aaron slipped into the doorway and finished eating. Tamara brought out paper towels and she and the man and woman who had come in with her took the bears' places and started on the food. Since I was still at the table, and I was still hungry, I got myself another piece. I could feel the bears eyeing me. I ate slowly and with obvious enjoyment. After all, it was delicious.

"This is my sister," Tamara told me, nodding to the woman beside her who had a huge slice of pizza draped over her small hands. The woman grinned at me. She had short red hair salted with gray, a round face and a nose with an incongruous crook in it. Her skin was pale and scattered with freckles. She wore a smartly cut business suit, and a merry smile.

I looked back at Tamara, whose scarlet and night-blue dress set off her dark skin. I was not going to say it. Obviously she was trying to get a rise out of me.

Tamara smiled in response. "She is the sister of my soul." She nibbled the point off her second slice of pizza. "She is a skilled diviner, so she may be able to resolve the problem of whether you are speaking the truth or not."

I put down my food. I felt my eyes changing color. I'd sat down to eat with friends. I hadn't realized they all thought I was a liar. Not only a liar, but a braggart besides, since I was claiming to have defeated the enemy they all feared.

Jonathan's huge hand came down on my shoulder, and he leaned to speak in my ear. "Look at it this way," he counseled, in a baritone that could be heard over at the shop, despite his speaking low. "In order for us to continue to defend you, we have to have evidence for why we believe in you, besides your beguiling ways and sweet smile."

I relaxed a little. Then I looked down and saw my food was gone. I turned around to him with a smile that showed all my teeth, but he was back up on the counter, the pizza was gone, and he was smiling too. He looked not only like he had more teeth than he should, but that they were bigger than could easily fit in his mouth. I decided not to look more closely.

"I'm Kat McBride," Tamara's sister told me. "The three of us," she included the man across from her, "met at a conference on neurology and music, many years ago. That's Sunny."

"Curt Sondstrom," he corrected her, turning my way.

"He makes instruments," Kat told me.

Curt suppressed a spike of fear as he offered his hand, which got my attention. He had a friendly smile plastered on his face, but he didn't meet my eyes. His little scraggly beard trembled a little, and his dark hair was beginning to escape from his ponytail. He hunched in his chair like a spider, with long arms and legs, but he wasn't tall. After a moment or two, he took his hand away.

When Tamara and her friends finished eating, the bears cleared away the refuse in a generous action that disguised the careful checking of the boxes for extra little scraps that quickly disappeared. Tamara wiped down the table and then covered it with a tablecloth of pieced-together African cloth. I was distracted for a moment by the engaging scent of the man who'd woven the cloth, sweating, impatient, cheerful, a long-held chancre of worry eating at him somewhere. The women who had sewn the pieces together were mother and daughter, and both of them had been pregnant, far away, but not too long ago.

Then Kat McBride picked up a cloth bag that she'd set down by her chair, brought out a hammered bronze bowl and a wooden rod, and set them on the table. Tamara brought her a pitcher of water.

I didn't know that I wanted to be divined. There were a lot of things about me that I didn't want generally known. The fact that I was an underage runaway, for one. The fact that I was in hiding from my family. And the wolf kind have always been careful with the secret of our nature. "What if I don't want to do this?" I asked.

Kat took off the jacket of her business suit. She removed the gold pin from her lapel, and took two rings from her fingers and gave them to Tamara to hold. "You don't have to answer any questions. There's nothing we can do to make you."

That was for sure.

"But not answering a question is an answer in itself, as you know." She smiled at me, like she'd just scored a point.

Huh. Tamara's soul's sister or not, I didn't think I liked this woman.

Kat raised a hand over the water in the pitcher and murmured a blessing. The air in the room changed slightly in response to her invocation. The attention of the folks in the room heightened, and that increased the energy that Kat had engaged. She poured the water into the bowl, and everyone was so still we could hear it ring on the metal, we could hear it slosh.

Kat lifted the stirring rod, murmuring again too softly to hear. The narrow end, carved with a fretwork leaf pattern, pleasing to the eye, fit neatly in her hand. The wide end was polished smooth with use. She touched this to the edge of the bowl and a bright tone rang out, hung in the air, and faded away. Kit closed her eyes, and whispered a few words.

The air changed again, tightening, beginning slowly to turn one way above us. Soon after, near our feet the air began slowly to gyre the opposite way.

Kat touched the rod to the outside of the bowl, below the edge, and slowly moved it around, rubbing the side of the bowl. At first the only sound was the wood rubbing on the metal, but then a low throbbing hum began. I heard it first with my body, before my ears registered it as sound rather than simply vibration. The sound increased, thickened, picked up overtones, until it rang through the room, pleasing to the ear, waxing and waning, the highest resonance only just within hearing.

Kat moved the rod to the top edge of the bowl, and produced a treble harmony to the deep low vibration that continued, even as the new note rang out. She spoke another incantation, and we saw the water begin to ruffle. Soon it hissed and danced. Kat left off rubbing the bowl, but held the rod close to the edge of it, as though as a reminder. The vibrations, high and low, continued to sound unabated, and the water continued to move.

"What is your name?" Kat asked me.

"Amber," I answered without thinking.

The ringing sound flattened into discord, rose into harmony, flattened into discord again. Kat broke into laughter. "Well, that was unusual." She looked hard at me. "That seems to be both a lie and the truth at the same time."

I nodded. "That's about right."

"Huh," she said, stirring the water again. "I can see this is going to be an interesting session."

"Ask her," Tamara said, "about the World Snake." She made her usual sign of aversion as she spoke the dreaded name. "Ask her what she knows."

Kat rubbed the bowl again, raising the dual notes, pure and sweet, and then asked me the question.

"So far as I know," I told them, as precisely as I knew how, "the demon in my service turned the World Snake at my command. I told him to see to it that she never swallows a city again, and he said he had done this."

I felt another spike of emotion from Curt Sondstrom, sitting to my right, almost out of my sight line. It wasn't fear this time, but excitement. I wondered briefly why he was being so thoroughly unobtrusive. He'd slipped just then, so I'd noticed him again.

The bowl continued to ring true and clear, the sound of my words picking up its resonance, and blending in a faint harmony.

"Well," Kat said thoughtfully, "that's true."

"I told you so," I said to Tamara. I tried not to gloat as it would only provoke the bears. The bear kind are very vain, and it is best not to try to outshine them.

Tamara nodded to Kat, and she sounded the bowl again.

"Where is the demon now?" Tamara asked me.

"I don't know."

"Can you call him?"

"I dismissed him from my service."

The sound from the bowl smudged into a slight dissonance. I frowned at it, and said again, "I dismissed him. I set him free. He's gone."

Another spike of interest from Sondstrom. I was careful not to look at him.

"That wasn't the question," Kat pointed out, as the bowl continued to sound a faint discord. "Tamara asked you if you can call him."

"Of course I can call him," I said. "But that doesn't mean he will come."

To my relief, the tone from the bowl became true and pleasing again.

"But you can call him," Tamara insisted.

I shrugged. "Anyone can call a demon."

"Perhaps we should have her call the demon," Tamara said to Kat, "and you can put the same questions to him."

That time, it was my emotions that spiked. "No," I said. "Really. You don't want to do that."

"Why don't you want to call the demon?" Curt spoke for the first time, but no one was listening but me.

"Because he might come," I shot at him. In all his writhing darkness, with who knew what animosity about the hundreds of years he was trapped here, and all his unknowable powers, he might come.

"She told the truth," Kat reminded Tamara.

"That only means that she believes what the demon told her he had done. It doesn't mean he did it. It doesn't mean the Great Snake isn't coming."

"Why not go and ask the World Snake?" I said.

Behind me I felt a new vibration, almost too low to hear, hard and dangerous, that raised the hair on my nape. I spun on my chair, opening my mouth in a snarl.

The sound from the bowl rose and rang loudly, as Tamara raised her voice to still us both. "Jonathan!"

The growl stopped. "Yes?" Jonathan answered politely, but his eyes were on me.

Well, that was some trick. He was still in human form, and I didn't know how he could do that. And to growl so low as to almost not be heard, and have such a visceral effect, that was just neat. I'd just learned myself how to be partly in both my forms. I started to growl myself, just to see if I could. Jonathan showed his teeth and I stopped.

Tamara glared at him, and nodded to Kat again. "Amber," Tamara said to me, when the bowl's song rang out again, "tell us again how you commanded your demon to turn the World Snake."

So I told it again, how I'd called my demon for the last time, how he had obeyed my commands, and received the dismissal he so desired. There were other things that happened between Richard and me, but they were private. The bowl didn't seem to notice my omissions, so that was all right.

When I had answered every question three times over, Tamara and the others didn't seem any closer to believing me. At last Tamara said, "Amber, would you be willing to call your demon, so that we may question it?"

"No," I said. "Let's not do that."

Tamara and Kat exchanged glances. "Why?" Tamara asked.

"It would be dangerous."

"Dangerous?" Sol asked. "This is the guy we met, right? Short, blond, blue eyes? The little guy?"

"He changed," I said. The bowl rang out in response to my answer. I almost grinned at it as it sounded "that's true!" to the company. Ha. Someone believed me, even if it was just the magic of the bowl.

"In what way did he change?" Kat asked.

"He got his powers back, and with them, his demon form. He looked like," I tried to explain, "darkness. If darkness had weight, and shape, and depth and will." I repressed a shudder. "The blond guy you saw was the form imposed on him by the magician who raised him. That's not what he was, not at the end. He was different. He's powerful. And he's not my demon anymore."

Kat let the vibration from the bowl fade, as they considered that. "Has anyone else seen a demon? Other than her demon, in the form it took while it was here?"

There was silence.

"So," she continued, "we have no way of knowing if what she described is true." She looked over at Tamara. "It could be just what the demon chose to show her."

Tamara shook her head. "Demons are dangerous. They are unknowable."

"Right!" I agreed. I loved Richard. Richard was gone. What he'd become was not something I wanted to see again. Really.

"I still don't see why we can't ask the demon some questions," Sol said. "Call him here, sort everything out."

"He didn't like being here," I told them. "He waited more than four hundred years for his freedom. He would not like being called back."

"What can he do?" Curt Sanderson entered the conversation once again. I glanced at him, but he still wouldn't meet my eyes. He was beginning to interest me.

"He could set the world on fire," I told them. The bears laughed. The humans smiled. They all thought it was a joke. I reached out and took the rod from Kat and swept it around the bowl so that it rang out anew. "He could set the world on fire," I stated. The laughter died away as the bowl sang true and clear in harmony with my voice.

CHAPTER SEVEN

Tamara took the others back to the shop, probably to decide who else they had to consult with, before disbelieving me some more. I was left to rest, which was fine with me because my wounds were throbbing again, and despite all the sleep I'd gotten, the idea of going back and curling up in that quilt for another couple hours was extremely attractive. But Curt Sondstrom didn't get up when the others did. His fear was spiking again.

Tamara took me aside before she went out the door and lifted an admonishing finger. "You will remember that he is a friend, and you are under my roof." With no further explanation, she went out to catch up with the bears and her soul sister on the way to the shop. When the kitchen door closed behind her, Curt met my eyes for the first time.

"You wanted to talk to me."

"I did?"

"Tamara told me what happened to you. Look, I didn't do anything to you, but something of mine may have helped."

He was tamping down his fear as much as possible. I could smell the sweat on his upper lip. "What are you talking about?"

"Tamara said you have some things that I made."

It took me a moment, but then my teeth bared. "Oh. You make instruments."

He put up his hands. He might be just a straight human, but he could feel what was flaring off of me just then. "Look, keep in mind, I didn't do anything to you, and I didn't know what was happening."

"No?" I smiled. It was not my nice smile. It was the smile that has more teeth in it than a human ought to have. I was gratified to see the metal worker guy lean back hard in his chair and make a smile of his own. His was the kind where you expect to see the tongue come out any minute to lick his lips. His little beard was trembling.

I went to the back room and got the bandana I'd left by the bed. I put it down on the table, opened it up, and pushed it over to Curt.

"You made these?" My blood and my gore were still on them, and the teeth marks on the leather, and the torn wire where I'd finally gotten myself free.

His eyes flicked over them uncomfortably. "Uh. Yeah."

I leaned over the table, and he flinched back again. "Did you make them for me?"

"No! I swear! Look, I really didn't know what they were going to be used for."

There were hollows in his words, covering his lies. I wondered if Kat had left, taking her singing bowl with her, just so that I couldn't be certain. "Did you do the magic in them that makes them work?"

"Uh, kinda. Well, yeah. Look, will you let me explain?"

"I thought that was what I was doing." After all, he was still completely intact. He wasn't bleeding one little bit. And I did not have his throat in my jaws. How much more reasonable could I possibly be?

"Would you back up a little then?"

I tried to straighten up and realized that I had grown very large indeed, as my anger rose. I stepped back and pulled myself together enough that I could stand upright. "Go on," I invited him. "Explain. If you can."

He gathered himself, his eyes moving, avoiding looking at me, and avoiding looking at the instruments on the table. He kept his eyes on his hands. "I take it you've met my Aunt Sarah."

I pulled out the chair opposite him and sat down. My ankle hurt. "Sarah. Yes. I have met Sarah. And she's your aunt?"

"Sarah's had some hard times. My brother and my cousins and I used to stay with her at the ranch, when we were kids. We were fascinated by the fact that she could—I mean, you know she has some skill as a changer?"

"Yes, I do," I said sincerely.

"Ah, well. When we used to stay with her, what she could do was change people, and animals, into other forms." His eyes lit, and suddenly he was staring into another world. "We'd be dogs one time, and once we were horses. But the best was when she turned us into Cooper's hawks. It lasted for an hour or two, shortest for the last one she did, longest for the first. And she couldn't do it again for awhile after that. Once, it was just me and my brother, and we spent a whole morning circling the valley, riding the updrafts high into the sky, and diving down again. Oh, my god, it was heaven." He met my eyes, his brilliant with remembered joy. "It was like Merlin and Arthur, being turned into different animals, and birds. Except, we got to choose. But it never lasted very long."

He pulled the bandana towards himself absently, and then realized what he was doing and pushed it away again. He gestured toward the hooks. "I was taking metal shop in high school. My brother Pete, too. We kept talking about how it would be if we could change for longer, for days even. Pete thought we should be able to make some kind of battery, some kind of holding or sustaining spell. You can put spells into metal and have them stay for awhile. So, that's what we worked on, me and Pete, some way to keep what Sarah did to us going for longer."

"Turn over your hands," I said. When he hesitated I reached over, grabbed his hands and turned them over myself. He was strong, being a metal worker and all. I stand five feet nothing, and I don't look like I should be that strong. Ha. He tried to pull away and was surprised when my grip held. I examined his wrists. There were no scars of puncture wounds. "So, either you didn't do it, or there's another way to do it than sticking a silver hook right into someone's tendon." My voice rose. Well, why not? My wrist hurt from grabbing him. I let him go and he sat back again, away from me.

"A bracelet will work too," he said, almost apologetically. "The hooks are, well, they're to keep the spell in place even if the... uh, subject doesn't want it."

"I see." I glared at him until he wilted. "How long does it last?"

"These?" He pushed the bandana and its contents further away. "They'll last indefinitely. As long as the silver is kept in contact with the flesh, the spell will hold. "

"So she could have kept me like that until she took the hooks out? She had me stuck two forms at once, part wolf, part human."

"Uh, is that your demon form?"

"What?"

"The demon, in the form of a wolf? See, Aunt Sarah was just making sure that the demon couldn't hurt anyone, including you."

"I don't have a demon! Weren't you listening?"

He dropped his voice, opened his hands. "People don't always know, when they're possessed. They can think they're perfectly normal, and all the time, they have a monster inside."

I didn't know where to start. I'm not people. I'm not normal, and what I carry inside, whether in human or wolf form, is not a monster. Some people just can't be told. "What did Madam Tamara tell you about me?"

"That you wanted to talk to me."

I sighed. Maybe I would just have to kill him later. I pushed the bandana his way again. "If you didn't make these for me, why did your aunt have them ready?"

"Oh," he said. "I keep her supplied. She's got a few favorites she uses them on."

"Her dog?"

He grinned. "Yeah, for one. Baz was useless as a sheep dog. He never got hooked on. Never noticed the sheep at all. But he was so friendly and willing, she thought she'd give it a try, and see what he could do around the house. I hear he's really working out for her. Makes the old place shine."

"That's not all he does," I said. I wondered if Curt knew.

"Can I make it up to you?" he asked with a smile. I did not like his smile. It suggested that he was off scot free, and I had forgiven him. My wounds had not yet healed, and I was still pissed.

"How?"

He opened his hands. "I'm a metal worker. I made that singing bowl of Kat's. I make gongs and bells, knives and swords. Maybe we could work something out."

"So that I don't bite you?"

His smile froze. I liked that. He looked at me very carefully, like I was going to grow another head or something. How little he knew. He said, "Tamara told me you weren't going to hurt me."

"She told me that too," I said. I let him relax for a moment and then added, "While you're under her roof."

He wanted me to come to his shop, up in Arcadia, and thought I'd be so enchanted by his instruments that I'd let him give me something and be appeased. This wasn't going to happen, but he didn't seem to understand that. He talked himself right out of the kitchen, and headed back to Tamara's shop. Half an hour later he came out and got into a big old blue hatchback parked down the street and drove away. I'd limped into the living room, where two comfortable chairs were set in a bay window. From there you could see the front of the shop, the patio, and up and down the street in both directions.

It was a very good lookout. Tamara's chair was the one that faced the store. Her mother used the one that looked down the street, but she often sat in Tamara's chair as well. I sat there now, and tried to figure out why Curt Sondstrom had suddenly stopped being afraid of me. Why, instead, he had quickly left the house tamping down on waves of excitement. What was he planning? I had an idea it wasn't something I was going to like.

I fell asleep in the chair. I was dancing in a sunlit glade in the dark forest, leaping about in my wolf form, chasing butterflies like a puppy to music that I knew was there, that my dream-form could hear, but I, though I was the one dreaming, could not. When I turned I saw Tamara's mother watching me.

She was young, in my dream, and strong, and danced barefoot in the grass. She turned away, walking off the grass and and onto what became a rocky wasteland where the sunlight turned hard and beat down on the sand. She began to dance, and the hard shadow she cast seemed to do a dance of its own across the rocky ground. It was a few moments before I heard the beat, and saw the drummer, hunkered over his drum on the desert floor, his face shaded by a wide-brimmed leather hat. He looked up and met my eyes. His were yellow. He bared his yellow teeth in a grin, and his face changed to one I knew. I started awake just as he began to speak. I hadn't seen him in more than two years, since he'd gone with my mother and brother to the Gathering, and not come home. It was my father.

Tamara sat opposite me in her mother's chair, sipping coffee from a big round mug painted with zebras. I sat clinging to the dream in my mind. I'd heard his voice, my father's voice, but the echo was fading, and I couldn't make out what he'd said.

"He's gone," Tamara said.

"I know." I realized a moment later she wasn't talking about my father. "Huh? Oh, Curt. Yeah. I saw."

She smiled at me, a spare and ascetic expression. "You did not bite him." I shook my head, and she nodded approvingly. "He told me about his aunt Sarah. Her husband used to beat her. And there were other crimes. Other tortures." Her eyes were deep and dark as she recounted them to herself. "If she called the police, the sheriff's deputy would arrive, and her husband would stand on the porch and tell him about the trouble he was having with his wife, while she lay on the kitchen floor, bruised, or broken, or scalded... Her husband was a former deputy himself, you see. That is why Curt helped her. That is how it began."

I turned away from the window to look her in the eyes. That's not what he'd told me. That wasn't how it began. What happened to Merlin, and the Cooper's hawks? Or maybe Tamara wasn't to know about that part.

"Every power wielder will at some time arrive at a moment where she must deal justice. Since we can, there will be a time when we must. You have dealt wisely today. I hope you do so always." She nodded to me. Warily, I nodded back. I thought she was talking about my not having chewed off Curt Sondstrom's face. What Tamara didn't seem to understand is, I'd heard him out, but I hadn't passed judgment yet.

"I must run. I've a delivery coming."

I stayed where I was. I tried to think myself back into the dream that Tamara had interrupted, but it was gone. I stared out the window, taking little note of what I was seeing outside. The street where the music shop was located had unusually mixed zoning, left over from the early days of Costa Mesa. The music store stood in the middle of the block, where most of the residences had been turned into professional office buildings. The handsome two-story house next door was a law firm. Down at the corner a beauty shop advertised itself as a spa, and next door a bakery that served coffee and sandwiches had a few tables and chairs on the sidewalk out front. On the far side of the music store, a row of shops sold jewelry, antique furniture, and bicycles. I sat thinking about my dream, watching the occasional foot traffic along the sidewalks. The late afternoon sunlight shone golden on the little flower gardens of the houses across the street. In front of one of them, gazing across at the shop, stood a slender, fair-haired young man in a dark leather jacket. It was Richard.

I limped back through the kitchen and out the back door. I was barefoot, because I'd kicked Elaine's shoes under the bed and hoped I never saw them again. By the time I reached the street, he was gone. Of course he was gone. I'd been imagining it, or it had been an extension of the dream I'd had, because not only was he not there, but he'd never been there. I stood downwind of where I'd seen the guy, and while it was possible to find minute traces of Richard around Tamara's store, because we'd been there together a couple of times, if he'd been standing just there his scent should be fresh and new, and it wasn't. So probably all that had happened was that I was missing Richard so badly, I'd begun to imagine I'd seen him.

I walked haltingly into Tamara's store, half-blinded by the evening light blazing in the windows, meaning to ask if anyone else had seen someone who looked like Richard, when I stopped at the sight of a big back-lit young woman in tight jangling braids, her dark skin set off by a blue, purple, and white African-style shirt over her jeans. I began to smile as I recognized her scent, until I realized she was very much not smiling at me. Her arms were crossed, and her face was hard, an expression I hadn't seen since I first met her. Not too far away, just happening to be idly looming by the counter, was the second biggest bear, Jason, not quite paying any attention at all to the two of us.

"Hey, Yvette," I said.

She was like iron, unyielding. "Tamara said you wanted to talk to me."

"Yeah," I said. "Come sit outside?" I glanced past her at Jason, who was looking a long ways down at me.

"No," said Yvette. "You got something to say to me, say it here."

"I'm going to go say it sitting out there," I said, "because my ankle hurts like sin and I don't want to stand anymore. So, come and talk to me out there, okay? Bring the bear if you want to. He's welcome to hear it."

A little wall ran around the patio outside the shop to the right of the door. People used it as a seat to drink coffee, or drum, or just hang out and talk or jam. Where the wall ended, Tamara had recently added an iron bench to increase the seating area out there. I chose an angle where the sun wouldn't be in my eyes, and sat down. It was also where I could see the spot where I thought I'd seen Richard standing only minutes ago. A little while later stony Yvette came out of the shop and stood in front of me, her arms still crossed.

I nodded. "Right over there, on Wednesday, after that meeting that turned into a jam—"

"Yeah?"

"You leaned out of your car window and called to me, 'Are you coming to the party on Friday? The one in Malibu?' And I thought you were going, so I went."

"What party in Malibu?" Yvette asked, her voice mocking.

"The one where I was shot."

"You got shot?" Yvette my friend was suddenly back, the iron gone in an instant. "You all right?"

"One of those darts they use on big animals. I was taken prisoner, kept in a cage."

"Oh, shit," she said, and sat down next to me, ducking from the blinding sunset. "What happened?"

"Well, I went to this party because I thought you asked me to."

"Uh huh. Because I know all kinds of people up there in Malibu." Yvette could do sarcasm so thick that it dripped. "So, tell me about my car?" I stared at her. She nodded when she saw I understood. "That's right," she said. "You ever seen me drive a car?"

I shook my head. "No."

"No," she agreed. "That's because I don't even have a license. In fact, I don't even know how to drive."

"It wasn't you."

"I'm glad we got that out of the way."

"But it looked just like you."

"From that far away?" She pointed across the street, where the figure in the car, whom I had been sure was Yvette, had leaned out to call to me.

"That's right. With your voice and everything, and that hat you wore all night." I'd seen her, but I hadn't smelled her. "Huh. Someone made me think they were you."

"Okay," she said. "Just so we're sure."

"I'm sure," I said. "But what the fuck is going on?"

Jason came out then, and walked over to stand behind Yvette where she sat on the bench. "So," he said, staring down at me, "everything all right out here?"

"Oh, yeah," Yvette leaned back to grin up at him. "She mistook me for someone who drives a car."

"A car?" He bent his head, so the two of them were face to face, Yvette grinning up, and Jason smiling down. He slid a look at me to make sure I saw this. I pretended I didn't.

"Yeah—" Yvette broke off on a gasp, because the bench was rising in the air. I kept my balance, and continued pretending nothing was happening as Jason lifted the bench up over his head, and Yvette laughed and shrieked at him, until he put it down.

And then there was kissing. Fortunately, a couple of drummers arrived and settled on the corner of the wall on the other side of the patio. Yvette broke away from Jason to duck inside the store and return with her djembe. The drummers greeted her as she took her place near them, hooking a leg over the wall and adjusting her drum on its strap over her shoulder.

Jason came and sat down on the bench beside me. Iron shouldn't creak, but I'm pretty sure the bench did. I asked him, "What do you do when someone tries to take something from you?"

"I stop them."

Well, it was a stupid question. No one takes anything from a bear. Except maybe another, bigger bear. Or two bears. Or a lady bear.

"What if a number of people are trying to take something from you, and assault you in the process?"

He broke his gaze away from the drummers and turned a long look on me. "What's going on?"

"My demon is gone, you know."

"So I heard."

Huh. He didn't sound like he believed it. And that made it just about unanimous. "Even though he is gone," I emphasized, "people still want my demon. They think they can make me give him to them."

"Can you?"

I raised my lip at him, in the human version of a snarl. "You, too?"

"Hells, no, I don't want your demon. Too much trouble. But folks have been asking how they would get it from you."

"Have they? They ask you?"

"Oh, no. But we've all heard them. Folks are worried."

"I know," I said, with an edge in my voice.

Jason's mild look took on a hint of amusement. "They think your demon can help."

"He *did*!"

"So you say."

"No one is getting him from me. Even if he was mine to give."

"So what are you asking me?"

"I think I'm asking what to do to get everyone to stop."

He shook his big head. A smile grew on his face, but that was because Yvette across the way was laughing and talking with her hands, her voice, and her drum, and then the three of them got down to it. The drums sounded out in exhilaration. The bright notes of Yvette's djembe rang out beneath her fast-moving hands. He caught her eye and grinned. Yup, I was looking at one infatuated bear.

The sunset left pink stripes reflected across the sky that intensified as the sun went down. "They're not going to stop," I said. I pulled my knees up to my chin and wrapped my arms around them, looking up at the changing colors in the sky. I thought when I left home, and got myself away from my abusive stepfather and his horrible sons, that my problems would be over. All I had to do was keep out of sight until I turned eighteen. Now, I had a whole new set of enemies after me, and Gray Fox still lurked in the mountains, waiting for me to show myself. I had to convince people that trying to take me was really not a good idea. I had to seek out everyone who was after me, and set them straight. Hunting was something I was good at, after all. This could actually be fun.

I didn't realize I'd spoken aloud, until I heard the sound of my voice: "I will find them out. And I will teach them not to mess with me."

I looked over at the bear, but he hadn't heard me over the pounding of the drums. Or he didn't listen. But still, my words sounded against the drums' resonance, and the harmonies rang out, doubling and redoubling in the open air.

CHAPTER EIGHT

S o, the first thing I did to get ready for my hunt was rest and heal up. That was only smart, after all. Tamara made it clear that if she was going to house me and feed me for a few days, then I was going to have to make myself useful, which is why I spent Saturday perched on a stool in the back room of her shop, unpacking boxes and checking their contents against the manifests. It was relaxing, and since I wasn't moving much, I was hardly in pain at all. I had time to think, about Sarah and her ranch, and seeing Richard again, and other things.

Tamara, with long-suffering patience, took me into town at lunch time to a place where I could buy some new tennis shoes. I got a couple of pairs of socks and some underwear as well, since I didn't know how many changes I'd need. At least, when she asked me if I needed money, I was able to tell her I could handle it. I spent the evil vet's camel money. I felt I'd earned it.

Aaron came to the house that night with a huge order of Chinese food. Sol joined us, and he and Aaron told of their adventures in the mountains, and in coming to and from the mountains, and Tamara told of some of her travels. I tried six different dishes, and felt left out. The places I had traveled, I couldn't talk about.

After another round of cleaning and ointment, and whatever extra healing was added by Tamara's concentrated touch, the following day I was back on my feet without too much pain. In the early morning I changed and in my wolf form trotted around the lot between the house and the shop, making myself small to avoid excited calls from the neighbors about seeing a wolf wandering loose.

I still felt a twinge when I put weight on my fore and hind feet and flexed them, but it didn't seem that I was going to be crippled, and that was a relief. If they had crippled me, I probably would have had to kill someone, though, if I were crippled, I didn't know if I could. What was I going to do to these people, in return for what they'd done to me? There's lots of biting you can do which creates lots of mayhem, blood and pain, without causing death. I thought about all the possibilities as I nosed around the lot, grinning to myself. Probably, when I met up with them, I'd just wing it. And that would be fun.

Tamara owned the lot behind the vacant one as well, that faced onto the next street over. On it stood a big old house surrounded by an eight-foot fence, that Tamara rented out. These days her tenants were the bears. A gate with a latch high near the top of the fence allowed them to cut through the yard between the house and the shop. Jonathan wandered through while I was trotting along the fence, and eyed me blearily. Bears tolerate wolves, but they are never happy about sharing their territory. I could see that I wouldn't be staying much longer.

Tamara went off after breakfast to the hospital to sit with her mother, as she did nearly every day. She had two or three employees who minded the shop at various times. There were also a dozen or so people who hung around and occasionally lent a hand because they were there, just as I was, while I convalesced. Today more and more people kept arriving, organizing, bringing in supplies, running errands, consulting about arrangements, hurrying around, putting up decorations of wreaths and flowers, setting up candle lanterns on the patio, stringing Chinese lanterns across the lot. A pickup truck carrying a load of wood backed over the curb and onto the vacant lot, and people gathered to unload and build the bonfire. Today was Beltane, one of the eight great holidays, so tonight there would be a gathering. There would be fire and food, dancing and drink. Power wielders planned to use the energy raised by the dancing and the drumming to help to strengthen the wards they'd been building all over the city against the World Snake. Well. It wouldn't do any harm.

I held things and carried things. I climbed up on the roof at one point to help string colored lights. I don't know why this annoyed the bears, but it did. I went inside and looked busy by grabbing a duster, a feather duster, made from the feathers of distant and probably long-dead ostriches. I dusted the shelf of foreign gods, the shelf of books about, guess what, music, and the thumb harps, the xylophones, and the many drums. I ignored the growing number of people arriving, gathering, greeting one another, carrying instruments, carrying plates or trays or covered dishes of food. I felt the rising excitement resonate with the magical buzz in the air. I kept near the walls and thought about Richard, who hadn't been Richard, and Yvette, who hadn't been Yvette.

By noon, my ankle was aching again, and despite there being so many people around I kept bumping into bears, whatever I was doing. So I went back to the house to lie down in the back room and take a nap on the quilt that smelled so comforting. I could hear some of the growing hubbub outside, as I rose from sleep to awareness, and relapsed into sleep again. I curled into a ball and wrapped the quilt around me. It wasn't that I was chilled, or lonely, or in pain. It's just that I still missed Richard.

Lying half asleep I remembered the smell of him in his wolf form; the scent of grass on his fur. The thoughtful, attentive look on his face that contorted into protesting laughter when I pretended to bite him. The evil, self-satisfied smile he had when he worked his long-honed wiles on me until I moaned. The smell of him, in his wolf form, the scent of grass on his hair…

Tamara came into the house, bringing with her four or five chattering friends. They laid out a buffet of ham, cheese, bread from the bakery, potato salad with dill, sodas and a bottle of wine, and talked and laughed while they ate. I went back to sleep. After a while I woke to the change of sounds, and heard them go. Tamara called and talked to some of them from the porch, and then she came back inside. I opened my eyes as she stopped in the doorway of my room.

"Come into the kitchen. I've saved some food for you."

Before I sat to eat down she took my wrist in her hand, felt the air over it with the other hand, and nodded. It had been giving me twinges, but now it subsided. When we sat down she held out a hand for my ankle, and with relief I lifted it, and felt the pain leak away. Wonderful. They'd left lots of ham. The bread was crunchy, and the potato salad was delicious.

Tamara offered me a cup of coffee. It was not as awful as the coffee they brewed in the shop and kept going all day, but it was pretty bad. Quantities of milk and sugar made it just about drinkable. Tamara sipped hers with apparent enjoyment, and picked at the last of the potato salad. She watched me take slugs of my coffee with laughter at the back of her eyes. I didn't seem to be fooling her one bit.

"I have taken counsel with many of the people who are concerned about what our next move should be. No one has yet been able to divine whether the Great Worm has changed its course. After tonight, I planned to meet with some friends in the desert. When we scry the stars together, we often receive a stronger, more powerful reading." She looked away into the distance, as though seeing the desert under the night sky. "But that isn't possible while so many are clamoring for action now." She met my eyes. "You are going to have to call that demon of yours. You're going to have to make him answer questions, to either set everyone's minds at rest, or figure out how to carry the battle further."

I shook my head. "I can't do that."

"Can't?"

"I set him free. I gave him his freedom. I can't call on him anymore."

She looked into my eyes searchingly. "You told Kat you can call him."

I shrugged. This wasn't going the way I wanted it to. "I can call him, but he isn't my servant anymore. It's different." I added, "It's dangerous."

She smiled wearily. "So, you understand at last what you are dealing with."

"I didn't say I understood him. But I do understand that, now that he's no longer bound by me, he can eat me for breakfast."

"Yes. Well, the hope is that there will be sufficient people of power present when you call him, to contain any damage he might wish to do."

"Have any of them had any experience controlling a demon? Ha. Or even seen one?"

"Nonetheless," she said, "this is what you must do. If you want people to believe you, if the danger is really past, we are going to have to hear the demon say so, and make our own judgment."

"Tonight? You want me to call him tonight?"

"On Beltane? Of course not. This is a celebration."

"But you want me to call him in front of other people?"

"That's the idea. You want to convince us that he defeated—turned—the Worm, yes? How else can you do it?"

"I thought I'd do it by having the Snake not come."

"People are too worried to wait for that."

"Yeah. I get that. But here's the thing. If I call him in front of other people, they'll know how it's done. They'll hear me call his name."

"So I suppose."

"But that's the problem. If they hear his name, if they can call him themselves, some of them may try to enslave him again, and I promised him that wouldn't happen."

Tamara thought a moment. I hoped she was thinking about all the power wielders she knew in this city, and what some of them might do with a powerful demon in their service. She said at last, "Then what do you suggest?"

I looked straight at her, with as much sincerity as I could muster. "Everyone there has to promise, has to swear, that they will never use what they see or hear to increase their own power. They have to give me their oath, on whatever they hold most sacred, that they will never call Richard themselves."

Tamara raised her brows. She suspected something. Her believing me depended on how stupid she thought I was. I opened my eyes a little and held her gaze, and finally she nodded. "It will be as you say."

Yeah, I thought to myself. And now we'll find the liars out.

So, the plan was that she would find an auspicious day, and all the interested power wielders would get together, and after everyone swore they wouldn't use this knowledge against him, they would watch me call my demon. Richard would come, he would tell them the crisis was over, and everybody would go away and be happy. Great plan.

Tamara said she would start sounding people out about the auspicious day, since many of the people she had to consult were here already for Beltane, or would be here in a little while. Finding the right day didn't mean throwing the bones, consulting the I Ching or meditating among three bowls of water, it meant finding a day and a time that interested power wielders could agree to meet. So, that was the first problem, and it was going to take a while.

Tamara finished her coffee and headed back to the preparations. I volunteered to clean up the kitchen, and she agreed, after I promised not to stay on my feet too long. I packaged up the food, washed the dishes and wiped the surfaces, standing on my good leg for the most part. I'd done this kind of thing with Richard, not too long ago.

Another problem was, Richard is not my demon's name. Richard is what I called him, because using a demon's real name for ordinary usage is asking for trouble. Richard entered my service for protection when he was powerless, and he gave me his true name. With that, I had complete mastery over him. Now that he was free, his true name was all that would summon him. Giving an all-powerful demon's true name to a bunch of power wielders was a really, really bad idea. Richard and I had talked about this, before he went. I'd given him a date for his freedom, but as long as I knew his true name, I could enslave him again simply by uttering that word.

If I called Richard, at the gathering that Tamara planned, I would be making a present to anyone who wished it, of the word that would call an all-powerful demon. If Tamara managed to invite all the people who were after me for my demon, she'd be doing my hunting for me, and all I had to do was watch who rose to the bait. This just might be fun.

When the kitchen was clean I wandered back over to the store to watch the preparations. I was crossing the vacant lot when Curt Sondstrom drove by. He saw me and came to a stop, double-parking across the street. He got out of the car and beckoned to me.

I took a moment to decide whether I'd seen him or not. I'm not a puppy. I don't come when I'm called. He looked over at the crowd of people, then came around the back of his hatchback and crossed the street toward me. I decided then that I had seen him, and I met him part way on the sidewalk. He glanced over at the gathering, where the preparations seemed to have melded with the party to come. The drinking, the laughing, the eating, and some preparatory drumming had already begun. Only the dancing would wait for nightfall, and the fire.

Curt turned so his back was to the crowd as he faced me. He had that plastered smile on again, and his tension was so strong I could practically taste it. He wasn't spiking fear this time, though, and that annoyed me. He should be afraid of me. I'd have to see what I could do about that.

"You wanted to talk to Sarah?" he said. "She's waiting to talk to you."

"Why would I want to talk to Sarah?" I said. I had spent some thought about what I should do about Sarah. I wasn't ready to talk to her because I hadn't decided which of the lovely scenarios were most fitting. Some of them, of course, were going to make some folks pretty angry if they found out about them, but there was no one here I answered to, after all.

"I'm sorry, I didn't put it right," Sondstrom said. I was interested in the fact that not all of his attention was on me while he was speaking. He kept a sharp eye on people coming up the sidewalk in our direction, or crossing the road towards us. He was not on the look-out for friends, unless he was looking for them in order to avoid them, I decided. "Sarah is waiting to speak to you." He dropped his voice, to sound sincere and contrite. "She has something she wants to say to you." He looked at me then from under his brows, giving the impression that he shared in this supposed apology. Of course, he hadn't said she was going to apologize, or maybe do anything but cuss me out one way and back for messing with her dog breeding program. But he was implying that she would.

"Oh?" I said. "Is she coming here?"

"No, no. She wouldn't. She's—some people don't understand the things she does, or why she does them. I'll tell you her whole story some day. She's at my shop in Arcadia. I'll take you there." He touched my arm to guide me to his car.

"But—it's Beltane!" I protested, child-like. "There's going to be a bonfire."

He smiled. "I'll get you back before the party gets going. I promise. It's not that far." He started walking, his arm not quite touching my back to herd me along. "You'll like my shop. Maybe you'll see something that appeals to you. I hope you will." His smile was tense, and fake. He was lying.

"I don't know," I hesitated. "I should be helping with the party. Tamara had some important things she wanted me to take care of." I tried to think what they were, in case he asked.

Instead, he said, "Oh, Tamara knows all about it. In fact, she suggested that the best thing you could do was meet with Sarah and make it up. Today, while there's time." There was that smile again. "And I'm to have you back in time for the barbecue."

Oh what a liar! I had to admire him, as I crossed the street with him to his car. "Should I tell Tamara I'm going now?" I asked, just to keep him jumping.

"I just talked to her on my cell. It's fine, she knows."

"Okay," I said, and stepped into the passenger seat of his car.

The car filled up with his tension as he drove off down the street, turned the corner, and then caught the main drag that would eventually take us to the freeway. I was wondering how long I should let this go on when he pulled in to a gas station and drove up to a pump. That's when Elaine, the evil vet, came out from behind the farthest set of pumps and got into the seat behind me.

"Go," she said. "I'm in," and Curt pulled onto the main drag again.

It is not good to let an enemy sit behind you, within the reach of her arms. I turned around in my seat to face her. "Hi!" I said, with fake enthusiasm. I could see both her and Curt at the same time from this position. "How are you? The hole you put in my hip is healing nicely, in case you want to know."

Elaine radiated tension in a different way than Curt. Hers had an intensity, like a low note on the scale, unlike the ascending chords that Curt was emitting. "I'm fine," she said evenly. "My truck is still nose down on the beach. They haven't managed to bring it up yet, because they haven't got a tow truck small enough to get around that bend, and big enough to tow it off the sand." Her mouth widened into an angry sneer, "And it's going to cost a fortune!"

I couldn't help my big fat grin. Honestly. I couldn't. "Oh, I'm really sorry," I said. I noticed that she was keeping her hands out of my sight. Unless I climbed up to look down in her lap, I wasn't going to be able to see what she was holding there. "So, do you want to talk to Sarah, too?'

She registered surprise and shot a look at Curt, who must have caught her eye in the mirror. He answered, "We thought it would be better if we were all there together when you and Sarah talk."

"That's right," Elaine concurred, following Curt's lead. "We're all trying to help you."

"Is that what this is?"

"We're perfectly serious. You don't know what trouble you're in."

"I told you I was sorry about the car. Did you find your gun yet?"

"That's not what we're talking about," Elaine insisted. "It's about your demon."

"My demon? You mean my ex-demon?"

She shook her head. "You can't pretend it's gone if you're still turning into a wolf."

"Oh, is that why I keep turning into a wolf?" I asked them. I wonder what my mother would think of that. And my father. And my brothers, and the whole great valley full of my kind.

"Don't make fun. We're going to help you."

"The demon has nothing to do with my wolf nature." I could see there was no point in explaining, but I tried.

"Then," Elaine's eyes gleamed, "it won't matter if we take it away." She moved forward to tell me earnestly. "Do you know that you're under a curse?"

I sighed. What an idiot. "Sometimes it sure feels that way."

"We want to help you," Curt put in. "There must be a cure."

"And that's what we're all going to talk about? You two, and Sarah, and me?"

"Yes," Elaine said.

"And is sister Holly going to be there too?"

The two of them must have conferred in the mirror again. There was a moment before Elaine answered. "She can't this time. She's out of town. But Holly says that as soon as we can get you to Cecil, Cecil will find the cure."

"Oh, is Cecil back in town?" I was looking forward to meeting him. I turned around to the front. Elaine was up to something. I gave her a little space so she could get on with it, since I wanted it to happen soon.

"No," Curt said, looking in the mirror again. "Where is old Cecil these days?"

Elaine's voice sounded distracted and a little strained. "He's still out on that yacht. He's trying to commune with the World Snake. He thinks he can talk to it."

"Well, good luck to him," Curt said. He looked in the mirror again.

And I just bet he was sure that my demon could help him with that. I was going to say that, but there wasn't time. I would have known that Elaine was making her move even if I hadn't smelled the chemical trace coming from the backseat, because the focus of Curt's eyes suddenly hardened. I didn't wait. I changed, and as I changed I let loose all my anger and pent-up frustration, so by the time I'd turned around, I barely fit in the car. She had a syringe in her hand, and had raised it to stick in my arm or my neck, but instead of an arm or a neck, she was facing a really large wolf's head, with its mouth open, snarling so fiercely that spit was flying. Elaine gasped. Curt lost control of the car.

I'd made sure to make my move before we got to the freeway. I didn't want to have a fight in a car going sixty-five miles an hour. Curt jerked left, really not a good idea, so I loomed over Elaine, who was screeching, and bumped the wheel with my forepaw and sent the car careening to the right. Curt yelled, grabbed at the wheel, I gave it another nudge and snapped at Elaine's head just to make her duck and jerk. She stuck the syringe in the uphol-stery and I snapped at her again to make her let it go, and nudged the wheel out of Curt's hands at the same time.

There was a bump as the car climbed up on the sidewalk, and then a crash that shook us all as we hit a fence, and then a breath-taking drop as I wondered if I'd aimed us at the river or some-thing, and tried to take a quick look outside, but the windows weren't sighted for something with its head pressed to the roof, and then we hit the ground, and Curt accidentally trod on the gas instead of the brakes and sent us roaring down the fake green hill of a golf course, over the rough and into the water hazard. I turned around and changed so I could use my hands, rolled down the window as we subsided into the pond, and changed again. Elaine was floundering in the back seat, trying to roll down the window, and then trying to roll it up again as the water poured through. Curt shouted something. He was having to fight gravity to try and get out of his seatbelt, and his seat, since his side of the car had listed downward. He was going to have to get past me, too, since my window was still out of the water. I wasn't going yet. I hadn't finished.

I leaned over the back seat. To ensure that I had Elaine's full attention, I took her head into my jaws. As she let out a mewling scream, clawing at me to no avail, and Curt shouted at me, I planted a huge paw on his chest, and then I let one canine pierce the skin on the back of Elaine's skull, until it touched the bone. Ouch! She shrieked at the pain. I didn't blame her. That must have hurt a lot. I tasted her blood as it bubbled up fast, all warm and sweet. Yum. I let go, her blood still dripping from my lips as she wailed and clutched her head and stared at me aghast.

I changed. Wolves can't talk. This wasn't the first time I'd wished we could. I'm not nearly as impressive as a human, damn it all, or this wouldn't have happened in the first place. I glared at her, my eyes yellow, and said, "If you touch me again, if you try and harm me in any way, I will tear your head off." I turned to Curt, who was lying half in the water by that time, his chest still under my hand. He gaped at me. "That goes for you too." Then I changed again, and hopped out the window.

The water wasn't deep, but you'd think Curt and Elaine were already drowning from all the yelling they were doing. I stopped when I reached the trees and turned around to enjoy the sight. Elaine had finally rolled down her window and was trying to climb out of it. Blood poured down her head. Head wounds bleed like mad. She must have thought she was dying. But all she had was one little puncture wound. I still had three.

Curt grabbed at her, trying to climb up past her to reach the window himself. She saw me, sitting there watching them, and she screamed something at me before Curt grabbed her and pulled her back. They were only trying to help me, is what she seemed to have said. Hah.

Golfers were descending on the car from all directions, faces alight with interest, because nothing exciting ever really happens on a golf course. Some were shouting about the damage to the course, and some were shouting about the idiot driver, one was shouting about calling 911 and getting help, and a couple of people waded in to make sure Curt and Elaine didn't drown.

Meanwhile I, a blameless little dog, trotted away from the scene with a big canine grin all over my face. I followed our tracks back up to the street and changed just before I climbed through the broken wall.

My ankle was hurting again before I'd gone a block, and it was a long way back to Tamara's, but it was worth it. Many blocks away from the store, I heard distant drumming. When I came closer, I passed through a complicated ward and suddenly I heard it clearly, loud and bright, sharp and joyous, the rhythm calling me to join in. I smelled beer and wine, excitement, and frying meat, I heard laughter and talking, and the burble of a lot of people having a great time. If I did not like the noise, or would be offended by it, or could be expected to call the fire department at the sight of a bonfire in a city lot, I guessed that the ward would distract my attention, push my senses aside. But if I was the kind who should be at that fire tonight, who should be part of that joyful sound, then the drums would call to me. Tamara told me she and her friends were powerful warders. Now I understood what she meant. In the brief days Richard and I had had together, after the crisis was over, when we were lovers and friends, we'd come to a drum circle at the music store, just because we were cramming as many adventures and experiences into our time as we possibly could. I was doing it to save up a score of memories, and Richard came because he was mine and I wanted him to. Now I came up to the crowd of people, some of whom I knew to nod to, most of whom were strangers, who hugged each other, exclaimed, raised their glasses, shouted stories over the noise. I limped through the folks as though I were alone in the woods. I found a seat near the food tables, grabbed a cup of cider and a handful of chips and sat down to get off my ankle at last. And I prepared to sit out the celebration.

Back home, in our valley, the bonfire would be built in the field behind our back garden. People gathered from all over, sometimes arriving days ahead of time, staying with cousins or friends, or camping out in the woods. They gathered at our place in the afternoon. Aunt Dora would supervise the tables set up and decorated for the enormous potluck that would feed people all night. When darkness fell, my mom would light the bonfire while all our family watched. I remembered dancing with my dad, leaping over the fire with my brothers, playing with cousins and friends, and the howl afterwards that only ended when my mom and dad chased off into the woods together. Later, other dark pairs, in their human form, or their wolf form, left the circle and made for the woods as well.

Last Beltane it had been my stepbrothers who had chased me into the woods. I looked down as I felt the liquid run through my fingers. I'd crushed my cup. That was the night I'd decided I had to leave soon, because if I didn't, someone was going to die.

As the sun went down, the drums were stilled, and people moved to form a huge circle around the artfully stacked wood of the bonfire. A group of women sang the four directions in haunting harmony. Tamara stalked into the circle wearing her robe of night blue scattered with stars, a black and purple turban wound tightly around her head and set with colored gems. She raised her arms, and the power that the singers had set into motion tightened and began to move widdershins around the circle of people. She invoked the Lady and Lord of the Dance, and invited them into the circle. She took the burning branch from Aaron, and touched it to the fire. The flames leaped with a woomph, and I gathered that the pyromaniacs in the group had liberally doused the wood with accelerants.

A buffalo drum sounded a heart beat. Tamara stood, silent and still, while it sounded half a dozen times. And then she stepped off on the beat, treading the circle, stately and fine, every motion a message cut in the air. Other dancers entered the circle, pacing the sound of the drum. Other drums joined the heart beat. The drummers watched the dancers, the dancers heard the drums, all the way through their bodies. Then one of the drums broke off, climbing a pattern of its own, talking back to the heart rhythm. One of the dancers began to bounce. More drums broke away, running up their own riffs, and coming back off time, on time, but always precise in relation to the heart beat. The dancers moved faster, moved up and down, side to side, made curvets around the fire. More drums joined in, until it sounded like a huge conversation all over the range of sound, sharp, deep, high, low, cacophonous and understated. Against this moving wall of sound other instruments set up their contrast. Rattles of seeds, rattles of metal, spoons beaten against a hand, bottles blown, fiddles screeched, flutes rose piercingly in their own stratosphere. Deep within the hammering of the drums I heard the uncanny susurration of voices, as though a group of people were talking distinctly, but far away.

The beat grew faster. The dancers leaped and clapped, throwing shadows that became a visual rhythm, in time to the rhythm of the drums, until the fire, the noise, and the dancers became together one wall of sensation, a complete cacophony that you could deconstruct down to the last tap and seed rattle, the last shout, shuffle and leap, but which altogether made a phenomenon so huge and compelling you felt it to your bones.

The crowd shifted, hopped, tapped, or gave in and joined the circle and danced. As darkness fell I sat on my corner of the bench, quite still, and alone. The drumming pounded through my heart along with the laughter and the noise. I couldn't sit still anymore. The sound drew me, but not only the sound. The drumming, the dancing, the excitement, the joy, the leaping forms drew and combined with the magic that had been raised in the place over and over again, year upon year. The accumulation of that energy came together, spiraling upward, drawing every living thing it touched in its wake. The compulsion to dance grew as my heart sounded in rhythm with the drums. But I couldn't dance. My ankle hurt as badly as it had the night of my escape. No point in damaging it further, especially when I'd been a fair way to healing.

In my own corner of the darkness outside the fire, I unleashed the pain and passion in my heart and changed, and as I changed I grew. I hopped up on top of the shop's roof and lay there watching the fire, tracking the spiraling energy, taking in the scent of sweat and joy, meat and alcohol. This was better. This was even enjoyable.

I spotted Yvette among the drummers, dancing as she drummed. I could hear the riff she laid down in counterpoint to the heart beat and the main rhythm, bright with joy, powerful and certain, as she threw her happiness into the air in sound, where all could hear it, where it became part of the magic.

Tamara stood now at the edge of the circle, wielding a shaker that rattled and cracked. The great bonfire roared, firelight reflecting on the dancers' ritual clothing, the flickering gemstones, the flying cloaks and scarves. The moving bodies spiraled around the flames, while dancers joined and left again, drummers spelled one another, danced in their turn, or stepped out of the firelight, into the darkness to eat, drink and talk, and more people stood around the circle, clapping, drinking, driving on the dance. All around the world tonight, bonfires were burning, drumming and dancing raised the power of life and joy into the night.

The dancing changed. Tamara joined the dance again, together with a group of men and women who moved together with intention, shaping the spiral of energy they raised, knitting it with the power already in the air to use for their purpose. Ah, yes. They were going to stop the World Snake from coming. I lifted my lip in the darkness. Because they did not believe me. How earnest they were. How certain, how powerful. Well. I didn't have to watch this.

Mindful of my wounds, I hopped down from the roof—after carefully checking my size, a lesson I had almost not learned in time not too long ago—changed and stepped on to two feet and limped toward the house. Two of the bears rose up in my path. They seemed bigger than usual. It took me a moment to recognize Jonathan and Sol, since their aspects had grown huge in the power of the night.

"Was that you up on the roof?" Jonathan asked.

"Who else?" I was not in the mood for conversation.

"Good view?"

"The best."

"Cool!"

They left me, and I crossed the yard, walking slowly around the people standing talking or drinking at the edges of the fire circle, and went into the house. I took a long shower, changed to my wolf form, where human thoughts were muted, and human feelings simplified, curled up against the wall and slept.

I woke briefly when the sunrise brought the sudden silence of the drums. I cocked an ear to the ending of the ritual, when the singers thanked the Lord and Lady, sang the four directions, wound up the working and opened the circle. Those women could really sing.

I ignored the sound of Tamara and her guests wandering into the kitchen, and the smell of coffee and toast. Since I hadn't actually taken part in the celebration, I didn't feel obliged to help with the clean-up. When Tamara and her guests had eaten and wandered out again, I went back to sleep for a few more hours. I got up later on and on two feet limped across the lot toward the shop. People were wandering around, haggard with exhaustion, but still exalted from dancing and drumming all night, taking down tables and decorations, taking apart the last of the fire and dousing it effectively.

I hobbled up to the patio and settled on the bench and watched everyone's exhausted industry. I nodded to the three bears who were sitting on the wall nearest the shop door, sharing a big bag of chips. Well, sharing in the way that bears share. That is to say, all three were helping to hold the bag open, and all three were scooping chips into their mouths as fast as they could. I sat there appreciating their efficiency and grace. I am a great admirer of the bear kind.

"Tamara wants you," Jonathan said, without stopping to swallow.

I nodded, thanking him.

"I think she wants you now," he repeated, when the next handful of chips had partly cleared his mouth. Sol and Aaron nodded in agreement.

"I look forward to talking to her," I said, but I didn't get up.

When the chips were but a memory, kept alive by Aaron seizing the bag, tearing it open and licking the salt and grease and tiny bits from the corners, Jonathan went inside. A while later Tamara came out with him, and sat down on the bench beside me. She showed her exhaustion from dancing almost all night, but she exuded energy, nonetheless. The working had fed her spirit as much as she had given herself to it.

She said, "I looked for you yesterday. Where were you?"

"I was there last night."

"Yes. I saw you on the roof." She gave me a disapproving glare. "I missed you earlier. No one knew where you were." She glanced at the bears, who were pretending as hard as they could that they weren't frankly listening in. They managed to look in all directions so I couldn't possibly think they were the ones keeping track of me.

"So," I concluded, "you did not in fact tell Curt Sondstrom that he should take me to meet his aunt Sarah and talk over our differences?"

Surprise cancels other feelings, every time. "No, I did not. Who told you I did?"

"Curt did. And so you didn't know that Elaine planned to bring a hypodermic to stick me with in the car?"

"Of course not! When did this happen?"

"Yesterday afternoon, a few hours before sunset."

"So that's where you went."

"Madam Tamara, if your friend tries to harm me again, I will bite him."

It is not a good idea to challenge a bear. All three of them turned and focused on me with such force that heads turned in our direction around the lot. But the sudden tightness in the air came as Madam Tamara straightened and glared down at me. It is *really* unwise to challenge a sorceress.

"You say this to me?"

I kept my voice soft. "We were not under your roof, so I dropped him in a pond. I didn't hurt him. But I will not allow him to come at me again."

After a moment, she nodded. I tried to let out my breath again without it being heard by the bears. Tamara asked again, "Curt told you that I said he was to take you away with him?"

"He said he'd called you on his cell phone."

Her dark anger spiked again. "I will speak to him."

I almost felt sorry for Curt.

She looked at me. "Where did this happen?"

"The golf course near the freeway. I had to walk back."

"And I told you to stay off that ankle!"

"Yes."

"I noticed you didn't join in the dancing."

"Not even a little bit."

"That was wise." Now she sounded surprised. I gave her a look, but she didn't catch it. She picked up my foot, put it on her knee, and held her hand over my aching wound. That's all she did, but I could feel the warmth of her hand even though she wasn't touching my ankle. The pain in my ankle began to fade away. I closed my eyes with relief.

"What do you think they wanted?" she asked me.

"They want my demon. They think I'm possessed. They're going to help me by getting it out of me. They think that's why I can change into a wolf."

I opened my eyes so I could see her expression. No, obviously she hadn't known that. She glanced over at the bears, who were trying to suppress expressions of amazed outrage, and outright laughter.

"Curt doesn't know…?" I nodded to the bears.

"He does not have your discernment," Tamara commented acerbically.

"You mean, my sense of smell." I smiled over at the bears. They smiled back.

Tamara was not pleased by the damage I'd done to my healing ankle. She ordered me to stay off my feet that day. I was happy to oblige her. I hung out on the patio eating leftovers, and being entertained by the bears.

Tamara offered, since she had some of the best ward masters on the planet staying with her, to ward my apartment, my town, my car and me, so that I couldn't be scryed, no matter who was looking for me. By the end of the day, the hilarity centering on the patio had ceased to amuse Tamara, especially now that I was taking up a guest room when she had friends in town. She came out in the afternoon after some particularly uproarious outbursts attracted the attention of actual paying customers and drew them away from admiring her wares, and suggested that either the bears might like to go home for awhile, or I might like to head back to her place for a nap—or something.

By the next day, even though I spent the morning helping out with the cleaning, unpacking, and stocking, Tamara decided that she had better get those wards in place and get me off her property because, she said, I was a bad influence on the bears. The bears were fairly low-key when most people around didn't know what they were (lady bears, back on the mountains, are pretty

fierce in April and May. Fierce, with claws and teeth. The four
bears had been spending spring and early summer at Tamara's for
years). But with a wolf around, they felt they had something to
prove. And this was true. Bears are strong, but they can be hard
on the furniture.

Tamara told Jason he was going to have to fix the new bench
himself. She told Aaron she expected him to find some new tiles
to match the broken ones on the patio. She told Jonathan and
Sol if they ever got on the roof again, she would personally use
a broom or a grappling hook get them the hell down, and if the
roof beam turned out to be cracked, they were in serious trouble.
And she told me it was time for me to go home.

That afternoon she called me into the back room where the
smell of burned sage hung in the air. She had cleared one end of
the long work table, and spread out two maps, a Triple-A map of
the Greater Los Angeles area, held down at the corners and side
by fat white candles, and a street map of Whittier, where I had
my apartment. Three of her friends bent over the maps in high
good humor, each working in her own way, making little figures
or decorations, adding them to one or other of the maps and
adjusting them, with a low-toned invocation.

Half a dozen candles of different sizes and colors stood on the
Whittier map, on little saucers, or scraps of paper to catch the
dripping wax, or stuck straight on the paper. A few birthday candles clustered around my neighborhood, the ends stuck through
a crust of bread that held them upright. A sprinkle of sand, and
one of cornmeal, drew the eye away from my street. Bright flowers and an aromatic spray of cedar leaves called attention to the
south city border. A little bridge of stones crossed the river into
Pico Rivera, and small dancing figures posed down and up the
605 freeway and off the map.

I moved closer, taking in all the details. A little black toy car
took up several blocks on my street. It had a tiny colorful paper

umbrella stuck to its roof. Near it was a little plastic wolf on the run, and she had a little umbrella over her as well. I reached to pick it up, but a heavy-set woman with silver hair caught my hand. Her ice-blue eyes held mine for a moment. "Don't touch." She let go of my hand before my anger rose. Her brown sweater gleamed with silver chains and bangles, and silver rings with colored stones flashed on her hands. "You don't want to add your own energy to the ward at this stage."

I nodded, and considered the maps again with my hands at my side. By concentrating, I could feel the energy of a working, but it was in motion, full of distractions. If this is what someone scrying for me was going to sense, a layer of misdirection, and a hodge-podge of diversions, then I really was going to be difficult to find. It was a truly masterful warding. If it worked. But I was too polite to ask them that.

"It will work," Tamara told me.

"Oh, this is going to work all right," the silver-haired woman said with complete assurance. She added a couple of jacks, like caltrops, in an annoyingly uneven circle around my street. She smiled at me briefly, a feral smile, and went to look over the larger-scale map of the city.

Tamara took her place over Whittier. She picked up a pinch of powdered thyme from a glass dish, and sprinkled it on the map along Philadelphia Avenue. The grains bounced away in different directions. Her voice softened. "My mother taught me this, a long time ago."

"How is she?" I asked.

"No better."

I thought about the frail old woman with the far-seeing eyes. "I'm really sorry," I said.

A tall, gangly woman in jeans, dark-skinned, her hands smelling of burnt sage, gave me a hard look. "Her absence is a great loss. We can hardly spare her now."

The fourth person, a slight Asian woman, shorter than me, with bright black eyes and a pointed chin, flitted to yet another point on the map, blowing tiny bubbles across it from a child's bubble bottle. She gave me a look too, but was too excited by what she was doing to make it stick.

Tamara shook her head. Her mother's last great working had been to create a talisman for me, that had saved my life. I'd given it back to Tamara, since after all it was made from a bit of her flesh, but I was still not forgiven.

It occurred to me that I'd been referring to the old woman as "Tamara's mother," for a long time. "What should I call her? Your mother?"

"And why should you call her at all?" She sounded tired again.

"I've been dreaming about her," I said.

That got the attention of all four of them.

"What have you dreamed?"

I told them about the glade, and about her mother, younger, happy, dancing there, turning to me as I came upon her. "She says something, but I can't understand her."

Tamara nodded. "I knew she wasn't ready to go yet. She's holding on so hard." And then she stunned me by dropping into a chair and bursting into tears. Her friends surrounded her, taking her hands, embracing her, bringing her a cool cloth, and stroking her head while she sobbed. I didn't know what to do. I stopped myself from changing because a big furry head in her lap right then was probably the last thing she wanted. I got another set of hard looks from her friends for just standing there doing nothing. Since they seemed to know what they were doing, I slipped out through the back door.

All four of the bears were standing there.

"What's going on?" Aaron asked me, his voice deep, with an edge in it.

"I didn't do anything," I told them. "Madam Tamara is upset about her mother."

"Oh." The bears looked at each other.

"Her friends are with her," I said.

"Oh. Well. She's all right then," Sol said.

Jonathan shouldered past me, up the two steps to the door to the back room. "I'll get her some coffee," he said.

When he'd gone in Sol and Aaron looked at each other. "Love!" Sol said, and strode off. Jason looked away. Aaron caught my eye and we laughed.

I went back to the house and fell asleep sitting in Tamara's chair. I started awake when Tamara put a tray on the table and sat down in her mother's chair.

"Where are your friends?"

"Gone out to dinner. Here. I brought you this." She handed me a bowl of hot lentil soup. I am not a bear. I ate with a spoon. And I did not lick the bowl afterwards, but that was only because of the thick ham sandwich from yesterday's leftovers that came with it.

"My mother's name is Imelda," Tamara said.

I nodded in thanks, still munching.

"I miss her. We… get on together." She was only toying with her soup. She gave me one of her looks over the rim of her bowl. "She liked you. I don't know why. You're a lot of trouble."

I nodded again. No question there. The ham was slathered with mustard and mayonnaise. The bread was fresh from the bakery, not from yesterday. It was still a little warm.

"We were going to have a sing for her, a healing, next week. But it seems that this is the only day that most of the same people can meet to consult with your demon."

I swallowed. "Can't they do both? The same night?"

She gave me a look that told me not to be so stupid, though I didn't understand why. "We must resolve this situation with your demon, before the community breaks apart. So that must come first. Mother… must hold on a little longer." Her eyes were suddenly bright, but her voice was steady. "I tried to call Curt. He doesn't answer."

I stifled a laugh. "His phone might have gotten wet."

"I see."

I thought I saw her crack a smile, but then it was gone.

She added, "I have sent word for him to call me. I will speak to him. I don't know why he did what he did."

"Holly asked them to," I mouthed, not waiting, bear-like, to finish chewing before I answered. "Holly and Elaine are his cousins."

"I will see that he, at least, does not bother you again."

I paused in my chewing as a frisson went up my nape. She was, after all, a woman of power. I'd last seen Curt the previous day clawing at Elaine who was bleeding on him as his car sank into the drink on the ninth hole. If my ankle wasn't still aching, I'd have had more sympathy for him. But still, at that moment, I felt sorry for the guy.

CHAPTER NINE

Tamara's friend Van followed me to Whittier the next day, as soon as we could miss the end of the morning rush-hour traffic. She was coming to finish off the wards on my apartment. I led the way on the forty-five minute trip up the 605 freeway in my Honda Civic, with Yvette sitting in the front seat, and Jason, who'd decided to come along, looming in the back. The only thing I'd taken away from Tamara's was the clothes she said I could have, my new shoes and socks, and the bandana with the leather bracelets and silver hooks, which I stowed in the glove compartment of my car. Sarah's old sweats, and Elaine's stupid shoes, I'd stuffed in the dumpster behind the shop before I left.

When we got to my street I parked a block away and gave my apartment key to Van, who was spiking with excitement over having been chosen to finish off this complicated ward. She explained that my presence during this last part of the warding was not desirable as she hauled out a bulging pair of heavy canvas bags full of supplies. She had to keep my energy out of her ward at this point or the whole purpose would be defeated. I nodded as though I understood exactly what she meant, and agreed to make myself scarce for a while.

I offered to drive Yvette to work down at Arches Auditorium, as it was still fairly early. She was part of the cleaning and renovation team, a job I used to have too until I lost it, but she told me the job was winding down and she'd worked her last day the previous week. So I got on Whittier Boulevard and drove up to Montebello to the Department of Motor Vehicles. When I pulled into the parking lot she gave me a look, then she got out and went into the building. I stayed in the car. So did the bear.

"Do you remember Richard?" I asked Jason, while we waited.

"Sure," he said.

"When's the last time you saw him?"

"Ah…" he stretched out his arms across the back seat of my car. I thought I heard the car creak. "Last week some time."

"How many times have you seen him, since I told you he was gone?"

"Two, three."

"So that's why you all think I'm a liar when I tell you I dismissed him."

"Pretty much. But then, maybe you did dismiss him. And maybe he didn't go."

"But did you see him up close, or just to look at?"

He caught my eye in the mirror. "Just to look at. He was on the sidewalk, outside the shop."

"Did you smell him?"

He was frowning. "No…"

"I saw him there too, on Friday." I rolled down the car window. It was going to be a warm day. And Jason is very big. "You know," I remarked, "the reason I went to that party last week, where I got shot and captured and all—"

"Mm hm…"

"—was because Yvette invited me."

"So you said."

I waited until I caught his eye in the mirror again. "I saw her."

"I heard you."

"Do you think I'm lying?"

He didn't react to my challenge. His eyes were as mild as though he were not one of the greatest predators on the planet, when he felt like it. The scar across one of his brows gave him a quizzical look, but his expression was serene. "Now that is the question, isn't it."

"You know anyone in this town who can take another's form?"

He did not look surprised at the question. After a moment, he nodded. "One or two."

I grinned. It was my hunting grin. "That's what I thought."

Jason has a huge smile. It came on slowly, in response to mine, and it was a sight to see. "Now what are you thinking about, wolf girl? You going hunting?"

"Me?" I said, in all innocence. "Who has to hunt when the salmon jump right into your arms?"

He broke out into laughter. "So, when do you think this fish is going to land?"

"Before next Monday," I told him, and he sobered.

"Ah," he said, "I see. That's when Madam Tamara wants you to call your demon."

"That's the schedule."

"And you think someone wants to gain control of your demon before that night."

"He's not my demon anymore," I said, but it was pointless. If Jason didn't believe me, why should anyone else?

Yvette pulled open the door and threw herself into the front seat, radiating excitement as though she was going to burst. In her fist she held a crumpled piece of paper. I got out of the car and went around to the passenger door. I opened it and stood there holding out my car keys. "You got your permit?"

"Temporary license."

"Then you drive."

"I don't know how to drive!" Yvette burst out wailing, while Jason shushed and patted her shoulder from the back seat.

I drove up the road to a big shopping center, where at this hour of the morning the most remote parking lot was almost empty. I showed her how to shift gears, and we switched places. I winced while she stripped the gears over and over, I braced myself as we jerked our way down the aisles, while Jason poured helpful advice, admonishment, praise, and swear words from the back until I threatened to bite him. Yvette shifted from first to second, to first, and to second again and again, and finally snapped at Jason so he shut up. Then she got into third, and the smoothness of the ride straightened her shoulders and relaxed her death grip on the wheel. Her turns became more assured, and when Jason ventured to make another comment, and she threw back a reply while turning, shifting, and remembering to signal, I told her to drive us on back to Whittier. And she did.

It wasn't time yet for me to go back to my apartment, so Yvette cruised down Greenleaf, negotiating the traffic with growing confidence, until Jason spotted a diner that promised meat, and asked her to find a parking place.

"I'm buying," he told me, as we walked back to the restaurant. He stared down my look of astonishment. Bears are very good at not being the ones to pay. "You made her happy," he said, looking at Yvette, leading the way. And it was true, she seemed taller. She seemed hardly to be touching the ground when she walked. And her smile must have been hurting her face by then. I let Jason buy my burgers.

As we wandered down Greenleaf after lunch, ducking into the bookstore, the antique stores, the clothing store where Jason tried on one hat after another—bears are vain—and then left without buying anything, I saw Richard across the street. That was interesting. Sooner than I expected, too. I didn't look at him directly.

I was wondering what he would do. Richard was straight and fine, with short blond hair and blue eyes. He was modeled by the magician John Dee when he captured him, and commanded him to assume the form of a beautiful young man. This version didn't quite walk like Richard. I looked away, and he was gone when I looked again. I was fairly certain he would be back. This was going to be fun.

Then Yvette spotted the music store. It hadn't been there very long. One of the windows was empty. The other held an artful display of gleaming violins hung around a large dark cello. A couple of drums lapped at the cello's foot, so of course we had to go in. The door stood wide open, but the store was just a shell, in the early stages of being stocked. Two of the walls had been primed, and waited to be painted. Newly varnished empty shelves were lined up on newspaper. Stacks of boxes stood against the far wall. The other wall was already painted and hung with brass instruments on specialized hooks against a black curtain. Several drum sets were already set up on the floor. Yvette made for the shiniest of them. She stopped when we heard the voices from the back.

"Get out of here! Get out!"

"You don't mean that." The second voice was sly, and it evoked a laugh from several others.

"Please… !"

Three men, young men, had crossed this way recently. Two nervous, one excited, and all just a bit rank. Jason started toward the back. I held out a hand and he stopped and looked at me, his brow raised.

"My town," I said. "My lead."

Jason smiled. He bowed and gestured me to the back room.

The woman's voice rose, suddenly fierce, "Don't touch that! No!"

"Nothing's going to happen to it," sly-voice said. "It's so beautiful—and expensive."

I walked through the door to the big back room—no wards had been laid, no surprise there, considering—and took in the three heavy-set youths, standing a little too close to the slight woman with the long dark braid. She wore smudged jeans and a paint-spattered work shirt. They had pinned her, by their positions, against a stack of crates and boxes, on the far side of the room from the land line that stood nearly buried under piles of papers on the desk. Her body was taut with fear and anger, her eyes were riveted on the violin in the hand of the tallest one, as though the intensity of her gaze could keep it safe. This guy spun around as I entered, holding the violin by the neck with one hand, and brandishing the bow with the other. This must be sly-guy, the excited one, and I marked him also as the danger man. His henchmen were slower to turn. One was almost as big as sly-guy, but more nervous. The other guy was heavier, and as his eyes fell on me, an unpleasant interest rose in them.

"Hi!" I said brightly, to everyone in the room. "Can I buy a drum? Are you open? Can I buy one today?"

"Get out," the big henchman said. He glanced at sly-guy for approval, and then moved to loom over me. "She's not open."

I'm five foot nothing on two feet. I look about as threatening as a glass of fruit juice. Until I smile. Then, I look disconcertingly as though I have too many teeth, and that's a little scary.

"Oh," I said, chipper and friendly, "oh, what a nice violin!" I walked up to danger-man and reached for the instrument, and as I did so I tried out Jonathan's trick. He'd been in human form, but his growl was pure bear, which meant he had to change just this much, just there—the sound vibrated deep in my throat and chest, too low for the human ear to register as sound, but I felt the reaction of the four humans in the room, and I plucked the violin and the bow from danger-man's hands before he could stop me. I stepped back a few steps, and then he reacted.

"Give that here!"

And then I smiled. Just for him. I felt my eyes turn gold. He stopped. The music lady shuffled to one side behind him, and the henchmen looked from him to me.

"But it's beautiful!" I said, to give her time, and hold their attention. "Don't you think so?"

"Girl, give that back before I—"

And that's when the unmistakable sound of a shotgun being racked came from behind the guys, and they all turned, mouths open. She held it pointed at the sly-guy's stomach. He put his hands out between the muzzle and his body, as though that would do any good. I took a long step to one side, just in case she was inspired to let loose.

"Get out of my store," she said, and her voice had a growl in it too, good for her! "Now. Or I will kill you."

Sly-guy paused just as long as he dared. He gave her a look that meant, "This isn't over," and "we'll be back," and he turned and shoved his way past his two henchmen, punching the second one hard in the shoulder just so everyone in the room knew that he was a really tough guy. The store lady's hands started shaking as soon as their backs were turned, but she clutched the gun and stalked after them to the doorway. She was stopped by shrieks and howls coming from the store. When we got through the door, the guys were gone, Jason was standing by the front door radiating innocence, and Yvette had a smirk on her face that meant she had just enjoyed a good show. There was a tiny tang of piss in the air. I gave Jason the eye.

The shop lady sat down heavily on a box by the door, cradling the shotgun.

"What did you do?" I demanded of the bear.

"Who, me? Nothing!"

"Oh, yeah? Well, you can put your head on straight now."

He looked up, guiltily. He was the one who'd taught me the trick of wearing both my aspects, one superimposed over the other. I saw again how impressive it looked. I didn't tell him, though. It had been my hunt, and I would have figured out how to finish it in another moment. Probably. And anyway, bears are vain enough.

"I'm sorry," the shop lady said, and now her voice was shaky with reaction. "Are you people all right?" She heaved herself to her feet. "I'm not quite open yet. I'm sorry you had to see that. I called the police the last time they were here, but they said they couldn't do anything. Not until something happened. But if something happened it would be too late." Her voice was rising. She was babbling to let her fear and rage run out, and that was fine.

"Don't worry," Yvette told her cheerfully. "They're not going to be back. Because—you scared them off with the shotgun, yeah. They went out of here so fast." She caught Jason's eye and they both stifled a laugh.

"I'm Ariadne Pierson. I'm just opening up this week—oh, I'm sorry." She realized she was still holding the shotgun, and went into the back room to put it away.

"Cool shop!" Yvette told her when she came back. "Are you going to have more drums? I have a drum, a djembe, it's from Ghana."

I offered Ariadne the violin. "Thank you," she said. She took it from me, and the bow, holding them delicately. "Thank you for coming in just when you did. That was lucky." She gave a laugh. "If I'd lost this…" She set the violin under her chin, and her body changed. She took on a posture that was practiced, certain, as different from her previous stance as though, like one of the wolf kind, or the bear kind, she had changed form. Then she drew the bow along the strings and the violin sang out with passion and fury, in beauty and marvelous joy. When she lifted the bow from the strings after just this brief music, each of us took a breath. We'd been holding ours.

"Oh!" said Yvette. "Do that again! Do it some more."

Ariadne broke into a smile so sweet, it was like an echo of the music that still hung in the air. She raised the violin and again she changed, again the music rang out, soaring, searing, delightful, but this time she did not stop. Yvette sat at her chosen drum set and tapped lightly on the edge of one of the drums, adding bits of percussion as she followed the music. I leaned against the wall, listening in Whittier, but seeing again, and smelling again, the forest at home, strips of foggy light among the dark trees, a long hunt with my dad, who'd been missing a long time now, and life the way it used to be, when I was younger and we were happy. Jason stared out the window, thinking in the manner of the bear kind. He came over to Yvette, laid a huge hand on her shoulder and bent and kissed her head. I missed Richard then. Richard, my dad, the life I'd expected, everything changed and difficult and uncertain... Tears welled in my eyes. I looked away. It was the music, that's all. That woman was good.

Yvette had us helping Ariadne move boxes around, the two of them talking up a storm, before we got away from the place. Not even the offer of letting her drive up to my place tempted Yvette from her enthusiasm for a ground-floor part in a local music store operation. When I offered to leave her there while I went back to my apartment, and come back for her later, she finally tore herself away, promising the music lady to come back and help another time. Yvette chattered on about the possibility of local drumming classes all the way to my place. I drove.

Van sat on the steps that led up to my apartment, her bags packed neatly at her feet, glasses perched on her nose, reading from one of those electronic books as we came around from the carport where I'd parked my car.

"Ah!" she exclaimed when she saw us. "Good timing, I just finished up. Here." She handed me my key. "You open it and walk in, and that will set the wards into play."

I could feel a strong organization of energy as I approached my door. I concentrated, and tried to track the energy to its source, but it wandered like little individual winds, leading my concentration astray. I thought this might really work. I shot her a glance, and she gave me a smug look. It was true, she was good.

"Maybe you should stay out," I said to Yvette and the bear. "You shouldn't get caught up in this working, or you might get scryed if someone was looking for me."

Jason raised one quizzical brow. "And this would be a problem, why?"

You can't tell a bear not to do something that might endanger him. They don't know the meaning of the word. I hesitated in front of my door. Bringing down trouble on your friends is a good way to lose them, and I didn't have any to spare.

"Me, too," Yvette said. "I'll go in too. 'Cause if they're scrying for you and they come up with me, they'll know they're a loser."

"We should all go through," Van agreed. "It will help to keep things confused. And if someone wants to try and scry me…" She left off there, but her smile was wicked.

So I opened the door, and we all trooped in to my little apartment where I hadn't set foot in a week. Van had lit candles in all the rooms, though they were gone now. She had sprinkled water scented with bay, and burned sage. The swirl of energy was stronger here, a little tangled, and even more distracting. We all trooped through the living area, which became the dining area because the table was there, which became the kitchen, demarked by the linoleum. We took turns going in and out of the bathroom, because we wouldn't all fit in there, and they all went into my bedroom, where there's a bed, by which time the energy Van had set loose in the place was sufficiently stirred up.

Beneath the traces of Van's presence this afternoon, Richard's scent was still everywhere. In the kitchen, where he had rearranged everything to his liking, there were traces of not only him, but of everything he'd cooked for me in the weeks we'd been together. Yvette wandered through, opening the larder door, looking out the window at the view of the building's back patio, discovering the linen cupboard, where the extra blanket lives, and going back into the bathroom and closing the door. Most of the apartments on this whole street were designed to be rented to students at Whittier College living off-campus, so they were partly furnished with battered, hardy furniture. Mine was just the same, and aside from the jumble of special kitchen equipment that Richard had insisted we acquire, there was nothing personal in the place.

Van finished her circuit and said she was off. She was going back to Costa Mesa to have dinner with Tamara and her friends, and wanted to beat the traffic. I thanked her again, but she waved it off. Her smile was still smug at the job she'd done. Jason said he would catch a ride with Van. Yvette wanted to go back to the new, local music store. She and the bear indulged in some cuddling on my front stoop while Van pointedly looked away, but then Yvette walked down to Van's car with Jason's arm draped over her shoulders, gave him another kiss, and headed back down to Greenleaf.

I was finally alone, which was good, because there was something I needed to do. I was safe from scryers seeking me, though people who already knew where I lived would probably show up. In fact, someone had hung out in front of my house for some time earlier that day. I'd caught his scent before, when I'd seen Richard at Tamara's. I was looking forward to seeing this Richard close up. And I was looking forward to dealing with the guy who was doing it. But first, I had to see someone out in Pomona.

I waited just long enough so that I would not pass by Yvette on my way out, since there was no reason for her to know any more of my business than she already did. I dog-legged onto Whittier Boulevard and caught the freeway up to the 60, and headed east, in good time to miss the rush hour traffic. The day was bright and the air was sufficiently clear I could see the mountains on my left, and the hills to the right. I took the 57 north and then exited onto the streets of Pomona.

The accepted method for contacting the Rag Man was to buy a bag of food for him from his favorite taqueria, sit in the park opposite, and wait for him to show up. I had an advantage, however. I knew where he lived.

I parked a few blocks down from the burned-out house behind the chain link fence on Garey. It was still light, so I walked on two feet along the fence line, turned down the alley and found the place where the fence was cut, leaving just enough room for someone to insinuate themself through the opening. By this time, I had sensed something wrong. If the Rag Man still lived here, I should have picked up his fresh scent already. His many comings and goings had led me to this place when I'd first found it. Now, I caught traces of him, because he'd stayed here for months, but none of the traces were recent.

I knew before I changed, slipped through the gap in the fence on four feet, and nosed into the lean-to he'd built himself under the porch of the collapsed house, that the Rag Man hadn't slept here in weeks. Dead end.

Back when Richard and I were trying to find out if his dreaded ancient enemy had come to town, Richard had introduced me to the Rag Man as the best scryer in the city. The Rag Man was cursed, but the result of it was that he could scry just about anything, a handful of stones, bits of broken glass, or even his oatmeal. Now, I needed to know if two people who had once been kind to me were all right. I'd come to ask the Rag Man if he could see what had happened to Marge and Andy, and why their cabin on Mount Baldy stood empty. But the Rag Man wasn't home.

I drove down to the taqueria. There was no fresh trace of the Rag Man there either. I went in and bought myself one of their pretty good burritos, and a burrito and some tacos for the Rag Man when I found him. I asked the woman at the counter if she'd seen the narrow guy with the unkempt straight hair, the knit cap, the layers of clothes, whose hands were tied up in rags, but she didn't seem to understand me. I walked across the street to the picnic table that was his usual rendezvous, but the Rag Man hadn't been there in weeks either. I sat down and ate my food. I wasn't expecting him to show by then, and he didn't.

I drove up to the reservoir, to see if the Holy Workers were still camped up on the hill over the city. The Rag Man was friendly with them, and they might know where he was. I was stopped at the electric gate by a big guy in dark glasses, who leaned down and asked what I was doing up there. His mouth was smiling, but his body was pretty clearly suggesting that I should turn back right now. He wasn't actually offensive, but part of me couldn't help working out the logistics of, say, biting off one ear without actually getting out of the car. And another part of me realized I just might have to do that to get by this guy, because I didn't know the Rag Man's real name. But I made an attempt to be civilized.

"I was here about a month ago," I explained. "We brought a friend, who's called the Rag Man—"

But it turned out, that's all I had to say. He straightened up, and his smile became real, and he pointed me down one of the new black roads between the meticulously marked out RV camping spaces, and the green lawns, and gave me a slot number to look for. There seemed to be more open spaces than there were a month ago, but groups of the Heiligen Arbeiters still gathered under each others' canopies, or by each others' barbecue set-ups, and watched my car as I passed by. Fires were burning. Meat hadn't been set to roasting yet, but barbecues were definitely in the offing. The stretches of grass between the precisely measured spaces were pristine, recently mowed, and all the painted white lines recently touched up.

The slot I'd been directed to was occupied by a little round steel trailer with no car to pull it, standing in a space meant for a mega-camper. I parked in the adjoining space, but even before I'd gotten out of my car I smelled him, though with some differences. He'd been around here quite a bit, his tracks traced and retraced routes in different directions. He smelled clean. He smelled of shampoo. And what was manifestly missing was the smell of sickness, charred flesh, blood, and pus. Still, knowing all that, when he stepped out of the trailer I didn't recognize him.

He walked up to me with a smile, holding out his hands, and I nearly snarled at him, because I don't care for familiarities like that. Then I caught his scent, and it was him, the Rag Man, but he was clean and neat, he wore new clothes and shoes, and his hands were not bandaged.

"Hey!" he said. "I know you!" He opened his arms, and hugged me. And I let him.

"Hey," I said. "You look great."

"Yeah," he said. "Check this out." He held out his hands to me. The flesh was pink and new, but there were no burns anywhere.

I was happy for him, but also disappointed. It was through his curse that he was the best scryer in all the land, and here he seemed to be over it.

"You don't scry anymore?"

"Oh, sure, I do that. Here. Come and sit. Want a beer? I got a beer."

I turned down the beer. I don't drink things that spit at me. I offered him the bag of cold greasy food, and he took it out of politeness. Before he would have scarfed it down, but now, he set it on a little camp table, and offered me the second handsome wooden camp chair. With a plump green cushion. His view looked out over the greater Los Angeles valley. The sun was beginning to drop into the haze in the west.

From this view the Rag Man had at one time pointed out the bite mark that the World Snake was going to make. Now he said, "She's gone, you know. The World Snake isn't coming."

"I know. Richard and me, we did it."

"That's what he said."

That got my attention. "He told you? When did he tell you?"

"Day after the earthquake. He came to my digs. You know the place. Down there."

I nodded because I did know the place, I'd just been there, but I was trying to figure out how he'd seen Richard after the last earthquake. Richard had been with me. Every minute. Right up until the new moon set him free. "The last earthquake? A month ago?" Richard couldn't have visited him.

"The one she did when she turned away, that's right. Richard showed up." His eyes met mine briefly. "I was in a bad way. Got sick." He cupped his hands in front of him. I still remembered the smell of the infection on his palms. He shot me another look. "I dreamed that someone came." He tried again. "A wolf. A woman in the form of a wolf. And she…" His voice lost some of its assurance. "Was that you? I thought that was you. But sometimes I can't tell…"

"You said that Richard came." That was what I wanted to hear about.

"Yeah." He shot me another look, still not sure about me. "But that was later. He… did something. In the back of my head. Inside my brain. You know he's a demon, right? Right. Right!" His voice rose as memory returned. "You told me that. That's why I couldn't scry him directly. Yeah. It was you. Hey, thanks." He reached out and touched my hand, briefly, so I did not bite him.

I'd cleaned his wounds, in the way of the wolf kind. But that was nothing, since he'd done his best to find Richard for me, when I couldn't.

"So, can you scry anymore?" I asked. "Now that you're better?"

He grinned. Now that was a new look for the Rag Man. "Oh, man, wait till I show you." He kept talking, while he reached down and gathered up a leaf that had managed to stray onto the lawn, a pebble from the asphalt, a few short blades of grass, a rubber band and a bit of string from the pocket of his new jeans, and a receipt that he tore into little bits. "Richard showed me. He didn't like me to call him Stan anymore, he told me why, no, I knew why when he told me. But watch this!" He dropped the tell-tales into the palm of his hand. "What did you come here to ask me?" I took a breath to answer, but he said, "No, wait. Don't tell me. Wait."

He held the miscellaneous bits together in both hands and shook them up. Then he bent and stared down into his hands. His energy changed as his focus strengthened. His eyes went blank and his body tensed, and then there was a soft explosion, a burst of orange light between his fingers. He opened his hands, releasing a puff of black smoke and a few traces of ash. With a wide smile he held out his open hands to me.

"And it doesn't even hurt!" he exclaimed.

"That's—just—"

"Yeah," he said happily. "Richard did it. So I'm not cursed anymore." He rubbed his hands and smelled them. "I still can't believe it. Man! I've had that all my life. All my life!" He looked away, out across the valley he wasn't seeing. After a moment he turned back. "So, I told these guys the Snake's not coming. Some of them believe me." He shrugged.

The Holy Workers had been up on this hill chanting protection and deflection from the World Snake for months, in concert with other groups of power raisers all over the greater Los Angeles area, all dealing with the World Snake in their own way, some of which worked contrary to one another. Power raisers working together is pretty much a contradiction in terms.

After Richard cured him, the next time one of the Workers came by asking for help, they'd succeeded in keeping the Rag Man with them.

"This is Fendor's place," he nodded at the trailer. "He had to go back to Wisconsin. That's where most of these guys are from, up around there. He gave me these," he wiped his hands on his jeans. "And the shirt. Said he'd gained weight, couldn't wear them anymore."

Fendor was a liar. The clothes still held the scent of a couple of young, tense women sweating over them as they worked their sewing machines. But that was all. The Holy Workers were treating the Rag Man all right.

"But, did you see anything?" I asked. "About my question?"

"Oh! Oh, yeah, sure. Two women."

"Andy and Marge?"

"I don't get names, mostly. Two women, right? Uh. One older, gray curly hair. One younger, fat, uh, happy. House, small house, stones everywhere, and trees. Uh, it's a cabin, up in the mountains, and it's empty, and there's—" his eyes shot to me. "Someone there. Dangerous. Waiting for you."

"Yeah," I said. "I met him."

"Not a man," he was frowning. "No, he is a man. But... Oh." He looked at me again. "Okay. It wasn't a dream."

"No."

"You can turn into a wolf."

"That's right."

He smiled again. "Good! See? I'm not crazy! Ha! So there."

"Me neither. But about the women. I just need to know, are they all right?"

He frowned, thought a moment, then shook his head. He reached down again and gathered up some more grass and rolled it in his hands. "Remember when this used to hurt? Oh, man, it is so much easier now that it doesn't hurt." He rolled the grass in his palms and a moment later it burst into flame. "Ha!"

"Andy and Marge?"

"Oh. Right." This time he walked to the end of the lawn where the sculptured landscaping ended and the hillside fell away to the natural California brown grass, low bushes, and aromatic herbs.

He picked some mustard flowers, a few dead grass heads and a pinch of dirt, sat down on the edge of the lawn. He shook the stuff in his cupped hands, and then opened them. He studied the mix for a while, and then looked up at me. "They're all right. They're happy. Excited. They've taken the moon road. You won't see them for awhile."

"They're alive?"

"They're on a kind of journey."

"What's the moon road?"

His eyes changed as he looked into the distance, but after a moment he shook his head. "I'm not sure. But they're going to tell you all about it. Soon, that will be your road."

He offered to take me along to the barbecue where he was going to dinner, but I was ready to head home. He squatted down at my car door to say, "Hey. You tell Richard hi for me when you see him. And tell him thanks." He stood up, so I didn't get to ask him any more about how I was going to see Richard.

If I did see Richard, I sure wanted to know when he'd managed to cure the Rag Man.

CHAPTER TEN

I drove home right into the rush hour, but after I finished creeping down the 57 and got on the 60, traffic was against me and
I sped along nicely, while across the median the endless lines
of people alone in their cars rolled slowly along. I wondered if the
Rag Man was right, and if I could believe that Gray Fox hadn't
harmed Marge and Andy. I hadn't smelled blood up at the cabin.
I hadn't smelled death. Neither of the women had been there
recently. Maybe they had gone on some kind of long hike.

I stopped at the grocery store before heading for my apartment.
I was thinking about the Rag Man, and the change in him, about
the moon road, and what that might be, as I carried the groceries
around the building to my stairs. And then I stopped, because
there he was. Richard.

He stood on the steps, waiting for me. It wasn't Richard, of
course, but it was a damn good imitation. The face was right,
the bright fair hair, the jeans and boots, even the leather jacket
was almost perfect. The stance was not quite right. Richard stood
straight as an arrow, and any deviation was a message. This one

said, "I'm not actually Richard," and I was trying not to read it. I stood there, taking him in. I couldn't help smiling. I couldn't even help the tears in my eyes, because I loved Richard, and he was gone. I tried hard not to look too closely at the details. I knew he was a fake. And I knew as soon as I came closer, his scent would be wrong, and that would ruin it for me.

There are a number of different ways you can react if someone impersonates your lover and friend, tries to step into the place that belonged to someone so dear to you. I'd thought of several of them, from the first time I'd scented the place where I'd seen Richard standing, and it had not been him. In the first one, of course, the imposter ends up running screaming down the avenue, back arched against the blow he can feel coming his way. I was going to personally guarantee that there would be screaming. And of course there could be other scenarios first, and the screaming and the running might come later.

I decided on the second course, because Richard looked so good to me, so fine, almost exact. And I missed him, and for all intents and purposes, there he was. No reason to chase him away just yet.

"Richard!" I said, and my voice resonated with love, and surprise, and happiness, all on its own. And my eyes widening, and almost starting to tear up, that wasn't exactly voluntary either. "You came back!" I exclaimed, and I almost made myself believe, just for a moment, that it was true. I took a step toward him. "You said you never would, but oh, you came back!" I wouldn't actually say something like that, but I thought I'd give the guy some encouragement. This might be fun.

Fake Richard smiled, and it was almost his smile. "I couldn't help it," he told me. "I had to see you again. I missed you."

He'd said that to me a dozen times in the last few weeks, in my dreams. Of course Richard would not miss me. He was free. He was gone, he dwelt in other worlds now, as a different being. But I was still enchanted to hear what almost sounded like his voice say those words.

"I thought I'd never see you again," my voice said, of its own accord.

"Darling," he said, "I couldn't stay away."

Okay, that wasn't Richard. The imposter recognized the false note at once, probably in my reaction, and tried again.

"I missed you so much!"

"I missed you too!" I indicated the door to my apartment. "Don't you have your key?" I was playing with him; Richard had never had a key, but this guy wasn't going to know that.

"I—lost it, I'm afraid. And I wasn't sure if you would want me…" He nodded toward the apartment.

"Oh," I said. I was trying to put off the moment when I would have to move closer to him, and the fantasy that this was really Richard would vanish. Ah, well. "Do you want to come upstairs?" I asked, and I canted my hips just a little, and I tilted my head and added just a hint of a pout. Because if you are going to play a role like this, you might as well play it to the max.

"Of course!" he said, dropping his voice. "Why else would I have come?"

I walked up to him, and he held out his arms for an embrace. I handed him the grocery bags and hurried past him up the steps. At my door I turned and looked down, giving him another one of those "come and get me" looks. He was disconcerted, shifting the grocery bags to get a good hold on them, but he smiled up at me gamely.

His scent told me he was almost twice as old as he looked in Richard's form. Richard's hair was smooth and soft, with only the aid of shampoo. This guy, this imposter, whoever he was, had some kind of hair goop on, as well as conditioner, and a strong deodorant. He'd had a fast food burger for lunch, and French fries; Richard ate that stuff, but only when he was starving. I beckoned, smiling, and the imposter hurried up the steps.

Inside, I took the bags from him. "Look what I got!" I told him, as I unpacked them on the table. "See how much I was thinking of you? Here's some of that pasta that you like, and basil and mushrooms. I was going to try and make that thing you make, but now that you're here, I can watch you do it one more time. Oh, I'm so glad you're here!"

This time I grabbed him and hugged him, hard. Richard was not a big guy, when he was in human form. The magician who raised him made him look as unassuming as possible, so his frame was slight, though his musculature was, well, terrific. When I grabbed and held the imposter, I squeezed hard. I could almost feel his heavy flesh, his girth, under the illusion that played on my senses. Unfortunately for him, he was only managing to blind the senses of mine that were the same as his.

"Now!" I said, letting him go, "let's see you cook!"

His uncertainty, his blush, his stammer, added to the comedy as I waited for him to figure his way out of this one. He made Richard's eyes go dark and bedroomy. "Haven't we got better things to do, after so long?"

I remembered that look on Richard. I caught my breath. It had been a prelude to so many delightful hours. I shook my head. "The moon hasn't set yet," I reminded him, my eyes wide.

I watched him do a double-take on that. "Of course," he said. "I'm forgetting. It has been too, too long." He moved to take me in his arms. Again I hugged him hard, avoiding his move to kiss me. Let him think the moon got in the way of that, too. For now, at least.

"So, are you going to cook my favorite dinner?" I asked teasingly.

"I will cook," he said playfully, "a whole new dinner, that will become your favorite henceforth, I promise you."

"Oh, terrific!" I said. I wondered how far over the top I could take the acting before he figured it out and gave up. But he smelled confident, not fearful. He was excited, not nervous. I figured I could play him a long, long way.

He made pasta, but he didn't use both butter and olive oil, the way Richard did, only olive oil. He cut up green onions and mushrooms, and grated a lot of cheese. He covered his not knowing where anything was by giving me the role of assistant, and calling for each implement like a doctor in an operating room. "Garlic press! Cheese grater! Colander!" It was a good guess that I even had a garlic press. Richard had bought all the gadgets in the kitchen. I let him get away with it all.

He put the yummy dinner on the table in front of me, and I grinned up at him like he'd done something amazing and clever. "Mac and cheese! I love mac and cheese!" I smiled to myself as he almost broke character.

My Richard's response to a crack like that had been a lecture on food that went on all through dinner. Fake Richard put his smile back on and said, "I'm so glad."

It was pretty good, with all the trimmings he'd added. I ate with enthusiasm. "Umph! Oh, you are so right, this is just delicious, Richard!"

"I'm so glad you like it," he said, his hand creeping across the table to stroke mine. "And now," he glanced toward the bedroom—not an inspired guess, since there was only the door to the bathroom to confuse it with. "Shall we?" he asked.

Again, I made my eyes wide. "Aren't you going to clean up?"

"Sweetheart—"

"'Sweetheart?'" I winced. "You never called me that."

Now his voice went all bedroomy again. "There are so many things I never got a chance to call you. Sweetheart, darling, precious girl…" He came around the table toward me. "But now at last we will have time."

"Oh, Richard!" I gasped. "Oh, Richard!" I grasped his hands, effectively keeping him from taking me in his arms again. I pushed him toward the kitchen. "You get cleaned up in there, and I'll…" I practically waggled my eyebrows at him. "… get cleaned up in there." I headed for the bathroom. I looked back to blow him a kiss. He was smiling. That wasn't Richard's smile. That was the smile of the guy who thought he was winning. I blew him another kiss. I knew just what that felt like. I almost smirked.

I detoured to my bedroom to kick off the clothes Tamara had given me. I pulled on a t-shirt and a pair of sweats of my own, and that was satisfying, to be wearing clothes that smelled like me, and had my shape built into them by use.

The imposter was making a racket as he did the dishes, whistling a show tune while he worked. I went into the bathroom and ran a well-deserved hot shower, and stood under it for a long time, laughing to myself about the guy who'd made me dinner, and was now cleaning my kitchen. I emerged from the bathroom in a cloud of steam, dressed in my own clean sweats, armed with clean teeth and clean hair for the fight to come. You choose your weapons and your tactics according to the field of battle. That's what my dad taught me.

I didn't give him a chance to think or react. I walked right up to him and started unbuttoning his shirt. That brought on a big smile, and that wasn't Richard's smile either. He reached for me, but I batted his hands away with a surprised look. "Richard!"

He stopped and looked down, and that gave me pause for a moment, because that was something I'd seen Richard do a hundred times. Close up I could see that the bone structure was right, but the little scar under his eye was missing, and his lips were odd. Close up, of course, I could smell the wax in the guy's ears, and the trace of athlete's foot in his shoes. Richard looked up again, and now the scar was there, and his lips were just as I remembered them. Huh. He couldn't be reading my mind, exactly, or he wouldn't think he was fooling me. But he had figured out about the scar.

I finished undoing his shirt and slipped it off his shoulders. I undid his belt, and slipped it off slowly. I doubled it up in my hand and saw his eyes widen involuntarily as he wondered, just for a second, what the fuck he was in for, before I threw it behind me and reached for the button on his jeans. I could smell his growing excitement, which fed my excitement. And it was lust, in a way, brought on by his nearness, by his close resemblance to my sweet lover, and by the thrill of the game I was playing. I manipulated the button open, paused a moment, and then pulled down his zipper, my hand feeling the warmth of his arousal under his briefs. I bent and quickly tugged his pants down to his ankles, and then, while I was there, I tugged his briefs off too.

Okay, that wasn't Richard either. Richard hadn't been anywhere near that—showy. And it wasn't a big reach to guess that Mr. Imposter wasn't nearly that well-endowed either. I wondered briefly whether, if I grabbed it, I would know its true size and shape. And I realized in the same moment that I really didn't care.

His pants and briefs down at his ankles, I looked deeply into his eyes, doing the bedroomy thing myself, and I took his hand. "Come," I said, making my voice husky. "Come, Richard. It's time."

I turned away and led him firmly to the bedroom, and was satisfied first to hear the startled exclamation, and then the hard tug on my arm as he stumbled and went down heavily with a thump and a cry. "Oh, Richard!" I cried, turning back to him. He was on his hands and knees, scraping at his pants with his shod feet. "Oh, no! I'm so sorry! Here, let me help you, please!"

"No, no, I'm all right, really."

I got down on the floor with him, and went to his feet and grabbed them, lifting them high. I smiled to myself when he registered how unexpectedly strong I was, how he couldn't shake my grip on his ankles as I pulled off each of his shoes and then his socks. I stood up, holding on to his pant legs, and pulled off his pants and his briefs while he still lay on the floor. I tossed them behind me and walked into the bedroom, leaving him to follow or not, just as he pleased. I was still smiling.

I pulled off my sweatpants, my sweatshirt, my t-shirt, and lay down on the bed as I heard him come in. I pointed. "Over there."

"Oh my god!"

I looked up. That hadn't been Richard's voice.

"What happened to you?" He was staring at my really impressive bruise, only just starting to fade on my hip.

"Oh," I said. "I got shot."

"My god!" Then he remembered, and the voice was like Richard's again. "My darling, are you all right?" He came toward me, but hesitated to touch me.

"I'm fine. Richard, over there."

"What?"

"The oil. In the dresser. You know."

And the fact was, Richard had bought the massage oil. He'd bought four kinds. He liked the strawberry, as he said there were some things in England he liked to remember. I liked the sandalwood. But that was a memory that belonged to the real Richard, and me. "The almond oil." After all, if I was going to play this scene to the end, I might as well get some good out of it.

Fake Richard sat down on the bed and opened the bottle. Again I turned to him in surprise. "Feet first, right? Watch out for my ankle. It still hurts."

Obediently, fake Richard moved down to my feet. "Ow," he said in sympathy. "What happened here?"

"I got in a fight," I said. There were constructs by which this statement was true. Besides. There's no point in telling the truth to a liar. He probably wouldn't even hear it.

"Oh, poor baby!" Richard's voice had never sounded so sappy.

"I'm all right," I said. "Especially now that you're back. It doesn't hurt at all." I'd never played sappy before, but it sure wasn't hard.

He began at my feet, and over the next half hour worked all the way up my body, had me turn over, and worked all the way down again, going very gently on my bruises. It was pleasant. It wasn't Richard, but it wasn't bad. I have had experiences, before the experience of Richard put them all behind me. Richard had made an art of love hundreds of years before I was born. He brought all that skill and understanding to my bed, in his efforts to bind me to him, to keep himself in my service while he needed my protection. So I'd learned from him that it could be fun. It could be a joy. And now that Richard was gone, I was wondering, will it be anywhere as good with anyone else? So, I thought, why not? By the time he had massaged me up one side and down the other, by the time I was slathered in almond oil, relaxed and at peace, that and his borrowed form might earn him my willing cooperation in what he seemed to have come here to do. So, when he got on the bed, I turned to him, and opened my arms.

He began to kiss me, lightly, following in the path his hands had already gentled and smoothed. I took the oil from him, dripped some on my hands, and worked his shoulders while he continued his way down my body. "Ah!" he said, and "Oh!"

His muscles were not Richard's muscles. I knew Richard's body very well. With my hands on the imposter's, I could feel his larger mass. His scent was not unpleasant. But then, not many smells are.

He pressed me to him, and kissed my ear. I squirmed and moaned a little, to give him encouragement. "Say it," he breathed. "Say my name! My true name! I want to hear you say it!"

Oh. And "Ah hah." So that was the idea.

"Mm," I murmured, "not yet, not ready yet."

That sent him back to the kissing. He worked his way down again. And it was pleasant. It just wasn't pleasant enough to make me forget there was a lying bastard in my bed under false pretenses. "Ooh," I moaned, and likewise, "Ohhh!"

He made encouraging noises. His hands began to roam. I sat up, "Now, darling, now." He moved up the bed toward me. I frowned and looked surprised. "Aren't you going to change?"

He was wearing Richard's face, but that discombobulated look was completely original. "Ah—" I looked sad. At least, I tried for sad. "My curse is still upon me. I cannot make love in any other form. You change first. Become my demon wolf!"

"Your... demon wolf?"

"Yes. Now, please, my own, my darling, I can't wait any longer..." I thought I might be laying it on a bit thick, but he didn't seem to notice. I added "Rrraaaarr!" like a human imitating the growl of a wolf. Badly.

He tried. And there was a wolf standing on my bed. He looked hesitant and confused. He looked at me as though asking what should happen next. And he didn't look anything like Richard did, in wolf form. I'd seen him first as a gray streak, leaping into the fray at my side. We'd run up mountains together in the snow. We'd roamed the hills beyond my house night after night. We'd slept curled up together on this bed.

The wolf image was drawn from my mind, somehow, for it was familiar. It had the shoulders and ruff of my brother Carl, but the lop-sided head of Tillman, my oldest stepbrother. In that proximity, with the smell of sweat and arousal in the air—his, and not mine—it's a good thing he didn't have my stepbrother's eyes, or I would have killed him on the spot.

The wolf form on my bed stepped forward. He nosed me in confusion. I drew in my breath. It had been Richard's wolf form that had seduced me into loving him. I am one of the two-natured kind, so when he followed me into wolf form, it was as though I had met part of myself. But this creature, who didn't know where the end of his feet were, or which way his legs folded, who wasn't seeing with different eyes, or taking in the room, or me, with new-lit senses, smelled exactly the same as a wolf as he did as a man. This was not going to work. It was time to put an end to this farce.

I changed, and as I changed I unleashed my passion, my cold fury at what he had attempted, in stepping into the place of one I loved, and pretending to be him, in order to fool me, in order to steal my demon from me. So as I changed, I grew.

The imposter suddenly found himself looking up at a very large wolf indeed, who smelled like a wolf, whose mouth opened in a snarl showing many huge, wet and pointy teeth, and whose eyes were lit with savage golden light. Curiously, he reacted like a wolf. His ears flattened, his eyes rolled back, and he crouched down on the bed, as though I were going to take him by the back of the neck like a puppy. Then his hold on his new form exploded and he lost his grasp on it, and he was a man again, and just himself, naked, sweaty, heavy, dripping with almond oil, and suddenly very much afraid. He yelled, and dove for the floor. I jumped on him and flattened him to the ground.

He tried to throw me off, he tried to reach back and grab some part of me with his hands to twist or rend or otherwise hurt, but I grasped his hand in my teeth and pressed down until he yelled. That panicked him and he twisted under me, and turned on his back to hold me off, and I stared down at him and snarled. Eyes wide, he held mine, and became very still, a stupid grin growing on his meaty face.

Good thing I was already full of yummy pasta. I changed, and sat down on his chest. He tensed to throw me off, and I just sat there, waiting to see if he'd try. After all, I can change as fast as I can blink. Sometimes even faster. He thought the better of it, and lay still. His excitement was high, but his fear had dropped. That's the trouble with being fairly small, and young.

"You're a shape shifter! A real one!"

"Yes." I reached over and grabbed my t-shirt and pulled it on.

"I've heard about it. I just never saw—" That's when he tried to buck me off. I changed and grew as he moved, planting a forepaw on his chest and bringing my head close to his. His fear spiked again and he subsided, letting his breath out.

I changed back.

"That's just amazing!" he gasped.

I brought my head close to his. "Want me to do it again?" He shook his head.

I smiled. That was better. I looked him over. "You're not a shape shifter. What are you?"

"You don't know? Can't you tell? I'm an illusionist."

"What the hell is that?"

He'd certainly put on quite an illusion. He was taller than Richard by nearly a foot, with big round shoulders and a torso running to fat, matted with gray-blond hair. He looked like a young guy in an older guy's body, with a round face, snub nose, vivid blue eyes, and pale blotchy skin. His mouth fixed in a smirk, watching me, watching his effect on me.

His voice shifted tone. "Try me and see." I almost bit him.

"Why don't you tell me, instead?"

"Let me up."

"I don't feel like it. I want to know how you did it. I want to know why. And I want to know now." I could feel my anger rising. His fear spiked when my eyes changed. I reached for my sweat pants and got off him to put them on. When he started to sit up, I raised my lip at him, and he subsided most of the way. I sat down in the doorway. "Now," I suggested.

"I just—I've always been able to do it. When I look at people— some people can see auras. I see patterns, colors, reflecting from inside their minds." He lay there more relaxed now, looking a little past me. He almost seemed to be enjoying himself. "The darker they are, the more tangled, those are the ones that are the most important. And I, well, I become the mirror." He looked at me then, and my mother looked up at me, with her little sideways smile.

I roared. "Don't do that!"

The illusion vanished, and the guy tried to lift his hands as he grinned up at me. "Okay, okay, you said explain. It's much easier just to show you. I look for the tangled dark spots in your mind, and I just—"

"Don't—"

"Some people like it."

"Then you've done this before."

"It's my power," he said modestly. "I can do other people too, once I've seen them. Check it out…" His form shifted under me, seeming to become a little smaller, his face smooth, hair light brown and slightly curled. His new form produced a winning smile and bright eyes. It was a movie star. I'd seen the face before, but couldn't think of the name. To go with the new look, a tang of sexual arousal rose. I wrinkled my nose. The movie star sighed, the illusion dissipated, the scent faded and the big guy was revealed again. He didn't really change. He coalesced into another form, which broke up like smoke when the illusion passed.

"How many times have you done this?" I wondered.

He shrugged, smirked again.

"And what usually happens when you're caught?"

"I don't usually get caught," he told me. "This is actually a first."

"So, I'll set the precedent."

He said nothing to that, not wanting to tempt his fate, I suppose.

"Did you pull Richard right out of my head?"

He shrugged. "I'd seen him, which helps. And love, longing, missing someone, creates certain shades of color. They're easy to spot."

"Where did you see Richard?"

"Can I get up?"

"No."

He sighed. "I saw him at Madam Tamara's store, after the bears defeated the Eater of Souls."

"The bears… ?" Well, if you'd heard the bears tell the story, that was the way it had happened. I curled my lip. "It is true, the bears were of some help in that action."

"Oh? Were you there?"

I thought of thirty different answers. I was the one who'd gone in, all on my own. I was the one who had found Richard, and obtained his release. I was the one Yvette had come to help. Yvette had brought the bears. There had been a fair amount of blood on the floor before the bears came in. "Yes," I said. "I was there."

He started to get up. I raised up my wolf head above my human head, and we both looked down on him, both aspects at once. "Stay where you are," I said, low in my throat.

His cheeks sagged, and his eyes opened wide. He lay still.

"Why do you want my demon's name?"

"Are you kidding me? Don't you know the World Snake is coming? We have to save this town! You may not care, but some of us live here. If you're not going to do it, somebody has to. A demon can do it, if it's treated right, if it's ordered correctly. There are thousands of things a demon can do, in the right hands…" His face grew cunning, as he imagined all those things a demon could do. I could see he'd thought about it. A lot.

"And yours are the right hands."

"Well, you're not doing anything with it!"

"With him." I stood up. It wasn't fun anymore. "Don't get up," I told him, as he sat up, so he stayed there, leaning on his hands. "We have one more thing to talk about."

"Oh, yeah?" His attempt at defiance was undermined by his winning smile, so I let it pass, offering my best attempt at a winning smile myself. It was probably just as fake, because he winced.

"You invited me to a party," I reminded him.

"Oh?"

"Yes. And I went to the party, and you weren't there."

"Oh."

I leaned over him. "And that's where they shot me."

"Uh. Look, I don't know anything about that."

"But you did ask me to the party."

"So? What's the harm in that?"

"You pretended to be my friend. You baited the trap. Who told you to do that?"

He looked confused all at once. He even blushed a little. I thought he didn't know how. "That was just a favor...for a friend."

"Who?"

I was betting on the evil vet again, but he named Elaine's sister.

"Holly. Look, if you've ever met Holly—"

"Not that I know of."

"—then you'd know. She's hard to say no to."

"You've seen Yvette, then."

He shrugged. "Everyone knows Yvette."

"Have you ever tried to pull something like this on her?"

"What? And piss off the bears? No way."

I kicked his clothes over to him, and walked away while he put them on. Not that I hadn't already seen everything he had, but I wasn't interested. I picked up my sweatshirt and pulled it on, and came back to find him doing himself up in my living room.

He smelled of sweat, saliva, tension, hair gel, and almond oil, and still his unlikely form exuded sensuality. "What's your name?" I asked him. "Your real name."

His fear had faded. His confidence and excitement were rearing back up. He smiled, broader than his smirk, but just as ucky. "Jack Collier. Call me Jack. I do insurance claims, up in Van Nuys." He got out his wallet and handed me a card. I didn't take it. After a second, he put it away, saying heartily, "So tell me, when did you figure it out?"

I shook my head. "You don't smell anything like Richard."

"Oh." His smiled wavered, and then returned at full wattage. "Well, we did have a good time, didn't we?"

I changed and launched myself completely without thought, my switch thrown and ready to kill just on that last smirk. I hit his body with my forepaws and bore him back, my jaws reaching for his throat. He choked a scream, and in that final second I turned my head, took his shoulder in my teeth and bit down. Hard. He shrieked again, and the blood streamed out everywhere.

I stood up on two feet and backed up as he fell. I stood looking down at him, gasping, bleeding, clutching his shoulder, staring at me in disbelief, horror and fear, trying to hold in the blood with his opposite hand, gulping in shock and sudden nausea, and all the time crawling backwards, backwards toward my door, all his illusions gone.

I threw him a dish towel to staunch his wound. It was stained, and had come with the place, so it was no loss. "Get out," I said. "Don't let me see you, in any form, ever again."

I wiped up the blood after he had gone. I had known it wasn't Richard. What had happened here had been with my full knowledge and understanding. But he had come to steal from me, under false pretenses. And in his past, I knew, there were others who had surrendered to him because with his form he had lied to them. For myself, I may have been a bit harsh. But all in all, I figured I'd gotten someone's own back again.

CHAPTER ELEVEN

I showered and soaped off the almond oil, but that wasn't enough. I opened all my windows, knowing I would be smelling traces of the illusionist, his blood and his sweat, for a long time. I needed to get out of there for awhile. Tamara had given me firm commands about staying off my ankle for a week, but I really was better now. I thought I would walk up to the hills. The sun was just setting, it would be light for another hour. If I took it slowly, by the time I got there the park would have emptied out, and I could change and go for a run. A short run, just see how my foreleg was doing. As I grabbed up my keys to go, there was a knock on my door.

Imposter guy was back for more? He'd forgotten something important he'd left here? Not likely. More probably my landlady was here for the rent, which I hadn't paid on the first of the month, for the first time since I moved in. When I got closer to the door, I could tell who it was. Yvette was on my doorstep.

"You know your phone number isn't listed? You have to let me have it." Yvette wore her happiness with the same force with which she expressed her displeasure. "Come down to the music store and help us," she said. "Ariadne wants to open this coming weekend, and she's got too much to do. I told her I'd get some help."

Well, I did have days of training now, in working in a music shop, so I pocketed my keys and went with her back down toward Greenleaf. Yvette explained about Ariadne being more into classical, Western-traditional music than Madam Tamara—as if I hadn't gathered that already—but that she was open to holding drum classes together with her current plans to teach violin, cello, viola, piano, and other music classes out of her store. Yvette talked so ardently and threw off such excitement I was certain she hadn't noticed the two guys who fell in behind us as we came down the hill, but when we reached the alley next to the Chinese place, she turned on them.

"Well," she said in greeting to the two big thugs we'd met before. "Got yourself cleaned up already?" And with no further hesitation she threw herself at the smaller of the two, the sly-guy, one fist launched at his face, the other hand held low. He raised his hands to protect his face, at the last second she dropped her fist and reached for his throat and bore him back into the wall of the restaurant, holding him there with the weight of her body, while her right hand went to his belly. When she touched him there he flinched back, pressing himself into the wall. Yvette, the graduate of nearly four years in juvenile hall, for a crime she did not commit, was doing fine, so all I did was prevent big henchman guy from butting in.

Yvette spoke in a voice I'd never heard, laced with fury and power. "You feel that?" She jerked her fist in his belly and he cried out, biting it off as she leaned into his throat. "That's my knife. You got a knife? What, no knife at all? Then what do you think you're doing, attacking two ladies in the street?"

Big henchman jerked in my grip. I bit down just enough for my teeth to puncture his skin, and he became very still.

Yvette continued, "Now, here are my choices. I can cut your belly open and leave you here to bleed out. I can cut a little lower—no, I see, you don't like that at all. Well then I can point it higher, here, and aim up, where the blade is just long enough to maybe reach your heart." She brought her face close to his and snarled, her eyes huge. "Or I could just cut your throat. Now, I never want to see you again. Which do you think is my best choice?"

Mr. Sly Guy Jerk did not express an opinion. It is possible that he couldn't actually speak, because her left hand still held his throat. She waited a moment, and then, lightning-fast, she cut her right hand across his belly and let him go. He shrieked and collapsed, clutching himself as though to hold together his innards and staunch his blood. In fact there was no blood, but Yvette was already walking away.

I released the henchman's head from my jaws and leaped after her, and changed, stepping back onto two feet just as we reached Philadelphia and turned the corner. Yvette was wearing a rather pleased smile.

'What was that? Did you have a knife?'

"Yeah, it doesn't do more than scratch if you use the back," she said with a smirk. "But it takes them a while to figure it out."

I lengthened my stride to keep up with her, and started to favor my bad ankle. "You could have let me handle it."

She looked at me, eyes wide. "It's my town too!"

So we spent the next couple hours taking it in turn to paint the two primed walls, and helping Ariadne move shelves, unpack boxes, and set up displays. Before we left, we both had job offers to help her get everything set up, at least until the store opened officially on Saturday.

Yvette chattered away as we worked, asking question after question until Ariadne finally suggested that more work would get done if she held all her questions until our breaks. But she was

BINDING   ⍥   157

smiling, and Yvette took no offence. By the end of the next day, Yvette had parlayed part of her pay into violin lessons.

It was a great pleasure to have somewhere I had to be every day, and work that needed doing. It got me out the apartment, where Richard's scent brought up memories in every room. It filled the days, especially since we worked late every night because there was so much to be done. Part of our pay that week was dinner, taken out from one of the local restaurants just a few steps away. It was pleasant, and on top of everything, we were being paid.

Ariadne was realizing a dream in opening her own music store. Her excitement and passion made her pleasant to be around. She was courteous and grateful, and that made her easy to work for. Yvette kept arguing for more ethnic and tribal instruments, and Ariadne heard her out. But it turned out she'd been teaching music in town for a lot of years, so even in the days before the store officially opened, people wandered in to congratulate her, to sign up for lessons, to arrange to rent instruments for band classes in summer school, or sign up for the local music camp that Ariadne helped to run. Some of them stayed to help for awhile, as there was still plenty to do. Yvette finally got her way by offering to teach the drum class she wanted. I took no part in these discussions, but I enjoyed them in my own way.

By Friday night, Ariadne had offered us both permanent positions. Yvette filled out the paperwork then and there. I had to tell Ariadne my wallet had been stolen.

One big problem with a fake I.D. is that you can't just go down to the DMV and get a new one, and they're hard to replace, especially in a town where I didn't know who to ask where to get one. I called the World Music store in Costa Mesa and asked Madam Tamara to ask Curt to tell his cousin Elaine I needed my wallet back. Now. When I called back the next morning, Tamara told me that Elaine would give me the wallet if I drove up and got it from her, or I could wait until she had time to drive down and give it back to me. There were several other possible choices, and I thought about that before I gave my answer.

"Do you think it's a trap?" Tamara asked when I didn't respond.

"Probably," I said. "Where did she say I should meet her?"

"It's up in Calabasas. Wait." After a moment, she read me the address and the directions and I copied them down with a pencil stub on the side of a piece of junk mail Ariadne had thrown away.

Then she told me, "I have arranged a meeting for Monday night. I expect you to be there."

"A meeting?"

"You agreed it would be best if you call your demon publicly, so that all may question it."

I remembered suggesting it. I didn't remember agreeing to do it. "It's dangerous," I said.

"Yes. We will take all possible precautions."

Tamara had never seen it, the thing that Richard had become. I'd known I might have to call him again. We'd talked about it. But I had seen that thing, and I didn't want to.

"You'll be there?" she insisted.

I hedged. "Well, if I don't show, you'll know where to ask after me."

There was a silence on the line. Then she said, "You are a lot of trouble."

"I know."

A short laugh. "Go well, wolf girl. The Lady speed your way."

It occurred to me, as I hung up the phone, that if I didn't show, Tamara and all those power raisers who were there on Monday night could have that healing sing for her mother. And that might be the best thing that could happen.

I stopped by Ariadne's in time to help her and Yvette put up the sign, "Amadeus Music Store," over the front of the shop, which was officially opening today. I told them my wallet had been found and I was going to go and pick it up. Ariadne gave me a smile and told me to hurry back. I was beginning to like her. Yvette gave me a look of suspicion laced with concern, and made a crack about getting out of working just before the opening. Yeah, I liked her too.

So on a bright sunny Saturday morning I headed across the greater Los Angeles basin down the 605, then up the 5 to the 101 toward Calabasas, enjoying the tiny clouds drifting across the sky from the northeast, until I came to a stop on the 101 just beyond downtown L.A., staring ahead at a long back-up of red brake lights on my side, and an empty freeway going the other way. Always a bad sign. After creeping along for a few minutes, I tried the charm that Richard taught me, for clearing the traffic.

"Does it work?" I'd asked him, Both hands on the wheel, I sketched the sign with my fingers and pronounced the charm.

"Does it matter?" he said. "While you're doing the charm, the roads may clear."

Just as he said that, traffic had picked up, and I glanced over at him and grinned, and he smiled in return. You would not believe the sweetness of his smile. The illusionist never got that right. I should have bitten him harder.

As I crept along in second gear I wondered what, if anything, would answer, when I called up the demon on Monday. But then, if I was about to walk into another trap set by the evil vet, and I was caught or killed, then I wouldn't have to worry about that in any case. I was prepared for another attempt to capture me to relieve me of my demon. If that happened, I decided, I was going to have to take care of the evil vet, and I was prepared for that. It was about time. What I was not prepared for was what would prove to be the fight of my life.

The traffic picked up a bit while I was thinking about what was ahead. As I shifted into third I smiled and pronounced the charm again. After all, it couldn't hurt.

As the freeway began to climb out of the L.A. basin, we passed steep hills with their tops flattened, and little oases of pink houses with red roofs on top, and spiky stands of palm trees. As it turned out, the accident that was holding up the traffic was on the other side, so my side didn't have to squash down into fewer lanes to pass by. As the speed of traffic accelerated to its usual tearing speed, I joked to myself that Richard's charm really had worked. The next set of hills were only sparsely built up, and further along there was actual open space up the steep slopes of a range of mountains. Not the forested mountains of home, but still enough space to rest the eye and make me think about how much I missed the pleasure of running for hours.

I got off the freeway and stopped to check the directions I'd gotten from Elaine by way of Tamara. I turned south and headed down the road into the hills. Here, every flat place seemed to have been scraped level and built up, right to the edge of the steep, brush-covered hills. From a distance the hills looked fuzzy, as though they were covered with green-grey brush. Closer to, the spiny bushes all seemed to be aspiring to become trees, and stood a lot higher than I do, in either form. Along the canyons and the seasonal creeks, and in green patches that marked springs or sinks, ancient oaks and sycamores grew, probably the same ones that stood there since before California was a state. Modern houses pressed up alongside old ranches with falling down fences. Bridle paths and hiking trails wound the uncultivated hillsides. Side streets were called after creeks, bobcats, coyotes, referring to sightings many years in the past.

Tree-covered hills sloped into tree-covered canyons watered with streams that were still running in early May. I hadn't seen country this beautiful since I'd come to Los Angeles. The wooded hills would smell of drying grass, of dust, of misty mornings and cool spring nights. The web of tiny lives would unfold before me with every step as I crossed foraging trails and hunting trails, telling their stories to me with my every breath. I promised myself that one day I would wander here for a day or a week or longer, until I knew every fold of earth, the view from every height, and every sweet little critter who lived there.

I drove down into a valley where the dwellings grew closer together, and everybody's territory was marked by fences. At a crossroads a trendy bar and restaurant with a sculpture garden terraced into the slope marked the center of town. I turned right and counted three mailboxes, and pulled over.

Elaine's house had a huge wall made of steel panels around it, articulated and painted to look like some kind of artistic state-ment in sheets of metal, but the prevailing message was clear: do not try to come in here. You are not wanted.

A heavy, lopsided gate of the same material had been shoved open across a rutted, sparsely-graveled drive, probably in invita-tion. Instead, I parked outside the fence, as far to the side of the road as I could, locked the car and left it there. First rule of walk-ing into a trap, leave your transportation outside of it.

Inside the gate a broad lawn needed cutting, and a wide border along the fence planted with native California plants had run wild, fighting for space and light.

The driveway led up to the house around a circular bed of ancient rose bushes, their trunks as thick as young trees, just coming into bloom. The house had been ultra-modern a couple of decades ago. It looked like a lot of glass cubes stacked on top of each other, overlapping in places, leaving gaps in others. These floor-to-ceil-ing windows were blocked out with shades or curtains or screens against the California sun. The front door stood behind a patio made up of huge squares of rough concrete, in a cave created by the overhanging cubes of the second story. Fat-leaved plants in big brown pots lined the sides of the cave all the way to the glass door.

You cannot just ignore a trap. If you stay away from it, the trap-per will become more wily, and try and find a way to drive you into it when you are most unwary. You have to defeat the trap, destroy it, and drive out the trapper. To do that you must first identify the trap, suss out all its workings from the buried chain to the straining spring to the deadly, pointy teeth. When you can see the trap in its entirety, you can drop a stone in its mouth, make it snap on itself, dig it all out, and throw it in the nearest lake. But leaving a trap unsprung in your territory is just foolishness.

I stopped at the edge of the drive. I didn't like the look of the cave. I didn't want to enter the house. Limited space limits choices. And before you walk into a trap, you want to know where all the doors are, so you can get out. So, I stopped at the patio.

A dozen or so people used this walk every day. Elaine used it frequently. Cousin Curt had been here recently. Elaine had crossed this way, either going or coming, just a short while ago. I was just going to back-track her, to see if she was outside or in, when the front door opened and she slipped out, snapping the door shut quickly behind her. Obviously she didn't want me inside the house either. The evil vet hurried out of the cave and started along her previous track, beckoning me. "Come this way." She pulled on a cardigan over her work shirt as I caught up with her. Her jeans had fresh stains. She'd euthanized a dog earlier that morning, a big tired old fellow who was sick with cancer, and hadn't changed her clothes. Poor old guy. There's a lot to be said for an easy death, except the lack of choice.

I caught up with her. "Nice place," I said.

"It's my parents'."

"Where is my wallet?"

Tension spiked off her. If scent were color she'd have been spouting rainbows. "Uh… I have to…"

"All right," I said agreeably. "I can wait."

I followed her around the side of the house, lengthening my stride to keep up with her, and limping just a bit on my bad ankle. In back there was another, bigger patio, bordered by pool chairs and palm trees. Orange and lemon trees alternated in big wooden planters along the fence. And of course, there was the big blue pool, smelling of chlorine, where not a leaf or insect marred the perfect, stinky water.

Elaine waved me along, walking so fast I broke into a jog to keep up, and changed from her right side to her left. My adrenaline started pumping as we passed the pool. I wondered if I should just throw her in now and save time. Elaine had washed her hands thoroughly with an astringent soap, since her morning's appointment bringing death to a dog, and more recently with a soap tinged with lavender, but she had missed a trace of the gun oil on her fingers. I couldn't see where she was concealing a gun on her at present. The pockets on the cardigan weren't big enough, and should have swung more heavily when she moved with a couple of pounds of pistol in it. She might have just been cleaning the gun before putting it away. Then again, she might have it hidden somewhere out here, ready to hand.

If she shot me again, I might have to bang her head on the concrete a few times before I threw her in the pool. I didn't think she could shoot me, since I was ready for her. The woman still didn't know how fast I could move. But if she made me move that fast, I swore she was going to be awfully sorry.

The evil vet led the way across the pool area, which no one had used in a long time.

"So, did you bury my wallet under a tree or something?" I wasn't expecting an answer. I was just talking to see her reaction. Like poking a snake with a stick. "Look, I don't care about the cash, I just need my I.D. Or don't you have it?"

"It's just—you have to see something."

I stopped walking. "I do? What would that be?"

"It's here."

The far side of the pool was fenced with high wooden boards that had once been painted dark green. She dragged open a groaning lopsided gate, and held it for me. "Just through here."

"My wallet is just through there?"

Elaine met my gaze briefly, then looked away into the field beyond the gate. "Go on," she said. "In there."

Through the gate I glimpsed green grass and the neatly spaced trees of an old orchard. "Why should I go in there?"

"Just—there's somebody waiting for you."

"Has she got my wallet?"

She still wouldn't meet my eyes. "I'll give you your wallet when you come out." The tension on her body reached a new height. I took one step toward the gate just to see if it could rise any more, but she seemed to have topped out.

I raised my head and opened my mouth a little. There was almost no breeze, and the air that was stirring came from behind and to the right. Curt had not come this way. Elaine had been through the gate earlier. She pulled it open a little more, invitingly. I smiled at her. I thought I'd better take a stroll around the perimeter of the orchard, outside the fence, before I walked through that gate.

A voice came from behind me. "Thank you, doctor. I'll take it from here."

I spun hard. My third oldest stepbrother, Finley, dropped lightly over the orchard fence onto the patio and stalked toward me. His eyes were already turning gold.

CHAPTER TWELVE

I grow bigger when I'm angry. I grow smaller when I'm scared. Another problem with fear is that you freeze, and you lose track of your surroundings as your attention telescopes on the threat coming at you. Time speeds up as you slow down, and you find yourself clutching at opportunities that have already slipped out of reach.

"You little bitch. Where have you been? You are in so much trouble!"

I managed to get an arm up before the first blow struck. I managed to ride the backhand that followed by shuffling a little out of range. I managed to back away before he grabbed me. I stepped to the side before he backed me against the tub with the lemon tree, or trapped me in the space between the tub and the gate, the heavy blows falling faster and harder.

"Bitch! Idiot! Cunt! I am so going to make you pay!"

I heard the evil vet squawking some kind of protest. He turned on her with a snarl, and I ducked back, out of range for a moment, and through the only opening available, into the orchard where I would have a bit more room to move. And there I was.

Right in the trap.

When my stepfather moved in, he made a point of teaching me and my brother Luke what the new pack order was. When he was certain we'd learned our place, his four sons took up the lesson. My oldest stepbrother, Tillman, chased me down every day, pinned me, held me down and laid into me until he was satisfied that I'd submitted sufficiently. He kept at it until he got me to submit without fighting him, through four memorable months. He left after that, since he had a job and a place elsewhere. His brothers stayed, though, and they picked up where he left off. Finley's smell, his sweat, his sneer, brought up the remembered rage and shame I'd retained from those lessons. That bile filled my throat and stomach again now as I backed away, step by step, holding off his heavy, open-handed blows, catching them on my forearms, riding them when I could not stop them, keeping them from landing where they would damage me the most, while I tried to blot out the practiced venom of his words. Ducking, blocking, keeping myself whole. Not on the jaw. Not on the joints. Not on the lower ribs. I heard myself make the little grunting noises that meant I was losing, and I burned with fury, hatred and shame at the sounds.

Deep in my belly my panic and fear told me again what I'd learned from all those old lessons: that I was already beaten, that it was only a matter of time before Finley did anything he wanted to me. I clenched my jaw against any further little noises. The rage rose in me, hopeless though I was. I was not going to give up.

I dodged a tree at just the right second, and the blow fell on the trunk instead of on me. I enjoyed the welling satisfaction, and the sound of his curses, and respite from the blows that didn't fall because the pain had disturbed his rhythm. One for me, and I hadn't even touched him.

I couldn't change, because the evil vet was over there somewhere, and she had her gun. If there's a gun around, you want to be in human form. Anyone can get away with shooting a wolf, especially one in their yard. In any case, changing to wolf form in a fight just meant that Finley, in his wolf form, could do things to me that humans couldn't get away with. Right down to my bones, I did not want to go through that again.

His hands came down like hammers, blows meant to disorient, weaken, diminish. Blows that I knew from experience would not stop until I couldn't stand up anymore. Stepping backward, I tripped over a pile of tree stakes, six feet high and almost as thick as my wrist. Someone had a plan to prop up this old orchard, but crashing down on the pile nearly ended the fight. Finley, grinning, launched himself to land on top of me. I twisted out of his way, pushed some poles between us and came up again. Finley was on his feet as well, with one of the poles in his hand. Oh, shit.

He tried to strike me with it, but it was too heavy to move very fast, and I avoided it easily. He stabbed at me with it, and I sidestepped, and then grabbed it and used the pole as a lever to shove Finley into a tree, but he dropped it before he struck, stagger-stepping to remain upright. Then he came at me in a rush, hammering at me now with his fists. He was angry.

The evil vet came into the orchard. I heard her crying out at him. He left me and headed for her at a run, and she backed out and slammed the gate shut. I moved to better my position, further out among the trees, away from the fence where he intended to pin me. Then he came for me again. Don't let him damage me, don't let him grab me. Once he had hold of me, since he was stronger and weighed more, he could throw me around however he liked, and I wouldn't be able to protect myself.

I was gasping now, as he laid in to me methodically, not hurrying, not breathing fast, the satisfied smirk on his face just like his dad's. Each blow falling on my bruised arms felt as though my bones might crack, they ached so much. But still I reached to block the blows that fell. My head rang from the ones that had connected. My lip was bleeding. I had to stay out of his grasp, hold him off as best I could, as long as I could.

He would beat me until I was exhausted. He would put me on the ground and beat me until I couldn't move. He would make sure I knew I was beaten. Then he would haul me off and take me back to my mom's place, where I'd have to go through this again and again. There were tears in my eyes, and I hated that too. A low growl started in my chest, almost too low for human hearing. Finley heard it, heard in it my defiance, and cursed me again. He came at me harder, and faster. If he grabbed me, I was done. I knew that.

I realized why he was holding back on me, why he hadn't ended this already. He wanted me to change. He wanted to pin me, screw me, roll me, make me piss myself. He wanted that complete subjugation. So his blows were a form of taunting, trying to get me to bite.

It's amazing how quickly you tire, when you're being beaten. I can run all day. I can hold my own in a fight for quite some time, but being beaten shakes you at your core, weakens you, drags out all your strength, makes you see only one way out of this situation, and that was to give up, to submit, or to die.

His blows slammed into me and I couldn't stop them. The anger in me rose and touched my heart. As I backed away through the thick grass, dodging the trees when he tried to drive me into one, turning away again so he couldn't back me into the fence, it occurred to me that this was taking longer than it should. He should have beaten me by this time. He always had before. I blocked another blow, and they were definitely coming slower now. It seemed to me that despite his weight and despite his strength, he wasn't as big as he used to be. I met his eyes. I didn't have to look that far up to do it.

My rage began to sing inside me, as I felt myself grow with my anger. Now a growl came from him, a purely human sound of fury and frustration. I grinned, showing him my teeth. He roared at me and lunged, and grabbed my wrists. He tried to pin both of them in one big hand, so he could beat me with the other one, but as he grabbed me, I changed, just my arms to my wolf forelegs, just for a moment, so when he grabbed, the shape he was expecting wasn't there, and I slipped out of his grasp, and in his moment of confusion, I gained a few steps on him, backing off and moving away from the high wooden fence. The growl deep in my throat was louder now. He stared at me for a moment in surprise. I was dizzy with pain, my arms, shoulders and ribs ached, and my stomach where he'd gotten in a good one. But I wasn't beaten yet. I was stronger now, and faster, and I knew more. There was a chance, just a chance, that I would get lucky.

He lunged and grabbed at me again, held me tight and tried to turn me and get an arm lock on me, and there I was with my head close to his shoulder, a bit bigger than I was before, and I changed, just my head, just for a moment, and in that moment I got his shoulder just below the neck in my wolf teeth and bit down as hard as I could. The taste of his blood was like the nectar of the gods.

He threw me off with a roar that was partly a scream, but I landed easy, out of the range of his arms, and grinning like a fool, his blood on my lips. He clutched his torn shoulder with his other hand, the blood welling through his fingers like the goo spilling out of a donut.

"You rabid bitch! I will get you for this. Dad told us to give it to you, but I was going to go easy. But you're going to pay for this now!"

His eyes slitted, he stomped toward me, his hands out, ready to grab. I backed away, still enjoying the sight of the blood that smeared his hand, and trickled through his shirt. He charged me, raining down blows with his fists. He didn't seem so fast anymore, or nearly so big. And it didn't seem so certain that he was going to be able to beat me. I tried to use new angles of my arms to block his blows, to spare the pulsing bruises I already had, but

I was sure now that they wouldn't fail, that they would be strong enough to keep the rest of me intact. I smiled.

As his fist rose again, I stepped in, instead of back, and unleashed my rage and grew, and again changed just my head, just for a moment, and snapped at his nose. He jerked back, but I hooked the edge of one nostril on a lower canine, and it tore. You gotta know that really, really hurts.

He screamed and changed and leaped at me all at once and I went down beneath a flurry of teeth and blood and fur, holding his jaws away from my neck with my hands, and laughing hysterically, because his wolf nose was askew, and it was bleeding like mad, and he snarled, trying to push his jaws between my hands and rend my throat. And then suddenly he jerked and yelped, and twisted off me. He staggered a few steps in a half-circle, and then he fell, partly across my legs.

Finley's big, as a wolf. I pushed him off me and got up, panting and covered with blood and saliva—his—and sweat—mine. The vet, a pistol held away from her side in one hand, grasping a big leather dog muzzle and a come-along in the other, ran toward me, her face as shocked and tearful as though she was the one who'd been attacked and beaten for the last ten minutes.

"Are you all right?" She dropped down next to Finley and looped the come-along around his neck.

"Me?" What a stupid question. I caught myself as I reeled, my body one big ache, with flares of more intense pain where I'd taken bad strikes. I was going to be red, white and blue for at least a week. I looked down at Finley at my feet, blood streaking his fur, and his nose all askew, still bleeding. I grinned. In fact, I really was all right. "Yeah. I'm fine. Hey, thank you."

"I didn't know he was going to do that. I swear, I didn't know."

"No?" I wondered why I was having trouble talking, until I realized I was still gasping for breath. "What—did you think—he was going to do?"

"He said he would take care of you."

"Yup," I managed. "That's how he does it."

"I'm sorry," she said again, while I just stood there and breathed for awhile, enjoying the view over the orchard, and up the hills beyond the fence, and the pointy mountains beyond. And the fallen foe at my feet. An elation grew in me as I stared down at Finley's still form. He hadn't beaten me. Not this time. And he wasn't going to. Even if the vet hadn't shot him, he wasn't going to beat me. I was going to beat him. I took deep breaths. My arms felt like professionally tenderized meat. My shoulders hurt. I ached almost everywhere. But deep inside I felt a tide of joy. I felt like throwing back my head and howling out my triumph. Ha.

"I was going to beat him," I told Elaine.

"He's awfully big," was all she said.

I looked at her. "You knew he was coming."

She held my gaze, the sunlight glinting on her glasses. Then she nodded. "There've been these cards. He sent them to vets all over the area. Maybe all over the city. You see them everywhere." She took a dog-eared postcard out of her pocket. It had a picture of a gray wolf pictured on one side. It wasn't me, but most people can't tell wolves apart, unless the markings are really distinctive. The other side of the card was addressed to Elaine at her office. A printed message said, "Have you seen or heard of a wolf hybrid in your area behaving oddly?" It gave Finley's cell number. A wolf hybrid? That was funny, in a way.

I sat down. It seemed like a good idea. I pulled my legs up and leaned my back against a tree, behind Finley's head where he couldn't see me at once if he came to. "So you called him?"

"I just thought he would get rid of you. Or know how to get rid of you."

"Get rid of me?"

"Because, you know—I though you were some kind of monster! I didn't understand you."

172 ◈ CAROL WOLF

I wouldn't have thought I had anything left in me, but I felt my eyes change. "And why do you think it is for you to understand me?"

She stared down at Finley. I closed my eyes. After a moment I heard her say, "I'm sorry."

I didn't respond. After a moment she went on. "He said... he said he raised wolf hybrids. That he'd sold one up in the San Fernando Valley, but it had gotten away. I didn't know—he didn't say—that he was like you."

I opened my eyes. "He didn't say that he's my stepbrother?"

She shook her head.

"Well. He wouldn't."

"You ran away from home?" Her eyes behind her glasses were tear-stained. No one had ever wept for me. It was disconcerting.

"Yeah," I said.

"I don't blame you. I couldn't... I saw my Aunt Sarah's husband beat her once. I was just a kid. He came into the house, roaring, and she just dropped into a ball on the floor and took it." She shook her head, trying to dislodge the memory. "I hid under the table. I can still remember the sounds. It was terrifying. When he went after you..." she nodded at Finley. Her glasses glinted. "I was wrong about you. You really aren't under a curse, are you?"

"Uh, no."

"No. And you don't change into a wolf because your demon granted you that wish."

"No."

"No. You're a shape-changer."

"I am one of the wolf kind," I told her.

"And so is he."

"Yes."

"And—there are others?"

"Lots."

"Oh." After a moment she said, "What do you want to do with him?"

"He's not dead, is he?"

"No, but he will be soon, if I don't do anything. The dart contains nicotine, which knocks animals out real fast…" She met my eyes and then hers wavered and looked away. I remembered how fast I'd been knocked out, not too long ago. She continued, "He's going to die if I don't give him the antidote." She took a small hypodermic out of the pocket of her sweater.

I looked down at Finley. He lay utterly relaxed, his legs splayed, his head back. His breathing had slowed. Blood still dripped from his slashed nose, and pooled under his shoulder. It was hypnotic to think we could just sit here, and do nothing, and he would die. And I hurt. I was tired. It would be easy.

"Is that what you shot me with?"

"That's right. But I gave you the antidote right away. We really didn't want to hurt you."

I thought about answering that. There was a snappy answer out there that would include my time in the cage, the time the wounds had taken to heal, the terror of being in two forms at once, at being helpless, and that stupid dog… I closed my eyes.

Elaine's voice jerked me back. "I'm sorry. I can't just let him die."

"When he wakes up," I warned her, "he will come after me again. And he will come after you. He won't stop. And he will mean to hurt you."

The not-so-evil vet stared down at Finley. "Maybe I'll try and call Curt. If he has some of those silver binders already charged we could try and—"

"Wait. Those little hooks?"

I got up, which was unexpectedly difficult, and made my way out of the orchard, which seemed like a long walk, and went back to my car. By the time I headed back, holding the bandana from my glove compartment, I'd gotten accustomed to the pain at every step, and my short-breathed exhaustion.

When I came back into the orchard, the vet was kneeling next to Finley, a discarded hypo beside her. She'd fixed the muzzle around his head, which almost didn't fit. From her pocket she drew out a lighter and a wad of tinfoil which she picked open. I jerked as I recognized the scent. It held a small block of that stuff that made the smoke, and she lit it like a cone of incense.

I moved to avoid the smoke and the memories it brought back.

She wrapped the burning block loosely in the tinfoil and fixed it inside the muzzle, near the corner of Finley's jaw.

"That'll hold him."

"Here." I opened the bandana and dropped it on her knee. "Will those still work?"

She recognized them all right. "Sure."

"So, stick 'em in, and let's put him on a plane to a country that doesn't accept wild animal imports." There was a story about a cousin who'd gotten stuck like that. Forever.

Elaine just sat there, staring at Finley. "I pinned your hind leg," she said. "I was just about to pin your foreleg when you moved. Your eyes opened, and you... you started to change. Your eyes... they were human, but yellow. And the foreleg I was holding—it was human."

"I was trying to change." Even mostly unconscious. Good instincts.

"I pinned it so fast. I was scared. I'd never seen anything... I couldn't stand you staring at me." She looked up at me, her face crumpled, like a kid caught doing wrong. "We took you to Aunt Sarah so no one would see you. No one goes out there. You looked so..." She shook her head. "That's why we thought it must be a demon. Or a curse. It looked like one!" She got up. "We can't just pin him. He'll get out of it, just like you did."

Well, I'd thought letting him die was the best idea yet.

"Watch him," she told me. "Make sure that tinfoil doesn't slip. I have to get my bag." And off she went.

I watched closely. Finley went on bleeding, but he hadn't stirred when Elaine came panting back carrying her big black vet case. She unlatched it and got out a set of wire cutters, picked up one of my silver hooks and started snipping it into little lengths.

"Hey!" Those were my trophies, and she was wrecking one.

"It's not the hook," she told me, not stopping. "It's the silver. Curt charged the silver to hold the spell that keeps you from changing back. I mean, from changing, in your case." She paused and looked up at me. "However did you... ?"

"I got them out first."

"Oh." She went back to snipping when she saw I wasn't going to tell her any more. Why give away my methods?

"Well," she said. "He's not going to do that."

She rummaged around and brought out a black plastic case from the recesses of her bag and snapped it open. It just held another hypodermic, but it had a big needle. "This is what we use when we tag an animal with a subcutaneous transponder." She set it aside and got out a bottle of alcohol. She dunked one of the little lengths of silver wire in a capful and loaded it into the syringe, and I began to smile. Finley was never going to change again. I leaned back against the tree and thought about that.

"I had another cousin," Elaine said, bending to her work. "Curt's little brother, Pete. Back when we were kids, and what happened up at Aunt Sarah's was our huge secret, Pete was the one who loved it the most." She shook her head. "I can still remember what it was like to fly, to see for miles..." She made a face. "Though coming back with mouse hair in my teeth wasn't so fun. Pete was nuts about it. He used to hitchhike out to Sarah's ranch, help her with chores. He got her to experiment with him. She doesn't do that anymore.

"He's the one who started working with metals, to find a way to hold the spell in place, make it last longer. He's the one who figured out that silver would work that way." As she spoke, she inserted the short lengths of wire under the skin between Finley's shoulder blades, and at uneven intervals along his spine all the way to the base of his tail. I thought the use of alcohol to clean the needle and the little wires was excessive, but she did a thorough job.

"Pete loved to be a hawk. He didn't get along with his folks. We thought it was just… After he figured out about silver, he charged up a piece, and instead of making wires out of it, he put it on the grinder and made a handful of dust. The next time he got Sarah to change him… we think he breathed in the dust as soon as she did it. She saw him fly away. He never came back."

She finished inserting the last little snippet of wire in the skin of Finley's neck, under his thick ruff behind his head. "He'll never get these out," she said, and sat back.

Good.

"That should do it. Now all we have to do is…" Elaine got out her cell phone and opened it. After a moment she got to her feet, cursing under her breath about how the damn thing never worked out here. "I have to make a call. Then we'll need to drag him to the garage. The cage is in there."

The way she said it clued me in. "My cage?"

She nodded and headed off. I got up and dragged Finley out of the orchard. Slowly, but not very carefully. Sharing is a virtue, right? I had a lot of bruises just then. And I was looking forward to seeing Finley in my cage.

Elaine adjusted the tinfoil packet in Finley's muzzle when she got back, and then the two of us slotted him into the big live animal cage that Elaine hauled out of the garage. She'd cleaned it, but my scent was still on it. Finley was going to be really confused. Then we put it on a dolly and wheeled it out to the gate. Elaine checked Finley's heartbeat and respiration. He was going to live, it seemed.

"I'm sorry I called him." Elaine poked the bars of Finley's cage with her shoe.

"Can I have my wallet now?"

"Oh. I'm sorry. I really don't have it."

"You're kidding me!" The least I could have gotten out of that great battle was my wallet back. "Where is it?"

"Holly's got it."

"And where is she?"

"Today? She's getting ready for Cecil's birthday party."

Elaine's friend Simon arrived before too long, driving a truck with double doors in the back, and a lift. He parked across the driveway and got out, a lanky guy a bit older than her, in dark jeans and a worn jean jacket. His short brown hair spiked in different directions, but his gaze on Elaine was intense with anticipation. "What've you got?"

Elaine told him imaginatively that I was a friend who lived along the road, and that I'd seen a hybrid wolf a couple of times, and this morning I'd called to report it, and how we'd gone out together and bagged it, and there it was.

Simon's glance fell on me. "Is that how you got hurt? Are you all right?"

I licked a drop of blood off my lip. "I'm fine," I told him. My arms were still throbbing, my bruises stung, but I'd won. I was walking away.

Elaine took back Simon's attention by showing him the wolf postcard.

"Seen 'em," he said. "So this was it?" He squatted down to examine him.

"I think so," Elaine said. "I called the number and talked to the guy. Finley something. He doesn't want it back, he just wanted to know what happened to it, make sure it's all right, and make sure no one was hurt."

"Huh. He doesn't look much like a hybrid. He looks like a full-blooded gray wolf."

"Yeah, he does. But that's what the guy said he was."

"Right. What happened to his nose?"

There was a silence. "Dogfight," I said.

"Huh," Simon leaned down to look closer. "He didn't win? A big fellow like him?"

"Couple of bitches," I said. It was all I could do to not start laughing.

"He's got a bite on his shoulder too," Elaine told him. "I cleaned it, but you'll need to keep an eye on it."

"Sure thing," Simon got up. "Poor guy."

"Yeah."

"He's a handsome fellow," Simon observed. "Does he have a name?"

I looked down at Finley, thinking, but Elaine didn't hesitate. "Butt Crack," she said.

"Butt Crack?" Simon smiled, trying to understand the joke. "Okay. You sure you want to get rid of him?"

"Yes," we both said.

"All right. I've got four stops. Any of them will be glad to have this specimen. I'm dropping a couple of rescues off at the rehab place near Big Bear, then I'm going down to the wolf center in Julian and picking up a pregnant bitch and a couple of yearlings for the new habitat near Phoenix. They've got a breeding pair they want delivered to the experimental station in Albequerque. So. Where do you want this guy dropped off?"

"Albuquerque," we both said.

"Albuquerque it is."

I grinned to myself. Albuquerque is deep in Lobo territory. Even if he got out of the station, he'd be in deep trouble, being so far off the Moon Wolf range. Escaping might even get him killed. What a happy thought.

We gave Simon a hand in dragging the cage to the lift, and then hauling it into the truck. One row of shelves held two wolf hybrids—and these were real wolf hybrids—wide awake and ready for fun. We shoved Finley's cage onto the empty shelf opposite and closed up the truck.

Simon studied Elaine for a long moment. "When I come back, maybe you'll tell me the real story."

She smiled at him. "Maybe. Someday."

I was tired, and I was hurt. I wanted to complete my errand and go home to a hot bath and relive my triumph. And this is why I made the mistake that would bring my enemies down upon me. Something was niggling in the back of my mind, but I was too tired to work it out. I forgot about Finley's truck.

"All right," I said, as Simon drove off, and Elaine finished waving at him. "Let's go find Holly and get my wallet."

CHAPTER THIRTEEN

"You can't go to Cecil's birthday party looking like
that."

I dabbed at the blood on my lip with the sleeve of
my sweatshirt. My head felt like it was bulging. My arms were
still throbbing. I ached in places I didn't remember being hit.
"I'm not going to any party."

"You are if you want your wallet back today. And you can't go
to Holly's looking like that."

I looked down at my clothes. "Oh." My black jeans were
smeared with dirt, and Finley's blood had gotten on them too. My
sweatshirt was dirty in places, and spotted with blood. I pulled
it off. My t-shirt was sweat-soaked. No, these were definitely not
my party clothes.

"Wait here," Elaine said. She went into the house and shut the
door behind her.

I sat down on a bench on the patio. Then I lay down, put my
sweatshirt under my head as a pillow, and fell asleep in the sun. I
woke up suddenly when Elaine loomed over me, holding a damp

cloth and an open bottle of witch hazel. I took the cloth and wiped my face, then poured the witch hazel on one corner and applied it to the bruises on my arms. I dabbed at my face and the bruises on my ribs. My lip had stopped bleeding.

She held out a liter bottle of water that had never been opened. I took it and drained half of it gratefully. She held out her cupped hand with two pills in it.

"What's that?"

I must have sounded suspicious. "It's just aspirin. You look like you need it."

I did need them. I gulped them down with some more water. I hoped she wasn't going to bill me.

Elaine had showered and changed into a green skirt and an ivory colored satin blouse that looked as fragile as it was revealing. She'd put on make-up that made her eyes look harder behind her glasses, and her lips and cheeks were as bright as blood. Her hair hung loose, and golden earrings tangled in the strands. A soft leather purse hung awkwardly from one arm. She held out a pile of clothes.

"I'm not wearing those."

Elaine's glasses flashed. "I brought pins. We can take in the skirt and pin it."

"I'm not wearing your clothes." The vet had shot Finley, but that didn't make us friends. The clothes smelled of her, and I didn't want anything of hers that close to me.

"Look," I said, "let's just go to Holly's, you go in and get my wallet, and we'll be done."

"I thought you wanted to meet Cecil."

I did want to meet Cecil.

"He's supposed to be back today. He's been out on a boat communing with the World Snake. He said if he meditated deeply he'd be able to communicate with it, and persuade it to move off, and spare the city."

I was going to try and explain again that Richard and I had already done this, but I didn't bother. "You really believe he can do that?"

"At least he's trying! What have you been doing?"

"Besides trying to get away from you?"

She decided not to argue anymore. "If you are going to Cecil's party, and you won't wear these, you are going to need some new clothes."

Elaine had been going to get a friend to take her to Holly's party, since her truck, she told me pointedly, was in the shop. So we went in my car.

I do not like new clothes. I do not like the way they smell. This is why, on the way to the smart clothing store in Canoga Park, with Elaine in the passenger seat directing me, I pulled over when I spotted a second-hand store. An embarrassed query by Elaine of whether or not I had any money I met with a grin. I still had almost all of the money I'd made her give me the first time we'd met. In any case, the clothes were pretty inexpensive.

I wandered along the aisles of women's clothes, and men's clothes, partly looking, and partly taking in the scents of the people who had worn them before. Much less annoying than sniffing chemicals for weeks until they wear away in the wash.

I got a new pair of black jeans, only worn a couple of times, but more form-fitting than the work jeans I usually wear. I bought a dark red silk open-necked shirt with wide sleeves and tight cuffs, and little pearl buttons at the throat and wrists. It had a little rip in the sleeve, but I didn't care. I found a black leather vest cut up into patterns like a snowflake, so my new shiny red shirt showed through.

We shape-changers have to be careful about our clothes. I like mine to be loose and comfortable, for running, fighting, or doing any work that comes to hand. Clothes that get in the way of what needs to be done are just foolish. Heavy clothes, like boots or big coats, tend to get lost when one changes back to human form.

Sweats are ideal, not tight enough to get hung up, but not so heavy that they don't come back with you.

The legends say that the wolf kind used to be able to run to battle in their wolf form, and then change into humans, dressed in full armor with their weapons in hand. No one can do that anymore, though the most powerful of the wolf kind can carry a fair amount of weight when they change, and bring it back. We practice, growing up. I thought about the things I'd left in that other place that, however often we change, we never seem to see, or don't remember, as I eyed a pair of short leather boots. They were a size too big for me, but I liked them, and they fit well enough. So I thought, why not? I'll leave my muddy tennis shoes in the car. If I end up changing, and change back and find I've lost them, I'll have a short walk to the car, and I'll be out thirty bucks.

Best of all, in the doorway into the dressing rooms, a tape measure had been tacked to the wall. I borrowed a plastic hanger, and measured myself. And then I had to measure myself again. I'd grown almost an inch since leaving home. An inch! I was taller! Not five foot nothing anymore! Ha!

This I had to celebrate, so I bought a lightweight silver and turquoise choker. It would probably be gone as soon as I changed, a gift to the dark. But until then, it looked nice. I already felt taller, wearing my new duds. I used the comb in my glove compartment to get the dried mud out of my hair, and off we drove to Malibu.

On the way, I had to hear all the details of all the damage Elaine's truck had taken, and what the estimates were to get it fixed, but when she realized I was enjoying the tale, she stopped talking. It must have been the big smile that gave it away. As I sat aching in all the new places, I could still feel the wound on my hip. It had finally closed up, and the bruise was fading to purple and yellow. Her truck didn't hurt her nearly as much.

Holly had her own narrow driveway off the Pacific Coast Highway, leading past the back walls of a set of tall beach houses, tight up against each other, and then curving onto a knoll overlooking the ocean on two sides. Turns out Elaine's little sister had married a Hollywood agent who'd died about five years earlier. Holly had inherited from him both his house and his fortune.

"He didn't disappear mysteriously, did he?" I wondered aloud. "We're not going to find a dog or a pony in the garage or somewhere, with leather bands on its legs?"

But in fact, Elaine said, he'd died quite publicly in a restaurant of a heart attack, and Holly had a certificate to prove it.

The driveway was lined end to end with parked cars, but the circle in front of the entranceway was clear. A stand of bamboo and palm fronds screened the house so all we could see from there were the red tile roofs. I could smell the ocean. I pulled up and parked at the walkway, since no one else had, and a slender, dark-haired young man in a blue uniform coat and a red bow tie and a happy smile appeared and opened my car door. When I got out without his help, he went around and opened the door for Elaine, who graciously held out her hand and let him assist her. He then came around again and held out his hand to me. Was I supposed to tip him? I hadn't needed his help, and Elaine was only playing along.

"Give him your keys," Elaine told me. "He's going to park your car."

"Where are you going to park it?" I asked him.

"Just give him the keys," Elaine said. "He'll bring the car back when you ask for it."

I handed him the keys. I could already tell this was not my kind of party.

Elaine took a long piece of white cotton cloth out of her purse, draped it over her neck and flipped her hair over it. She pulled another one out and handed it to me. "Put this on."

"What is it?"

"When you meet Cecil, take it off and give it to him."

"It's his birthday present?"

"It's just the custom. Come on. It doesn't hurt."

I took it from her, wrapped it around my fists and tested its strength. It would certainly do to strangle someone. Under Elaine's unamused gaze I slipped it around my neck.

Beyond the bamboo screen an ornamental waterway wound back and forth. We had to cross three little arched bridges hung with flowers to get to the big square front porch decorated with more baskets of fresh flowers, where a young woman in a black uniform waited to greet us. A tall, heavy woman in a flowing flowered dress and short, flat, dyed blond hair stood up from the rail where she had been leaning, smoking a cigarette, to greet Elaine as she approached.

"Sally!" Elaine said, and went to her.

"Don't say a word!" Sally held her cigarette at arm's length as she whisked her long skirts around to face Elaine and embrace her. "Good to see you, too." She also wore one of the white scarves around her neck.

"Holly's in great form, I see," Elaine said, examining the flower baskets.

"Never better." Sally reached out and put her cigarette out in a basket of peonies.

Neither of them sounded sincere. In fact, that was definitely sarcasm.

"Is Cecil here?" Elaine asked.

"I haven't seen him. I thought I'd hang out here until he arrives," she confided. "Otherwise I'll never get a word in edgewise."

"Not once Holly gets in range," Elaine agreed.

"Who's this?" Sally asked, looking at me.

"Oh, just some werewolf I know."

Sally barked a laugh. "If you decide to bite Holly," she told me, "give her an extra one for me."

What an evil vet! Didn't she understand that was supposed to be a secret identity? I'm the only one who gets to tell people what I am. I glowered at Elaine. Her glasses glinted as she smiled back.

The uniformed woman ushered us into a big immaculate room where all the furniture was the same light beige. Here the walls were hung with colorful banners, so long they draped over the floor, decorated with signs within circles, strange gods, and what looked like abstract pictures of the same flower, in different forms and colors. Here we were greeted by two more young waiters in black, who welcomed us and offered us necklaces of golden flowers from a big platter. Elaine bowed her head and let them deck her with one. I already had an extra scarf on, so I declined. Elaine picked up a second one and dropped it over my head.

"It's for Cecil's birthday."

"But you said Cecil is an asswinding jerk."

"Shush!" she said, and asked the male waiter, "Where is Holly?"

"She's on the meditation lawn, ma'am. Shall I take you there? The birthday meditation is about to begin."

Elaine waved him off. "I know the way."

"Birthday meditation?" I asked as I followed her.

"Yes," she said. "It will be lovely." More sarcasm.

At the far end of the living room a huge floor-to-ceiling window looked out over the wide ocean. The blue, green, gray and silver water changed from moment to moment, reflecting the bright sunlight. High scattered clouds scudded before the winds. A couple of paragliders were out playing in the sky. Far out near the horizon, a dark gray tanker stood out to sea.

Elaine directed me out a door beside the big window, and that let us out onto a wide wooden deck. There, several beautiful people stood about, smelling faintly of cosmetics, looking out at the view of the ocean, drinking from plastic wine glasses and snacking off little plastic plates. The guests, male and female, perfectly groomed, well-fed and healthy, all wore loose, pastel-colored clothes, and those white scarves and flower necklaces. Some of them greeted Elaine. As I passed one of the women, my attention was seized because I'd scented her before. She was at the party where Elaine had shot me. I tried to meet her eyes but she turned away from me. I was wondering whether I should bite now and explain later, when Elaine came back and took my arm. She couldn't move me on the first yank. She didn't understand how strong I am. I decided that this was small fry. I could mop her up later. After I'd taken down the main prey.

I followed Elaine down a set of steps that led onto a perfect rectangular green lawn, decked with canopies of pale blue, white and yellow cloth wafting in the ocean breeze, to shade all the beautiful guests in their flowing clothes, flowers and scarves, to the drifting sound of wind chimes.

As we descended the steps, just about all of them turned their heads, took in who it was, and turned away again, except for a few who waved or came to greet Elaine. The birthday boy's arrival was breathlessly anticipated.

"Where is Holly?" I asked.

"She'll be in the thick of things," Elaine told me. "She just loves these parties. Just look for the densest crowd, and she'll be in the middle of it."

The canopies obscured some of the groups of people, but we wandered among them, looking for our hostess. On the side closest to the sea, a small hedge bordered the lawn. Beyond that the hill dropped steeply away to a terrace about thirty feet below, where paths wound around a formal garden. A set of steps at the end of the lawn led down to the garden, and then further down to the beach. I recognized that beach. Sure enough, at the far end, a steep road led up to a dirt parking lot. This was the private beach where I'd been at the party. And, not surprising, several more of the people that we passed smelled familiar. How many of them had been at that party? I was going to find out.

"There she is." Elaine changed course toward the patio bordering the lawn on the side away from the ocean, where a dark blue swimming pool gleamed like a jewel in the bright sunlight.

No one was swimming. A group of people stood in a cluster, from the center of which black-clad servants erupted on errands, or arrived carrying trays. Occasional gouts of hilarity burst forth. As we approached, the cluster seethed, and a tiny, intense woman wearing a white linen scarf that draped over her head, around her neck, and fluttered behind her, made her way out of it, pulling flunkies, waiters, and guests in her wake.

She lifted her hands. "Darlings, Beloveds, I have an announcement!" Her voice pierced all the bright conversations and got everyone's attention. Behind Holly stood the only guy at the party in a suit, short, dark-haired, with a chiseled black beard. He directed three of the black-clad wait staff who carried a table across the grass, on which they balanced a heavy, cloth-covered object. Behind them them another flunkey doled out a power cable from the house

"Elaine!" Holly cried, and changed direction toward us, her entourage tacking in her wake. "You came! I'm so glad you came! Darling!" She reached up and grabbed her sister in a fervent embrace. There were tears in her eyes when she released Elaine, but not enough to damage her artful make-up. "It's so good to see you." She kissed Elaine's cheek once more and turned to me.

I saw her breath stop, and started to grin, but the look in her eyes gave me pause. Desire, hunger, and fear made her shifty and hopeful all at once. I was pretty sure she didn't see me. She was looking at a whole bunch of plans, made and unmade over the previous weeks, that were now standing before her, offering new possibilities. Well, one of the possibilities she was not taking into account was that I might bite her head off. So I smiled at her. It was the toothy smile. It's not a smile you take in so much with your eyes. Somewhere in the back of their brains, humans remember when a wolf in your face meant that you had been asked to dinner, and you weren't going to be offered any dessert. Holly's eyes went still all of a sudden, and then she remembered to breathe again.

"Hello!" she cried, her voice high and fake. "And who is this?"

Elaine, her voice heavy with sarcasm, reminded her, "You remember Amber?"

"We met at a party." My teeth still showed. I did not offer my hand, and she did not try to kiss me.

"Oh. Yes," she said. She let herself be distracted then by a round man with a round face and thinning hair, wrapped in cotton robes damp with sweat, who told her what had been done about the placing of the table. She turned away gratefully to contradict everything he'd just said, and then turned back to say, "We'll talk, we have to talk," and then started to turn away again, but I moved to stand in her way. I was still smiling.

"I came to pick up my wallet," I told her.

"Oh, not now, darling, can't you see I'm busy? We'll talk afterward." She waved a conciliating hand at me, and turned to give half a dozen more conflicting directions to the guy in the suit, who listened with patient gravity, and then went away to make sense and order out of her spontaneous utterances. Holly gave more orders and suggestions to the round guy, and to any of the flunkies who came into earshot. She and the round guy sent servers off in several directions. Some never returned.

I told Elaine, "I could go search the house," but she shook her head.

"Everyone!" Holly cried again. No one paid any attention. She clapped her hands. Her voice rose higher. "Everyone!" The guy in the suit offered her a hand mike, and she spoke into it. The suit guy took the mike back, turned it on, and handed it to Holly again. Her voice blasted out from all corners of the garden. "Can you hear me? Namaste!"

That got everyone's attention. Conversations died, people turned her way, and raised their hands to the prayer position. "Namaste!" they said back to her.

"My Beloveds, I'm so glad you came."

"Where is Cecil?" someone called out. "Is he coming?"

The fixed attention of the guests was suddenly tangible. Holly smiled and waved her hand again. "That is what I have to tell you."

The sound of disappointment rose from the crowd. Some of the people turned away, and conversations started up.

Holly's amplified voice sounded over them. "Cecil has decided that it is his place to remain in communication with the Great Enemy. But he will join us for his birthday meditation, by ship-to-shore radio!" With a flourish, Holly grabbed the cloth that covered the object on the table, and yanked it off, with some assistance from the guy in the suit when it got snagged, revealing a radio and a set of speakers. "Cecil? Cecil, can you hear me?"

One of the staff finished plugging the radio in, and leaned over and turned on the on button. A green light gleamed. Bearded suit guy picked up the radio's microphone and handed it to Holly, and very firmly took the hand mike away from her.

"Hello? Darling? Hello? Is this on?" she asked the suit guy. He leaned over again and touched the volume. A mellifluous voice blasted over the lawn.

"Beloveds, I hope I am speaking to you—" A voice like dark molten caramel rolled out from the speakers. The crowd leaned into it as though it were food. The round man stepped in, waved off the suit guy and dialed down the volume to a bearable level. "I am on a boat, with only a few friends, but I am thinking of you all the time. Can you hear me? Is anyone there?"

"We are here, Cecil! We can hear you!" Holly cried into the mike, but Cecil's voice kept right on talking over her.

"I hope I have not mistaken the day, or the time," he gave a little laugh. "The days are so much alike out here, and Beloveds, I am working very hard, meditating night and day."

The suit guy took the microphone from Holly's hand, and showed her how to depress the button before she spoke into it.

She took it back from him. "Cecil! Beloved! I am here! We are all here, gathered in your honor. Speak to us, Master!"

"Holly!" the voice boomed back. "How wonderful. And who else is there?"

And Holly proceeded to introduce every guest at her party. After the first few, one of the guests came up and seized the mike from Holly's hand, and spoke back to Cecil directly. After that, everyone had to speak to Cecil. I looked over at the house. How big was it? How long would it take to search it? The suit guy had gone to the patio, and was giving low-voiced instructions to a group of waiters. Black-clothed flunkies stood in bunches by the pool, on the deck, by the glass doors into the house from either side of the patio. I wondered if part of their job description was to keep certain people from wandering around the house.

The introductions, the scrimmages to seize the mike and talk to Cecil, continued. It looked like this was going to take a long time. Among all the canopies one large, heavy tent sheltered the refreshments, and except for the waiters, right now it was empty. I made my way over there. A little fountain burbled on the table that held stacks of glasses. You were supposed to drop a piece of cut fruit, strawberry or peach, into the bottom of a glass and hold it under the fountain to have it filled with chilled white wine. The waiter demonstrated for me, but I declined. I let him give me a glass of orange juice, and then four more.

I cruised the food tables, while Cecil's voice still boomed in the background, like a roar of surf, rising and receding. Tiers of platters of hors d'oeuvres, laid out artistically by color and shape, filled up again by the numberless waiters as soon as they were depleted, covered three tables. I hadn't had lunch yet, and fighting makes you really hungry. I grabbed a big plate, and went hunting and gathering. But no little sausages did I find. No cheese, no deviled eggs, no crab or caviar. No animal protein of any kind. "Don't tell me," I smiled back at the smiling waiter. "Vegetarian?"

"No," he smiled back again at me. "Vegan."

I had hummus. And bread. Four kinds of hummus. Three kinds of bread. I chewed quickly, and promised myself a whole lot of meat for dinner. The sound of a gong, and the shifting of people, brought my attention back to the lawn.

"My Beloveds," Cecil's voice intoned, "let us take this chance to meditate all together."

"Grab your mats and pillows, everyone!" Holly directed. "Mats are over there. Pillows if you need them. You'll find incense sticks ready in each pavilion…"

"For the length of one joss stick," Cecil continued, oblivious of the people hurrying to grab what they needed and take their places, "let us join together in the face of the coming disaster, on what may be our last day of this joyous life, and think of love, and what the power of love can do for us. Let us embrace the World Snake with the power of our love, in colors of blue and gold and white. For we know, Beloveds, that love will always win. Always. Namaste."

"Namaste!" they all murmured in response, with their hands palm to palm at their hearts, and bowed their heads.

The smell of incense drifted over the lawn. I stood chowing down on another piece of flat bread smeared with hummus and thinly sliced cucumber, and watched all the lovely people fold themselves onto thick round pillows, or wooden benches, or prayer mats, or combinations thereof, hands clasped at their bellies, facing toward the sea. I felt the power of their attention rise, gently. This was not a powerful bunch. The energy wasn't shaped or organized, it just rose because they were all doing the same thing together, more or less. But no one here knew how to do anything with it, so it just rose up and floated away.

I wandered among them as though I just hadn't found my pillow yet. I identified seventeen of the people who had been at the private beach party, who had joined in deceiving me, and who had stood by while I was shot.

And Holly had arranged for the party, the deception, and the trap. She took her place now on a kind of platform, decked with colored cloths, in a three-sided tent hung with more of those banners. Three other people took their places on a rug at her feet. The round guy was one, Sally, the big woman I'd met outside, was another. A tall guy who wore an orange ceremonial robe hanging open over regular clothes was the third.

Holly lit a stick of incense and stuck it upright in a holder on a table to her right. Next to the incense stood a gong. On her left, a round meditation pillow had been decked with flowers, I guessed for the absent birthday boy. Over the amplifier, we could hear him breathing into the microphone. His followers breathed slowly and audibly too, all making the same sound together.

"How long... ?" I mouthed at one of the servers. He shrugged and shook his head that he didn't know.

I snagged a couple more pieces of bread. If I stood around much longer, my bruises were going to seize up, and then they would really hurt. Just standing there doing nothing, so I had a moment to think about them, made my arms start throbbing again. And besides, I didn't want to be part of the breath-fest, and I wasn't one of their flunkeys.

Down below the cliff was one of the sovereign remedies for aching muscles. I walked around the edge of the lawn, stepping past peoples' prayer mats, until I reached the steps that led down the steep slope to the terraced garden below. I trotted down, though not at my usual speed. I crossed the garden, short-cutting across the winding paths, and found the next set of steps that led right down to the sea.

The private beach was fairly narrow at this time, since the tide was almost at its height. A couple of the black-clad staff walked along the shore near the surf, probably taking a break. They weren't looking my way. I changed with relief onto four feet, trotted to the water and waded out into the tide. The salt water eased my bruises that were just beginning to stiffen up. I paddled out into the surf and then back again, remembering running down a beach with Richard, not too long ago. A wave smacked me down, and I hauled myself out of the water and shook myself hard. I looked up and down the beach, glanced up at the garden and the top of the cliff, and then trotted to the steps and ran up them on four legs. Running on four legs is so much faster, and I thought the exercise would keep me from stiffening up again. The pain in my wounded wrist and ankle was nearly gone. My hip was stiff, and the dart wound still hurt, but the pain of it now blended together with all my new aches and bruises. Salt water would diminish the swelling. Now I just needed rest and sleep.

I poked around the garden, stopping here and there when something interested me particularly. I found a bench in an alcove shielded from the wind and looking out to sea. I changed and sat down.

I was pleased to see that my new boots were still with me. The white scarf and the flowers were gone, but the silver and turquoise necklace had made the change this time. I rubbed my arms, working out the lumps so they would heal faster.

I'd grown up near the ocean. The sound of the surf, the smell of salt, the fog sitting far out on the horizon, reminded me of home. But it isn't home anymore when you are abused. The home I was sick for only existed in memory. This was my home now; this was my territory. On the cliff above were people who had done me harm. How should I deal justice to them all?

Elaine had hurt me the most, and I'd taken it out on her car. Come to think of it, I'd taken Curt's transgressions out on his car as well, and given them both a ducking. Serious dents or window cracks? Sand in the engine? Slashed tires? But would that teach them anything? And what did that make of me, except a vandal? *Every power wielder must deal justice, because she can*, the sorceress had said. But what I chose to do to those who had hurt me must leave me stronger, not weaker. And it must disincline any of them from ever challenging me again.

On that resolve I drifted into sleep, shielded from the wind by a corner of the bench. I woke up just a few minutes later to the sound of voices. The two staff members had come back from the beach and were climbing the stairs. I followed after them, still on two feet. At the top of the cliff, the heavy breathers were still entranced in their meditation. I got past the staff at the door by asking for the bathroom, and went inside to explore the house.

CHAPTER FOURTEEN

The house had four different roofs because it was built in different sections. I guessed it had once been a small house, and the sections with the bigger rooms and the bigger windows were added on later, as the succeeding owners got wealthier. The middle right-hand section had a ground floor recreation room with two glass walls, one looking out at the sea, one opening on to the pool. It held a maze of weight lifting machines, stationary bikes, stair machines, rowing machines, a punching bag, a pool table, and a ping-pong table. And a full bar, for when the recreaters got thirsty. One door led to a big bathroom with a whirlpool, and one led to a sauna, and that was the whole ground floor. A winding circular staircase led up to the second floor, and here I found Holly's bedroom, wreathed in flowing hangings, flowing curtains, tapestries of angels, and a really thick violet carpet. She had the biggest bed I'd ever seen, flooded with purple, white, and red silk cushions. This room was probably off-limits to guests, but there was no one around to ask. I thought my wallet might be in there, but I couldn't catch a whiff of it.

The far right-hand section held an office, a den, an entertainment room on the ground floor, and above, a couple of guest rooms, each with its own bathroom. Every room had a color scheme, and all the furniture and even the art work matched.

I was still wandering around the guest rooms when I heard Cecil's voice come up over the amplifier again. I continued my snooping while Cecil pronounced a series of blessings, and his followers called out together in answer, and then clapped twice. It sounded like the session was breaking up. I'd learned some interesting things about Holly's household arrangements, but if my wallet was here it was well hidden, even from senses as keen as mine.

I wandered down another twisting wrought-iron staircase listening to Cecil thank everyone for his lovely birthday party, and his followers called back wishes for his safety and success in his attempt to save Los Angeles. And when everyone realized it was all over, and the World Snake really was gone, he was probably going to take the credit, too.

At the bottom of the steps, a lithe olive-skinned man with a little mustache waited, looking up at me. I'd known he was here, because I scented him, but I hadn't seen him yet. The last time I'd seen him, he'd been manning the gate at that private beach party. You could say we were acquainted, since I'd bitten him once. I stopped a few steps up, where I could meet his eyes on a level. He wore loose, light-colored clothes like the others, but his were somehow elegant. His rose-colored shirt glowed against his skin, and his tan trousers fit his dancer's form neatly. He had on a white scarf, like the others, but his was shiny and silken. He'd managed to ditch the flower necklace too.

"I wondered if you were looking for me," he said. "It's Oliver, if you don't remember."

He was one of the Thunder Mountain Boys, a dance group I'd run into a few times, literally, when I'd lost Richard and was trying to find him. I hadn't known his name. I'd always thought of him as Honey, because he'd been insulting. He looked awfully respectful now.

"I remember a lot of things," I told him.

"I didn't know they meant to harm you," he said, "at that party. And I was still manning the gate when it happened."

"When they took me down."

"Yeah."

"Did you see me down?"

He nodded, barely smiling. "I helped carry you to the truck. There's Marlin, you see. He's still not right."

Marlin was the leader of the Thunder Mountain Boys. He'd taken Richard at one point, so I'd thought he deserved the state he'd been left in. Still, I reminded him, "That had nothing to do with me."

"All right," he allowed. "But there is the matter of the roof you left me on."

My turn to smile. Barely. "How did you finally get down?"

"I finally got down when I managed to attract someone's attention in the street the next morning, and they called the fire department."

I couldn't help smiling then. "Cold night."

"Yup. And they billed me, for bringing out the fire department. Especially since I couldn't give them a rational explanation for what I was doing up there. 'Carried up by a giant wolf' just wasn't going to wash."

"I can understand that. A lot of things I tell people don't wash with them."

He took off his white scarf and held it out in both hands. "I want to ask you to accept this, and let there be peace between us."

"I thought you're supposed to give that to Cecil."

"Cecil isn't here. You can consider it an apology. A flag of surrender, if you like." Slowly, carefully, he draped it over my neck, and stepped back. I nodded.

"I thought you were one of the Thunder Mountain Boys."

Now he smiled, as much in relief as pleasure, it seemed. "I can do both."

"So what is it about Cecil, anyway?"

Oliver-who-used-to-be-Honey's scent changed. His eyes changed, too. "Wait till you meet him," he said. "It's quite a trip."

Oliver followed me out onto the lawn where a hundred or so long good byes were going on. These included everybody exchanging scarves with one person after another, and grasping hands, and kissing cheeks, and fervent protestations of love and care. I noted the more enterprising folks making one last foray at the food tables, some equipped with bags. I headed that way myself, since hummus is not filling.

"There you are!" Holly shrieked behind us. "Dear child, I am so glad you came to our little party. I so wanted you to meet Cecil, but it was not to be, this time. But come, come and meet some of my dearest friends. We've been longing to have a talk with you." Holly took me by the arm in a grasp that was not friendly, and pulled me along with her. I let her. I wanted to meet some of her closest friends. And I wanted to have a really good talk.

"Oliver, darling, so good of you to come, mm, mm," she grabbed him with her other hand and kissed him on both cheeks. "So sweet. See you soon." She patted his cheek and dragged me off with her. I was given a short tour of the house along the way, so I learned that the comfy little room we ended up in was called "the nook." Big fat leather furniture was grouped around a fake fireplace and a mantel lined with leather-covered books no human hand had touched in years. Framed photographs covered the walls. The same short, plump, smiling man stood next to one movie star after another, his arm draped around them. Some of the pictures were signed, with lots of exclamation marks. The sun, just beginning to set, shone fiercely through the three windows that looked out onto the ocean, silhouetting the three guys that stood there holding drinks. They turned as Holly drew me inside.

It was no surprise who her special friends were, after all. The round guy wiped his balding head with the end of his whitish scarf and gave Holly a big smile. The suit guy detached himself from the other two and made his way to a sideboard, where he poured a drink for Holly. He offered me one silently, raising a glass. I smiled, because of course I would be so comfortable taking a drink with these people, especially after the last time. I shook my head.

"Darling," Holly cried, "this is Stuart." She took the little round guy's arm, and then she touched the sleeve of the remaining guy, and looked up at him. "And this is Benjamin."

Benjamin was the guy with the orange robe over his regular clothes. He nodded, looking at me with interest from serene gray eyes. He had a square jaw, a big build, and weathered skin. His scent was pleasant, untinged by cosmetics or chemicals. I nodded back at him.

Sally and Elaine came in behind us. Sally grabbed a drink from the suit guy, whom Holly called Phil, and Sally and Elaine called Jeeves, like it was some kind of joke. Sally plopped down with Elaine on the big couch, as Holly took for herself the big chair next to the fireplace. She gestured to me to sit on the couch. I went to stand by the mantel, across from Benjamin. Honey—I mean Oliver—had come to lounge in the doorway. He accepted a drink from Phil as well. Out on the horizon, the fog began piling up. Soon the sun was was going to sink right into it.

"I am so glad you came today," Holly trilled at me. "Won't you sit down?" She leaned over and patted the couch. I pretended I hadn't heard. "I can see that we got off on the wrong foot with you," she confided to me. "But really, we do want to help you."

I lounged on the arm of the couch. She winced, and so did suit guy. "Oh, good," I said. "You're going to give me back my wallet."

"Of course!" Holly said. "Of course, that was all just a terrible mistake."

For which my wounds had still not fully healed.

"We just want to have this little talk first."

I was willing to tolerate talking, for the time being. Later, there might need to be some biting, perhaps chewing, perhaps deep bone bruises and puncture wounds. It remained to be seen how they would tolerate that. I felt my eyes begin to gleam. I was looking forward to this conversation.

Stuart the round guy sat forward in his chair. He used both hands, so I would know how important what he was saying to me was. "We have learned through the guidance of Cecil, our Teacher, that certain kinds of meditation can create within you a kind of self-control that is so powerful that no external force can influence you."

"Is that right?"

Oliver, leaning in the doorway, smiled.

Stuart gestured some more. "We would like to offer you a chance to study with us, and with our Teacher, so that all that we know of this power can be yours."

"Oh, wow," was all I could think to say.

Benjamin looked at me sharply. "A demon on the loose, with power over a person, is a danger to everyone. That's what we think."

"Oh, no," I said. "Is it?"

Stuart nodded. "You have no idea the power something like that can wield."

"I don't?"

"They can trick your mind," Benjamin said. His eyes weighed me gently. "They can make you believe things that aren't true."

"Have you ever raised a demon?" I asked him.

He shook his head. "I've only seen—"

"Darlings, let's not frighten her," Holly interposed. She focused on me. "We think that as soon as Cecil gets back, you should embark on a series of personal tutorials, with Cecil and with us. We are," she said, "the Inner Circle of Cecil's students."

"I should study with you?"

Stuart, Holly, and Benjamin nodded.

"But, why?"

"Darling, don't fool yourself. A powerful demon is in possession of you."

"Oh, my gosh," I said. "How do you know?"

Elaine bent over her glass, hiding her smile.

Holly fixed me with her eyes. Her makeup was perfect. "Are you aware that at certain times, you turn into a wolf?"

"Huh?" I stared at her, open-mouthed. In the doorway, Oliver snickered. "A wolf? An actual wolf? Really?"

More nodding around the circle.

"We saw you."

"It was terrifying."

I almost smiled, but stopped myself. Not yet. "Oh, my god! How did this happen?"

"We don't know," Benjamin told me. He had real sympathy and concern in his voice.

"Sure we do," Stuart told him. "Either you summoned the demon, or you were tricked by one into allowing it to possess you." He shuffled forward in his seat. "Do you remember, at any time, holding some kind of ritual, where you called up a demon? Or any strange event, something that seemed even supernatural at the time, and after that, you sometimes had blackouts?"

"Ask her first if she's ever had any blackouts," Elaine suggested.

"Yes, good," said Benjamin. "Have you ever had a blackout? A period where you lost time? You found yourself in one place, and you don't remember getting there?"

I did, in fact. It involved waking up in a cage. I was about to bring that up, when Stuart grabbed my hand. "Do you know how you called the demon?"

I looked at Stuart, and he removed his hand.

"But now is not the time for that," Holly interrupted. "I'm sure you'll be able to tell us all how you did it—when Cecil comes back, of course." Her voice rose as she overrode the protests of the others. "What we need to arrange is for you to begin classes in meditation as soon as possible."

"Advanced classes," Benjamin suggested. "And don't worry, you won't be charged. The four of us have decided that your education right now is important enough, we will be covering the cost of your first set of classes."

I looked over at him, but I couldn't find it in myself to thank him.

Stuart said to Holly in a low tone, "I thought we were going to get her to pay in part, you know, so it will mean more to her?"

"Stuart, not now."

"But we said—"

"Later!"

Sally put in, "We can talk to you now about the special ways you'll need to purify your body for correct meditation. An all-vegetarian diet—"

"A vegan diet—"

"Not necessarily a vegan diet, but certain kinds of animal fats must be restricted."

"All the time?" I asked Stuart.

"All the time," he agreed. "And then you'll be ready for special tuition when Cecil arrives."

"What is it about Cecil?" I asked. "What's so special about studying meditation with him?"

"Tantric meditation," Sally corrected. She wore a secret smile. "You'll like it."

"You rise," Benjamin said.

"What?"

"When you practice Tantric meditation with Cecil, you are raised up. Literally raised up."

"In the air?" I asked.

They all nodded. Clearly they'd all had this experience.

"So you're saying that when you study closely with Cecil—"

"Closely," Sally chortled.

"Oh, I get it." And finally, I did. They were thinking about it, about studying closely with Cecil, and so their scents changed. "You have sex with him. And when you have sex, you levitate?"

More nodding. I couldn't believe it. "How high?"

They each considered the question. "About two feet?" Benjamin said.

"Three," Oliver said, from the doorway.

"I have no memory of how high," Sally breathed, her eyes closed.

"I'm sure it was higher than that, when I'm with him," Holly opined.

"And that's why you have the great big bouncy bed," I realized. "So you don't break anything when you land."

More nods.

"How long does the levitation last?"

"During orgasm. It's incredible."

"Levitation does something to your orgasm?"

"Not mine," Sally corrected. "His. Cecil's."

"Just his?"

"It's quite an experience," Benjamin offered.

Sally explained earnestly, "It's not just about having sex. It's about distilling the vast power of your sexual energy and focussing it so that your will can transcend to a higher level of personal achievement. That's why you have to refrain from all other sexual activity, except while you are guided by Cecil. And then it works."

"So, can you all levitate, now that you've... studied with him, how long?"

"Four years," Holly said.

"Almost four," Stuart asserted.

"No, darling, I'm certain—"

"Two."

"Three."

"Six," said Elaine, looking at Holly. Holly looked away.

"How long before you can levitate? And how long does it last?" I imagined it for a moment. Being able to fly. A flying wolf. Ha.

"No," Stuart said. "It doesn't work that way. At the moment of exaltation, you rise up together. But it only works with Cecil."

"So, Cecil can levitate. But you can't?"

"I'm sure I can too," Holly said into the silence, but no one believed her.

"No wonder he wants a powerful demon," I realized.

"We want it for him," Holly said. "Why should you have it? You're just a child, you haven't the slightest idea what it could mean, how it could be used. A great man like Cecil could save the world!"

Already been done.

"It seems to us," Benjamin said, "that such a power loose in the world needs a great man to control it, to bind it, to harness it so that it can do the world some good. Whereas having such a power running loose could be dangerous, especially to you."

"Oh, no!" I said. I lifted my hands. "I feel it coming on! I can't control it!"

"Concentrate on your breathing," Holly cried. "In, in, in, and out, out, whoosh!"

"Picture a line of light, see it distinctly—"

"Close your eyes and imagine you are in a deep forest—"

"Close your second chakra like a fist!"

"Ah! Ah! Ah!" I yelled. I couldn't stand it anymore. I let my wolf head grow above my human head, and I leaped off the couch and ran on two feet around the room. Oliver lifted his glass to me in a toast as I passed, grinning his head off. Holly was up on her chair, Phil pressed himself into the window frame, Sally stared with amazement. Elaine sat back smiling. Benjamin reached out his hand to touch my wolf head. I let the eyes go gold and flare, and he backed off. I reached for the fury that lived in a knot above my heart, and it was there. I released it, and grew as I changed. The room was suddenly quite small. I took a turn around on four feet, making sure to knock over anyone who was standing. Oliver dodged my head, and I let him, because there was peace between us now. When I'd gotten my fill of their amazement and terror, I let go of my anger and got smaller. I tore around one more time and then got up on the couch where Holly had first offered me a seat. I started to sit down as a wolf, and finished as a human. Damn! One of the boots was gone. Well, at least Oliver's white scarf was still around my neck. Maybe it was static cling.

"Now, I will give you a class of my own. As for what it will cost you, I haven't decided yet." I surveyed them where they sat, pressed back into the furniture, or against the wall. I certainly had everyone's undivided attention. It felt good. "I am not possessed, or controlled, by a demon. I am a daughter of the wolf kind. And we change form at will. As for your Tantric meditation, you all seem to go in for a lot of extra workouts, from what I gathered. Jeeves, over there, had a practice session on the beach early this morning, and another one in the left hand guest room at the top of the stairs, just before lunch. And as for yesterday…" I looked pointedly at Holly, whose eyes were wide with fury. Within them gleamed something else.

Phil stared at me, his mouth gaping. Holly's head whipped round on him, glaring. All other eyes turned to him, taking in his amazement and guilt.

"Why, you bad boy," Oliver had moved in to lean against the wall by the door.

"Oh, Phil, how could you!" Holly shrieked.

I looked over at Oliver, and everyone followed my glance in fascination and terror. Oliver smiled, and raised his glass to me. "Cecil and me. In the hot tub. The last night before he embarked. We made quite a splash." His eyes gleamed.

I raised my brows. He raised his back at me. I left it at that. It had been Phil with him in the hot tub, just a few days ago. But I kept the truce.

"But that's—Cecil wouldn't—" Stuart protested.

"And as for your vegan diet," I said to Stuart, who turned to me like someone just glimpsing a tree about to fall on him, "that bacon sandwich you had this morning is probably not on the list of pure, healthy foods."

"No—turkey bacon!" he croaked.

"Nah," I said. "It was pork. And so was the chili verde you had for dinner last night."

"Stuart! No!" Holly's hand raised to her lips in horror.

Benjamin was laughing.

"And as for you," I said to him—

"No, no, don't spoil it," he raised his hands.

"No?" I asked, my eyes glinting.

"I'll confess," he smiled ruefully. He looked around at the others, who gazed at him with bated breath. "It's the milkshakes. I can't give them up. Or coffee. Or beer. Gotta have them. I'm so sorry."

"Oh, Benjamin!" Holly's hand came away from her mouth. "I thought you were so advanced!"

He shook his head, smiling.

"And," I turned to Holly. Her eyes changed. Something feral gleamed there, something that said to me, "don't you dare!" But I did. "You've been practicing awfully hard too, for Cecil to get back. With Stuart in the bed, with Jeeves on the bench in the garden, and there was another guy, this morning, also in the bed, who smelled of chlorine…"

"No! It's not true! You're lying!"

"I so am not. Just some extra workouts, right? So should I mention the waiter in the rec room?"

"No!" Holly shrieked.

Actually, that one wasn't true. "No, but Cecil and you did some practicing on this couch. Several times."

"Here?" Stuart asked accusingly. "You were with him here? You told me—"

"How do you know it was Cecil?" Benjamin asked, with academic curiosity. "Have you ever met him?"

"I saw him once, at a meeting." I had, at Tamara's. The white scarves were a clue. "But I'm pretty sure he gave her the scarf she's wearing."

"Ah," he said, satisfied.

"Stuart, you have to understand—"

"No, no I don't understand! We had an agreement!"

"We were studying!"

"And as for you," I turned to Sally. Her mouth opened, and her eyes opened, and suddenly she looked very small, waiting for a blow that would knock her down. "Completely vegan diet, month after month, yuck! How can you stand it?" Her mouth relaxed and began to smile. "Does all that great sex you've been having really make up for it?"

Sally gleamed at me for a moment, then glanced around at the others. "I'll have to think about that."

"You! Get out of my house! Now! Now! Now!" Holly shrieked.

I turned to her, and changed, and grew, and lunged. I took her head and shoulders into my jaws and pressed down with my teeth just exactly enough, and let go and changed again before anyone in the room had a chance to react. She was still opening her mouth to scream. I leaned over and spoke in her ear. "Don't touch me again. Ever."

There are lots of ways to bite. They don't all involve drawing blood. I must really be growing up, I thought, from the vantage of my glorious new height of five foot almost one inch.

And then she did scream.

CHAPTER FIFTEEN

Holly's screams followed Elaine and me down the stairs and out of the house. They wafted us across the bridges, along the gravel to the four-car garage, where Elaine retrieved my wallet from the glove compartment of the dark green Porsche, whose keys Holly had thrown at her, "Take the damn thing, you sickening horrible bitch!" followed by another scream, "Don't scratch the paint or I will fucking kill you!" And hey, the clothes I'd been wearing when they caught me lay in a wad in the passenger foot well, together with—hooray!—my tennis shoes. And all this would have gone much faster if we didn't have to keep stopping while Elaine leaned on the wall or another piece of furniture or a fence post and howled with laughter, again.

Sally drifted out with us, wearing a smile of peace and satisfaction. It must have been the meditation.

By the time we got back to my car—and there was no one to bring it to us by this time—Elaine's laughter had subsided to occasional gurgles that bubbled up, with gasping reminders about the look on Holly's face, or had we seen the spittle in the corner of her mouth, or the way Stuart had looked at her. Elaine leaned over the hood of my car for one last howl. Then she straightened.

"Oh, god, that was the best party I've ever been to."

"Yup," Sally agreed.

"Listen," Elaine said to me, "I am going to take you out for the best dinner we can find. And there's going to be a whole lot of meat in it."

"Can I come?" asked Sally.

"How about me?" Benjamin came crunching across the gravel in the twilight toward his car, parked nearby next to Sally's. "I'd love a good dinner. With lots of meat. And a chocolate milkshake."

"Sure!" said Elaine. She directed me back to Calabasas, and led the caravan of three cars to a steak house. And there was a whole lot of meat, and laughter, and milkshakes all round, and together we made a much better party than the one earlier.

I dropped Elaine off at her place and headed back across the great city toward Whittier. She still hadn't forgiven me for her truck, but that was all right, since it wasn't back from the shop yet. The not-so-evil vet and I parted on fair terms. It had been a really good dinner.

Traffic was light for a Saturday night. I hit a slow-down on the 101 near the city center. Some event breaking up and everybody heading home. My arms and body throbbed from the beating I'd taken. Now that the party was over, now that dinner was done, all I wanted was to curl up in bed until I stopped hurting.

When I got to Whittier, heading down Greenleaf for my turn onto Philadelphia, the downtown seemed more lively than usual, so I continued down the street, looking for what was going on. The club on the corner in the building that used to be a bank had a line around the block—the Whittier College students had to have something to do on the weekend. The cinema down the street was letting out its last show of the night, and a couple of the coffee shops were open, but the real noise and energy came from further along the street, on the other side.

The Amadeus Music Store's sign was lit, people crowded the sidewalk outside, and through the windows churning bodies bobbed to the sound of drums and fiddle playing. I found a parking spot around the corner and made my way back. Yvette was dancing to the sound of her own drumming, with half a dozen fellow drummers from the Wicca group, in counterpoint with a clutch of solemn young fiddlers, beating out a tide of joy to fill the room and spill out down the sidewalk. I got it, finally. This was the store's official opening day, and Yvette had organized a proper celebration. I went to stand by Yvette, and she nodded to me, without missing a beat.

"Hey," she shouted. "Nice outfit!"

"Guess what?" I yelled back, "I'm taller! I've grown! Almost an inch!'"

She nodded to me, smiling. She hadn't heard a word I said. And it wouldn't mean anything to her; Yvette was tall as a mountain, maybe almost five ten. Well, I was probably going to grow even more. I wasn't done yet.

I found Ariadne in the midst of a crowd of well-wishing guests and future customers. She wore a long black gown and glittering silver earrings, with her hair hanging loose down her back. One of the counters offered an array of snacks, and another offered drinks. I grabbed one of each and wormed my way in to greet my boss.

"I got my wallet!" I announced to her over the din. "I can fill out the application now!"

She nodded and leaned closer, so she wouldn't have to shout. "You're hired. Start tomorrow. Eight-thirty."

"Thanks!"

"And Amber—"

"Yeah?"

She nodded at my clothes. "Nice look. Keep it up, when you're working in my store."

I could see that my days of dressing without looking at what I pulled out of the closet were about over.

I saw Jason in the doorway to the back room and headed that way. I thought if that's where the bears were, there must be better food back there, but I was mistaken. Tamara and the sorceress, head of the local Wicca group, were making signs over the back door with candles, incense, and salt. Well, that made sense. If Tamara was coming here to do a working, it would be only courtesy to contact the local sorceress. To get her to help was even better.

Jason and Jonathan stood watching. I waited until the two women of power finished what they were doing before going to greet them.

Jason took my shoulder and stared down into my face. "What happened to you, girl? You been in a fight?"

"You might say that."

"You win?" Jonathan asked.

I grinned at him, showing my many white teeth.

"That's good."

"All right, then," Jason said, nodding, and let me go.

"Yvette arrange for this party?"

"How did you know?"

"The drumming pretty much gives it away."

"She told me about Ariadne opening today," Jason said, "and I told Tamara that this shop had no wards, and Tamara said she'd come and see to it, and we brought some friends, like, to help with the buzz." He raised his arms and pointed one toe.

Jonathan bent down and pointed, and raised one huge leg behind him. "The groove!"

Jason twirled. "The atmosphere!"

Jonathan turned the other way, stamping his feet. "The beat!"

They both raised their arms and posed, big finish. If you have never seen bears dance, it is a sight to behold.

"The magic is definitely working," I pronounced, and they both laughed, deep and loud.

"Looks like the ladies are finishing up," Jonathan observed.

Jason agreed. "Shall we—?"

"Check on the supplies again?"

And the bears headed out to the food tables, clearing the way before them like a pair of tankers at a small boat regatta.

Tamara came over to me and examined my face, frowning. She raised her hand over my forehead, and held it there, not touching me. "What trouble have you found now, child?"

"It was a trap," I told her. My head felt better, the ache lifted a little. It clouded again when she dropped her hand, but I still didn't hurt quite so much.

"You're all right?"

"I'll be fine. Nothing damaged." I couldn't help it; I added, "You should see the other guy!"

Tamara was not amused.

"You were right," I told her. "I was wrong. I'm going to have to raise my demon. In public, in front of everyone, so everyone can see him and talk to him. This has got to end. I keep being attacked, kidnapped, seized on for no reason. People are making stuff up about me out of their heads. And a whole lot of people are wasting a whole lot of time and energy fighting a fight that is over, and has been done with since the last earthquake. Did you know that Cecil, the Tantric Meditation teacher, is out on a boat trying to commune the World Snake?"

A burst of laughter greeted this news. The sorceress had finished sprinkling salt along the windowsill and came up behind us. "Oh, funny," she said. "He gets seasick, you know."

"He's been out there for weeks," I told her. I looked at her speculatively, wondering if she had ever, ah, studied with Cecil.

"Yes," she agreed, still chuckling. "And he will stay out there until he knows the danger is past. Our Cecil doesn't take any chances with his current incarnation. He's having too much fun."

"He's having too much sex," I murmured.

"That too," the sorceress agreed. She must have read my thoughts. She was a sorceress, after all. "Oh, not me," she said. "I never needed anyone to help me fly."

"I see you two have met," Tamara observed. I was still staring at the sorceress, wondering if she meant what I thought she just said. Wondering, too, if she would give lessons. A flying wolf would be so cool.

"We have," I nodded.

"But—" the sorceress added, "I don't know your name."

"And I don't know yours. I'm called Amber, here."

She bowed. "Well met, Amber. I am called Fireheart."

"Lady Fireheart," I nodded.

"I hear you found your demon boy."

"I found him. I let him go." I turned to Madam Tamara. "Do you still want me to call him publicly?"

Tamara nodded gravely. "I think you must."

"So do I," I admitted. "Everyone has got to finally figure out that it is over. The World Snake isn't coming, and Richard isn't mine anymore. And then everyone can damn well leave me alone!"

Lady Fireheart raised her brows. "Still trouble over the demon. Much as it grieves me to say it—"

"Yes. You told me so. But if it weren't for him, we'd be snake food by now, so it's a good thing I didn't listen to you."

"You said it was dangerous," Tamara reminded me.

"It is dangerous. And I don't know if it will work. I did dismiss him, I don't know if he will answer me anymore. But if he does come, and he can convince people, it will be worth it to try."

"Then we will see you Monday night," she nodded.

"I'll be there."

"Wow," said Lady Fireheart. "This I must see."

Tamara reminded me, "Everyone who comes will see how you do it."

I met her eyes. "Yes," I said. "That, too."

The wards were not quite working, or they weren't set up soon enough, because the police came before too long and broke up the party because it was spilling onto the sidewalk and people with drinks in their hands were dancing in the public thruway. Ariadne thanked them politely, apologized gracefully, and gave them food, but not drink. The drummers finished their last stomp while she did this, and the party broke up.

Yvette went off with Jason, and I drove home. Climbing the steps to my apartment door I realized all at once how tired I was. I ached in places I didn't remember being hit. Once inside, where there was no one to see, I pulled off my clothes and made my way to the bathroom. I turned on the taps and drew a deep, hot bath, and sank into the water. I traced the lumps and lacerations on my arms, the white stripes edged with pink where the bruises went so deep, it would be days before they colored up. My bruises hurt all the way to the bone, where they throbbed in time with my heart beat.

I remembered Finley, beating on me. I remembered backing up, blocking his blows. I remembered thinking that he didn't hit as hard as he used to, that maybe he was going easy on me, taking his time. And I realized again, as I'd realized it then, that he didn't have it anymore. He couldn't beat me. I had beaten him. If the evil vet hadn't shot him, I could have killed him myself. And now he was on his way to Albuquerque. I sank under the water, eyes open, and softly sang my victory song.

CHAPTER SIXTEEN

I drove down to Garden Grove the next Monday night, with a shopping bag of paraphernalia for the public raising of my demon, and Yvette in the passenger seat. Yvette said she wasn't going to miss this for anything, but probably she was coming because Jason would be there. Garden Grove is about ten minutes north of Costa Mesa, and forty minutes south of Whittier; not what I'd call half way. But Tamara had chosen the ground for this event with care.

One of Tamara's friends had the keys to an outdoor amphitheatre, and this had been determined to be the best possible space to do the raising. First, because it was outdoors and not indoors, thus preventing the possible destruction of a perfectly good building. Second, because the amphitheatre, though outdoors, could be closed against any uninvited observers. And because it had comfortable seats and accessible parking. But mostly because Tamara's friend was giving her the use of it for free, for the evening.

My bruises had stiffened up so that when I woke the previous day, it was an hour before I could raise my arms as high as my head. I was better today, though still sore. The bruises on my arms and body had begun to come up in all shades of red and purple. In another day or two, they'd be glorious.

I'd been told to come to the amphitheatre at eight, when the sun was just setting, but the parking lot held about twenty cars when we drove in. An old guy with a down-turned mouth and puffy, shoulder-length gray hair, bald on top, wearing a suit he'd had for many years, stood nodding at us by a locked gate leading into the Festival Amphitheatre.

He started talking as soon as we came in range, while he unlocked the gate with one of his many keys, let us in, and locked it behind us again, and then escorted us along a passageway until we emerged in the amphitheater. He told us that the theater was dark, but that wasn't true. The sun hadn't set yet, and besides, half a dozen really bright lights shone on the huge concrete half-hexagon that was the stage. The red folding seats rose up for dozens of steps on three sides to the high wall behind them. The middle section was divided from the two small side sections by a pair of aisles. Most of the people who'd come to watch had found seats in the center.

As I came into the amphitheater it became clear why everyone else had gotten there early, or I'd been told to come later. A dozen different wards had been laid in the theater in the last few hours, some set to protect the people in the audience, some to isolate the stage, and anything that was on it. Which was going to include me, thank you very much.

The theater itself had been in use for decades, and the tangle of energy that had been raised there, over and over, in one performance after another, lay like dormant fretwork in the air. Tonight's workings had been woven into it, so they stood out strongly and were easy to sense.

Yvette broke away from me and climbed up the steps to the top row, where the four bears sat together, looking down on the rest of the audience. No surprise, they'd brought a picnic, and handed Yvette a bottle and a sandwich even before she finished hugging them. She sat down next to Jason.

My guide with the keys brought me to Tamara, who sat in the prime seats, four steps up so that she was just a little higher than the stage, and in the center. She wore her ritual clothes, her deep blue gown and robe of stars. Her turban tonight was black and purple and jewels gleamed blue and silver in her hair. Her eyes were distant, still tranced from the powers she had been raising. She nodded to me. "Wolf child."

"Madam Tamara," I nodded back.

"Are you ready?"

"Are you?" I asked.

She smiled slightly, acknowledging the edge in my question. "It was necessary. It will keep people from panicking."

"Do you think it's enough?"

"How strong is your demon?"

"I guess that's what we're going to see."

I went down the steps, hopped up on the stage and turned around to view the audience. Some of them clapped. They stopped when I looked at them. It seemed as though all of them had brought food and drink. I guess they were expecting quite a party. And I would bring the entertainment.

I nodded to them, and some of them clapped again. I'd seen most of these folks before. A half-dozen Goth kids in black magician robes occupied the first row of seats at my feet. Each held a wand in one hand, and passed bags of chips with the other. At least they weren't wearing the pointy hats with the stars on them. In the next row three people sat as far apart from one another, and the rest of the crowd, as they could get, like touchy wizards choosing distant territories. The two women, one sylph-like, wrapped in ceremonial clothes from her head to her slippered feet, and the big woman with the round face in a medieval cloak with the hood pulled up, I hadn't seen before. The heavy-set guy to my left wearing glasses, with straight black hair and a sheathed sword resting on his knees, I'd seen once before at Tamara's.

Tamara's friends grouped around her seat in the middle like a star cluster, passing each other food from baskets and a hamper, leaning over to whisper or make comments. Van sat beside Tamara. On her other side, the sister of Tamara's soul, Kat McBride, held her singing bowl on her lap. The guy from the theater with the keys sat in a seat by himself above the little group, in a proprietary way, looking around at the other folks as though keeping an eye on them on behalf of the Festival Amphitheatre.

Three of the Thunder Mountain Boys sat with Marlin along the aisles about halfway up. I nodded to them, and they nodded warily back. Oliver was not among them. Marlin gazed around the place indifferently. He'd had a run-in with the Eater of Souls not long ago, and hadn't been the same since. The Boys had probably brought him under the mistaken impression that Richard had something to do with it, and could put him back the way he was. As if he would.

I recognized Lady Fireheart, and some of the women from her Wicca group wearing their ceremonial robes, seated together high in the middle seats on the left. I nodded to her, and she nodded regally back. A scattering of other power raisers, in small groups or alone, dotted the back seats, but everyone had left a big circle of empty seats around the bears. And so it should be.

"I am going to call the demon that was once in my service," I began, without preamble. It's not like I needed an introduction, after all. They all knew why we were here. But I did need to make a few things absolutely clear. I didn't raise my voice very much, but it was an amphitheater, so I didn't have to. The tension in the theater rose as I started speaking. The attention of the power raisers, focused on me by people for whom concentration was an art form, set the residual energy of the place into a spin. I felt the gyre rising clockwise above me, slowly lifting out of the bowl of the theater.

"I am doing this," I continued, "because a lot of people in this city don't believe a couple of things that are true. One. The World Snake is not coming anymore." I felt the audience's reaction to my pronouncing the name in this place of power, a frisson in the air. Some of them jerked back. Idiots. I'd just said she wasn't coming. Calling her name wasn't going to make her come after all. "She has turned," I told them, in case they weren't listening. "She is not going to swallow Los Angeles, and she will not consume the cities of men again." Some of them looked at each other. They still didn't believe me. I felt the anger rise, where it sits above my heart. They had forced me to do this. And I did not want to do this. And by the gods, if my demon showed up, they were going to know why. The energy of the place was working on me too.

I went on, my voice rising. "My demon did this at my command when he was in my service. And in return for this great work that he did for me, and for all of us, I dismissed him, and gave him his freedom.

"But some people in this city are under the impression that he still belongs to me. He doesn't. Just as some people still don't believe that the World Snake—the World Snake—really isn't coming. This needs to end. So, Madam Tamara told me if I call the demon one more time, and let him explain to you what he did, then everyone will be on the same page. He's free of this world, and we're free of the Great Snake. All right?"

I looked around in the fading daylight. The bright lights gleamed from above, making pools of sharp light on the stage, but I could still see the folks in the seats, staring at me. Some of them were nodding. Some of them spoke aside to one another.

"You are going to see me call the demon. Before I do this, I must have your word, your solemn oath, on whatever you hold sacred, that you will never call the demon for yourself. You will not attempt to command him, or take his freedom, or bring him into your own service. I will continue when everyone everyone here—" my eyes gleaming yellow, I raked them all "—has sworn."

I sat down on the edge of the stage. I folded my arms. Tamara got up from her seat. She went from group to group, person to person, and spoke to each of them. The light faded from the sky. In the peaceful twilight, crickets began to call.

The stabbing bright lights seemed to grow stronger, but it was just the contrast of nightfall. Moths danced in the spears of light, seeking the source. At last Tamara came down the steps toward me. She nodded to me, almost a bow, and took her seat again.

I got to my feet. The air seemed to tighten, but it was just the energy of everyone's attention gathering in anticipation, because I was going to call the demon. One of the Goth kids up front stood up. He was holding his phone up, using it as a camera. Well, that was all right. He'd get the preliminary stuff I did, but as soon as I did the summoning, something would happen. You can't film a working. I looked up and saw that, nonetheless, a couple of other people in the seats were planning to try.

I opened my bag of stuff. I dug out a big fat piece of chalk, and drew a circle on the concrete stage, as round as I could get it at that scale, a little wider than my reach. Then I drew an even wider circle around it, with about four feet between the two. I felt the audience's prick of interest at that; that wasn't how it's done. But this is what we'd worked out, Richard and I.

I was about to lose a bet. We'd been walking back up the hill toward my place, after dinner, not long before the end of his time with me, when Richard said to me, "You aren't going to be able to let me go."

"Watch me," I'd replied. I thought he meant I wasn't going to keep my word. It made me angry, because I didn't want to. I didn't want to lose him, I wanted our love, our companionship, to go on like this forever, when I knew that four days from now he would be gone forever, and I had made it happen. I had set him free.

I climbed the hill as though charging an army. Richard kept pace. He always kept pace. "I mean," he said quietly, "you will still know my name. And as long as you know my name, you will always possess me. Whether you call me or not, I am still yours to command."

I stopped and turned to him. His pale hair gleamed in the reflected light from the streetlamp up the road, but his face was in shadow, and his eyes were dark. "I know," I said. "I was planning to forget it."

"Oh." He didn't move. After a moment he added, "Do you think that will work?"

"No," I admitted. I started toward my place again, and then stopped. "Can you make me forget it?" I turned to him. This time his face was in the light. He nodded once, as though he was afraid to speak. "Then, that's what we'll do." I headed for my steps.

"Amber…"

I turned.

"Do you mean it?"

I came back to him. I took the edges of his worn leather jacket in my hands, and looked up at his face, not much above mine. A stray lock of his hair lay askew on his brow. I breathed in his scent, better than Christmas, and leaned up and kissed him on the lips. "When you go," I said, "take your name with you. Right out of my head. Gone."

In his eyes, hope flamed, like a glimpse of heaven. He closed them, leaned forward and gently kissed my forehead. "It shall be as you say." He held me close then, and before he let me go he said softly in my ear, "We'll think of another name, that you can call me by."

"Why?" I straightened.

"Just in case."

"In case of what?"

"In case you need me. Just once."

We climbed the steps together. "How about DeNinny?" I suggested.

Richard aimed a punch at my head, and I ducked away, laughing.

Now, on the stage of the Festival Amphitheatre, I drew a pentagram centered in the inside circle, whose five points touched, but did not cross, the second, outer circle. When I had done this, I got out a box of cornmeal, and poured it in a circle around the center of the pentagram. I heard whispers in the audience. I hoped they were all taking notes.

Next, I got out my packs of candles, and the new set of little glass bowls I'd bought. I set a candle in a glass bowl at each point of the pentagram. Then I got out the small, colored chalk, and drew signs on either side of each point. There are runes of protection, deflection, guard and ward, but I don't know them. I know a few signs that my kind use, so I drew the ones that said Safety, Friendship, Welcome, Good Food, Health, and Fair Dealing. I drew Watch Out for Traps a few extra times. If anyone in the audience knew the signs, they could figure out for themselves what they meant in this context. What they actually meant was that raising the demon needed to look complicated, it needed to look like an art that I had mastered with great effort and endless diligence. The fact was, this was all just distraction. When I knew the demon's name, I could summon him by pronouncing it correctly, and he was compelled to come by the last breath of the last syllable. But most of my audience probably didn't know that, and if they did, it was better to confuse the issue for them. In any case, I no longer knew the demon's name. I was relying on the good will of a being that no longer actually existed in the form I had known. I hoped that the demon I was about to call would keep the bargain I had made with Richard, who was only a tiny construct of itself.

And then I did a few things just so that, if anyone else tried this, they'd look as silly as I did. I lit the candles. I got out a silver bell, and a golden whistle. It was brass, really, and I'd borrowed it from the music store, but it looked golden, and that was good enough. I walked around the outer ring of the circle, intoning nonsense syllables under my breath. Every five steps I stopped, held up the bell, rang it, and blew a blast on the whistle. I repeated this until I'd gone all the way around the circle. Then, I pocketed the instruments and stepped between the two circles. I raised my arms, intoning some more nonsense words. I turned in a circle, and clapped my hands three times. And then, in a clear voice, I pronounced the name that Richard and I had agreed on.

"Bellsandahisnlianamene!" I clapped three times. I turned around again. I raised my voice. "Bellsandahisnlianamene!" Not a word you'd ever say by accident, under any circumstances. I clapped, turned, wove a weird pattern in the air with my hands, turned, and clapped again. Who said this couldn't be fun? I raised my voice once more. "Come to me! I summon you! Bellsandahisnlianamene!"

Silence. The people in the audience behind me seemed not to breathe. Then, just as a tiny, impatient rustle began among them, the air in the theater tightened. The space in the center of the pentagram darkened. Again I heard the audience breathe, this time in gasps. The darkness within the pentagram thickened, as though a different kind of density erupted there. Behind me, I heard exclamations, and a few swear words. The darkness took on shape, and then it took on size. The hair on my nape rose. The air tingled with energy. My eyes tried to figure out the shape of the darkness, even as it kept changing, even as my stomach tightened and my heart began to race. I'd seen that darkness within darkness before, and I knew to be afraid.

I stood between one circle and the other, not in the demon's part, nor outside the circles, where the watchers sat. We'd agreed on that, too. I could hear a wind blowing. The candles at the points of the pentagram burned steadily, as though nothing touched them. But the lights above and behind me in the amphitheater danced, bouncing on the cable that held them, and the shadows trembled, but where I stood, there was no wind.

We hadn't agreed that the demon wouldn't eat me. We hadn't agreed that it wouldn't turn me inside out for the fun of seeing all the living colors blend. I hoped that my surviving this was implicit in our understanding. At that moment, I wished we'd talked about this just a little more.

And then the demon was there. He was enormous. It was impossible that he fit in the space defined by the center of the pentagram, but he was there, he didn't cross those lines, and yet I could see that he was huge. I felt his will, his power, as my mind was drawn in to the layers of darkness that seethed, that emerged, fell away, and erupted again, as though another universe lay open before me, and I had only to step in to understand it all. I felt my panic rise, as every hair on my body stood on end and signaled that I should run, run now, run very fast away. I stiffened with fear, I let my panic show, because this, too, was for my audience.

Just when I thought he could grow no larger or he would somehow collapse the tiny space I stood in, and the whole theater, and perhaps the city as well upon himself, the form coalesced, and seemed to kneel before me.

"YOU SUMMONED ME!"

He roared, and the sound seemed to come as much from inside my head as from the being before me. It reverberated in the air as though sound itself could hold a shape in the darkness, drawing meaning and form out of my mind, and it was angry. Panic rose in my body. I braced myself against the assault of sound and fury, and held my ground.

"Yes—"

"YOU SWORE YOU WOULD NOT!"

"I did, but—"

The shape that whirled within the darkness within darkness, emanating from a deeper darkness beyond, coalesced into a form that seemed to suggest a head, which bent in my direction, the eyes flaring like distant red suns in the grip of a massive solar storm, his face in a rictus of fury.

"YOU GAVE ME YOUR WORD! YOU SAID I WAS FREE!"

I bent backwards, aware of the edges of the circles I stood between, knowing that it would be better not to find out what would happen if I was forced over either of the concentric lines. I looked him in the eyes, holding myself up even though my legs, like my voice, were shaking. "I did give you my word. You are free," I managed to pronounce, just as the face coalesced for a brief moment in front of me, and one suggested eyelid dipped in a wink, and the eye flared a heavenly, remembered blue. I held on to my fear so that my overwhelming relief would not show, as the pandemonium of sound mounted, and the figure rose like a towering storm above me.

"THEN WHY AM I HERE?" it demanded, and the concrete floor beneath me, and the walls of the theater trembled in the torrent of sound.

"Shut up!" I shouted, and my voice broke as I raised it, "and I will tell you!"

A silence, as though the demon was transfixed by my effrontery. Behind me I felt as much as heard the terror, the attention, the heavy breathing of the amazed audience. "Oh, shit," someone said, very softly.

The demon gathered itself in a whirlwind of gyrating darkness, and shaped itself into something suggesting human form, over which was imposed, spinning leisurely, a depthless hole into the darkness. The human form seemed to diminish in size, while the vast dark layers it emanated from grew, pulsing, collapsed, spinning, and grew again.

"SPEAK!"

"All right. These power raisers of this great city—"

"PAH!"

For a thing that didn't, couldn't, spit, it sure could make the sound.

"Stop that!" The form stilled itself. "The power raisers of greater Los Angeles want to know from you what you did about the World Snake. They're still worried that it might come here and destroy the city." I glanced back as I said this, and caught a satisfying glimpse of the whole audience pressed back in their seats, agape, figuratively if not literally, at the stage. The wind might not be blowing where I stood, but it sure was blowing them around. So much for their wards. Ha. At the top of the theater, all four bears were on their feet, in their bear forms, braced against the gale. Yvette knelt between the legs of one of them, holding on to the back of the seat in front of her.

The darkness whirled again. I seemed to be staring out into layers of reality, a being of darkness, a greater, denser being of layers of darkness, a mouth of deeper darkness from which all of this emanated, and a view as wide as a new, lightless universe, all impressed itself upon my sight at once, dizzyingly. But more than that, the sense of the being's consciousness, the power of its will, was like being pressed by huge stones.

"I DID AS YOU COMMANDED. I TURNED THE WORLD SNAKE. I ALTERED ITS PATH SO THAT IT WILL NOT DESTROY A HUMAN CITY IN ANY TIME TO COME. I DID THIS, AND YOU SET ME FREE."

"Yes," I said. "I know. But they don't believe me."

And now the shapes all exploded outwards, and the demon's wrath blasted out in a storm of force, that flayed senses I didn't know I had. "BELIEVE!" a wind of other worlds screamed. "BELIEVE!" And now I felt the wind, I felt the cyclone erupt in the amphitheater. The demon's face rose huge, its eyes red, its jaws wide. "OR SHALL I BRING ALL NON-BELIEVERS TO THE PATH OF THE GREAT SNAKE, SO YOU CAN MARK IT FOR YOURSELVES FOR THE NEXT SEVERAL EONS?"

Silence. With a huge effort, I turned again to look at the audience. They were shrunken, clinging to their seats, their hair and robes flung every which way. Food and wrappers, cloths and utensils flew through the air and piled up against the walls of the theater. Above the amphitheater, the structure that held the lighting cables rocked ominously. The Goth kid with the camera lay on the ground by his seat. The other Goth kids were piled up, clutching each other. Tamara sat straight, but held her hands together very hard. She looked grave. She also looked angry. Kat McBride clutched her broken singing bowl with tears tracking her face.

"Anyone still not believe me?" I asked. Silence. I waited, just to be sure. "Anyone at all?" No one spoke, and no one moved. "All right then."

I turned back to the demon. Only he could see me grin. "Bellsandahisnlianamene, I thank you. You are no longer in my service. I swear, by my name, never to call upon you again. You are free to go."

"MISTRESS," the voice hissed, like the roar of the sea, like the distant sound of cannons, like the susurration of wind, all at once, "I HEAR YOU." Then the voice rose like a siren, as though a million voices in a million paths of air spoke the words, "AND I WILL HOLD YOU TO YOUR WORD."

And at the last sound of the last syllable, he was gone. I almost staggered in the vacuum of sound and form he left. The absence of noise rang in my ears. The stillness in the theater was like a death.

And that was it, then. It was over. I would never see him, in any of his forms, again. I stood there for a moment, staring at the place where something, at any rate, had been. And then I remembered to breathe again.

I turned and brushed at the chalk of the outer circle with my foot, and stepped out of the circle. The audience still sat there, though the bears had changed back to their forms as men. Yvette was holding hard to Jason. I didn't blame her.

I took another deep breath. "Any questions? Anyone think the World Snake is still coming? Anyone not believe me now?"

I saw some people shake their heads. The Goths at my feet got up, several of them still clutching each other. The one on the ground got up, holding his phone. He poked some buttons, shook it, poked at it some more. Ha. I was as sure as I could be that this working was not going to be the one that made it onto film.

Madam Tamara stood. Somehow, she had straightened her clothing and her turban, and looked as grand and impressive as ever. She pitched her voice so that everyone could hear it, and it did not tremble. "Thank you. That was certainly most impressive."

Kat McBride piled the pieces of her shattered bowl together, and fit them into her cloth bag. She stood up next to Tamara and wiped her tears with her sleeve. "I heard only truth. Did anyone else hear otherwise?"

The audience made very little response. It was as though they were all recovering from a storm, one that had blown them from the inside as well as from without. And I knew exactly how they felt. Not much like discussing the phenomenon, for one thing.

People got to their feet, smoothed their hair, re-draped their clothing, and then clambered around the theater gathering their scattered belongings and the debris from their suppers. Then they climbed down the steps of the aisles toward the exit. The Goth kids were among the first to leave. The Thunder Mountain Boys escorted Marlin away gently in their midst. Tamara's friend with the keys of the theater finished supervising the picking up of all the litter, and climbed down to the floor of the amphitheater. His hair was puffed and tangled by the wind, though he didn't seem to have noticed. He walked over to the stage and glared across it. "Are those marks going to come out?"

I'd blown out the candles and gathered them up with the bowls. The theater guy brought me a bucket of water and a mop, and I slopped over the circles and the pentagram, and scattered the cornmeal until nothing was left while he watched, stalking the stage as I worked. When I was finished I passed the mop and bucket back to him, and he took them away.

Tamara stood on the theater floor in front of the stage, talking to some of the power raisers, while others threaded past them toward the exit. The guy with the sword stopped, caught my eye, drew his sword, and lifted it in salute. I nodded to him. He nodded back, sheathed the sword and headed out.

Tamara turned to me. "Thank you. We are finished here. That was a very convincing demonstration."

"So, you think that will do it?"

"I think—"

But I never found out what she was going to say. A scream erupted outside the theater, in the direction of the parking lot, followed by a number of rising shrieks, and we all charged out there to find out what the hell had happened. I knew, though. In fact, it was part of the plan.

I'd bet myself that the Thunder Mountain Boys would be the ones to do it, but my second guess would have been one of the Goth kids, and in fact, it was. The four remaining wand-wavers stood by a blackened hole in the pavement, three of them still shrieking, one lying down at the edge of the hole, trying to get up the nerve to reach inside. One of the bears got to her first and hauled her up away from there.

The yelling and demands and the attempted explanations, all drowning each other out, came to a stop when Tamara's voice cut across the noise.

"What have you done, you stupid children?"

The kid with the camera told her, "It was Keith. He said the name. That's all he did. He was making a joke about remembering it, and he said it—"

"You dared him!" the Goth girl who'd been on the ground screamed at him, right from the edge of hysteria. Her long hair had been dyed silver, and tied up in little braids adorned with stars. Her make-up was smudged. "I heard what you said, Joel! You dared him to say the name out loud, and you made fun of him that he couldn't remember it! But then he did!"

"No I did not!" the Goth boy choked out, but his voice was shaking.

The three other Goth kids stepped away from him, looking down on him. The silver girl, breathing hard, pointed her wand at him. "You did. I never want to see you again."

"That's not what happened!" Joel cried.

"What did happen?" Tamara asked.

The other Goth girl wore a coronet beaded with tiny skulls under the hood of her black mantle. Her fingernails were very long and black. "They were walking ahead of us, and they were joking and everything. And I heard Joel dare Keith to say the demon's name. And Joel said Keith couldn't remember it, and Keith said he could, and then Keith said it."

"And there was a crack—" Silver Goth girl took up the story.

"And there was a roar—"

"The ground exploded," Joel said. "Right next to me. And Keith was there, right beside me, and then he was gone, and now…" He turned and gazed down at the hole. "He's gone." He gazed at the other Goth kids. "I didn't do it! I didn't do anything! I don't know what happened to Keith but—" He spied me, standing beyond Tamara. "It's her fault! She brought the demon here! She knew he'd have to be fed."

One of the bears—I saw it was Jonathan—went over to loom above the Goth kids. His voice was so low it rumbled. "Don't be a fool. You did it yourselves. Your friend summoned a powerful demon without taking the slightest precautions."

"We're still at the theater! You warded the theater, I saw you!" Joel accused Tamara.

Jason came up then and joined Jonathan. "You can't ward against stupidity," he said. "You want to call the demon and ask for your friend back?"

Tamara turned to me. I shrugged. "I thought it would be one of the Thunder Mountain Boys. Richard had it in for them."

"Yes. Well, it may still be. Only they may be wise enough to wait until they can choose their ground and fortify a circle before they call the name."

I shrugged again. I could hope. Because I'd made sure they had the wrong name, they would invite the demon in, but then have no more control over him than their wards could give. And the best wards that Tamara and her friends together could produce hadn't kept out the storm.

Tamara turned back to the Goth kids. "You were told of the dangers. You agreed that you understood them before you were let inside. You each one gave your oath not to do what one of you has done. Go home. Put away your toys. Learn some wisdom. If you can."

I thought I would do the same. Yvette went off with Jason in Tamara's friends' car. I got in my Honda Civic and drove home through the deepening night alone. Road work on the 405 brought traffic down to a crawl for a short time. As I passed the scorching bright lights illuminating the guys and equipment tearing up the highway, I wondered what would happen if I called that name again now. Would there be an explosion, and a big black hole in the road? And what would be the explanation? But I kept my word. I did not even think the name.

When I turned up the alley to pull into the carport behind my apartment building, my headlights swept the steps leading to my apartment, and I saw him standing there. My heart clenched. I felt breathless with hope, and at the same time, stiff with fury. If that imposter had come to my place again then he was going to die tonight.

I parked my car and walked around to my steps, the bag of stuff banging against my leg in my hurry. I stopped when I saw him. It's never quite dark on my street, but the moon was behind me, and I could see his face, his form, his boots, his old black leather jacket. He tipped his head at me, smiling a little, and his eyes gleamed. I began to smile. I opened my mouth, and it was there. The scent of him, clean and new, the spice of his sweat like an aftertaste, and the musk of his hair.

"Well," he said. "Wasn't that fun?"

"Richard!" I breathed. I ascended the steps, my smile growing, breathing him in. "Did you come to say good bye?"

"We already said good bye." His eyes took me in like a lover's. "I came to say thank you."

"I'm taller," I told him. I was grinning like a fool.

"I'm sure you are."

I laughed then, and hugged him, and he kissed me, and both our scents changed, and I took him inside.

CHAPTER SEVENTEEN

My lover was enslaved for four hundred years to a succession of human masters, and sex was one of his best weapons to control the conditions of his servitude. So my lover is patient, and he is thorough. Since he was raised by the magician John Dee, who specified his looks point by point to a demon who was required to obey him, my lover is beautiful, from the shape of his toes, to the muscles of his thighs, the planes of his belly, the bones of his chest. His fingers are long, his face as fine and fair as a Greek hero, his skin smooth and pale.

When I first knew him, he smelled of fear. He played me the way a slave must always play its master, to get the best deal for himself. Now he smelled of himself, and sex, and joy, and his eyes lit with the pleasure of it.

I put away my memory of the towering being of darkness and power I had raised on the stage in Garden Grove, because Richard was back, of his own accord, and what I could see and touch and taste, I loved.

When I lay spent, adrift in delight, my head on his chest, his arms loose on my back, I asked him, "Why did you come back?"

I felt his smile as his hand lightly moved along my spine. "You can't tell me now that you aren't pleased to see me."

"Of course not." I brushed my fingers down his belly, to the hair on his groin, and stroked him there softly, just so that his scent would change again. "But I wasn't going to see you again. You said so."

"Yes," he said. "Stop that, or stop talking."

"Mm," I said. "I'm listening."

And then there was some laughing and some wrestling, and I let him win.

"Time is different there," he told me, when we lay relaxed again. He lay holding me against him, both of us lying on our sides. Richard spoke softly, almost into my ear. "And so is form, and senses don't precisely translate. I looked back on a wearying and miserable interlude on this plane, in this form, and a few things stood out. Here, and in this form, I can touch you." He kissed my shoulder and his arms tightened around me.

"What's it like? Where you come from?"

He breathed out, considering. "It is a universe as infinite as yours, where I am the darkness, the wind, and the stones, all at once. I can wear it like a cloak, if it pleases me, or reach out to other worlds and enter them like bees, all their minds my own."

I turned around in his arms, so I could see his face. "Can you take me there?"

He smiled. "I could, but then you wouldn't be what you are now. You would be changed, and there would be no returning."

"You came back."

"For the pleasure of it." He bit my nose, gently. "I had to stay nearby for a while anyway, until you called. After this," he lay back, drawing me with him, until my head lay against his shoulder again, "I'm going far away. Ha." He said the words again, as though tasting them. "I am going far away, which is one way to put it. You won't see me again. And so, I came to see you, of my own free will, under no compulsion or geas, but one."

I raised myself up to look at him. "And that is?"

He smiled. "For the joy of it. For the joy of love."

I walked out of my room the next morning, dressed for work in my party clothes, my heart expanding with joy at the smell of the breakfast Richard had cooked. Just like old times. Brief, happy times.

"That's new," he said, looking at my outfit, an admiring glow in his eyes, and I preened. So this was why women buy clothes. Huh.

Over buttery French toast, fresh orange juice, fried eggs and peaches with cream, I got up the nerve to ask him, "How long are you staying?"

He sat down across from me, his plate as laden as mine, and passed me the syrup. "Three days. When you wake up, day after tomorrow, I'll be gone."

"I have to go to work," I said, testing the words, to see if I really did. I'd lost my last job over Richard, and it seemed like a good plan. But I wanted to keep my job at the music store. "My boyfriend's back in town," just wasn't going to cut it, when Ariadne's staff was just me and Yvette.

"I'll bring you lunch," Richard said, "if you show me where it is."

Ariadne's shop was open from nine in the morning until nine at night. I was there from eight-thirty until five, and Yvette came at one, so I could take a lunch break, and then she and I covered the store while Ariadne gave music lessons in the back room, and couldn't be interrupted. I didn't tell Yvette that Richard was back. Yvette had seen Richard briefly a few times at Tamara's, during the two weeks before I'd set him free. Today, Yvette wanted to talk about the cyclone of darkness that spoke both inside her head and out of it, about the smashed picnic basket, and the beer cans that had been turned into strange shapes, about the blackened hole in the parking lot, and the fact that Goth-boy Keith hadn't been seen since. Obviously, she had a bigoted and prejudiced idea of what a demon was really like, and wasn't going to look at Richard, in his current form, with any kindness.

Yvette wore her African shirts and beaded hats to the store. She'd sold two drum sets to customers simply by playing them with all her passion and verve, which drew the customers in, and then encouraging the customers to try one themselves. Ariadne suggested gently that Yvette try any of the instruments she liked, and had started giving her lessons on the flute as well as the violin, whenever a regular pupil did not show up.

That morning, Ariadne had brought her cat, Minto, to work. I caught the scent the moment I came through the door, and knew exactly what she was. It didn't surprise me that Ariadne spent the morning searching for the cat, who was keeping out of my way.

I met Richard for lunch and he brought meat pies he'd found somewhere. We ate them in the park and then wandered the streets until I had to go back to work.

Ariadne had gone for a walk, thinking the cat might have gotten out when the door was open. I went in the back and found the heavy gray tabby stretched out in her fur-lined box on the shelf Ariadne had built for her, with her cream saucer and her food bowl, and her toys within reach. I was going to ask her if she ever changed to her human form, but I knew the answer as soon as I met her eyes. If she changed, Ariadne might make her open her own cat food cans. I told her what I thought of her, and then went out and informed Ariadne where the cat had got to. The cat made a big show of hating me after that.

When I got off work, Richard was waiting outside. He took me to a second-hand clothes shop he'd scoped out. Clothes shopping with Richard was like playing dress-up. I bought him a new red shirt, just because I could, and we found a couple more outfits so I wouldn't just have one to wear to work.

When we got home, Richard made dinner, his chicken with a golden mushroom sauce that I'd asked for. After we ate, we headed up to Hellman Park, and there we both changed form and charged straight up the steep hillsides, just two little dogs off leash when we met people, but farther out, deeper into the open country, we ran as wolves, and played and hunted, long into the night. And that was my night, the night that I would remember always. All Richard's beauty, and all his wiles, had not been able to seduce me, when he took service with me. But when by chance I ordered him to change, and he took on a wolf form, then it was like meeting myself. And how could I say no? Richard in his human form is beautiful, clever and fun. Richard as a wolf is my mate.

There was no moon that night as we traversed the trails through the grass and brush and the drying herbs. We surprised a couple of dogs who'd jumped their fence and were out for the night being bad dogs. We stalked them, cornered them against a rise, and sent them running for home, their tails between their legs, with just a look from our yellow eyes. We made love in a hollow of the hill, in one form or another, and the scent of the dirt, and the grass, and our sweat, and the smell of Richard as a wolf caught in the back of my throat. For a long time after that, I could bring back that night, and those scents, and Richard, and my love.

At work the next day I was tired but functional. It doesn't take a whole lot of energy to clean floors, dust shelves, arrange goods, and help customers, especially when Ariadne or Yvette did most of the customer assistance. I'm not that good with people. They don't like my smile. The next night was my last one with Richard, and I had a different plan in mind.

Richard bought the fixings for the chicken mushroom dinner again, but this time he stood over me and made me make it, so

I'd know how. I didn't know cooking could be that easy, though fiddly, since all I'd ever done was fry meat. We lingered over dinner, and we still hit traffic on the 605. We crept along to the 10 and then headed west, toward the city, and beyond, up to West Hollywood. On the way, I asked Richard, "Where is Keith?"

"Who?"

"The kid in the parking lot, who called your name—your fake name."

"Oh, that fellow with the wand. Why did he have a wand?"

"Current fashion."

"I see."

"What did you do with him?"

"I ate him. Why? What did you want me to do with him?"

"You ate him?"

"I can, you know. I have a big enough mouth, in that form."

"Where is he now?"

He turned his head to me. "Wherever I like. I told you, time is different across that boundary."

"Can you drop him back here, alive?"

"I can drop him anywhere. Down a chasm where he'll fall forever. Into my own world, where he can be a piece of dust. Alive, dead, mummified, eighty years old, or an egg."

I laughed. "Can you turn him into a dog?"

His smile was wicked. "If it's your pleasure. He did break his oath to you."

So he did. But if I thought someone needed to die, I should do it myself, and I didn't know this guy. I thought about it. Something that wouldn't hurt too much, but would leave him really wigged out. For the rest of his life. "Can you drop him in a hospital in some foreign country, with a broken arm, a strange bite out of his leg somewhere, and no memory of Monday night at all?"

Richard laughed. Now that was a sound worth hearing. "Lovely. What country?"

"Um. What's a country pretty far away that we're not enemies with right now?"

"Poland?" he suggested. "I liked Poland."

"Yeah," I agreed. "Poland. That'll teach 'em."

"Not really. The Thunder Mountain Boys are going to draw up the strongest wards they know, and call Bellsandahisnlianamene."

"Oh. Is that why you have to go?"

"No. I have to go because I'm not from here, and I don't belong here anymore."

"I know." After a moment I asked, "What are you going to do to the Thunder Mountain Boys?"

"Have you ever heard the story of the red shoes?" His voice was light, but I heard the anger underneath. He'd had a bad night with them.

"No."

"Look it up sometime. I thought I'd eat them afterwards."

"What are they calling you for? I'd have thought they'd know enough to be afraid of you."

"They want me to put Marlin back together again."

"Will you?"

"No."

"Can you?"

"I don't care."

"Oh." I fell silent with disappointment. I took my foot off the gas, and started looking for an off-ramp to turn around. Then I thought, what the hell, and put my foot on the gas again. I might as well check it out myself.

"Amber?" Richard had taken all this in. "Where are we going?"

"Someone I want you to meet."

"All right." After a silence he said, "You would prefer I did not eat the Thunder Mountain Boys."

I shrugged. "Whatever you like." He had an edge in his voice. Richard had never had an edge in his voice. Every now and then, for a moment, despite his scent, I remembered that this was not really Richard anymore.

"It shall be as you please," he said. "I will have my... fun, but they will survive the night."

I said, "Thanks," because I supposed he was sparing them on my account. And it was true, I didn't want Oliver to die. Somehow I thought I owed him that.

"It will be a very long night, though." After a silence he added, "But the next one who calls me, I will eat."

I looked over and saw his eyes flash. Not blue for that instant, but some color of darkness, very deep and very black. I let out a breath. "Fair enough."

"So, if I'm not to eat the Thunder Mountain Boys when I'm finished with them, what shall I do with them?"

"Where are they going to do the raising?"

"Their studio."

"Just blow a big hole in their floor. That'll fix 'em."

"So it will," Richard said on a laugh.

I smiled at the thought. After all, they were trying to take possession of my demon The last time they'd had him, when they'd finished with him they'd betrayed him to his death without a second thought. Richard owed them a bit of payback. So did I, come to think of it. "Feel free to take out some of their mirrors, too," I suggested.

He met my eyes with a smile. They were blue. "I will consider it a command."

I found a parking place down the street from our destination. We walked up the sidewalk as the sun set, and I took Richard's hand, because he was there and because I could. When we reached the bookshop, Richard stopped.

"I know this place."

"Have you been here? Do you know Darius?"

He shook his head. "Couldn't get near it. His wards were too good."

"Oh." I hadn't thought of that. "How about now?"

He smiled. He really wasn't quite the same as when I'd known him before. He'd never had a smile that mocked others. "There are very few wards that can touch me now," he said. "In any case, these are in tatters." He held up his hands, as though feeling the shreds of spider webs in the air.

"I want you to meet Darius," I said.

"If you wish," he shrugged.

We set off the little bell walking into Darius's bookshop. Two heavyset bikers looked up from opposite corners to check us out as we came in. Darius sat behind his desk, looking down at his hands. He was not reading. The desk before him was clear. The woman seated beside him checked us out too. None of them seemed friendly.

The rows of shelves from the front windows to the back wall were no longer orderly and well-stocked. Shelves had long bare patches. Books were piled sideways, and some were stacked on the floor. A pair of young women were going through the books and setting them up on shelves in some kind of order. They glanced at us too.

"Can I help you?" The woman sitting beside Darius pitched her voice as a challenge. I walked toward the desk, and Richard followed. "If you've come to browse the books, that's fine," she continued. Her red hair was cropped like a helmet on her skull. She had large eyes, enhanced by make-up, and a square jaw. Her suit coat and soft blouse said clearly that she didn't normally work in the bookshop.

"You've had trouble," Richard stated.

"Darius has been ill," she said, setting a hand on his shoulder. He didn't seem to notice. "Some people took advantage."

"Robbed him blind," one of the bikers muttered. "Bastards."

"We're looking after him now," the woman said. "Can I help you?"

I ignored her. "Darius?" I crouched a little so I could look into his face. "Darius?"

He raised his head, his deep eyes haunted. He smiled, but it was just a muscle memory. "Hi," he said, hardly raising his voice. "Can I help you?"

I reached out and took his hands. "Darius?"

"You a friend?" Helmet woman asked.

I nodded. I didn't have to tell anyone that I'd only known him for a few hours as his real self, a geomancer of considerable power. He was known as the one person who could keep all the power wielders in the greater Los Angeles area talking to one another, and even in some sense working, if not together, then at least in the same direction. Shortly after I met him, Darius had been attacked by the Eater of Souls, and this was what remained.

He caught my eye again. The smile creaked into place once more. "Hi. Can I help you?" He stared at me and the smile faded.

"We think he had a stroke," helmet-woman said. "He just sat here, day after day, and somebody took the cash box, and then other people started just walking out with all the books they could carry."

"We put a stop to that," one of the bikers came up to eavesdrop.

"We took him to the clinic, but they couldn't find anything that might have caused this."

Yeah, they probably never even heard of the Eater of Souls. Though in the last few months, there'd probably been a rash of people like Darius around here. Marlin, for example, lived right across the street.

I looked over at Richard, but he wasn't giving anything away. He looked Darius over, and then wandered off to look at the backs of the books, favoring big fat old dusty ones, that he pulled out and examined. I trailed after him. I can be patient.

"What's in it?" I asked, after he'd leafed slowly through a heavy book with thick black writing.

"It's a history of one of the princedoms of Germany, from the eighteen hundreds."

"Huh," I said. I knew where Germany was. I knew there had once been two of them. I didn't know one was a princedom.

"I spent some time there," he said lightly, and put the book back. "It's like getting to read the end of the story."

"Can you help him?" I nodded toward Darius.

"No."

I had not expected him to say that. "But—you fixed the Rag Man. He told me."

Richard has a really sweet smile at times. "Yes. But that was different. That was a, a cog out of place, is all. His gift was not meant to hurt him, and all I did was an adjustment. The Rag Man didn't have anything wrong with his soul."

"Can't you just magic Darius back, make him the way he was?"

Richard laid a hand on his chest. "I am here in my accustomed, severely limited form. As you see."

"Yes."

"In order to bring enough of my power into this world to aid Darius, without killing him at the same time, it would take a gateway more complicated than you know how to create, or we have time for."

"I thought you had mastery over space and time."

What looked at me suddenly through those eyes was not Richard. A jolt went through me and all at once I was braced to kill, while part of my brain screamed Run Run Run! It was gone in a moment, and his blue eyes were just Richard's again. "Yes," he answered quietly, well aware of the tension in me. "But you truly do not want any more of me in this world."

I let my breath out on a little laugh. "You're right."

"Well then. There is nothing I can do for Darius. But you can."

And that is why I spent the last night I had with my lover breaking in to the back room of a bookstore in order to bite the head of a geomancer.

Richard explained while we sat in the car eating fast food and waiting for a better hour to commit breaking and entering, and assault and battery.

"He had his soul cut out of him, as you saw. But he fought hard. He may even have fought them off at the end. You say there was a fire in his room?"

"Scorch marks. Still smelling of fire." I chowed down on my burger. Richard picked out the best fries and laved them with salt and ketchup.

"Mm. He has some soul stuff left. He can attract more, and make use of it. His spirit is strong. But you'll need to bite his head open."

"I'll need to—? I did mention I kind of like this guy?"

Richard looked at me shrewdly. "You respect him."

"Yes."

"You feel guilty about him."

And he was right. I did. I had an idea that I had somehow led the Eater of Souls to Darius, and but for me, the guy would have been fine. "Yeah. So?"

"And that's why you want to fix him. And to do that, someone needs to cut a hole in his head. You're not going to get anyone else to do it. Medicine has gone on another path here. But if you puncture his skull, just here," Richard touched the middle of the crown of my head with his finger. His greasy finger. "He'll be able to attract the kind of human energy that he can use as soul stuff. To make a gross, inaccurate modern analogy, it's like giving him a way to access stuff he can reprogram for his own use."

"How the hell do you know that?"

"I've been here a long time. And I was raised by one of the greatest scholars of his age, after all. And unlike you, I like to read." Richard took my hamburger from me, turned it, and took the best bite. I did not snarl. I did not savage him. I waited for him to give it back to me. Truly, I was in love.

So, at about one o'clock in the morning we parked around the corner, sauntered along the street past the darkened front of the bookstore, and then cut down the passageway between Darius's building and the one next door. We could try and break in through the shop, but we risked being seen from the street, and all the unpleasant complications that might bring about. Darius had one narrow window in the back room where he slept, but it looked over a neighbor's yard, and that was my second to last choice. The back door that led to his room was at the end of this passageway. He still used this door. In fact, he'd used it recently.

When we got there, I tried knocking, just in case Darius would simplify matters by simply opening the door and letting us in. No answer. The door was steel, close-fitting into the frame. I leaned down to examine the lock, thinking over everything I knew about burglary, which wasn't much, and Richard reached past my head and tried the knob. The door opened.

Well, that made things a lot simpler. I stepped into the dark back room. No one was there. I changed to make sure, and so that I could see in the dark. The bed was empty. Darius hadn't slept there tonight. Someone had tidied up the room since I'd last seen it. The smell of scorching was still discernable, but the marks were gone. The bloody rug had been removed, and the books had been stacked neatly against the wall. Darius hadn't touched them since that was done. One of the stackers was helmet-woman, and one was the talkative biker.

Darius had eaten a plate of beans at the table, earlier tonight. So, when he'd used the door recently, it hadn't been to come in. I went out to follow his trail and track him down. I trotted into the passageway just as the end of it was blocked by a car pulling up. Doors opened, doors slammed. I smelled gun oil, a trace of vomit, fear and fury. A cop car. I backed quickly into Darius's doorway, as people came down the passageway, two flashlight beams stabbing the darkness ahead of them.

"Okay," said a heavy, tired-sounding voice. "Here you are, home safe."

"Oh, shit," a younger voice, a woman's voice said. "He left the door open."

"All right, check it out. I'll wait here with him."

Darius's voice, strained, confused. "I have to find... I have to go..."

"Don't worry. We won't let anyone hurt you."

A flashlight beam hit the back wall and played around the room. I dropped on to Darius's bed and made myself as small and harmless looking as I possibly could. When the flashlight caught me, I heard the woman cop's indrawn breath, and felt her jolt of fear.

"There's a dog in here!"

I lay quite still. I wagged my tail just a tiny bit. And gods help me, I let out a little, pathetic whine. I had no idea where Richard had got to. I had a moment of panic that my last hours with Richard had been used up, that he'd gone forever and I'd wasted our final night. But at the moment, I kept my eyes on the woman with the gun, who was looking back at what she might in her crazed imagination consider to be a threat to her safety. And it was true. I was. And if she went for her gun, she was going to find out just how fast one of the wolf kind can be. But I did my damnedest to look just as harmless as I knew how.

The other cop came to look, holding Darius by the arm. I wagged my tail at him, too. "Huh. Is that your dog, Mr. Kolpak?"

Darius shuffled into the doorway. The cop found the light switch and turned it on.

Darius looked around stupidly, as though he didn't know where he was. His feet were bare, and he wore only a pair of pajama bottoms. His long body was thin from recent malnutrition. He took a few steps into the room, and then he noticed me. "Hi, there," he said, sounding pleased, and reached out a hand to me.

I got up slowly on my four feet and walked over to him, head low. I wagged my tail and nosed his hand. He crouched down and hugged me hard. He turned his face into my head. His voice, though quiet, was raw. "Please, please, help me," he said.

"All right, then," said the cop. "We're going to go now. You go to bed, okay? It's bedtime. Don't go outside again until it's light, understand? But if you do, take the dog with you, why don't you? Then the creeps out there won't bother you."

"You lock this, now. Hear me?" The cops closed the door firmly behind themselves. But Darius didn't move. He buried his fists in my fur and began to sob.

As they walked back to the car the woman cop asked, "What happened to him?" and I heard the older guy reply something about Darius having been robbed and attacked, and hit on the head, and his store broken in to. And that was part of the story. The real robbery that the Eater of Souls had carried out was invisible to him.

When the car had driven off, Richard was in the room again. I looked up at him curiously. He no longer smelled of burgers and grease. He nodded to me, looking down at Darius's bent head, and he was right. Darius was still holding me hard, crying into my shoulder. He took no notice of Richard. There would be no better moment.

When I grow large, it's usually because I am angry. But this could not be a moment of raging passion. If I missed the exact place Richard had pointed out, which is where the three seams on the skull come together, I risked projecting a bit of bone into Darius's brain, and that wouldn't help him a bit. And I needed my head large, but the rest of me could stay as it was, since Darius was holding on to me, and that would serve to keep him in place. So I drew on my passion for the first time in a measured way, and nothing happened.

Well, that pissed me off, and since I'd already set myself to grow, the next moment my head was brushing the roof, so that was all right. I worked on toning the size-thing down a bit, while I focused on the top of Darius's head, and then planted my pointy upper-left canine just—there. I steadied myself for a moment, leaned in to Darius to hold him steady, and then dropped my tooth hard onto the top of Darius's head and heard the bone crunch.

I tasted blood, and Darius let out a choked scream, shoved me away hard and grabbed his head. Richard was there with a towel and pressed it down hard to stop the bleeding.

I backed off, and when I was far enough out of reach I changed. I crouched on the floor where I was to try and keep from panicking him any further. "Darius? Darius! Listen, I'm sorry I hurt you. But I think it's going to help, it's going to make you better. Darius? It will be all right." At least, I hoped it would be.

Darius grabbed hold of the towel and pressed it to his wound as though doing so would stop it from hurting so much. He was still crying, which disconcerted me. Honestly, I hadn't wanted to hurt him.

Richard brought another towel, took the first one away from Darius, and bent to examine the wound. Then he covered it with the second towel, and guided Darius's hand back up to hold it in place. The first towel was fairly soaked, but the wound didn't seem to be bleeding so much anymore.

"How is it?" I asked. "Did I do it right?"

"It looks right," Richard said uncertainly.

"You weren't sure!" I heard it in his tone. "You don't know!"

He shrugged. "How much can anyone know, caught in a form like this one? It should work."

"How long before we know?"

"I have no idea. But this is a good place to try what you did. He has done many workings here over the years. A lot of energy has been raised, and he put a lot of himself into his work. If this works, he should be able to call that energy to himself."

"If it works."

Darius's panic decreased as he seemed to realize that no one was going to attack him anymore. I sat there talking to him, saying anything I could think of, so he would calm down. I was well aware that the night was leaching away, my last night with Richard, my last hours with my love. And I couldn't tell if all this had even done any good.

Richard brought a third towel, and Darius focused on him as he took the other one away and guided Darius's hand to hold the new towel in place. When Darius turned back to me, his eyes had changed. They weren't empty anymore. There was, in their depths, a gleam of awareness.

"Darius?" I said.

A moment later I thought I'd imagined it. He went to his futon and lay down, still holding the towel to his wounded head.

The freeways were as clear of traffic as they ever are as we sped home. The streets of Whittier were empty and dark. I let us into my apartment, and we went straight to bed. And perhaps he was a master of time and space, because despite the lateness of the hour, we seemed to have all the time in the world to say good-bye once more. I did everything I could to impress his form, his scent, and his laughter into my memory. This extra visitation was a gift, and I made the most of it.

When I woke, Richard was gone, as he told me he would be. Not wholly gone. He'd left his jacket, neatly folded on the chair. It smelled like him, and when I put it on, it just about fit me.

CHAPTER EIGHTEEN

So, the demon was gone, everyone finally got it about the World Snake not coming, my lover had come back of his own accord to be with me and ravish my senses to unparalleled bliss, I'd defeated Finley and sent him into a miserable exile. I had a job, I had a friend or two, and I'd grown almost an inch, and might grow some more, so now I could settle down and live happily ever after, sad about Richard going away, but joyful that he'd come back at all.

Not unexpectedly, it did not turn out that way.

I flitted around the music store all day in a state of hyperactive bliss. I dusted every shelf and every object, reorganized the sheet music, cataloged and shelved the new CDs for sale, and even greeted and helped customers using a friendly voice and a nice smile. Ariadne looked at me askance. I think she was considering a drug test. When Yvette came in at lunch time, she told Ariadne not to worry, it would wear off and I'd be back to normal again.

I'd been ignoring Minto, Adriade's cat, and she didn't care for that. After lunch I went into the back room where Minto was sleeping, and a moment later the cat ran out into the shop hissing and yowling. When I came out, she hissed at me and struck out with her tiny paw, and then ran and hid under the counter where she made yowling sounds. Ariadne looked over from where she was showing a customer how to assemble their new music stand. I could see her wondering just what I'd done to that cat.

I got down on my hands and knees and stuck my head under the counter. Minto backed away and growled, but I saw her smirking at me. I propped my chin on my hands and smiled. She flinched back. "I've only ever once eaten cat," I told her. "It was pretty stringy. But if I lose this job, I'm going to be hungry, and I'll bet you're not stringy at all." I smiled wider. Minto slowly crouched down. Her tail stilled, and she stopped making those noises. I got up. Ariadne was watching me. "She's fine," I told her.

After that, Minto made a point of greeting me when I entered the shop, and otherwise left me alone. I could feel her watching me sometimes from her various hiding places, but that was fine. Now that she knew her place on the food chain, she was just as respectful as she needed to be.

I walked home after work, enjoying my melancholy at Richard's departure, which was overshadowed by my glee that he'd come back, he'd come back to see me, he didn't have to, he just wanted to, and the joy we'd made together, and the fun we'd had. His smell was still on me, in places. And I was thinking about that chicken thing with mushroom sauce, that we'd made so much of the previous night that I was going to eat it for dinner again. Up the street a guy got out of his truck and came toward me, flipping the keys and pocketing them. I noticed him first because he looked a bit like my defeated stepbrother Finley. It wasn't Finley, of course, but that's the moment I realized I'd forgotten all about Finley's truck.

Finley's truck was better than a scent marker. It was a beacon that would summon someone from the family. And for anyone from my family, Finley's trail would lead directly to Elaine, Elaine's house, and the fight I'd had with Finley in the orchard. Anyone who came looking for that truck would be able to tell that I'd been there, that his blood and mine had been shed on that ground. Since Finley was gone, they'd know where to start looking for me: they'd start with Elaine, and she knew where to find me. Was the truck still there? Had it been towed away? Or had he been in a rental car, which was now overdue and being tracked down? Had Finley told anyone where he was going that last day?

I called Tamara's shop as soon as I got home, to ask her to contact Elaine. Tamara wasn't there. The shop worker didn't know Elaine. She'd heard of Curt, but didn't have his number. She said she'd have Tamara call back, except Tamara wasn't expected back in the shop that night. Since there wasn't any point in trying to cross the greater Los Angeles valley right smack in the middle of rush hour, I had my dinner, and enjoyed the last of the chicken with mushroom sauce, breathing in the scent that Richard had left in the room, on the things that he'd touched, remembering his smile, the look in his eyes, before I caught the freeway and headed back out to Calabasas.

And I hit traffic. It was dark by the time I got to the exit from the 101 that would lead me to the little hamlet where Elaine lived in her parents' house. It was true that my family could use that truck to hunt me down. On the long drive out, I realized that it didn't necessarily have to work that way. I could instead use the truck as bait, to gather information on who was hunting me, how much they wanted me, and what they knew. I thought of Gray Fox, and how this would put me one up on him. So now this was not their trap to catch me, but mine to catch them. And that was a lot more fun.

I parked in the parking lot of a trendy restaurant some miles from Elaine's place. The dirt lot backed up against a scrubby hill, with a bigger and steeper hill beyond it. I changed in the twilight and leaped the fence, and loped up and along the hillside. I made a loop around the steeper hill, then came down the rocky, scrub-covered slope to the dirt road that ran behind Elaine's orchard. No one of the wolf kind or the fox kind had been on this hillside. I moved closer down the slope. Finley's truck was there, parked a hundred yards down the road and around a slight bend from the back fence of the orchard. Finley had made sure that if I circled Elaine's house before going in, I wouldn't see his truck, and I wouldn't catch his scent. As it turned out, I hadn't bothered to check, since I hadn't expected Elaine's call to be Finley's trap. I told myself to be more careful next time. And of course, this was next time.

So I moved parallel to the road for a couple of hundred yards, to catch any scent of anyone looking for me. I came down to the main road and walked along it on two feet for a half mile, passing the start of the dirt road, some ways from where the truck was parked. I completed the circle without scenting anyone recent, anyone hanging around, anyone who wasn't a human who passed here often, or a critter who lived in the neighborhood. No one had found the truck yet. So this would be my trap.

I walked on two feet down the road in front of Elaine's house, and then changed and trotted along her fence line, and turned up the far end of the dirt road behind the orchard. Somewhere back there I remembered seeing a sagging section of the fence. What I wanted to do was change the story that our scent traces told about what had happened in the orchard. Right now, you could scent that Finley had walked from his truck to Elaine's house, gone over the fence into the yard, and gone into the orchard, where he'd met me. We'd had a big fight on two feet, then he'd changed, and there was blood from the wounds I'd given him on his shoulder, and of course his nose, and a tiny bit from the dart wound. All of this would tell the hunters to go knock on Elaine's door on two feet, and ask questions. I didn't want Elaine brought into this, since she knew how to find me. So I had to prevent anyone from finding her, by making the scents tell a different story.

The fence to the old orchard had been repaired a number of times, but for the last few years no one had bothered. I found the sagging boards, got up on two feet and manipulated them until I'd made a gap. I changed and went through on four feet.

It was easy to find the place where Finley had fallen. He'd lain there bleeding for quite a while, spreading his scent with his blood, sweat, saliva, and fur. In my wolf form, I rolled in this, until I carried his scent on my back and sides.

Then I went back and forth through the gap in the fence, until you'd swear that both of us had come in this way. If someone found the place along the way where Finley had touched the top of the wall jumping over into Elaine's yard, they wouldn't know what to make of it, because it didn't fit the story. I went out onto the dirt road and wrote a new story. I trotted over to Finley's truck, and then on the way back I rolled every few yards, rubbing my back on the dirt road. In a day or two, when the wind and weather, fog and traffic had erased the marks, a scent tracker would be led to believe that I'd met Finley at his car, that we'd both come back this way on two feet, and then we'd gone into the orchard through this fence, and fought all over the place, on two feet and on four.

On four feet, I rolled over the ground where I'd dragged Finley to the garage. I left a few more odd traces of Finley in the yard, and then came back into the orchard and messed up the story some more. There'd been a big fight, obviously. And then I'd run away straight up the hill across the dirt road from the orchard. I laid that trail, and then I laboriously laid the scents that would tell them that Finley had followed me in his wolf form, up to the summit of the hill. I took both his scent and mine up and back down the trail I was laying. When I got back to the dirt road I walked back the way I'd come on two feet, until I crossed a stream. I changed onto four feet and followed the stream for miles, in and out of the water, and then made a huge circuit around the whole base of that mountain, and then ran up to the top of it and caught up my trail and Finley's again, and took it in another direction.

My kind are air as well as ground scent trackers, so water by itself won't cause us to lose a trail. What confuses a tracker the most is circles. One trail crossing another, concentric circles with tracks crossing through them, makes the path hopelessly confused. I made four concentric circles, the first two a hundred yards or so apart, and each succeeding one farther apart until the last two were miles from each other. Then I crossed through all of them again and again, laying spokes across these great wheels, with both my scent and Finley's, in different directions. It would take a month for someone tracking this to figure out who was going where, and in that month the traces would degrade and make it even harder to understand. Some trails I went over again and again, some only once, touching the ground, or the foliage, as little as possible.

You can fool a tracker into thinking a trail is fresher because it is stronger. I confused the story for ten square miles moving out from Elaine's orchard. Ha. Let them try to figure that out. This is what I'd done when I'd run away from home. I'd laid tracks of concentric circles for weeks beforehand, and then joined them up just before I left, so they'd be tracking me in circles for a month, while I got away by car. I couldn't say I wasn't having fun. I giggled to myself every time I crossed the track again, with yet another misleading trail.

I got home a couple of hours before dawn, even before the morning rush hour began. I took a hot shower and fell into bed for a few hours' sleep before I had to go to work. I drifted into dreams, my feet twitching as I ran my trails over again while I slept.

At work the next day I was as slow and dragging as I'd been hyper the day before. Ariadne was amused. Yvette gave her an "I told you so" look. I planned a quick dinner after work, and then three or four hours sleep before I headed back to Calabasas to see if anyone had walked into my trap.

Instead, Jason arrived about fifteen minutes before I was due to clock out, looming through the shop doorway and staring askance at the cat on the counter. Ariadne didn't have any students on Fridays, so she was showing Yvette how to draw the bow across a violin, and we were all, even Minto, being polite about the sounds she made. Jason greeted Ariadne respectfully. Yvette turned at the sound of his voice and lit up at the sight of him, though being on duty she did not throw herself into his arms, as she usually did.

"Hey! I didn't know you were going to be up this way tonight."

"Madam Tamara sent me." He turned to me. "Madam Tamara would like to see you."

"Oh? When?" A drive down to Costa Mesa that evening was really not in my plans. I'd had a long night, and I was in for another one later.

"Now, of course," the bear replied.

"Now?" I said, and I put every bit of resistance I could into the syllable.

"Yes," he said, meeting my gaze. "Now."

A wolf can take a bear. Bears know that, too. The trouble is, what's left of the wolf afterwards is usually not worth much.

As it turned out, Tamara was in Whittier, at the home of Lady Fireheart. I drove there with Jason hunched in the passenger seat giving directions and making unspoken but unmistakable complaints about the head and leg room. I felt the wards guarding Lady Fireheart's house from two streets away. I went past the house and parked in front of the next one. Wards incline you that way, and hers were strong. The name on the mailbox was Ortiz. Jason opened the front door without knocking and led the way through another powerful set of wards that parted for us, through the living room redolent with ancient incense, with floor to ceiling bookshelves on every inch of wall space, all stuffed with books. On a few empty surfaces heavy glazed pots were displayed. We passed a couple of young kids in front of the TV who didn't look up from the computer game they were playing together.

In the kitchen, Madam Tamara sat at the table cutting vegetables with a long knife, while Lady Fireheart fried meat on the stove. Jason made a slow circuit of the room, sampling whatever food he could reach. I stood in the doorway with my arms folded, making my own unspoken statement.

Madam Tamara looked up at me. Her hair was twisted up in a simple blue cotton kerchief, and she wore a long white cotton shirt over a pair of light blue trousers. She took in my expression and asked, "What did the bear tell you?" She shot a look at Jason, who looked unconcerned.

"That you wanted to see me. Now. Tonight."

Lady Fireheart gave the bear a look. "Trust Jason to put it like that."

"We do have a few questions to put to you," Madam Tamara said. Her voice was remote, not friendly.

"Yes," Lady Fireheart turned to me, the hand without the wooden spoon in it open. "But I sent Jason to ask if you would join us for dinner. If you please. People of power are so prickly!" She slapped Jason's hand away from one of the pots she was stirring. I thought she was brave, to come between a bear and food, even in her own kitchen. Also, whatever she was cooking smelled really good. And anyway, it wouldn't do me any good to leave this early for Calabasas and my stake-out of Finley's truck. If I left in an hour and a half, I'd get there at the same time as if I left right now, since rush hour was just gearing up.

"Thanks," I said. I stepped into the kitchen. Lady Fireheart turned back to the stove. She was barefoot, and wore jeans cut off below her knees, and an old t-shirt. She told me to call her Susan.

"Perhaps you would like to tell us," Madam Tamara began, but the sorceress interrupted, admonishing her with the spoon.

"Wait until after dinner. Everyone will be in a better mood."

"I won't," I said. I went to stand across from Tamara at the table. "What do you want to ask me?"

Susan turned and pointed the ladle at me. "After dinner." She licked it before it dripped red sauce on the floor, but I got the message. Susan might be making dinner for family and friends, but Lady Fireheart was still in the room.

Susan made vast amounts of taco salad, so there were leftovers despite the two starving children called in (over and over) from their game in the living room, the silent gangly boy who was my age who emerged from one of the bedrooms, and the bear at the table. I had several helpings myself. After dinner she put a plate of homemade butterscotch brownies on the table while the kids cleared the plates to the sink. They grabbed their share and went back to their game. Jason grabbed more than his share and cadged a ride from the boy back to Whittier, to hang around Amadeus Music until Yvette got off work. Susan made a pot of sharp, smoky tea and served it to me and Madam Tamara.

"We have to ask you," she said to me, as she sat back down at the table, "if you know anything about what happened to Keith."

"Keith?" I asked.

"The boy who called your demon's name in the parking lot."

"Oh."

"No one has seen him since that night," Susan said. "His mother is a friend of mine. I don't know what to tell her."

What was I supposed to tell them? That he was either drifting somewhere in the universe where Richard was the wind, the stones, and the spaces between, or still falling down a bottomless pit to the center of this or another world? Or maybe in a hospital in Poland, with a broken arm, a bite mark, and a case of amnesia?

"Two other people who were there that night are missing, too," Tamara added.

Whoops, I thought. So he had gotten to eat a few. "Any Thunder Mountain Boys?" I asked.

"Funny you should mention them," Susan said. "There's been some kind of explosion at their studio. They said it was a terrorist attack."

I started to laugh. "And it blew a big hole in the studio floor, right?"

"How did you know?"

"Are any of them dead?" I asked.

Tamara and Susan shook their heads.

"Then let them be grateful. Richard owed them."

"You admit your demon is at work in this?" Tamara asked.

"No," I said. "You took their oaths, didn't you? Anyone who's missing, that's what's at work. They saw what they were dealing with. They had fair warning."

"That's true," Susan said.

I grabbed another one of the brownies. "So, what's the new plan for dealing with the World Snake? Any meetings ahead? New workings? Coordinated power raisings?" Tamara and Susan looked at each other. I sat back. "So. You believe me. You finally believe me. The World Snake isn't coming."

"It was a very convincing demonstration," Susan allowed.

"And various diviners have concurred." Tamara added.

"She's turned," I finished. "She's not coming. Ha." I grabbed the biggest brownie left on the plate. After all, I deserved it.

"Then, is your demon still with you?"

I shook my head, my mouth full. "He's gone. He's not coming back." I swallowed. "Unless someone calls him. I know I'm not going to." I met Tamara's eyes. "Ever again. He said he'd eat any-one who did." She nodded. That was good enough.

"We heard a rumor that you attacked Darius," Susan said. She poured us all more tea. "Is it true?"

"I attacked him?"

"You bit him in the skull," Tamara stated.

"Says who?" I wondered who had seen us.

"I say so," a voice spoke from the doorway.

I looked up, and there was Darius. Kat McBride followed him into the kitchen, and set a chair for him. Susan went to hug him. He and Tamara nodded to one another. I sat there grinning like a fool.

"He has a lot of questions," Kat told us, "so I thought I'd bring him along. The people who have been helping him found him in his shop yesterday morning, taking inventory."

"They told me I'd been attacked and robbed," Darius said. His voice was thinner than I remembered, from when I'd first met him. He seemed frail and wan, and the bandage on the top of his head looked like an absurd little hat. But it was Darius, not some empty shell. He fixed his gaze on me. "You attacked me the other night. You bit me in the head. What did you do to my store?"

I shook my head. "I didn't do anything to your store."

Helmet-woman from the bookstore followed him in and was introduced as Patricia. The talkative biker we'd met at the book-store loomed in after her, carrying a case of beer. He said he was called Terry. More chairs were brought, the circle expanded. Susan produced a second pan of brownies, which quickly disappeared.

"You were angry with me, for what I asked of you," Darius said to me. "But I didn't think you were going to come back and attack me."

"She attacked you?" The biker stared down at me. "Which time?"

"It wasn't an attack," I tried to tell him. "I did put a hole in your skull. And it worked! You're better now."

Some of the women from Susan's Wicca group came in. They made greetings and then went on through the kitchen and set up tables on the patio outside. Helmet-woman sat down close to Darius, and explained to him that he had had some kind of stroke, and had been nearly unresponsive for weeks.

"What are you talking about?" He stabbed a finger at me. "She came to my shop a couple of days ago. She was looking for Marlin, and I explained to her that the World Snake is our first priority. And it has to be."

"Ask him what day it is," I suggested.

Darius heard me. "What day—? It's March 18th."

In the silence that followed, we could hear the women talking out on the patio, and voices in the living room that signaled more people arriving.

"Darius, it's May 6," Susan told him. "The World Snake has been turned, you're back, and everything's all right."

"It's… ? No," he said, shaking his head.

"You trepanned him," Susan said to me. "What made you think to do that?"

I shrugged. I wasn't going to bring Richard into this discussion, because that would confuse the question of whether or not he was truly gone. "I just thought it might help."

More people came into the kitchen and I got up to make room for them. I let the crowd push me out onto the patio, where a string of bright lights criss-crossing the yard had just been lit against the twilight, and tables were being loaded with snacks and drinks. At the end of the patio a building with a roof and three walls stood next to a huge brick oven. I wandered over to the shed where shelves of ceramic pots stood, identical plates of fresh brown clay, rows of cups, pots, bowls in pale brown, without decoration, and bright glazed finished teapots, vases, platters, more mugs and bowls, with slashes of fierce color, or intricate decoration, all drying row upon row in the open air. Lady Fireheart was a potter.

A drum started up on the patio, joined a few moments later by several others. Women and men carried instruments out, found their places in the growing circle, and joined in. I slipped along the side yard to the front of the house where the house and the wards together muted the sound of the drums. Madam Tamara had wanted to see me, and see me she had. I had a trap to tend.

"Amber!"

I recognized the tall, heavy-set woman on the sidewalk, a white scarf draped across her shoulders. The flowing green gown was new, though, and the air of replete satisfaction, and the scent of lavender soap.

"Someone I want you to meet," she said with a smile.

A big shiny car had stopped in front of Lady Fireheart's house, and all the doors opened. A quick little woman hurried around the back to help a guy out of the backseat. He wore a gleaming white robe that buttoned to his throat, and a short purple robe over it. His long black hair hung to his shoulders, beautifully combed and oiled. I didn't need the white cloth around his neck to recognize him. I'd seen him once before at a meeting at Tamara's, but it was the scent of lavender soap that told me who he was. And the smell of sex. The danger was over, the World Snake was gone, and Cecil was back in town.

"Master," Sally conducted Cecil onto the lawn, her hands in prayer position. "May I present Amber, of whom you've heard so much."

Cecil flowed toward me with his hands outstretched. "My dear girl, how wonderful to meet you at last. We have heard so much."

The bony little woman who had helped him out stood on his other side, her hands also in prayer position, her eyes down. She also smelled of lavender soap. The two men who'd been in the

BINDING   ❧   265

front seats stepped up to flank Sally. The stocky one with the deep tan had recently bathed, and before that he'd had sex with the bony woman. The other one, dark and slender, dressed in dark jeans and a white linen shirt, wore a little smile a lot like Sally's. He also smelled of lavender soap. Honestly.

Cecil grasped my hands in his and pressed them. "Wonderful! Wonderful! What you have accomplished! The World Snake has turned, and we have you to thank. I felt her, I felt her mind as she changed her course. And you, you are the cause. We have so much to thank you for!"

Well, that's what I wanted, wasn't it? Praise and thanks? Kudos and acknowledgment? And it was true, but just... not from him.

"You have so much to teach us. A demon, under your command! So advanced! And perhaps we can teach you a little as well. You must come to us, you must come and study."

The little smiles of the people around him increased, and their scents changed just a little.

"Where's Holly?" I asked him.

He stopped smiling. "Ah, Holly. My dear disciple. She mistakenly took a wrong path, we think it was through improper meditation, and worldly pursuits. We have suggested that she withdraw for a time, and purify herself, and meditate anew." He squeezed my hand again. "We won't be seeing her for awhile. But come and see us! We have waived all initial fees, in honor of your accomplishment."

I didn't even want to bite him. I didn't like his scent. I grasped his hands in turn, leaned forward and reached up to speak softly in his ear. "I'm sixteen."

I let go as he stepped back so fast that he fell over the tanned guy behind him. I left him in the arms of his disciples, and headed for my car, smiling. I was learning lots of new ways to bite. I drove off to Calabasas to see if I'd caught anything in my trap.

CHAPTER NINETEEN

When I got to Calabasas I once again parked a mile away from Elaine's place, this time in a different direction, and approached on foot, walking along the left side of the deserted highway, where my scent would be obscured by traffic the next day. Finley's truck was still where he'd left it, but it had been tagged with a yellow warning card from the local sheriff's office, saying that it was about to be towed.

The house next door to Elaine's place stood empty. It had been built by someone from the same school of geometric house design, though this one looked like it was made from cut-out metal rectangles instead of giant sugar cubes. In one place the brick wall was only a few feet from the side of the house. I changed, took a bound from the far side of the road, made myself big, touched down on the wall and leaped up to the roof where I hunkered down small again. From the far side of the roof I could look over and down onto Finley's truck. The little breeze blew down the road in my direction. If anyone came along, I would be sure to notice. I went to sleep.

After two more nights of commuting to Calabasas after work, my patient hunting was rewarded. I was roused at about midnight from my nap on the roof by the sound of quiet voices and softer steps walking along the dirt road. When they were almost at the truck I caught their scent, and crouched lower, afraid they might sense my excitement. It was my oldest stepbrother, Tillman, and with him was Gray Fox.

I made myself as small as I could in my wolf form. The air was not moving very much, and it moved from up the road, across the roof, and down to the yard below. It would be difficult for them to scent me. And if they did... I noted again the best direction to run and make my way back to my car. After all, there were two of them. I hadn't planned that there would be two of them.

The voices stopped as Tillman changed to his four-footed form and cast around the truck, and up and down the road, scenting the ground, the air, the standing grass, the bushes. Tillman is big as a wolf, with a heavy black head and a patch of pale fur on his back. Luke and I used to say it's because he likes to roll in filth. I watched as he returned to the truck, stepped onto two feet and struck the side of it for emphasis. "She was here!"

"They both were," Gray Fox agreed in his measured voice.

"What do you think happened?"

"Lower your voice, sir," Gray Fox advised. "There are people about."

"People?" Tillman mocked him, but he did lower his voice.

"My cousins are casting for scent over these hills. It is possible that one or the other, or both were hurt, and went to ground near here."

"You think my brother was hurt?" Tillman sounded like this idea would never have occurred to him. I remembered Finley's nose, how it had looked so cockeyed, and bled so much. I smiled to myself.

Gray Fox leaned easily against the door of the truck, his arms folded. "The scent of his blood is on the grass beyond that fence," he nodded in the direction of Elaine's orchard. "Not enough for a death wound, certainly…"

Tillman had already changed and dashed off. The Fox waited for him, bending his head in patience. Tillman came back a little while later and stood up again. "There was a fight!" he announced.

The Fox nodded concurrence.

"How could she give him a fight?" Tillman asked.

"Probably he gave her a beating," Gray Fox suggested.

"Yeah, but then where is he?" He stared up at the hills, as though he'd spot his brother just by looking.

"Do you think he might be holding her himself?" Gray Fox asked him. "That he's found a den and means to keep her as his prize?"

Tillman's head came around, startled. "No way!" He thought a moment and then said, "You think?" And then he added, "Dad will kill him."

"Very true."

"I'll kill him! Hell, that's not in the plan!"

"None of this is in the plan." Gray Fox sounded bitter.

"Yeah, well, who'd have thought the little bitch would take off like that?"

"We all thought it," Gray Fox corrected mildly. "What we didn't think is that she would succeed."

Up on my roof, I grinned down at them. Ha.

"When we catch her, it would be best if you cripple her," Gray Fox told Tillman. "There will be no more running away after that. She has shown herself to be resourceful. She must be disposed of in such a way that she won't be in a position to provide a rallying point for the others."

"I thought you wanted the little bitch dead?"

"Not yet, sir," Gray Fox cautioned, touching a hand to Tillman's arm. "Not just yet. She'll need to be seen at home, and seen to have lost, badly, before she dies. And she must die before your father kills her mother."

"Dad said to kill her," Tillman said uncertainly.

"Yes. But his orders to me, after we discussed it, were to bring her home broken. I'm certain you can manage that."

"Right. But what if Finley's got her? What if he's now her mate?" Tillman's voice rose again. "What if he's got her pregnant?"

"What do you think your father would want you to do?"

Tillman thought for a long moment. Then he shrugged. "Beat the shit out of them both, I guess. If she is pregnant, that should take care of any pups."

"We will make certain of that." The coldness in Gray Fox's voice reached me where I lay. I felt a pulse of anger in my chest. I welcomed it.

Tillman stared up the road, and then took a step to stand closer to Gray Fox. This time he really did lower his voice. "Do you think Finley heard the rumor? You know, about the... you know."

"The demon?" Gray Fox's voice was mocking.

"Yeah, and maybe that's why he's keeping her for himself?"

"There isn't any demon," Gray Fox told him. "The little bitch never had that kind of power. If she had, I would have known it, and I would have let your father know long before he came and took the old bitch her mother for his mate."

"Right," Tillman agreed. "That's right. Still. A demon. That would be so cool!"

"Yes, sir, but it is not to be. Now, let us see if we can run down these errant pups of ours. I have sent my cousins to each end of this valley and the next, to cut either of them off if they bolt. Let you take up the hunt, and I will follow."

"Yeah," Tillman agreed, and I could taste his rising excitement. The memory of what Tillman's excitement had meant for me in the past rose up in me. I quashed it. I was older now. Really. I was stronger. I'd beaten Finley, after all. And still the cold knot of fear was there, closing my throat, tightening my limbs.

"The trail splits up that hillside. It may be an old track, or just another way to their den. I'll take the north fork and you the south, if you like."

"I'll take whichever one is fresher," Tillman corrected him.

"As you wish, sir."

"Let's go find the bitch, and give her what she deserves. And if Finley's got her, I'll make him watch. Come on!" He leaped out onto four feet and tore down the road.

Gray Fox started after him on two feet, taking his time. I saw him reach into his pocket, and heard the static as he thumbed on the radio. "Anything at your end? Very well. We're at the truck now, and Tillman is taking up the trail from here. I'll be following. No, it went exactly as I told you it would. Same stupid boy. Thank you, Cousin. Call me if you see anything. I'll do the same. Out."

I hugged the cold rooftop as I listened to Gray Fox reveal his treachery against my mother, and his plan to destroy me, and became as small as I could. As he made his way after Tillman to follow my trail, I put my head down between my paws and tasted bile.

Gray Fox had been the ally and henchman of my family for time out of mind. He lived at the top of our valley, our gate keeper, our first line of defense against any enemy who came to find us. I remembered the sound of his voice in our living room, while we kids were in bed upstairs, talking for hours with my mom and dad. I remembered the respect my parents both had for him, and how they'd taught that respect to me and my brothers. And he was a traitor, who had plotted with Ray before Ray stole my dad's place. Who was planning my mother's death sometime in the future. Who wanted me broken, and then dead.

The knot of anger in my chest expanded. I took deep breaths. My eyes hurt. They were aflame. And I found I had grown so large that I had only to step off the roof onto the dirt road, and two more bounds sent me up my carefully laid trail after the villain, after the traitor. And I came upon Gray Fox so fast that he never heard me, never saw me, until I picked him up by the back of the neck and shook him hard, like a rat. I heard his neck snap.

There was hardly any blood. I flung his carcass high and far off the trail, so he would be hard to find. And then I went on after Tillman.

I'd laid the trail that Tillman was heading up night after night in exhaustion and hope. Now my trap was sprung, I was rested, I was angry, and all I needed to do was run him down in the night and take him out as I had Finley. The plan was that Tillman would track me the way I would track someone, choosing the strongest scent at each crossing, because the strongest scent should indicate the most recent trail, and that way I'd lead him down one of several tracks that looped back on themselves. Loops I'd picked because they provided good cover for an ambush. So, whichever trail he picked, he would eventually end up running around in a circle, where I could find him and attack him. His only other choice was to backtrack, which would only lead him to a different choice of loop. I'd laid a labyrinth to catch my enemy, and he had walked in. All I had to do now was follow, and make the kill. Why do these things never go as planned?

The cool damp night did not offer the best conditions for tracking, but that wouldn't matter because once I knew what track he was on, it would be hard to go wrong. I set out up the hillside, the traitor Gray Fox's scent still in my nose, his blood in my mouth, his fur in my teeth, looking forward to running down my second prize for the night.

It's very difficult to run silently through California scrub. The rocky paths, the thick ground cover, mean that stones turn under your feet, and branches break or shake back into place wherever you pass. I made myself as small as I could along some narrow game trails where I'd laid the path, but my elation, my joy of the hunt soon made me large again, and I pressed on looking forward to the ambush, the catch, the kill.

Turns out I didn't know Tillman that well. Suddenly, his trail simply stopped. I halted and cast about, confused. I had a dawning feeling that he'd turned my trap around on me, that he was out there in the dark, watching, about to leap on my back. I crouched down, listening. No more than me could he move silently in this cover. Nothing. The crickets began to call again. I turned and back tracked, and found his scent again. He'd left the trail, the perfectly well-marked trail, and dashed down a slope into a narrow clearing. He'd gone chasing after a rabbit. A rabbit!

I picked my way along Tillman and the rabbit's trail, the rabbit radiating fear, and Tillman happy excitement. I found the place where the rabbit had doubled back and hidden under a bush, while Tillman bounded on, still on the chase. I glared at the rabbit in her little hollow as I passed. She held perfectly still, pretending I hadn't seen her. But now Tillman was out in the brush somewhere, off my carefully built system of tracks and round-abouts, and he might turn up anywhere—because he'd gone after a rabbit! If he wasn't already lying in ambush, he might just blunder upon me, which might be just as bad.

I changed course to move down-slope from Tillman's trail, and traveled parallel and downwind, so I didn't miss the spot where he finally realized the rabbit wasn't in front of him anymore, and cast around in a loop to pick up the scent, before he finally trotted back to where he picked up my trail again, and headed along the track I'd made. Except this was a different track, slightly older, without a trace of Finley's scent with which I'd baited the trail near Elaine's house. But he loped along, his tracks as wide apart in their stride as they had been before, showing he traveled at the same speed.

I followed along a bit more carefully, knowing now that Tillman's tracking was not dependable. And I wondered if the reason he hadn't stayed with us, after his father moved in, wasn't that, as we'd been told, he had a job elsewhere, but because he was not reliable when he was on the hunt. That would explain, too, the Gray Fox's care in guiding him to make the right decisions. I laughed to myself, looking forward to catching up with my oldest, dumbest stepbrother.

Tillman left the track three more times. I was starting to think he'd blown off the whole idea of tracking me and Finley down and was just having a fine old time trekking through the woods. When his trail came to an abrupt halt, I realized he'd backtracked and gone off the trail again, and I'd missed it. I'd reverted to my usual size again by this time, and moved more slowly so I wouldn't miss my prey. When I found his trail again, I realized he'd gone up one way, and then back down the other, and I would have to do the same, and hope I didn't meet him at the wrong moment. The web I'd laid seemed by that time just as likely to catch me as it was to catch him.

I wondered if at some point, the scouts that Gray Fox had watching the ends of the valleys were going to decide that Gray Fox had been out of touch too long, and come in looking for him. Or was their discipline so strong that they wouldn't move from their posts until Gray Fox called for them?

But meanwhile, I had to avoid ridgelines, I had to stay in the underbrush. I had to make sure I didn't come close enough to the end of either valley to be scented.

When I backtracked Tillman for the fourth time, and found my own recent trail instead of his, I had to admit to myself that my whole elaborate web of trails was a complete failure, because Tillman didn't act the way he was supposed to. He could be anywhere in these hills. He could be lying in wait for me after all, or I could stumble upon him scarfing rabbits.

I stopped, listening to the night. The fog had come in so gradually I'd hardly noticed it, except as increasing dampness. Now, trees loomed out of the gray mist, and a smattering of rain made air scenting difficult. Ground scenting is much slower. I thought about high-tailing back to my car, some miles away over a few rough hills up the valley, parked behind a small country store. But then I would have given up being the predator. I would be the prey. And I'd have all this to do over again. So I cast back once again to the last place I'd scented him, stopping to listen for some large predator crashing through the brush, panting after the critters, and tried again.

He was off my track again, coursing down a well-used hiking trail. Then he left that too, and it took me several casts to find the next trace since he'd made a huge leap off the trail down onto a little open space, but here the mystery cleared up. He'd charged into a whole bunch of rabbits. I found the place where he'd landed, and the pair of rabbits in front of him had split, and he'd gone one way and then the other, and half a dozen other rabbits had lit out in different directions, and Tillman charged straight down the slope after another one, and down along a dirt road into the flatlands.

I followed, making myself small to get through the thick brush. Wherever he was, I didn't want him to hear some large animal crashing through the brush toward him. A handful of lights shone dimly through the trees up ahead. I heard the sound of a car traveling fast in the distance, and saw the glint of headlights as it passed. The lights must be near the main road. It was getting late, and I still hadn't found him.

The path crossed a streambed. So had Tillman, in a leap, and so did I, moving slowly. I was beginning to think that, in his wolf form, Tillman was nuts.

The path widened suddenly and opened onto a grassy verge. I stopped, tasting the air. From up ahead, beyond the shapes of old buildings lit by dim lamplight, and the smell of dust and decaying wood, came the scent of fresh blood.

The dirt road I was on carried the scent of bunches of people. Only a handful came over again, and some smelled of strange food and spices. The wind picked up and blew a clear patch in the fog, and I found myself pacing down the center of an old western ghost town, lit by intermittent old-fashioned streetlamps. The ghosts at present were the visitors who weren't there, but probably would come again after the sun came up. But the weathered boards, the signs, the wooden sidewalks were right out of the movies. Or right in the movies. Of course, it was some kind of movie set. A figure turned the corner at the far end of the street and came toward me, licking his fingers. Tillman. At last.

I charged him, just as he caught wind of me and changed and leaped toward me with a snarl. I opened my heart to all my rage and fear, and grew. My jaws opened wide and I slathered for that first satisfying grip, the chomp that would break cartilage, rend muscle, bring up blood and screams and even life itself. And then I was upon him, and he slammed me to the ground as though I were a rabbit, and was on me at once.

They say some lessons stay with you forever. Even if you don't remember them all the time, at certain points they will come back to you as fresh as the day they were pressed into your skull and bones. Tillman's weight, his scent, his saliva, made me fourteen again, a spoiled child, loving and beloved, who'd never been badly hurt. Ray was first, of course. But Tillman had been next, and I'd already been beaten when he started in on me. He'd broken my will, then waited around to see if anything grew up in its place, and when it did, he'd broken that as well. All this I remembered as he rolled me over and over, worrying my ruff and biting for my throat. I was dead, as soon as he willed it. It was over and I was dead.

I arched to escape his weight, I rolled to escape his pin, I snapped at his eye, I kicked at his belly, I grabbed at his foreleg and bit down and he leaped off of me and stood panting, ready to slam me down again. This was not going to be like Finley.

All I had to do was get angry, I told myself. All I had to do was find my fury, and I would be able to withstand his blows, I could bear the pain. I could hold on to some part of myself when he broke me, crippled me, worked me over, and dragged me back home. And went on with the plan to kill my mother. I felt the fear, I felt the memory of my terror, but somehow the anger didn't come.

I grew as small as I could and leaped away from him up a set of wooden steps, but he came bounding after me. I couldn't seem to find the emotional traction to grow large, but I found it awfully easy to get really small. I slipped between a couple of the steps and dropped to the ground. I hit hard, but staggered to my feet again and charged off down the dusty street. He had to turn around on the stairs, but in a few bounds he was after me.

If I could get enough distance, I might still find a vantage point and be able to ambush him. If I could get far enough away from the smell of his sweat and his excitement, I might be able to find all the strength I'd acquired since I'd been away. If I could find a hiding place, I might be able to keep him from killing me.

I took the corner and dashed for a gap between the buildings on the far side of the street. Across the field the smell of freshly killed rabbit raised the hackles on my neck. Because I was next. If I could find a hiding place, Tillman might get bored eventually and go away.

Or I could get to the road. Traffic. People. It's a lot harder these days to beat someone publicly without someone stopping you. But it was still the middle of the night, hours before many cars would be on the road again.

I tore around the next corner, along a wooden sidewalk where my nails clattered, and I heard the thump as Tillman hit it on the bound. I'd gained half a body length on him. Or maybe he was just playing.

I heard his teeth snap behind me and I pulled my tail as far under my butt as it would go. I reached out with my forelegs, but shortened my stride with my hind legs because in my back brain I thought I could feel his breath on my heels. I tore up the ground as I grabbed for it to give me purchase. I don't think I've ever run so fast.

I reached out farther with my forelegs. The act of running, the act of staying ahead of him, allowed my panic to subside a little, and the thought of gaining just a little more distance in my stride raised my heart. I reached out with all my power, farther than I had before. My forelegs grew. I did it again, and I gained on him. My body reached my normal size, and longer, as I tore around the side of the next building and down another foggy street.

Behind me Tillman leaped, and snapped at my tail once again, and I turned on him, teeth bared, my front end much larger than my hind end, and I was as big as Tillman, who put his forelegs down and sat on his butt to screech to a halt and not run into my teeth. I leaped for his nose. You can end a fight, even if you're little, if you bite their nose.

Tillman batted me aside, and I turned my head, and sank my teeth into his foreleg.

He changed on a roar, grabbed me by the scruff, and shook me. He fumbled with one hand for his zipped pocket, pulled out a gun and shoved it into my mouth. "You damn bitch, you damn fucking bitch!"

Tillman's arm—the one in which he held the gun—was bleeding. His hand shook. I changed, as gently as I knew how. I didn't want to take the chance of getting shot as a wild animal.

"You are so over!" He clubbed me in the head with the gun, and it went off. My ears rang, and the blackness behind my eyes lit with orange and scarlet fireworks. I thought he'd shot me. The light behind my eyes went green and then faded to blackness. I came to I think only seconds later, with Tillman crouched on top of me, quite still, listening. Listening to see if anyone had heard the shot. Idiot! The light of the streetlamp glinted on his wide-open eyes.

"Okay," he said in my ear in a hoarse whisper. "You've got one chance, and then I'm going to put a bullet through your hip, understand me?"

He had me by the hair. I nodded, and the fireworks went off in my head again. I thought my head would split, it hurt so much. He was on top of me. My feet were free, but had no purchase. One of my arms was under him, and the other was trapped under me. And of course he had that gun. For the moment, I was stuck.

His rancid dead rabbit breath whistled close to my ear. He whispered, "Tell me about the demon. Is it true? That you got hold of a demon?"

I made a sound in my throat, as though to deny it. He shook my head by the hair and I almost blacked out again. Yellow lights spun behind my eyes and his voice faded. When I could hear again, he was listing all the things a demon could do for him. He put his knee in my back, pulled my head back and my arm up. I let out another sound, not quite a whimper.

"Give me his name, isn't that right? If I have the demon's name, then I'm in control, right?" He spoke in my ear, a growl in his voice.

"Yes!" I started to cry. For me to give Tillman my demon, I would have to be broken, and he would have to believe it. So I started to cry, and tried as hard as I could to hold it back, and I didn't answer him.

He shook my head again. "Tell me! Did you give it to Finley?"

I whined, "It wasn't my fault!" A useful phrase in any discussion where you're pinned.

He banged my head on the ground. I almost threw up.

"How'd you get it? What'd you do with it?"

When he shook me again, I whispered, "Three wishes. He gave me three wishes." I mean, honestly, what could Tillman know about demons?

"Yeah?" His voice was salacious. After all, three wishes could add up to a whole lot of rabbits. "How'd you get that, huh?"

I cried some more. I whined that Tillman would make the demon kill me, which hadn't occurred to him, because he wasn't about to waste a wish on me. And after some more sniveling, and some more pounding, and one point where I really did throw up, I told him that you just have to clap your hands, and on each clap, you call the demon's name. And that the demon had the power to give you a new car, or make you super beautiful, and the sex was awesome, but that if you called him again after your three wishes, he did horrible, unnamable things to you, and I was really, really scared.

And then there were some negotiations, which I pretended to believe. And some awkward contortions because he didn't have any paper on him, and I wasn't about to say that name again. I carefully and laboriously scratched the name Richard and I had agreed on, on the glass window of one of the buildings using a small pointed stone. The letters reflected in the light from the streetlamp and Tillman followed the syllables with one big grubby finger as he read the name over to himself several times.

I lay on the boardwalk like a bleeding, exhausted, beaten piece of meat. And that was not hard to pretend. And I waited to hear him clap his hands. And when he did, I looked up to see him form all the syllables and say them out loud, correctly and audibly. When he clapped his hands again, there was a sound like thunder going off inside a metal barrel, and there was a shape in the air around him and over him, a blackness within blackness. I saw Tillman open his mouth and his eyes in surprise. I lifted a hand in farewell, and the whole construct, with Tillman inside, folded away into itself and vanished.

And he was gone. And I had won. I put my head down and cried, this time for real.

CHAPTER TWENTY

The night was very still. The fog drifted among the buildings, now cloaking and now revealing them again. I could lie there for the rest of the night. Tillman was gone. I'd done for Tillman. And that was two. Ha.

I got my legs under me, and lifted my head. And then I did vomit, and that hurt too. I went to look at the hole in the ground, and the mark left by my dear demon as he swallowed my enemy. I wondered if my stepbrother was falling forever, or drifting in the cosmos of another universe, or if Richard had thought of something new this time. I changed onto four feet. Unfortunately my ringing headache came with me, though it was a little easier to bear in my wolf's head. I headed softly back through the town and up the hill, running Tillman's disappearance over and over in my mind, a big grin on my face as I made my way back along my trail.

I found Gray Fox on the slope above Elaine's house, about fifty feet off the track I'd laid. I located him more easily than I might have, by the static from his radio. I pushed my way through the bushes and found him lying twisted, one leg under him upslope from his head. He'd changed to his human form. He lay on his back with his arms oddly outstretched. He watched me come up to him.

"You!" His voice was a whisper.

I changed and hunkered down by him. "Who did you think?"

He didn't answer. The radio in his pocket blurted again, and a muted voice spoke. I saw him try to move his fingers toward his coat. I saw that he couldn't.

"You betrayed my mother," I stated.

His lips rose in a smile. "No, little wolf girl."

"I heard you." My head still felt wobbly, and the headache hammered me with every pulsebeat. But I was still strong enough so that my eyes turned yellow as I looked down on him.

"No," he whispered. "It was your great-grandmother who betrayed the grandsire of my master. My line have lived in exile for more than a hundred years now, to keep you in his eye."

I stared down at him. I had no idea what he was talking about. Only one thing was clear. "You're a spy."

"I did my duty."

My head was spinning, and it wasn't just the blows that Tillman had given me. What the hell was going on? "You got rid of my dad. You brought Ray and his sons into our house. You…"

I could hardly hear him. "I serve my master's plan."

"Who? Who were you spying for?"

Again that little smile. "Soon, you will meet him." He whispered a name, and his eyes grew fixed. I didn't look behind me. I knew no one was there.

I took the radio out of his pocket. At the bottom of the hill, I tossed it over the fence into Elaine's swimming pool. I found the keys to Finley's truck in the predictable spot, on top of the visor. I started it up and did what I should have done in the first place. I drove down the road that led to the beach, and then along the highway until I found a well-used parking lot, and left it there with the keys on the dashboard. I expect some smart guy soon made it as hard to find as it could possibly be.

I made my way back over the mountains on four feet. At any other time it would have been a joy to lope across the open country, smelling the dawn and crossing through the traces of the night creatures' journeys. My splitting head and the new bruises Tillman had given me were an unwelcome distraction.

What was I doing here? What was the plan? To lie in wait for each of my stepbrothers in turn, and anyone else Ray sent after me, and take them out one by one? But no, the plan had been to hide. I'd run away to hide like a kid pulling the bedcovers over her head to escape from a nightmare. All right, fair enough, it was good to get out, and it had been a nightmare. But what was the plan? To stay down this hole until someone from home cried ollie ollie oxen free? To come back when it was all over, and Dad had somehow come home again at last, defeated the bad guys, taken up his rightful place, and everything was once again as it used to be? That was stupid. It was childish. And it was young.

Wasn't I supposed to be growing up? Getting stronger? Finding my powers? The powers I would need to deal with the situation at home? Well then, I needed to know what the hell it was. What was going on? Why was my mom so weak? Why had my dad been defeated? Had he been killed, or just run off? And if he wasn't dead, then where was he? Where was my older brother Carl? Ignoring these problems because I wasn't ready to deal with them was no longer an option. I had to find out. I had to figure out what to do next. I had to grow up.

When you're a child, the sounds of the larger issues echo through the house, and you ignore them. Gray Fox's frequent journeys. Dad asking Mom about them, and getting an off-hand answer. Oh, that's just his way, we have to accept him the way he is. Aunt Dora talking to Mom, trying to get Mom to do something, to act. Mom slipping away. Dora fighting with Dad, Dad telling Aunt Dora it was just Mom's way.

Grown-up's problems. Adult issues. Not mine, when I was a pup. Well, they were mine now. I had to grow up, and I had to do it right now. Gray Fox's whisper, his last words to me, almost inaudible, sang in my mind. *"Sun Wolf is coming. He is going to kill you."*

Who the hell was Sun Wolf? I'd never even heard the name.

I made it back to my car before the sun rose. I went the long way out of the valley, because I remembered where Gray Fox's sentries might still be watching the passes. I stopped at a gas station and filled up, and while I was there I left a message at work, telling Ariadne that I might be late this morning. It was dawn, but morning rush hour traffic could start this early, and I had the whole Los Angeles basin to cross.

I drove home, thinking all the way. I showered and changed into work clothes. I clocked in just half an hour late, and I worked all day. I listened to my boss going on about the history of music, and I smiled at Yvette's clowning on the drums, even though it felt like my head was going to explode. I went home after work and ate some dinner before I went to sleep. Because that was the grown-up thing to do.

Two days later, on my day off, I drove out to Malibu to find the ranch where I'd been held prisoner all those weeks ago. I wanted to talk to Sarah. I should have done it long ago, but between being attacked, and recovering from attacks... the fact was, Sarah was one more enemy at my back that I had hoped would just stay away. But my plan was to be wiser now. So I was going to have a talk with Sarah.

I drove with my windows open because of the heat, though Yvette told me the previous day that this was nothing to what was

coming in July and August. It took a couple of casts to find the
dirt road Elaine had bumped her way out of when I was hiding
in the backseat of her truck, but by mid-afternoon I drove up to
the bungalow where the beat-up truck and the dented hatch-back
were parked at the side of the barn. I parked next to them and
got out. No dogs barked. Out in the pasture some of the sheep
were carrying on, trying to convince somebody that they hadn't
been fed in weeks. I knocked on the door but no one answered,
and I didn't hear anyone inside. I sat down on the steps to wait.
Sarah had gone up and down these steps half a dozen times today
already, with Baz at her heels. Holly had been here recently, perhaps even this morning. Elaine had been here not long ago as
well.

It was cooler in this little bowl of a valley, and this much closer
to the ocean, than it had been further inland. A breeze came
through the gap in the two hills to the south, and brought the
smell of salt and water. I heard Sarah out in the pasture yelling
at her dogs, and then Baz's black and white form came around
the corner of the barn on four legs, barking his head off at me.
He skidded to a stop when he caught my scent, backed up and
disappeared into the barn. Sarah was still calling him when she
saw me.

"Can I help you?" She had on the same work boots and stained
corduroy pants. The sleeves on her shirt were rolled up, and she
wore a leather hat pushed back on her head. Her voice was hard.

"You don't remember me."

"Can't say I do."

I opened my heart to my anger at this woman, and released my
wolf aspect so that I wore it above my human form, and I let the
growl sound in my voice. She stepped back even as I said, "Does
this remind you of anything?"

She collected herself and stopped. "Oh. The wolf girl. I wondered when I'd be seeing you again."

"Yeah?" I let my wolf aspect fade. "You thought Elaine or Curt or Holly would be bringing me back to you shot, drugged, and in chains again?"

"No." She glanced over to her sheep pastures behind the barn. "I thought you'd come and take it out on my flock. I stayed up nights with a shotgun for days after you took off."

I smiled. "I was busy," I told her.

"So I heard."

"Oh?"

"Curt, Holly, Elaine, they've all been telling stories about you."

"I met Cecil."

"I hope you bit him," she said darkly.

"You don't like him?"

"Never had much use for a preacher who needs so much money."

I stood up. "Then why did you do that to me? Treat me like I'm some kind of animal?"

She folded her arms, but she didn't back up anymore. She shrugged. "Holly asked me to. She told me you were possessed by a demon, and that Cecil was going to cure you. I should have known it was a lie. Cecil couldn't cure rabies with a shotgun."

"So, Holly is the liar." I looked across at the pasture where a couple of late lambs were bouncing around. That is the moment, that must have been the moment, when I missed Sarah's glance up at the house.

"I suppose you'll want to talk to her next."

"I suppose." I looked back at her. "Is it true you can make people shape change? Curt said you used to make him, and Holly, and Elaine shape change when they were kids."

She shrugged. "Can't you?"

"No."

"Oh. I thought you were like me."

She held on to both her wrists with her hands, and made some kind of tug. And then there was a border collie looking up at me with tired eyes. She shook herself, and then Sarah stood there again.

"Huh! I didn't know people could do that."

"Then you don't know much. There's always been people who could do that."

"And you can do it to other people?"

"For a little while. Made babysitting a breeze, with those kids. Always did." She looked smug.

"I'll bet."

"You waiting for me to say I'm sorry? Or are you going to chew my liver out?"

"Do I need to?"

She shook her head. Her eyes were still tired. "Not if you're willing to let bygones go."

"All right," I was going to add that if she made me sorry, I was going to come back and burn down her barn, but that's when Holly slipped out of the house and down the steps along the banister. I turned as she came, and only thought this made one less trip back up to goddam Malibu. She had her hand cupped in front of her, and lifted it as she reached the steps. She was lit with tension, but didn't seem to have a weapon, and I knew I could change and rip out her throat before she did anything serious to me, so when Sarah yelled, "No! Holly, don't!" I just stood there, my mouth open to finish what I'd been saying to Sarah, or say something to Holly, or ask Sarah what she was going on about.

Holly blew the fine sparkling dust right in my face, and then backed up fast, her face leering into a grin. "I got you! I got you!"

I was brushing the grit out of my face, and off my tongue as Sarah marched up the steps, grabbed Holly's hand and her neck, scraped her hand over Holly's and then made that odd tug, and changed her into a sheep. The ewe bleated and leaped, but Sarah didn't let go. She'd wiped some of the last of the dust out of

Holly's hand as she changed her, and she stuck her fingers in the sheep's mouth as deep as it would go. And then she let her go, and kicked her the hell down the stairs. If I had known at that moment what Holly had done to me, I would have given her an awfully good kick as well.

Sarah stared down at me.

"What?" I asked. "What just happened?"

"Silver," she said. "Silver dust."

CHAPTER TWENTY-ONE

I tried to change, right there at Sarah's place, and I couldn't. I threw myself into the change, rode the pain in my head, my throat, my lungs, until it topped out and I fell, still on hands and knees. I called up my wolf aspect and I was able to raise it, but not make that turn to where I wore my wolf's form. I tried again and again. I blacked out twice. The second time I came to lying in front of the steps, with my head on Sarah's lap. I pulled myself up. I still didn't like her smell.

"It'll wear off, right? It's just temporary."

She shrugged. "I don't know. Curt's brother, Pete, he did something like that. He did it to himself, and he never did come back."

I tried every day. I spent whole nights at it. I walked up the hill of Hellman Park and tried my heart out until I lay screaming. I am a daughter of the wolf kind. I have my father to seek, my history to discover, my would-be assassin to defeat. I am one of the two-natured kind, but if my wolf nature is never to be seen again, then what? If I cannot change, then what am I?

সমাপ্ত

ACKNOWLEDGMENTS

First and foremost, thank you to Laurie McLean, Agent Extraordinaire, without whom . . . as well she knows.

Grateful thanks to Skyhorse and Start who resurrected the beleaguered Night Shade Books, and with it *Binding*, *Summoning*, and the Moon Wolf Saga.

Thank you, Ross Lockhart, my most excellent editor, for asking pointy questions in all the right places. Thank you to Cory Allyn, and to Jeannine Hanscom and Shannon Page, for saving me from error.

Thank you to Sarah, for friendship, and for Writing in the Library, and to all the WITL gang. And loving thanks to Riva and Rebecca; and to Bill Jouris, for his long-sustained and continuing support and encouragement, which means more to me than he can ever imagine.

I would like to thank my beta readers, Doug, Laurie, Bill, and Eric, for raising useful doubts in good time.

And as ever, and always, to Eric.

ABOUT THE AUTHOR

Carol Wolf earned a B.A. in History at Mills College, an MFA in Drama-Playwriting at Rutgers University, and pursued a life in the theater, which resulted in about thirty productions of her plays on five continents, including her feminist musical farce, *The Terrible Experiment of Jonathan Fish*, and the award-winning *The Thousandth Night*. She wrote the scripts for the blockbuster video games *Blood Omen II: Legacy of Kain*, and *Legacy of Kain: Defiance*. She co-founded the micro-budget film company, Paw Print Studios, and produced and directed the feature films *The Valley of Fear* and *Far From the Sea*, available on Amazon. She studied broadsword fighting in the SCA, Uechi-rhu karate, and earned a black belt in Toyama-ryu Iaido. She has lived on both coasts, and in Europe, and presently lives in the Foothills of the Sierra Nevadas with her husband, two border collies, and a varying number of sheep.